The
Midnight
Bakery

BOOKS BY EMMA DAVIES

Lucy's Little Village Book Club
The House at Hope Corner
The Beekeeper's Cottage
The Little Shop on Silver Linings Street
My Husband's Lie
The Wife's Choice
A Year at Appleyard Farm
After the Crash
The Little Island Secret

THE LITTLE COTTAGE SERIES
The Little Cottage on the Hill
Summer at the Little Cottage on the Hill
Return to the Little Cottage on the Hill
Christmas at the Little Cottage on the Hill

THE ADAM AND EVE MYSTERY SERIES
Death by Candlelight
Death at the Dinner Party
Death on the Menu
Death at Beresford Hall

CLEARWATER CASTLE SERIES
Secrets of Clearwater Castle

Letting in Light

Turn Towards the Sun

The Mystery of Montague House

The
Midnight
Bakery

EMMA DAVIES

bookouture

Published by Bookouture in 2025

An imprint of Storyfire Ltd.
Carmelite House
50 Victoria Embankment
London EC4Y 0DZ

www.bookouture.com

The authorised representative in the EEA is Hachette Ireland
8 Castlecourt Centre
Dublin 15 D15 XTP3
Ireland
(email: info@hbgi.ie)

ISBN: 978-1-80550-300-2
eBook ISBN: 978-1-83790-333-7

For Sarah. For keeping the faith (and my copy of Duncton Quest)
all these years

1

_____

Frankie

Frances let the door of the bakery close slowly behind her,
leaning against it for a moment to breathe in the warm, familiar
smell. It was welcoming, redolent of childhood afternoons spent
baking with her mother: rich, buttery pastry and the heavenly
scent of bread, fresh from the oven – like coming home, or at
least the kind of home Frances dreamed of. The kind of home
she had, once. With her back to the door, she could already feel
her shoulders relaxing. She was safe.

Turning, she relocked the door and moved swiftly through
the shop – past the counter and the rows of shelves behind,
which, come morning, would be filled with bread and pastries
ready for sale, and onward towards a door at the back. The
bustle of the shop in daylight, filled with people and conversations, was not for her, but through here was her sanctuary – the
beating heart of the bakery.

She slipped through the door and took off her coat, hanging
it on a peg before swapping it for her apron which she had hung

there the night before. The room was dark and still, silent save for the hum of refrigerators. She could just make out the large metal worktable which almost spanned the width of the room, and the huge mixing machines illumined by glimmers of moonlight which fell through a window at the rear. But she could walk the room as confidently as if it was lit by the brightest of beams – she knew it as well as she knew the pattern of freckles across her nose. It was only when she was ready for the night of work ahead of her that she flicked a switch on the wall, watching as the overhead lights blinked slowly into life.

By two thirty in the morning, Frances had been at the bakery for over three hours and, despite the time, wasn't even halfway through her shift. She had moved on from making the first batches of bread, those which took the longest, and was now mixing up the paste which filled the cinnamon buns she was working on. Even after all this time, she couldn't get enough of its sweet scent, and the thought of it mixed with butter, oozing from between the layers of rich dough was enough to make her mouth water. And her stomach rumble. With a quick check of the clock, she smiled: she was bang on schedule.

Time ran differently at night and Frances liked the calm, slow passage of hours, the rhythmic nature of her tasks allowing her mind to slip its gears and freewheel. It was amazing the things which tumbled into her head when this happened. And her name was just one of the things she liked to think about at night. Frances Nightingale...

For most of her early life she never even considered how she felt about it. A happy childhood morphed into an equally happy adulthood, her whole life ahead of her, alive with possibility. It was only much later when all that changed. When Frances turned fifty and found herself looking back on her life more than she looked forward. When she counted all the people who had come and gone from it. When she looked in the mirror and realised she didn't know who she was any more. When she realised that the way Robert said her name raised the hairs on the back of her neck. Becoming a Nightingale again was easy, she would always be one of those, but Frances was different. Frances would have to go. Before it was too late. Before there was so little left of herself that she disappeared altogether. But who to become...?

A rebellion was taking place, and its tiny shoots had taken hold with a tenacity which surprised her. She had a notion that she could be something else, something wilder, more carefree, some*one* wilder... So, now that she *was* allowed to choose her own name, she wanted it to be Frankie.

It was a name for the kind of person she'd like to be. Someone optimistic, happy, an extrovert even. The only thing she wasn't sure about was whether or not it suited her. Was Frankie an appropriate name for someone in their mid-fifties? She didn't know. It could be, perhaps, if she changed a few things. But, at this moment in time, she was still very much a Frances, and she wasn't sure how long it would take for Frankie to fully emerge – that's if she ever did. She liked to think of her as a beautiful butterfly, struggling towards the light as it climbed free from the darkness of its hard and crusty chrysalis, but once she *was* free, oh, then how she'd fly...

The pinging of the oven timer brought her out of her reverie with a start. She was on schedule, but there was still much to do and she daren't get behind. To others this job might not look like much, but to her it was everything – it was her lifeline.

She had worked at the bakery for nearly eighteen months. Only small, it was just off the centre of town where there were still plenty of older buildings, and although Duggan's was the least prepossessing of them all, Frankie loved how no two were the same. There was so much to see beyond the plain glass panes of the shop fronts, but only if you looked upwards to the ornate stone arches above the windows, the jagged rooflines filled with chimney stacks and decorative balustrades, and even stone balls sitting high up on carved plinths. And from her tiny flat perched way above the bakery, these were the views she was lucky enough to see every day. Or rather every night, because it was then that she liked to look out upon the world – upon the sky, swathed in darkness and sprinkled with stars, and the quiet streets, where light pooled on the cobbles and reflected in windows.

And mostly what she saw was the aloneness of everything. Not necessarily loneliness, but the lone woman who nursed her child in the house at the top of her street; the solitary man who sat writing at a desk each night; the dim lights glowing in the distant houses of those who couldn't sleep; or the pavement sleepers just trying to make it through the night. They were things most people never saw.

Once blind to them too, she had worked during the day and slept through the night, but now that the night-time was her realm, her eyes had been opened and she saw things differently. Or perhaps it was just that in the dark things were easier to see. The way she thought about it, the daytime was for busy, for rushing around, and it was easy for things to get lost in all the noise. People got lost too, but the daytime hid them. It buried them under all the things there were to think about and all the things there were to do. With so much else going on, how could you possibly see it all? At night though, things were different. The world was quiet, was still, and the invisible was seen far more easily. Sounds daft, doesn't it? How could you see things more clearly at night? Frankie used to think the bright colours of daytime would be more revealing, but they weren't, they just added to the noise.

None of it really mattered anyway. Everyone else was asleep, so even if Frankie did have something to say, who was there to listen? And she actually liked the night. She was free to think whatever she wanted to, and when she was done working, she got to go home to bed just as other people were leaving theirs. She got to sleep through all the noise and confusion of the day. She missed the sun, but that was about all. If you gave up something for long enough, you forgot about it after a while. And there was much of Frankie's life she'd do anything to forget.

2

Beth

Beth couldn't remember a time when she wasn't tired. Not just a little weary, but the bone-numbing, mind-cauterising kind of tired that stalked your every move. It was just one of the things which had changed about her life since the accident.

It was noon, so by now Jack would have eaten his breakfast and probably attempted the washing-up too, but the other thing he would have done is to switch on the coffee machine for her. She raised her head a little from the pillow and, sure enough, the smell was like a siren song, dragging her body towards it as if she was caught in a tractor beam. She threw back her covers and slid her feet into her waiting slippers. It was time to get moving.

Jack was reading the newspaper as she entered the kitchen, no doubt still wrestling with the crossword. He did this most mornings while he was waiting for her to rise. His wheelchair prevented her from giving him the hug she would have liked, but she approached him from behind, and did what she always did – slid her arms around his neck to lay her head on his shoulder. Her lips touched the warm spot of skin above the collar of his tee shirt, one of her very favourite places.

'Morning,' she murmured, leaving her head where it was for a moment. She could feel Jack smile and he pressed his head against hers in reply.

'Morning,' he said. 'You're just in time, three down is a killer.'

Beth peered at the paper over his shoulder. *Aurally challenged aviator, anag,* she read. *Nine letters.* She stared at the page. 'Nope,' she said. 'I need coffee first.'

She backed away so that Jack could reverse his chair and manoeuvre across the kitchen. 'Coming right up,' he said. 'Although there was only just enough left in the packet, so it might not be as strong as you like it.'

'Sorry, my fault,' said Beth, following him to take down a fresh pack of coffee from a cupboard he could no longer reach. She placed it beside the coffee machine so it was ready for later. Jack didn't say anything else, even though Beth suspected he wanted to. One day, they might be able to afford to have the rest of the kitchen modified, but that was a way off in the future yet. Converting the downstairs to provide usable spaces for Jack had taken all the money they had, and some they hadn't, so, for now, it was up to Beth to second-guess a lot of what Jack might need – or want – while she was either asleep or at work. She took a seat at the table so her husband could still bring her a coffee as he'd intended. It was a small ritual, just one of many they fitted in to each day but, like a lot of things in their life now, vastly more important than its simplicity might have suggested.

Inhaling the fragrant steam from her mug, Beth sighed in anticipation. 'So, what's on the agenda for today?' she asked. 'Did you still want to go to the library?'

A cloud crossed her husband's face. 'Maybe. Not sure it's worth it, really.'

Beth nodded. 'I reckon we should. They've had a rubbish

selection the last three times we've been. Which means that today all the gems will be back on the shelves just ripe for the picking.'

'What's the weather like in cloud cuckoo land?' asked Jack with a wry smile. 'No, don't tell me... the sun is shining.'

'You'll be eating your words later, Mr Millner, you'll see. Besides, I want to see if they have any books on slow cooking.' She didn't, but that wasn't the point. 'Let me just finish this and sling on some clothes, then we can get going. If we've got time we could go for a walk across the common as well.'

Jack smiled and gave her one of those looks, the ones which had melted her heart when she had first met him all those years ago. Nowadays, he didn't always say how he was feeling, although she knew how grateful he was to her, just as she knew how much he loved her. Saying those things felt too poignant somehow, but he could still give her the look, and that was enough.

She took a deep breath and swallowed a mouthful of coffee. Then she tapped the newspaper. 'Fieldfare,' she said. '*Aurally challenged aviator... deaf flier... anagram...* fieldfare.'

'Oh, for goodness' sake,' muttered Jack.

Back in their bedroom, Beth sat on the edge of the bed for a moment, trying to gather her thoughts. All too often she found them straying to what would await her during that night's shift, when what she should have been doing was focusing on the present. It was a promise she had made to herself a long time ago – that even though she had to sleep during the day, what-ever time she had with Jack would be time spent *with* him, fully in the moment, not distracted or only half paying attention. They had so few hours together it was important to make them count. It was hard though. There was so much to think about. So much to plan for.

She had already taken care of all the morning stuff, she did it as soon as she got home, before she went to sleep – helped

Jack out of bed, helped him to get washed, dressed, to take his medication and make breakfast – but there was also the rest of the day to think about too. And the night. All those long hours when she wouldn't be there.

What she mustn't do, under any circumstances, was think about the life they had before. The one where Jack was a farmer and spent his days outside whatever the weather. The one where they had dreams for the future, dreams of a family – a trio of rosy-cheeked little Millners running around with bare feet and tangled hair. That life died on the day Jack nearly ended his.

He was a gardener when Beth first met him, happy, but largely unfulfilled. But it was a job which paid the bills, and so although he had always longed to own a smallholding, that didn't come until much later, his father's premature death leaving him with just enough to kick-start their dream. They bought a ramshackle farmhouse with several acres, plenty to allow Jack to put his plans into practice, and for a few years he was the proverbial pig in clover. Until a moment's inattention robbed him of everything they once thought would be theirs. Beth could still remember that day vividly, as if the nine years which had gone by were nothing more than a heartbeat, but she reckoned it would take a lot longer before her memory of it began to fade. She had saved his life that day, and on more than one occasion had found herself thinking it might have been better if she hadn't. Trouble was, she knew that Jack thought the same thing and so she never, *ever* let it show. Even on the very worst days.

When she had reached him, pinned beneath the bulk of the huge machine, it had been one of those beautiful spring days which made you feel glad to be alive. Yet his eyes had told her that being grateful for it was not enough. He knew he had changed their lives forever. He knew he might die, in all likelihood probably *would* die, but what he couldn't know was what

Beth, with all her years of nursing, could foresee, and for that she would always be grateful. If he had known what living might mean, he'd have begged her not to fight for him, to loosen his hold on the gossamer-thin thread that still bound him to the earth and set him free. And what scared Beth most was that she might have. Instead, she had been calm and rational. She had phoned for an ambulance, knowing that however much she wanted, she mustn't try to free him from beneath the crushing weight of the tractor. So, she had held his hand, pleading with the universe for clemency, and talked to him, refusing to let him die, knowing that in many ways this was the easy bit. If Jack survived, the pain would come later, for both of them.

They had a different life now, that's all. So, Beth gathered up her thoughts, placed them firmly into the different compartments she kept for them and then reached for her clothes. One thing at a time, Beth. One thing at a time.

The library was quiet and the desk deserted when they arrived. Beth unloaded the pile of books Jack had borrowed the last time and left them on the returns side of the counter. Then she followed him to the fiction section, offering up a little prayer to the reading gods that there might be some crackers there today. Scanning the shelves Jack couldn't reach, she spotted one immediately and took it down, showing it to him with a told-you-so smile before cradling it in her arm as she continued to look. It was a practised routine – she checked the top two shelves and Jack did the bottom three. It never took long. She realised a long time ago that if anyone else was browsing the same section they would melt away, lured by the pull of some fictitious book elsewhere. But that was okay; they hadn't got much time as it was.

Less than ten minutes later they returned to the counter where the librarian already had Jack's account to view on her computer.

'Hit the jackpot today,' she said. 'The Kate Atkinson came

in as well as the Anthony Doerr. That should keep you going for a while.' She reached beneath the counter to pull out the books which had been put aside for him.

'You're a star, Libby, thanks. I've got another list of requests though, sorry.'

The librarian nodded as Jack struggled to reach inside his pocket with his only good hand. She affected a patient smile although Beth knew she was desperate to help. It wasn't impatience, just human nature. It's hard watching someone wrestle with such a simple task.

Eventually, the hard-won piece of paper was handed over and Libby glanced at it briefly. 'Brilliant. Leave those with us, Jack, and we'll see what we can do. There might be quite a long wait for a couple of them, but the others shouldn't take too long.'

Libby said this, or some variant of it, every time Jack handed her one of his lists. Beth knew she couldn't read half of what Jack had managed to write, but a quick phone call to Beth later would clear that up and no one would be any the wiser. Except Beth, of course, and Jack, because he wasn't stupid.

They waited while the rest of Jack's books were checked out and were about to leave when Jack stopped suddenly. 'We didn't look at the cookery books,' he said.

Beth was torn. She knew she should go and look but by the time she'd got Jack back in the car, driven to the common and got him back out of the car again, they'd have precious little time to walk as it was. She smiled. 'Won't be a tick,' she said.

'What is it you're looking for?' asked Libby.

'Just a book on slow cooking, if you've got any.'

Libby pulled a face. 'Only one or two, I'm afraid. Shall I see if they're in, save you rooting for them?'

'Thanks.' Beth smiled, complicit.

'Just the one, sadly,' said Libby, returning moments later. 'Do you want to have a look?'

'I'll take it anyway,' replied Beth. 'There's bound to be something useful in it.'

It took Libby less than a minute to discharge the book to Beth's account and then they were on their way again. She flicked a glance at her watch. It was going to be a rush today, but maybe if she cooked something which took less time for their tea, it would give her more time for all the things she still had to do. She gave a friendly wave to the staff as they left. 'Bye. Thank you.'

The trouble with the library was that the staff had worked there for so long, they'd forgotten how quiet it was, how much their voices carried. And if Beth could hear the things Libby said to her colleague, then so could Jack. It angered her. Not because she said such things – she was only expressing sympathy – what angered Beth was that people always commented about *her*. *That poor woman*, they said. *It must be so hard for her*. Maybe it was, but had they never stopped to think how hard it was for Jack? After all, Beth still had the use of her arms and legs.

It was quiet up by the common today. In the summer it was heaving, the numbers of habitual dog walkers swelled by children playing, groups picnicking and sunbathers making the most of the warmth. Early February wasn't a time to loiter though, and as she and Jack crested the slight rise from the path by the road, a gust of wind sliced through her. That would certainly explain the lack of people. Beth always forgot how exposed it was up here.

She stood, as she always did, on the side which shielded Jack from the worst of the buffets, grateful that she had to walk at a fair lick to keep up with his electric chair. But Jack didn't have the benefit of exertion to keep him warm and, after a few minutes, she stopped.

'Sorry,' she said. 'I didn't think it would be so cold.'

Jack eyed the path ahead of him. 'I'm okay for a bit if you

are. Or would you rather go home? You could grab a couple of hours' more sleep.'

Would that she could. 'No, I'm fine, let's carry on.'

Jack nodded and they silently continued. It was at times like these that Beth wondered what life would be like if they were both absolutely honest with each other. Would they ever do half the things that filled each of their days? She knew it sounded awful, but she wasn't sure their relationship would survive without the myriad number of small white lies they told, or accommodations, as Beth liked to call them. Walking was good for Jack, or rather fresh air was. It was good for her too, and so they came to the common several times a week. Sometimes, it was the last thing she wanted to do, but she did it because she knew that if she didn't, Jack would hardly ever get out of the house. By the same token, she was pretty sure that Jack stoically agreed to come because he knew how much she cared about him – about, and for him. Refusing that help would be like a kick in the teeth, given all that she did for him. And so, they carried on, *accommodating*...

As if reading her mind, Jack halted beside her. 'What would I do without you?' he said.

Beth held his look. 'Don't,' she said softly, seeing the emotion written there. 'We both know you'd be okay. And at least you'd be free from being nagged all the time.'

'I mean it though, Beth. I couldn't do this without you. But you work too hard, and...' He didn't need to say the rest.

It was exactly what Beth was afraid of. Every day, Jack told her to sleep, told her he was worried about her. But to do the things she did there just weren't enough hours in the day to sleep as well. And she was so, so tired. It scared her that one day she wouldn't be okay, that her body wouldn't be able to keep up with the demands she made of it, and everything would go bang. She had no idea what would happen if it did.

Turning, she dropped to her knees, ignoring the cold of the

hard ground beneath her. 'I love you, Jack Millner,' she said. Some days she couldn't tell him hard enough.

Leaning forward as far as he could, Jack slid his good hand around her neck, pulling her closer so his lips touched hers. Some days she knew he worried he didn't tell her often enough. 'I love you too,' he replied. And then he sat back and smiled that smile. 'But can we please go home? It's flippin' freezing…'

3

Frankie

It was twenty to eight in the morning and Frankie was just about to head home, another night shift completed. She was tired, and living above the bakery meant she could be in bed in about three minutes flat if she really wanted, but a pearlescent sunrise drew her away from her front door and out into the streets. Frankie loved the town when it was like this, just waking up from its nightly slumber, stretching and yawning as it limbered up for a new day. She loved how it always seemed cleansed of all that had gone before, each morning a brand-new start, the slate wiped clean, full of promise and as yet unsullied by the day's events.

On mornings like these she would wander – up through the market square and away from the shops, through the passageways of ancient timber houses before finally turning into the green swathe of the churchyard. Today, she had a fresh loaf of bread in her bag which was meant for her breakfast, but she broke up the crust to share with the flock of starlings that roosted in the old trees. It was a small thing, but the birds'

squabbling antics made her smile as they fought over her offer-
ings. She waited until they had feasted, disappearing as fast as
they had arrived, before breaking off another piece of bread for
a shy robin who hopped from branch to branch eyeing her hopefully with a cocked head. Then she sat, just for a few minutes,
on the sagging bench by the memorial garden and thought
about how lucky she was. She might not have much in her
world, but she had everything she needed.

Stretching out her legs, she breathed in the chill air, feeling
it fill her lungs, cold and clean. The bakery was always boiling
at night, and much as she was grateful for the warm fug in
winter, by morning she always felt the need for contrast – like
when you overheat in bed and slide your legs over to savour the
coolness of the sheets on the other side. But the very best thing
about mornings like these, and indeed every morning, was that
now she had finished work she had the whole day to herself and
probably wouldn't see another soul. Occasionally her boss at the
bakery would pop up to see her, but Vivienne's visits were infre-
quent. If she wanted anything she usually left Frankie a note,
which suited her just fine.

It wasn't that Frankie didn't like people; she did, but over
the years the ones which she'd had in her life had all drifted
out of it. She understood why. She hadn't needed anyone else
and so she'd given them no reason to stay. That wasn't true,
but it was what she'd thought at the time, or rather, what
Robert had taught her. Now she knew better, it was too late to
do anything about it, and although back then she'd thought
losing them didn't hurt much at all, she'd later discovered that
it did, very much so. Now, the thought of getting close to
people only to watch them leave again was akin to having
sensitive teeth. It made you wary, but the only real pain came
if you drank iced water. So, she didn't drink iced water –
simple. She didn't need any reminders of what she'd lost and
so she kept herself to herself, and she'd got used to being on

her own. It was easier than she'd thought, and working the night shift helped.

When Frankie had first started working nights it had taken a while to get used to the new routine. Not so much the sleeping and being awake, but the when and what to eat – that was what had really thrown her. But then she realised there was no need to change things round at all and so, even though she would soon be having breakfast, perfectly normal for the morning, for her it was actually the last meal of her day. Later on, when she got up, she'd have her main meal – dinner – which became, in effect, her actual breakfast, and then during the night, she'd have lunch. It sounded confusing, but it worked. This morning she was going to have boiled egg and soldiers on account of the fresh loaf, and then finish off with her hot chocolate. She swore it helped her drop off to sleep.

Frankie's flat was only small, but she was lucky to have it at all. Perhaps Vivienne had sensed her desperation when Frankie had asked if she knew anywhere reasonable for rent, but then again, maybe it suited her to have Frankie on hand. Vivienne lived right on the other side of town – if there was ever a problem, Frankie could be there long before she was. And it was cheap, too, but that was more on account of it being little more than a glorified storeroom for the bakery when she moved in. Goodness knows why Vivienne had hung onto half the stuff she had, but as long as Frankie didn't throw anything out, Vivienne was happy for her to live there. Once Frankie had cleaned out all the years of dust and cobwebs, and moved the junk into the box room, piling it high, it wasn't too bad at all. It was an old building and, perched up under the eaves as she was, the ceiling slanted this way and that giving it bags of character. With a couple of lamps and a few brightly coloured throws she'd scavenged from the local charity shops, her odd collection of furniture was transformed. It was warm and cosy, but most importantly it was hers. Frankie wasn't much bothered by material things. She had her freedom and that made her rich beyond her wildest dreams.

The door at the top of the stairs opened on to a tiny square space, which wasn't really a hallway, but was big enough to hang a coat and kick off her shoes. Then, it was straight into the kitchen, where she was greeted by the bunch of daffodils she'd popped into a jug to sit on the wooden counter nearest the door. They were bought cheaply from the local market, something she did every week if she could, the sight of them never failing to lift her spirits. The other thing which helped was her music.

She grew up listening to 1970s and '80s bands but it was music from a much earlier era that was her go-to whenever she needed a lift. Her first real boyfriend had introduced her to it, and during the years they were together she'd grown to love those songs too. They were such sweet melodies, old-fashioned and romantic and she and Shaun had danced to them for hours. This morning her playlist would have to include 'A Nightingale Sang in Berkeley Square' – she'd been humming it, she realised, ever since she'd been in the churchyard. Given her surname, Shaun used to tease her that she was his very own nightingale, while she used to dream of being one of the angels who had dined at the Ritz, just like in the lyrics... But she'd given Shaun up for Robert and, as a consequence, hadn't listened to those songs for years. It was only recently that she'd taken to playing them again, perhaps as a reminder of a past life, one where she'd been happy, or perhaps as a kind of apology, to let Shaun know how wrong she'd been to let him go.

Setting a pan of water to boil, Frankie went to get changed out of her work clothes. Putting her pyjamas on now meant that she could pretty much fall into bed once she had eaten and done her few odd jobs, none of which would take very long. She used to have a big house, spending hour after hour cleaning, but not any more. Admittedly, her flat wasn't very big, just a kitchen, bathroom and living room-cum-bedroom, but one of the things which had most surprised her when she left Robert was just how few things she had of her own. Their house had been stuffed with belongings, but when the time came to leave she realised there was virtually nothing she wanted to take. And those things she'd lovingly cared for year after year? She didn't really like them much at all. So that was another benefit of being on her own – the dusting didn't take up much of her time now. Plus, of course, she was nowhere near as fussy as Robert was. She'd succumbed to tears on plenty of occasions during those first few weeks, looking around at the bleak and unfamiliar space, but when she'd cried herself out, she'd blown a huge raspberry at him and hadn't cleaned for a week.

4

Beth

It always took Beth at least an hour to settle into her shift. Once the staff handover was complete, she spent a while revisiting each patient's notes and charts so that everything she'd just been told embedded itself. She was tired, and anxious she might make a mistake, but that wasn't why she did it. The patients on this ward were so poorly, it wasn't just about the physical care she could give. It went way beyond that.

There were no doctors' rounds at night. No consultants, no physiotherapists, no rehab or palliative care nurses either, so it was much quieter than during the day. For most it was the only chance to sleep without being interrupted, but for many, night-time was when fear crept in, when facing their own mortality became almost too much to bear. And for those patients, Beth was a friendly face and a sympathetic ear. She was hot buttered toast and cups of tea among the whispered confessions of the endless hours until dawn.

Strictly speaking, none of these things were what Beth was paid to do, but she and all her colleagues did them because if they didn't, what was left of humanity? They worked in a profession which had become hobbled by a lack of resources with little money to reverse the situation. As nurses, what they offered had become driven by cost, and ruled by targets they hadn't a hope of reaching, but a kind word or a gentle touch still meant far more than could ever be quantified. And the day she forgot that would be the day Beth turned her back on her career forever.

She smiled as Lisa came into view. Beth was a senior staff nurse, so as ward sister Lisa was one step up from her and, although fairly new to the hospital, she and Beth had hit it off from day one. Beth appreciated her no-nonsense, common-sense approach, which also came with a priceless sense of humour. Today though, Lisa's usual sunny smile was absent from her face.

'You didn't hear this from me,' she said as she reached Beth, adding several charts to the pile already on the desk beside them. 'But the memo is going in pigeonholes in the morning.' Beth didn't need to ask which one; talk on the wards had been about little else for weeks.

'What does it say?' asked Beth. 'I know you're not supposed to tell me, but—'

'But I'm going to because I'm an angel. Plus, it's unfair and we all know it.' Lisa crossed to a filing cabinet behind them, pulling out a single sheet of paper. 'Like I said, you didn't hear this from me, and you haven't seen this either,' she added, sliding the memo across the desk. 'Basically, it's as we thought. A restructure, which means we're all going to have to reapply for our jobs.'

Beth scanned the letter in front of her. 'How many have to go?' she asked, looking for the detail.

'Altogether…? Two,' replied Lisa. 'And of those remaining, four of us will effectively stay on the same grade, although we'll be called something completely different.' She tapped a paragraph at the base of the letter. 'While sadly three will have newly created roles, on the newly created grade structure which doesn't fool anyone. You can call us and the grades anything you like, but we can still spot a pay cut when we see one.'

'Jesus...' said Beth under her breath. It was even worse than they'd feared.

Lisa was studying Beth intently. 'How's Jack?' she asked.

'Same as usual,' Beth replied. 'And yes, completely oblivious to what's going on here.'

'*Beth...*'

'I know. And you're right, I should have told him. But we can't exist on any less than I get now, so as long as it doesn't affect him, he doesn't need to know about it. *If* things don't work out then we'll have that conversation, but you know how tough it is, Lisa. I can't heap any more shit on him.'

Lisa raised her eyebrows. 'But you'll happily wallow in it yourself?' She tutted. 'Sorry, I shouldn't have said that, but I worry about you, Beth. You have enough on your plate as it is.' She nudged Beth's arm. 'Obviously, lucky old me is going to be asked for my opinion of those applying to stay on your grade, so I hope you know that I will be singing your praises at the top of my lungs. *And* I will be *extremely* unpleasant to anyone who says differently. Not that anyone would,' she added quickly.

'How long have we got?'

Lisa blew out a stream of air. 'Not long. Applications have to be in by the end of the month.'

'But that's only three weeks away.'

'Yep. So, shout if you need any help. Anything at all.'

'What about you, though?' asked Beth. 'You've still got to apply for your job.'

'Yes, but I've been buying Matron chocolate Hobnobs for weeks now. I'll be a shoo-in, don't worry about me.'

Beth rolled her eyes. 'Honestly, Lisa, I—' She stopped abruptly as a raucous noise sounded from the electronic board which covered one wall behind them. As one they both swivelled to face it.

'*Shit*, it's Bernard...'

'I'll bleep the crash team,' replied Beth, but Lisa was already racing down the corridor.

It's not like it is on the television when someone dies. In reality, the battle to save someone's life takes much longer. The team had already discussed with Bernard his right not to be resuscitated, just as they did with all patients in his situation. It was different for everyone. Some categorically did not want to struggle, but Bernard and his wife had both agreed that a few weeks, or even a few days longer would be worth it. It would give them time to say all the things they needed to, and for Bernard to hopefully see the faces of his grandchildren for one last time. So, the crash team worked on him for nearly half an hour before they agreed that nothing further could be done.

It was almost half past one in the morning and in the hours since the crash call had first gone out, the doctor had been to certify Bernard's death and the routine wheels which were required to turn had been set in motion. Beth had also sat with his wife, Irene, holding first her hand and then her shaking shoulders while the initial shock and emotion had poured out of her. It was only now, with the arrival of Bernard's other family, that Beth was free to check on how Lisa was doing.

'Why do we let ourselves get so attached?' she said, giving Beth a wan smile. 'Every time someone dies, I think I won't let myself do that again. I'll remain professional, impersonal, just like everyone tells us we're supposed to be. But I don't. You'd think I'd have learned my lesson by now.'

Beth looked at Lisa's weary face, seeing the faint lines where tears had tracked their way down her cheeks to drop off the end of her chin. She pushed a mug of tea towards her.

'We do it because we're human,' she said. 'Because Bernard wasn't just a patient in a bed with a whole set of problems to resolve. He was an eighty-six-year-old man who had lived a whole life, and in the time we were privileged to know him we learned all about that life – about the hardships he and his family faced when he was young, about his love of engineering, about how, as a little boy, he would tinker with any bit of machinery he could find, and how that love led to his first job, working on the canal. He told us about his favourite boats – the ones he built which made him really proud. We know how he met and fell in love with Irene, and how the first of their three children was born just seven months after they were married. Now that child is grown up with two children of her own, and we've met both her and her siblings, and all the children they've got between them – Bernard's grandchildren, the loves of his life. So, you tell me how, knowing all of that, we can possibly remain detached.'

Lisa sniffed, her hands wrapped around her mug of tea, taking comfort from its warmth. 'He was such a lovely man,' she said.

'He was,' replied Beth. 'Which is exactly why we fought so hard for him and, at the end, when it was obvious we couldn't save him, we gave him back his dignity and, I hope, the reassurance that he was among friends when he died.'

Lisa nodded gently, silent for a moment as she thought about the truth of Beth's words. They didn't change anything, but then that wasn't why Beth said them. It was a reminder that whatever else this job forced them to be, above all else they remained human.

'How's Irene doing?' asked Lisa.

'She's with her daughter,' replied Beth. 'And both of her sons will be here soon. Time is the only thing we can give them right now, but they know where we are when the questions come.'

Lisa looked up, a resigned expression on her face. 'And in the meantime, we offer tea and sympathy,' she said. 'One of the things we do best.'

'And there's nothing wrong with that either,' said Beth. 'Small kindnesses become very large at times like these.'

Beth remembered them well from the time when Jack had hovered in the space between life and death. How for days she had sat beside him not knowing what the future would look like, her head full of questions she hadn't a hope of answering. She had felt scattered, adrift, as if her tether to the world was working its way loose, and it was only the care and caring from the hospital staff which had kept her grounded. For months on end Beth's world had become, at best, complicated chaos, and at worst, something she wasn't sure she wanted to live through herself. Those times each day when she had sat in the hospital were the only constant through it all.

It was almost three o'clock before she and Lisa had caught up with their workload sufficiently to allow Beth to take her break, by which time Jack had already been lying on their bedroom floor at home for well over two hours.

5

Beth

It was the thing Beth feared the most. That something would happen to Jack while she was at work, and she wouldn't even know about it until she got home. She'd turn her key in the lock and open the door, thinking that in just a few short seconds they'd be together again, she saying good morning and he groaning at the thought of getting up. And then she'd find him, and her life would come crashing down around her.

Almost as bad – or was it worse? – was knowing that something had *already* happened and there wasn't a single thing she could do about it. She couldn't just drop everything and rush straight to his side, however much she wanted to. She had patients to look after and, like tonight, might even be in the middle of trying to save someone else's life. The choice of who might live and who might die simply wasn't hers to make. She was miles away from Jack. It was the price they paid for living. Some days it was thoughts like these which felt as if they were pulling Beth apart.

She forced herself to breathe, to calm her racing heart and

still her trembling fingers. Be logical. Jack had texted her, so he was okay. If he could still use his phone, he was conscious, *and*, she hoped, able to ring emergency services if he needed to. Her fingers jabbed at her phone's keypad.

Are you okay? she asked first. Followed in quick succession by, *What's happened?* and *I'm sorry I couldn't get to my phone, we lost a patient tonight.*

There was an agonising wait, but then three little dots appeared which Beth had never been so pleased to see – Jack was typing a reply.

Okay, it read.

Cramp.

Fell out of bed.

Beth swallowed. *I'll leave as soon as I can*, she replied.

K. Not going anywhere 😌

The strings which Jack had woven around her heart pulled tighter. God, how she loved this man.

How are you? Are you hurt?

Sore arse. Bit cold. But have pulled cover and pillow off bed so no rush

Beth could see him, lying on the floor, with neither the strength nor the means to alter his position. He would be lying where he'd fallen, limbs bent, twisted... or broken— She pushed the scene from her head. Now wasn't the time to dwell on such thoughts; she needed to get home. Sending a quick kiss and *I'll*

see you soon to Jack, Beth threw her phone in her handbag and
rushed back to the ward to find Lisa.

To Beth's way of thinking, staff relations were a two-way street.
If you pulled your weight, or in Beth's case always strived to
overdeliver, then it was reasonable to expect your boss to cut
you a bit of slack every now and again. It didn't always follow,
though. Beth had worked under countless ward sisters or
matrons for whom an employment contract might as well be the
actual law, and there had been no room for deviating one iota
from its terms and conditions. Thankfully, Lisa was of the same
mind as Beth and so a short while later Beth was able to leave
the hospital, well before the end of her shift.

St John's Hospital was one of the very few locally that
hadn't been swallowed up into a brand-new, huge, multimillion-
pound   redeveloped   everything-under-one-roof   'service
provider'. It was an old building, crumbling around the edges,
but with its red brick and mullioned windows, still managed to
hang onto a degree of charm. Over the years, however, what
little space it occupied had been nibbled away, sold off to raise
much-needed cash, and so parking was virtually non-existent. A
small area had been designated for staff, but it hadn't a hope of
accommodating everyone who worked at the hospital. The cost
of it was subsidised, but even if a space came free, Beth couldn't
even consider using it; it was simply beyond their means. Given
its age, the hospital was just off the centre of town, though, so
was only a fifteen-minute – ten on a good day – walk to a tiny
private car park where Beth could leave her car overnight for
free. She hurried through the warren of hospital buildings and
out into the night.

It wasn't until she had been walking for several minutes that
she realised how anxious she was feeling. She was frantic with
worry about Jack, but that wasn't the only thing troubling her.

Her shift started at nine thirty each night and finished at seven each morning, times when the streets had a little life to them. There were people walking dogs or leaving for a night out. There were cars, too, and an atmosphere to the town as it prepared to either wind down for the day or wake up. Now, it was the dead of night, silent and absolutely still. There was no moon, and cutbacks had meant that streetlights were lit for fewer hours, so although not normally blessed with a vivid imagination, the hairs on the back of Beth's neck were beginning to rise. Dark things happened at night; you only had to read a newspaper or listen to the news to know that. She swallowed and, pulling her raincoat tighter, hurried on.

By the time she reached the town centre a steady drizzle was falling, and although she was relieved to be almost at her destination, the buildings there were more cramped, huddled together, throwing heavy shadows onto already dark streets. Beth picked up her pace even more.

Soon, there was only one more street to go before she reached the car park. It was more of an alleyway really and, as she hurried down it, a lighted window drew her attention. She was walking behind the bakery – she could tell by the incredible smell which wafted from a vent in the wall – and, inside, a woman was dancing. Beth slowed automatically, pausing to watch, curious, but also comforted by the sight of something so ordinary, so joyful, among the dark streets.

The woman was singing, too; Beth could hear her through the glass, and she smiled. It was a song she recognised as one her mum used to sing when Beth was still living at home – a romantic ballad by some Hollywood starlet, Doris Day perhaps. The woman was cradling an enormous bowl in her arms as if it were her partner and, completely oblivious to the outside world, was twirling around the room.

Still smiling, but not wishing to disturb the baker's reverie, Beth roused herself and, head down against the rain, began to fumble in her bag for her car keys. Why was it that you could never find the flipping things when you were in a hurry? They must have dropped to the bottom amid all the other debris, and Beth pushed her hand deeper, wrestling with her bag while still hurrying as best she could. Just as her fingers touched metal, her foot slipped on cobbles slick with rain and, with no hands free to balance her, Beth pitched forward, crashing to her knees. Pain shot through them and up into her hip.

For a second, she couldn't work out which way was up. One minute she was standing, and the next she was sprawled on the ground, the contents of her bag rolling around in the wet. Both knees were throbbing, and one hand stung unaccountably as she tried to stand. From nowhere, she felt a hand on her arm.

'Gently, you've taken quite a tumble. Catch your breath a minute.'

Beth startled, looking up into the face of the woman she'd seen dancing.

'Thank you, I—' She broke off, sagging back down as her head began to swim.

'That's it, just sit a minute, and then we'll get you in out of the rain. Let me know when you want to try standing.'

The woman's smile was kind, her face etched with concern. She still had hold of Beth's arm and Beth could feel her fingers through her coat, holding just tight enough to be reassuring. After a minute, Beth took a deep breath and gestured with her hand.

'Up you come then,' said the woman. 'Here, lean on me.' The woman was half Beth's size but had a surprisingly firm stance. Slowly, Beth was able to draw her feet under her and, grimacing with pain, stood shakily.

'Oh dear...' The woman was looking at her anxiously. 'These cobbles are murder in the rain. I've nearly gone over myself on countless occasions.' She pulled back to better see what the damage might be. 'Where are you hurt?' Beth lowered a hand vaguely in the direction of her knees. 'Ouch... I hope those weren't your best tights. You've made quite a mess of them, I'm afraid. Come on, let's get you inside and I can take a better look. I think you might be bleeding.'

'No!' Beth shook her head. 'Sorry, I didn't mean to shout, but I have to get home. My husband... he's fallen and...' Her vision swam with tears.

'Then all the more reason to get you home in one piece. It won't take long.'

Beth shook her head again, harder this time, but all that did was set things spinning.

'You've had a nasty shock apart from anything else, and if you're intending to drive, at least wait until you're feeling less dizzy. You'll be no use to your husband if you have an accident on the way home.'

Beth felt herself being pulled in the direction of the bakery and although her heart told her that Jack's need was far more urgent than her own, her head would quite like her to sit down.

'Just a minute then. I'm sure I'll be fine, I'm a nurse.'

The woman regarded her for a moment. 'And that makes you immune to getting hurt then, does it?' Swivelling slightly, she made sure that Beth was stable on her feet before quickly crouching to scoop up Beth's possessions, sweeping them back into her bag. 'Right, let's get you sorted out.'

The bakery door was wide open, music still drifting through it, although a different song was playing now. It was blissfully warm inside the kitchen and Beth had no hesitation in sinking onto the chair the woman provided. She set Beth's bag down on the table beside her and studied her intently.

'I'll get the first-aid kit,' she said, crossing the room to a shelf on the far side. She switched off the music before taking down the universally familiar green box. 'Shall I let you do the honours? You'll probably do a much better job than I will. And while you do that, I'll put the kettle on. Don't argue.'

Beth, whose mouth had been open to do just that, closed it again and accepted the kit with a wry smile. 'Thank you.'

Wincing, Beth pulled at her tights where the gauzy material had stuck itself to her knees. The woman was right – she had made a real mess of them. They were wet, muddy, gritty with something, and a trickle of blood had rolled down one of her legs. Seeing that the woman's back was still turned, Beth quickly fished under her skirt and rolled down her tights, kicking off her shoes so that she could take them off entirely. By the time a steaming cup of tea had been placed in front of her, she'd cleaned and dressed one of her knees and was just tackling the other. They stung like crazy.

'I don't know if you take sugar,' said the woman. 'But I've put you some in anyway. It's good for shock, isn't it? Or is that just an old wives' tale?'

Beth smiled. 'Whether it is or it isn't, it's still my go-to cure-all at work,' she said. 'We lost a patient tonight and...' She stopped, swallowing. 'I sat with his wife afterwards and the first thing I did was make her a cup of tea.' The image of Irene's distraught face swam into her head, and it was all Beth could do to stop tears from spilling down her own cheeks. She bent to her task again in order to thrust them away.

'That must have been tough,' said the woman. 'I don't know how you nurses do it, coping with stuff like that.' Even though her head was still bent, Beth could feel the woman's watchful gaze. 'Would you like a tissue?' she added. 'It sounds like you've had quite a night. A good cry would probably do you the world of good.'

Beth looked up in astonishment. She'd held her tears inside herself for so long now she'd almost forgotten how to let them go, and yet a perfect stranger had seen the one thing which Beth was sure would make her feel better.

'You're probably right,' she said, again choosing not to give in. 'But I can't do that to you. And I ought to get going. My husband...'

The woman nodded. 'Why don't you ring him or message him? Let him know you'll be on your way in a few minutes. Then at least you won't feel so anxious driving home. You'll only rush even more than you're already going to.'

Beth fished in her handbag. 'I will, thank you.' She pulled out her phone, praying that it was undamaged. 'He's disabled,' she added, feeling as if she owed the woman some sort of explanation. 'And he fell out of bed. Normally he's okay until I get home... he just sleeps.'

The woman nodded.

'But he got cramp, and... I guess he must have rolled over too far and couldn't right himself. His arms and legs don't work very well.'

Again, the woman nodded. 'So, there's just you looking after him?'

Beth could feel herself blushing. 'We can't get anyone else... it's too expensive.' She started to type a message on her phone. 'Sorry, you've been very kind.'

The woman pushed the mug towards her as if sensing her sudden desperation to go. 'At least drink that before you leave,' she said.

Her message sent, Beth quickly dressed her other knee and, with a cursory glance at her palm which was also grazed, picked up the mug and drained half its contents in one go. 'Thank you,' she said again. 'That was lovely, but I'd better be on my way.'

The woman got to her feet and darted to a rack on the far side of the kitchen. 'Hang on, let me get you these...' She came forward bearing a paper bag. 'There's a couple of pastries in there. Make sure you eat something.'

For the second time, Beth stared at her, completely taken aback by the woman's kindness. 'Thank you. I don't know what to say. Did you make them?'

The woman dipped her head. 'White chocolate and rasp-berry croissants. They're my favourite.'

'Oh God, Jack will devour these. I'll have to fight him off.' And suddenly, just like that, Beth knew that everything was going to be okay. A little chink of light had just appeared in the night. She got up, collecting her handbag. 'I don't even know your name,' she said.

The woman smiled. 'It's Frances... Frankie.'

6

Frankie

Frankie didn't used to be the kind of person who watched from the sidelines, but she was now. On days when she was trying to be kinder to herself, she realised that not everything that went awry was her wrongdoing. If *she* didn't understand why she pushed people away, why would they? Sometimes though, she wondered whether all it would have taken was for someone to ask the right questions, someone astute enough to see beneath the perfect veneer of her life. Trouble was, she hadn't peered beneath it either, not for a long time, and by the time she did, everyone had gone. Moved on.

It sounded harsh, but the truth *was* harsh. It brought with it a lengthy period of self-loathing which had stuck to her like glue. It wasn't until she realised she could peel it from her skin that she began to understand that what happened wasn't because of the choices she'd made, but because those choices only *seemed* like hers. They weren't though, they hadn't been for a long time. But some of the glue still stuck to her, in the tiny nooks and crevices where it was hard to get at, which was why thoughts about what happened last night were still swirling around her head.

She hadn't even stopped to think about the consequences when she saw the woman fall. She'd instinctively rushed out to help but, afterwards, when she started to dissect what had happened, the doubts began to creep in. At first, she had been pleased – what she'd done were the actions of the woman Frankie used to be, and the fact that she could still behave in this way was reassuring. Then she realised she had broken free from the sanctuary of the bakery, and the thought sent a sharp flick of fear through her belly.

A cup of tea and some deep breathing had calmed her, as had the fact that in all likelihood she would never see the woman again but, hours later, she was still on her mind. She'd hurt her knee, and was anxious to get home to her husband, but there was something else about her which had pricked Frankie's thoughts, as if looking at her was like looking in a mirror and seeing something of herself reflected back. It wasn't until much later, when she was taking a tray of morning rolls from the oven, that she understood why she couldn't get thoughts of the woman from her head. What she had seen mirrored in the woman's eyes was pain – not from the graze on her knee, or the anxiety over what had happened to her husband, but the kind that ran deep, just like Frankie's did.

She'd remained distracted right until the end of her shift, yearning for the oblivion of sleep, but then, twenty minutes ago, her boss, Vivienne, had rung to say she was poorly and that eclipsed everything she had been feeling. Vivienne wouldn't be able to take over from Frankie as she normally did. Instead, Frankie would need to stay on for another hour or so until someone came to cover for her. It would probably be Melanie, who normally only worked on Vivienne's days off, but Melanie had children she had to take to school. At such short notice, Frankie reckoned the earliest Melanie could relieve her would be half past nine, and while the thought of adding another two hours on top of her normal shift wasn't pleasing, this wasn't what had made her stomach lurch. The morning rush started just after eight. And Frankie would have to cope with it, alone. All those people...

Frankie knew what needed to be done to get the bakery ready for customers; that wasn't what worried her. Nor was it setting aside bread for the regular orders or accepting the deliveries which often arrived first thing. What terrified her was the sheer number of people who would come through the door – having conversation after conversation till her head rang with voices which would still be there long after she left. It would be exhausting. And she always felt as if she were on a stage, projecting an image of herself which was based on reality yet was not truly her. Would she ever lose the self-consciousness which made her feel so detached, as if she were looking at her life through a window?

She stood in the centre of the shop for a few moments, pulling her mind into order, listing everything in her head which needed to be done, and then, with a deep breath, she went through to the rear of the bakery, the space she still thought of as her sanctuary, to collect the first of the loaves.

Duggan's wasn't the smartest of shops. The fittings were old and showed their age, but every morning, before her shift was due to end, Frankie made sure she left everything just as she found it. She wiped down the work surfaces and mopped the floor, and also washed and dried the equipment she'd used overnight, before returning it to the huge storeroom. For as long as she had been there, not only had this room housed all the things she used on a daily basis, but also a fair amount of old and obsolete equipment, including display materials and damaged shop fittings. Not quite as old as those stored in her flat, but it was evident that they hadn't been used recently. To make her life easier, she had separated these from the rest of the things, relocating them to the furthest shelves. She had, however, kept them just as neat, clean, and organised as everything else, and among these were three beautiful wicker baskets. She assumed they had been used for display in the shop at some point, and yet although there was still room for them, Vivienne preferred to put the loaves straight onto the shelves.

Frankie went to look at them again, regarding them with a critical eye, and to her mind they were still the only thing about the shop which had any charm. She'd never really considered how it looked before – not her job – but it was bland, basic, utilitarian even: the display cabinet for the pastries was made from plain glass, the shelves for the bread had once been painted but were now turning yellow with age, and the counter where the till sat was covered in Formica, off-white and chipped at the edges. She was halfway to the shop floor, baskets in hand, before she stopped herself. What was she doing? If Vivienne had wanted to use the baskets she would have. Similarly, if she'd thought placing a vase of fresh flowers on the counter was a good idea, she'd have done that too, and replaced the board with prices on it where the letters kept falling off. Imagine how Vivienne would feel when she came back to work and found Frankie had taken it upon herself to change things? She returned the baskets to the storeroom and firmly closed the door. She was procrastinating, inventing things to take her mind off opening the shop when what she really needed was to get on and do it.

They say that people are often hard to recognise when seen out of context, and it must be true because, when a woman came in an hour later and stood right in front of Frankie with a big smile on her face, and a cheery 'hi' on her lips, Frankie stared at her blankly for far longer than she should have. Goodness only knows what her face must have looked like as her brain trawled its data banks for a clue as to the woman's identity. Her memory had definitely got worse as she'd got older, but the woman must have thought she was a complete idiot. Frankie had literally seen her only a few hours before but now her brain had stuck fast.

Thankfully, the woman just laughed. 'I don't think I even told you my name, but it's Beth. And you're Frankie, right?'

Finally, the penny dropped. Frankie nodded, smiling as her cheeks bloomed with embarrassment. 'Was everything okay? How's your husband?' Frankie couldn't remember if she'd been told his name or not. She suspected she had, but her panicked brain was refusing to yield it up.

'Oh, he's okay...' Beth rolled her eyes, but it was a reflex action. Frankie could still see anxiety etched in the creases of her face. 'He's got a massive bruise on his backside, and a similar dent in his pride, but nothing broken, thank God.'

'And how are you? Did you get home all right?'

'I did. My knee hurt like buggery changing gear but other than that, it was fine. Scared myself senseless in the car park, mind, but that was me just being silly.'

Frankie turned away for a moment to serve another customer. 'Sorry, go on,' she said, turning back. 'What scared you?'

'I park in the little place around the corner, you know where I mean?' She paused fractionally for Frankie's answering nod. 'It's usually pretty empty overnight, aside from the odd car or two, but you get to know which ones are the regulars. I've never noticed anything out of the ordinary before, but last night as I walked past this one car, there was a bloke inside with his head lolling against the window. I honestly thought he was dead.' She shook her head in amusement. 'But like I said, just me being silly. After a few seconds, with me peering at him while trying not to look like I *was* peering at him, he gave a massive snort, and his head lolled the other way. He was just asleep. Mind you, that's a bit worrying in itself, but...' She smiled. 'Anyway, never mind that. I hoped you'd still be here. I wasn't sure what time you finished.'

'I'm usually gone by now,' replied Frankie, eyeing the street. 'But the owner's poorly so I'm helping out for a bit until the cavalry arrives...'

Beth nodded. 'I'm glad I caught you then. I wanted to give you these...' She laid a box of chocolates on the counter. Posh ones, too, from Hotel Chocolat. 'First, for coming to my rescue, to *Jack's* rescue, and also because those croissants you gave us were the best we've ever eaten. Honestly. We had them for breakfast.' She inched the box forward. 'I wasn't sure if you like—'

'Oh, I do,' Frankie replied. 'I absolutely do.' She stared at the gift which Beth had no need to bring her but had done so anyway. 'It really wasn't necessary, and I should probably modestly refuse them, saying you shouldn't have. But I'm not going to, because I bloody love these.'

Beth grinned. 'In that case, I'm even more glad. It's just a small kindness to say thank you for a big kindness, that's all.'

Frankie would have said it was the other way around. Either way, it was a lovely thing for Beth to do and she suddenly felt quite emotional, reminded of a quote she'd always loved: *So shines a good deed in a weary world.* But Shakespeare had written another line before that and Frankie wracked her brain trying to remember how it went; something about candles. That was it – *how far that little candle throws his beams...* Which one of them was the candle, she wondered? Or perhaps they both were. She, holding out a hand to Beth in the dark, or Beth standing before Frankie now and reaching back with a good deed of her own. Beth's smile was a bright flicker of light in a world which for a long time had felt dark, and overwhelmingly weary – not just for her, or for Beth. Everywhere she looked were people just trying to make it through the day. A tiny glowing filament had strung itself between them, so when Frankie saw Melanie coming through the door to relieve her, just at the moment Beth invited her for a coffee, she did something she hadn't done in a long time. She said yes.

7

William

William was six foot three and around fourteen and a half stone, or ninety-two kilos in new money, and, standing as tall as he could, gave the impression of a force to be reckoned with. He had learned from an early age that standing tall was his best option, and just in case he didn't, his mother had constantly pulled him up for slouching. Now, even though he was in his early fifties, her voice still sounded in his ear if he did so.

None of that made him feel any easier, however. It really didn't matter how he looked, or how he sounded, because as far as Stuart was concerned, he was Bill, should-be-eternally-grateful-for-your-job-and-you-don't-get-paid-to-think-you-get-paid-to-do-as-you're-told. He'd heard that line so many times, he'd almost come to believe it himself. Almost.

What rankled most was that William *was* extremely grateful for his job. The club's boss, Danny, had taken a chance on him when no one else would, and William knew he wasn't prime employee material. The wrong background, the wrong age and the wrong experience saw to that. But his job was the difference between eking out an existence or going under completely, and Stuart used that to his advantage whenever he could. As Danny's right-hand man, he clearly believed that gave him licence to treat William any which way he pleased.

Nevertheless, William would have to talk to Danny tonight because the situation was getting out of hand, and the longer he left it, the worse it was going to get. If Danny wasn't careful his club was going to get all sorts of attention, and all of it the wrong kind. In all likelihood his boss wouldn't listen, but William's heart still urged him to try. Then, at least, he would have done his best – his conscience would be clear. He would still be keeping his promise to Louise, even after all these years.

So, it was a slow trudge through the streets this evening as William made his way to work. The town was filling up with the party crowd; everyone else had long since gone home and every building he passed was closed for the night. Shadowy lights spilled from shop windows onto the pavement, but inside, all was dark. Offices were darker still, just the odd security light, and the only 'life' came from the flats above them. William often wondered about the lives of the people who lived there. Were they happy? Were they warm? Were they settling down for a relaxing evening after a good day? He could picture it if he tried, and he would have that kind of life one day. He had to.

He paused in the alleyway beside Duggan's bakery. There was a vent from which the most heavenly warmth wafted into the air. Warmth that was laden with a smell so intoxicating that William liked to stand still, breathing it in, imagining eating a breakfast that would smell just like it. He did it for as long as he could before his stomach growled with hunger, but for those few moments he could almost taste the sugary glazed pastries and the loaves of bread, fresh and doughy, slice after slice smothered in butter.

With a sigh he carried on down the alley, leaving the shops behind. He crossed over the road, walked through the car park and then down the tiny side street where the club's neon lights were stark against the dark sky. His heart began to beat somewhat quicker at the thought of the conversation ahead of him.

Heading around the side of the building, William pressed the buzzer beside the scratched and dented blue door which only the staff used and waited for Rick to let him in. Rick spent most of his time on the phone inside a small, windowless office. What he did, William had no idea, and he'd never had a conversation with him that was long enough for him to ask. William bade him a good evening as he passed, the same as he did every night, but today there was no reply at all. On the few occasions Rick did reply it was mostly words of one syllable, or a grunt. Being polite never hurt anyone though, so William would continue to greet him for as long as he worked there.

There was almost half an hour to go before William's shift started. He liked to get there early, to ready himself for his duties without feeling rushed or underprepared, and tonight he was earlier still. What he had to say to Danny wouldn't take long but he didn't want their conversation to eat into his normal routine.

Opening his locker, he eased off his raincoat just as a gruff voice came from behind him.

'Stuart wants to see you,' said Rick, turning on his heel before William could reply. 'He's out front.'

William stared at Rick's retreating back and swallowed, straightening his shirt and hitching his trousers a little higher. He didn't want to give Stuart any excuse to pull him up. He passed a hand over his hair and checked that his shoes were still gleaming before pulling open the door which led inside the club.

Stuart was behind the bar flirting with Linda and Sam, two of the VIP waitresses. They were all laughter and smiles, happily engaging in the banter, and William often wondered what they really thought of the oily barman – whether they actually liked him or whether it was just part of the job. Either way, William liked them both. They probably thought he was old enough to be their grandfather, but they'd always been really nice to him, and Sam had even brought in extra food for him on a few occasions. She said it was leftovers she didn't have room to freeze, and William was pretty sure that was just a little white lie, but he was very grateful all the same. Sam smiled as William approached before melting away with Linda in tow. Whatever Stuart needed to talk to him about it was obvious that both women had been told to make themselves scarce.

William prepared a smile. 'Evening, Stuart, Rick mentioned you'd like a word.'

'I do indeed, Bill. Walk with me a moment.'

William nodded and followed Stuart to the edge of the stage. There was no live event on tonight, so the area was dark and full of shadows.

'So how long have you worked here now, Bill?' asked Stuart. 'It must be a fair few months.'

'Nearly nine,' he replied, trying to keep his voice steady. He didn't like the overly chummy tone in Stuart's voice; it sparked of insincerity and it occurred to him there was every possibility Stuart would ensure he didn't make it to ten.

'And everything going okay, is it?' asked Stuart.

'I'd have said so, yes.'

'Excellent.'

Stuart paused a moment, his eyes roving William's face. He leaned in. 'Thing is, Bill, I've been watching you and you strike me as the kind of person who knows what's important in life. And it occurred to me that we might be able to help each other out.'

William nodded. He hadn't a clue what Stuart was talking about.

'It's not something I offer to everyone, but it strikes me that you have some special qualities, which might mean you're open to certain possibilities...'

'Possibilities?'

'Yeah... like a little bit of extra work... and no questions asked.'

A hot flicker of alarm stirred William's stomach. 'I'm not sure I understand. I did explain when I came for my interview that I was putting my past behind me.'

'Not that easy though, is it?'

William dropped his head. 'No, but, like I explained, this is a fresh start and—'

'Bill, Bill, I believe you, mate,' interrupted Stuart with a lazy smile. 'We wouldn't have taken you on if we didn't, would we? But you have to recognise that you're not everyone's cup of tea, are you?'

'Maybe so, but I deserve to be given a chance, same as the next man.'

'It's a nice thought, Bill, I see that. But you and me both know that in the real world it doesn't happen like that. I don't like it any more than you do, but I don't make the rules.' He sniffed and wiped the back of his hand across his mouth. 'And we're getting away from the subject in hand, so let me put it like this. I have a very special friend who's having a party next week, at a nice little private venue, with some... special guests. And I need a bit of help to ensure that everyone has a good time. You understand?' He smiled again. 'Bit like you do here, only this time it's cash in hand because you're going to keep your mouth shut, okay? It's the kind of party that no one else needs to know about.'

William swallowed and his heart sank. 'The illegal kind, you mean.'

'Bill, don't be like that... It's just a few games of cards, where's the harm?' He narrowed his eyes. 'I wouldn't have thought I'd have to tell you what a good opportunity this is. I'd have thought a man in your position could always do with a little extra cash, and if you do your job well then there could be a lot more where that came from.'

'I'm grateful, Stuart, don't think I'm not, but I'm trying to do an honest day's work here and be paid for it, that's all. I don't think the kind of offer you're talking about will do me much good. So, if it's all the same, I'd rather pass.'

'That's a shame, Bill, it really is.' Stuart stared at his fingers and picked a bit of dirt from beneath one nail. 'I like you, and I'm offering you something when others wouldn't have given you the time of day. It saddens me you don't want my help.'

'It isn't that,' replied William, heat prickling the back of his neck. 'I'd just prefer to keep things as they are. But you needn't worry about me keeping my mouth shut. I won't tell anyone what we've discussed.'

'Glad to hear it, Bill. But I'm not sure you understand. See, Danny's a good businessman. He has a reputation to uphold and he runs a good club here. People come to have a good time, and you and I ensure that's what they get. So I'm wondering how Danny might feel if he finds out you're not quite as honest as he thinks you are. He might worry about what that would mean for his business, and that really wouldn't be good for you. I'm just trying to ensure that doesn't happen.'

Stuart's eyes were fixed on William's in a way that made it hard for him to look away. And their meaning was clear.

'How much money are we talking about?' replied William.

'Normal wages, plus another fifty for any extra nights you do.'

'And how many will that be?'

'A few. Two or three to start with, and we'll see how things go.'

William studied Stuart's face but it was clear there was only one response he could give. He nodded as if he was considering his offer. 'Danny know about this, does he?' he asked. 'Only that's why I'm early, I wanted to have a bit of a chat with him.'

Stuart lifted his head, nostrils flaring. 'He's not here tonight, it's just me... looking after things...'

William was meant to feel intimidated but he could see the clench in Stuart's jaw. He straightened himself to his full height. 'Shame... not to worry, another time will do.' He paused, as if thinking. 'So maybe I'll pass on your offer this time round. Thanks all the same.' He was taking a big risk and he was fully aware of what could happen. He needed this job but he wasn't about to give Stuart even more power over him. Not yet anyway. Not unless he had no choice.

Stuart leaned forward until his face was only inches from William's. 'Yeah, it is a shame. Okay then, big man, suit yourself, but I'm watching you, Bill. I'll always be watching you.'

He didn't say it, but William would be watching him, too.

With a snide grin, Stuart patted his arm. 'Good man,' he said.

William stood his ground as Stuart walked away. It might not have been the most sensible thing to make an enemy of him but William was angry. He was fed up of being made to feel a nothing, a nobody... His fingers clenched against his palms. 'It's *William*,' he murmured under his breath as he tried to calm his breathing. 'Not Bill, Billy, Will or anything else you want to call me. It's William. *William...*'

8

Tam

'What can I get you this evening, Eleanor? Tea, a hot chocolate or some Horlicks?'

The elderly lady gave Tam a look that twinkled in amusement. 'You won't get me that easily,' she said. 'It's a slippery slope, I tell you.'

'So you always say,' replied Tam with a smile of his own. 'But have you ever tried Horlicks? I quite like it.'

'Yes, but it's fine for you, you're only young. If I have it, I'll be drooling, babbling and behaving like Betty in no time.'

'Naughty,' chided Tam, but he grinned. Eleanor had such a wicked sense of humour. 'So, last chance to change your mind, or is it to be your usual eye-wateringly strong black coffee?'

Eleanor dipped her head. 'I won't be swayed,' she said.

'Fair enough.'

Tam ducked his head back through the door and headed towards the kitchen, still smiling. He always left Eleanor till last on his final nightly round of drinks. There was only an hour left to go before his shift finished and if he was lucky, he'd get to have a chat with her for a while before anyone else needed him. The residents at Chawston House were a mixed bunch. All elderly, of course, but there was no one who made him smile quite like Eleanor did. She reminded him of how his mum used to be before her stroke, so maybe that's what it was – both as feisty as each other, both determined not to act their age, and both able to argue with themselves in an empty room.

Returning to Eleanor, Tam placed her coffee on the small table beside her chair. Eleanor had already added her nightly bribe to it, not that she needed an inducement for him to stay, but she did it just in case.

'Jaffa Cake?' she said, picking up the box.

'Don't mind if I do,' replied Tam, watching her struggle with the packaging. Her hands were twisted now, wrecked by arthritis, but only when she gave up would Tam take over the opening of her favourite treat. He never offered. Tonight, she made it as far as the cellophane wrapper before giving up in disgust.

'Don't ever get old, young man, you'll live to regret it,' she said.

Tam, who felt every one of his forty-nine years, smiled as he ripped open the packet and offered it to Eleanor. 'I shall bear that in mind,' he replied.

It was one of the things which worried him, actually, living the way he did. He'd never been pernickety about his appearance, but even basic maintenance wasn't so easy now. He worried that, like an old house, the moment he started to neglect it, however slightly, his body would wear its age far more so than it did now.

He checked his watch. 'Just in time,' he said, although, of course, there was no coincidence about the timing of his arrival. 'Shall I switch on the telly for you?'

Eleanor nodded. *Gardener's World* had been one of the things which had got them talking in the first place, and now, time permitting, they always watched it together. 'Don't tell anyone,' she said. 'But you're my favourite.'

Tam glanced towards the door. 'Don't tell anyone, but you're my favourite, too.' While it was true that Tam said that to all the residents, in Eleanor's case, he meant it. He turned on the television and perched on the only other armchair in the room. It wouldn't do to look too comfortable.

Once upon a time, Tam would never miss an episode of *Gardener's World*. Gardening had been his livelihood, and it never ceased to amaze him how much call there would be for a specific plant or a particular colour of rose if it had been featured on the nation's favourite programme on the subject. Now he no longer had a garden. Nor a television set on which to watch it, but he still liked to keep his hand in. One day those things would change, and he wanted to be ready when they did.

Tonight, he was able to watch for a full thirteen minutes before he got called away by another member of staff. Trish was running late so he was needed to help with the drug trolley. He stuffed another Jaffa Cake in his mouth as he left Eleanor's room and winked. 'See you tomorrow, milady,' he said.

Eleanor waved a hand as if to dismiss a recalcitrant servant and snorted with laughter. She was definitely one of the things which made his job worthwhile. Perhaps the only thing. She was certainly the only one who knew the truth of his circumstances.

Working in a residential care home was not a career move Tam had ever seen himself making, but then a lot of the events of recent years weren't what he'd foreseen either. Bankruptcy being one of them. He shouldn't have been so trusting, he knew that now. But hindsight was a wonderful thing, and it was very easy to be wise after the event. Going into business with his best mate had seemed like one of the most logical decisions he'd ever made, at first anyway. His horticultural business had started off small, selling to just a handful of garden centres, but as it grew it had made sense for him and Chris to work together – more manpower, for one thing. But he should have realised that Chris wanted different things than he did. And, when it inevitably fell apart, Chris hadn't been the one to take responsibility – that had been left to Tam. Chris might have walked away with a bankruptcy label around his neck too, but even that hadn't bothered him. He was free to carry on, to start up a new business any time he liked. It had been Tam whose conscience wouldn't rest. Tam who sold his house and everything he owned to pay off his creditors, and even that wasn't enough. They were small businesses like his; it wouldn't have been right to let them down. It was the only time in his life he'd been grateful for his divorce – had he still been with Sandra the devastation caused to their lives would have been unimaginable. As it was, Tam had lost everything apart from his integrity, and yet on most days he still thought he had done the right thing.

The job at Chawston House had come about through a friend of a friend, and Tam had jumped at the opportunity – he couldn't afford not to. It had been a lifeline for a drowning man and without it, things would have been so much worse. And it wouldn't be forever. In another year or so his debts would be clear and then he could start thinking about saving for his own future. Perhaps he'd even be able to rent a flat, or afford the deposit, at least. After that, who knew? He still had another fifteen to twenty years ahead of him before he could even think about retiring. Not that he wanted to, he still had far too much life to live, but what he couldn't get his head around was that those years might be spent working at Chawston House, or somewhere similar. The cold wasn't the only thing which kept him awake at night.

Once Tam's shift had ended, he finished handing over to Trish and then it was only a matter of minutes before he walked out, bag slung over his shoulder, into the night air. It was nearly eight, time for relaxing and settling down for a few hours before bed. Not for Tam, though; he still had a few things to do before he could turn in.

One good thing about his shift pattern was the opportunity it gave him to have an evening meal. It was a perk available to all staff who were on duty at that time, but not many took advantage of it. Most of them went home to cook, but without that luxury Tam ate whatever was on the menu. Tonight, it had been sausages and mash, with cabbage that was more mush than cabbage had any right to be, and carrots as hard as bullets, but he had eaten it all without complaint. Breakfast and lunch he had to provide himself, but it was surprising how little he could get by on.

Food was something Tam had stopped thinking about – in any pleasurable way, that was; it had simply become fuel. But in every other regard Tam took care of himself as best he could. It had taken quite some time, of trial and error, awkward confrontations and a few heated discussions, but eventually he had found a small gym where the staff were a little more relaxed about security. He was pretty sure they knew why he was there, but he was just as well dressed as any other member and unfailingly polite, so mostly they didn't give him a second glance. He was able to shower, wash his hair and, importantly, have a shave every night. There was never the opportunity in the morning, but he was lucky – his ginger hair was inclined to curl and his five o'clock shadow was barely noticeable, so he was able to get by with just a cursory wash and brush-up.

His evening ablutions completed, Tam headed towards a small car park where he had been staying for the last few nights. It was nudged in between the buildings down a small side street and wasn't far away from his work. It was quiet enough, and there was a streetlight too, for which he was always grateful. There was a downside to that, of course, but so far he hadn't incurred any unwelcome attention.

More than once he had thanked his lucky stars for having

had the foresight to buy an estate car and, opening the boot, he clambered inside the spacious interior. His boots came off first, then his jacket, and once he'd stowed both carefully away, he took his uniform from his bag and laid it out so he could fold it ready for the morning. Placing it on the passenger seat ensured it never got creased. He had already changed into his tracksuit at the gym, so now it was simply a matter of climbing inside his sleeping bag.

Five minutes later, with a library book in hand, Tam settled down for the night.

9

William

Back in the day, the club had been called Oasis and William had been a frequent visitor, just like all of his mates. Not that he let on, but he and this town knew one another well. William had grown up here, gone to school here. It was only later that he'd moved away. But although he knew these streets like the back of his hand, they had a different feel about them now.

He could still remember his teenage self, walking down Bridge Street on a Saturday night, with far too much beer in his belly, laughing and carousing with the lads. They'd had a favourite spot down by the river where they used to smoke and neck cider straight from the bottle. It was also where he'd had his first kiss, with a girl called Michelle. That was before Louise, of course. Good times. Yes, they'd drunk too much, been loud and no doubt obnoxious on occasion, but it had been fun, none of it had felt threatening – they were just having a lark. But William had been only too aware when the fun had stopped for him and it had all become desperate instead. When the object of a night out changed from enjoyment to seeking oblivion.

Some of the memories were good ones, but there were many more which weren't and it wasn't the first time William wished he'd never come back. But he'd made a promise, and what would he have to show for the last few years if he didn't take the opportunity when it arose? It might be the last chance he'd ever get. He must remember that.

Of course, the club hadn't been called Oasis for years now. It had had a number of names over time, the most current of which was Vipers, a name which William thought highly appropriate. And Stuart was the biggest snake of them all. It sickened him to think that Danny might turn out to be like him, only putting on a show of being respectable when, in fact, he didn't care one jot how he made his money. Only time would tell though, and tonight William had a job to do.

It was Tuesday, traditionally a night when the club was quiet, so unlike on other days when most of his time was fully occupied, either on the door or dealing with club-goers outside, William had more opportunity to get a better feel for what was going on inside.

Most of the staff at Vipers were like William – people who wouldn't necessarily have chosen to work there given their pick of jobs going, but who, like him, didn't have the luxury of being choosy. Everyone, that was, except for Stuart. Somewhere in his late twenties by William's estimate, Stuart's habitual expression was middle distance between a sneer and a knowing arrogance, as if he believed that not only was he better than anyone else, but that he was also in possession of knowledge only he was privy to. It made William uneasy, and perhaps it was a sixth sense he'd picked up over the years, but William had been wary of him from the get-go. Now, knowing what he did, he was even more wary. Admittedly William hadn't worked at the club all that long but he had a feel for when a situation was right and when it was wrong, when a situation would resolve itself or when intervention would be needed. And on quiet nights like these, William's antenna had time to finely tune itself.

The first few hours of his shift were relatively relaxed, but once the night got going he was quickly able to spot the most serious contenders for making trouble. They had a hard edge to them, and whereas the rest of the punters were just out to have a good time, these few had eyes which glinted with something much darker.

He had been watching three men in particular, drawn to his attention by the fact that they seemed to know Stuart well. Initially he thought they were simply getting quietly and steadily drunk, but following a trip to the bathroom, William saw their behaviour had changed – from amiable and relaxed to something that seethed with a bright and brittle energy. It was something he'd seen on far too many occasions before. What was worse was that he was powerless to do anything about it. Unless, of course, anything untoward happened.

By one in the morning, adrenaline had been coursing through William's body for hours, and with neither fight nor flight to make use of it, he felt jittery and nauseous, a raw headache beginning to gnaw at his temples.

The spark, as sparks did, flared briefly, but with so much combustible material in the room, caught rapidly. The fire flashed, and for William that meant he was up against five men intent on trouble. He was bigger than most of them and two immediately melted into the background, but it was the three he'd spotted earlier who were most likely to cause him problems.

For the most part, the altercations at the club which William had got involved in previously had been short-lived. It had been enough to point out that if their behaviour continued they were likely to get chucked out and, by and large, their friends convinced them to stop being stupid. Few of the argu-ments had ever been serious enough to warrant William physically restraining anyone. Tonight, though, he knew it wasn't going to be as simple as a few quiet words. He had placed himself between two of the men, holding the bicep of the one on his right in a very firm grip, when Stuart suddenly materialised beside him.

'Looks like you can handle yourself,' he said to William with a snide grin. 'But I can vouch for these fellas personally. They're just a little excited, aren't you, lads?' he added, turning to them. 'No need to get alarmed, William.' He stressed the pronunciation of William's name as if he thought his request to be called anything other than Bill was frankly ridiculous. As if he was doing William a favour. It made William want to prove just how well he *could* handle himself.

There was a moment when things could have gone either way, but then the ringleader gave a dismissive shrug and leered at William. 'All right, Grandad, I'm cool,' he said, wriggling his arm in an attempt to release William's grip.

William let go, ignoring the jibe. None of these men were worth losing his job over. But he waited until he was sure they had cooled off before moving away. He was well aware, however, that Stuart's gaze had moved with him, and he was now regarding William intently. His message was clear. These men were his, and therefore untouchable. If William had any doubts about Stuart before, then this little encounter had caused them to multiply rapidly.

The thing about people like Stuart was that they considered themselves invincible. It probably never occurred to him that William might talk to their boss if he had any concerns, at least not until William mentioned the possibility. Now William was even more determined to follow it up. If he was to make any difference at all, he had to give it a try. He'd never forgive himself if he didn't.

10

Tam

'Hello, Tam.'

Tam stared at the neatly dressed man blocking his path. Too neat. The Chris Tam knew of old never ventured sartorially past jeans and a tee shirt. Now he looked as if he might have on his best suit for a court appearance. Not that Tam gave a damn, not any more.

'It's good to see you,' he added. 'You're looking well.'

Tam refused to be drawn, remaining silent. Chris wouldn't have failed to clock the length of his hair. He used to tease Tam about it, about its ginger colour, but also how it grew ever more curly the longer it got. Now it was far beyond what Tam used to tolerate. He surreptitiously pulled his coat together a little more. If Chris's memory was any good, he'd also realise that Tam was still wearing his favourite shirt, only instead of crisp and well laundered, it was now a little rumpled, with a slight fraying to one cuff.

Chris tried again. 'No, really, you look better than you did the last time I saw you. Things must be on the up.'

They weren't, not really; Tam had just got better at looking after himself with no money to speak of, but he was damned if he'd reward Chris with a response. He checked his watch. 'I have a job I'm going to be late for,' he said.

'Good... that's good.' Chris paused, as if weighing something up. 'I was hoping to catch you,' he continued, opening his jacket to fish inside. 'I have some more post for you. Sorry, some of it might be a couple of weeks old, I haven't seen you and—' He stopped to pull out some letters from an inside pocket.

Tam's gaze was cool as he looked at the envelopes Chris handed to him. 'I don't suppose there was anything important. Thanks anyway.' He moved to walk on by, but Chris stepped sideways, blocking his path.

'Look, I know you don't believe me, but I do feel bad about what happened. I feel awful, actually. But it happened and, well, you handled it the way you felt was right, while I—'

'Walked away abdicating all responsibility.'

'I chose a different way,' corrected Chris. At least he tried to. He would never convince Tam his way was better. 'And it's taken me until now to really find my feet again. Which is why I've come to see you.' He gestured at a pinstriped leg. 'I've just come from the bank.'

Tam supposed his interest was meant to be well and truly piqued, but there was nothing Chris could say to him that would have him wanting to hear more. He stared down the street. A tabby cat was sitting on a wall cleaning itself, one leg stuck in the air at an absurd angle. He watched for a moment, smiling gently before turning his attention back to Chris, the smile instantly falling from his face.

'What do you want?' he asked.

'Nothing, I just... So, no permanent address yet then?'

'I'd have told you if I had.'

'Yeah, right, course.' Chris picked at the edge of his nostril, before rubbing his nose. 'Only it's been a while and... not that I mind bringing your post but—'

'I should hope not, given that it's entirely your fault I'm homeless in the first place.'

'Mate, are you ever going to let up about that?'

Tam glared at him. '*Really*? You're really asking me that question?'

Chris looked away. 'Okay, okay, I get it. But look, I'm asking because I might have a proposition for you. Something which could solve your... problem.'

'My problem? Assuage your guilt, more like.' He swallowed, trying to tamp down his anger. 'How can I make it any clearer, Chris? I want nothing to do with you, or any *propositions* you may have. I did that once before, remember? I should have thought allowing me to use your address for mail would be the least you could do, but if it's a problem I'll be happy to make other arrangements.'

'It's no biggie,' replied Chris with a steady gaze. 'But don't forget that without our little arrangement your employer might not have given you a job in the first place, or be quite so happy to keep you on.'

Tam was finding it increasingly hard to keep his anger in check. 'You're actually threatening me with blackmail now?' He shook his head. 'You know, I used to think you were a decent bloke, but with every word that comes out of your mouth you prove to me how wrong I was. I don't even know why I'm still standing here. Excuse me, I have things to do.' He shoved at Chris's arm and pushed past.

'At least listen to what I have to say,' Chris argued, catching hold of Tam. 'I came to offer you a job. I'm going into business again... not quite the same kind of thing as before, just a shop this time, but I've got the details sorted out, my eye on the perfect premises and now I've been to the bank the finance is ready to go too.'

Tam gave him a long look. 'Yeah... I wondered why the suit, but you know, Chris, wild horses and all that.'

Chris pulled in his neck by several centimetres. 'It's a good job... better than the rubbish one you've got at the moment.' A vein was beating at the side of his wide forehead. 'But if you're not interested then... Look, mate, what happened was ages ago now, and I'm in a position to make it up to you. So don't go getting all snarky on me until you hear what I'm offering.'

Tam wrinkled his nose. 'I'd rather not, if it's all the same. And snarky doesn't begin to cover how I feel, so I'll make it clear, shall I? You took my dream, Chris, pretended it was yours and then shat all over it. So no, I don't think you can make it up to me, and I'll take my chance with my rubbish job, thanks. At least it's honest.'

Chris glared at him, looking hot under the collar despite the cold wind blowing down the street. 'Fine. Have it your way. But you're making a mistake here, Tam, and you know what they say – pride comes before a fall.'

'I've fallen further than I ever thought possible,' replied Tam, jaw clenched so hard his teeth hurt. 'And I've made all the mistakes I'm going to. Now, in another five minutes I'm going to be late for work, so if you'll excuse me...' He took several steps forward as Chris moved to one side to let him pass.

'I bumped into your mum the other day,' said Chris from behind, his voice suddenly silky smooth. 'She doesn't know, does she? She asked me how the business was, and if the next time you visit her you could bring a nice little potted plant for her friend Marjorie's birthday.'

'Leave my mum out of this,' growled Tam. 'And no, of course she doesn't bloody well know. It would break her heart, literally, if I told her, and she's not to get stressed. She's been pretty stable this last year, and I aim to keep it that way.'

At that, Chris's stance changed. His shoulders dropped and his chest deflated. 'I'm sorry, Tam, I really am. Look, if you change your mind, you know where I am. It's a good job, and it could be the start of something better for you. You'd have more money, you'd be able to get a place of your own again. Think about it at least. The offer still stands.'

Tam gave him one last look and carried on walking.

He didn't look back. He'd made a pact with himself to never look back. But even so, he hadn't gone more than a few yards before he wondered if his pride had been doing the talking for him. Except it wasn't pride, was it? There might be something puritanical about the way he lived now, but he wasn't wearing a hair shirt for no reason: it was the principle of the thing. He had to make amends for what he'd allowed to happen. Behaviour like Chris's was infectious, and Tam was scared that if he was exposed to it again for any length of time, he would end up thinking that dodging the consequences of his actions was okay, just as Chris had. He'd forget all the people who had been hurt when his business went under, the stress he had caused them, the livelihoods that could have been ruined had Tam not sought to repay them by any means open to him. Knowing that he had made things right was the only reason he could sleep at night. He shook his head at the thought. That was a joke in itself.

He could remember vividly the first night he had slept in his car. How naive he had been, thinking that he could just park up and sleep the night away. He'd only managed two nights in the same street as Chawston House – not right outside, just a little further along the road – but those two nights had clearly been two too many for the other residents in the street. And on the third he had been 'moved on'. It had been the same story ever since. Remove the four walls of a house and Tam instantly changed from a respectable, law-abiding person to someone you would cross over the road to avoid. Scum, in other words. And what hurt was that, inside, Tam was the same person he'd always been, and always would be, but that wasn't enough. He'd never be a part of the world again until he could acquire four walls, and that was what almost made him turn around and run back after Chris. Almost.

There was always something going on at Chawston House. Gemma, the Pets As Therapy lady had been in that morning, and he waved as he spotted her and her two huge golden retrievers on the other side of the road. And, as usual when Gemma had been in, Tam was met at the gate by Eric, one of their residents, who would have gone home with Gemma if he could. As it was, once the visit was over, he insisted on accompanying Bonnie and Tyler right to the front door of the house, holding both dogs while Gemma signed out, before escorting them all down the driveway. Once there, he would stand, waving, until Gemma and her dogs disappeared from view.

'Morning, Eric,' he said, as he slipped through the gate, smiling at the staff member who stood beside him. He liked Marina; you could always tell when she was on duty because you could hear her laughing long before you saw her. Today, she had a look in her eye that Tam knew well: a warm, compassionate sadness. 'Hey, did you see those dogs, Eric?' he asked. 'Beauties, weren't they?'

Most of the time, Eric returned to the house without any issue. Sometimes, it took the suggestion of a cup of tea to entice him back inside, but on occasion, like today, Chawston House had simply slipped from Eric's memory.

He was still staring down the road. 'I had a dog once,' he said. 'Just like those two, only black... and a bit smaller.'

Tam laid a hand on Eric's sleeve. 'I don't think you've told me that before. What was his name?'

'*Her* name,' replied Eric, smiling. 'She was called Floss, the best sheepdog, she were, for miles around.'

'Really? So, were you a farmer then?'

'Oh aye, one hundred and forty-five ewes, we had.'

Tam flicked a glance at Marina. 'Blimey, I bet they were a handful. No wonder you needed a sheepdog to keep them under control. Did you whistle for her, like you see on the television?'

'Course...' said Eric, staring at him, puzzled. 'How else do you get her to do what you want? That's how she were trained. I had her right from a pup.'

'I've never really understood how that works but, tell you what, Eric—' He broke off, rubbing his hands together and shrugging his shoulders. 'It's freezing out here. Would you like to come inside for a cup of tea, and you can tell me all about it? I'd love to know.'

'Only if you've got time...'

Tam checked his watch. 'I have. Lunch won't be for an hour yet.' He touched Eric's sleeve again and began to slowly walk towards the house, waiting a second or two to make sure Eric was following. 'Actually, you could stay and have some if you like. I think it's fish and chips today.'

'Is it? That's my favourite.'

'Blimey, what are the chances? Good job you stopped by then.'

'Are you coming too?' Eric asked Marina. 'You look like you could do with a warm through, you're shivering, girl.'

'If that's okay,' she replied, smiling. 'I am a bit cold. And I'd love to hear more about Floss, too, she sounds like a darling. I've got a spaniel called Jasper but he's mad as a box of frogs. He definitely wouldn't be any good with sheep.'

'That's because he's a retriever,' said Eric. 'Not his job, is it?'

Safely through the front door, Marina steered Eric down the hallway. 'Shall we go and put the kettle on?' she said.

'Aye, my room's this way...'

She turned to smile at Tam, who was hanging back so he could pop into the office to sign in. 'Trish asked if she could have a word,' she whispered. 'See you later.'

Tam grinned and ducked through the office doorway.

Trish had been at Chawston House for eleven years now, and Tam had liked her from the moment he met her during his interview. As deputy manager, she'd played the role of good cop alongside her colleague, Donna, who was definitely happier playing bad cop. Tam had wondered whether it was just the way they'd decided to conduct their interviews, but since joining the staff he'd discovered it was how they always were. Both were fair and straight talking, but, as the more senior manager, Donna maintained a rather aloof approach. You could have a giggle with Trish.

The office, however, was empty, so Tam stayed no longer than the minute it took him to sign in and check his pigeonhole for notices. It was more than likely that Trish wanted him to swap a shift, or, with any luck, work an extra one. With that thought in his head he went off to say hello to the residents and see if he could find her.

As it was, it took until well after dinnertime before they both had a moment to chat.

'Just pop to the office with me a minute,' she said. 'I need my diary.'

Tam followed her down the hallway, thinking that whatever it was he would say yes. Any extra money was a help. The quicker he finished paying off his debts, the quicker he could start saving for his future.

It didn't even occur to him that something might be amiss until Trish closed the office door behind them and asked him to take a seat. Routine business was usually conducted standing up, occasionally perched on the edge of the desk, but sitting down was serious. Sitting down was trouble.

'I'm not sure whether you've realised but your six-month review is coming up in a couple of weeks,' she said, opening the big black book at the side of her desk. 'And Donna has asked me to get a date in the diary.'

'Okay.' Tam nodded. That wasn't serious. So why did Trish have trouble meeting his eye?

She flicked over a couple of pages in the diary before settling on a week Tam couldn't quite see. 'It's not until the twenty-first, so how about we make it for the week after? The twenty-eighth? It's a Wednesday, so you'd normally be on duty.'

Again, Tam nodded. 'Any day is fine, whatever suits you best.'

She looked up. 'Although I had been thinking of taking some holiday... I've a few days left which I'll lose if I don't take them.' She studied the diary once more. 'But if I do that, it would mean pushing things back a bit. It might give you a bit more time though,' she added.

'Time?' queried Tam, not quite sure what she was getting at.

'Yes. To... prepare.'

'Oh, I see, yes, sorry. I wasn't sure how you did things here. There's a form, is there? Like for an appraisal?' He smiled. 'Happy to do that. Do you need it in advance, is that it?'

'On the day is fine,' Trish replied, still staring at the page. 'I think I *will* make it a bit later. How about the thirteenth of March? That gives you two more weeks.'

'Whatever works best for you. I don't want you to lose your holiday.'

Trish plucked a pencil from a pot on the desk. 'Shall we say four o'clock? If we need to change anything we've got plenty of time. I'll book my holiday with Donna later. It won't be a problem, she reminded me about it the other day, and look, no one else is off if I go that week.'

Tam was too far away to make out the dates clearly, but he nodded and smiled. There wasn't much else he could do. Not until Trish revealed why she was behaving so strangely. This was very much a standing up kind of conversation.

'Right, there we go then. Four o'clock on the thirteenth. I'll get that form for you, shall I? You won't have any problem with it, it's quite straightforward. Really just an opportunity to say how you're feeling about your role here. How you've found your induction, that kind of thing.'

'I've enjoyed it,' replied Tam. 'As you know, it's not the kind of work I've ever done before, but the residents are a great bunch.' He grinned. 'As are the staff. And I think things have gone well.'

Trish held his look for just a second before glancing back down. 'It's been good having you here,' she replied. 'I don't think there's any argument about that.'

Comforting words, but Tam had the strongest suspicion she was still leaving something unsaid. He stared at her back as she fished through the sections in the filing cabinet behind her desk.

'Here you go.' She handed over the form with a tight smile. 'I'm sure everything will be fine.'

Up until the last few minutes Tam had been sure it would be too. He took the piece of paper and turned for the door. He'd almost made it through before Trish spoke again.

'Erm, Tam...? Sorry, it's just... it doesn't matter to me in the slightest, but you know what Donna's like...'

Tam turned around slowly. 'I'm not sure I follow,' he said, anxiety flicking around the pit of his stomach.

Trish's cheeks had flushed bright pink and it was clear she was struggling to find the right words. 'I was in town the other day. In that little car park up behind the baker's... and I couldn't help noticing... Is everything all right, Tam?'

A wave of heat made its way up his neck. 'Perfectly,' he replied. 'I'm fine.'

Trish nodded. 'Right... Well, I won't say a word to anyone, you don't need to worry on that score, only...' She tapped the sheet of paper. 'Perhaps when you fill in that form, when you come for your review meeting... it would be really good if you had a proper address... a permanent one.'

11

William

Since the last time they'd spoken, Stuart had made no more mention of needing William's help at any 'special' parties, but he was pretty certain they were a regular event. If he had to make a guess, he'd say the games being played were poker, and not just the friendly kind either. Instead, the kind where large sums of money were bet, the kind which were illegal because Stuart certainly didn't hold a gaming licence, nor was he running a casino. So, apart from anything else, if William had helped him out, it would have made him complicit simply by being there. He didn't need that kind of complication in his life. Not now.

The fact that in all of William's nine months of working at the club he had never twigged what was going on was of little comfort. Stuart might be good at keeping his money-spinner a secret, but even so much as a whisper in the wrong ear could change all that in a heartbeat. If William was to do what he came here to, he needed to stay as close to Stuart as possible even though his instincts were telling him to run. He might be

trying to do the right thing, but he'd learned the hard way that
there were special rules for people like him. It wasn't so much
about being honest, it was about never becoming involved in the
first place.

At first, gaining the job at the club had seemed as if the
universe was finally giving him a helping hand, but things were
turning out to be far more tricky than he'd imagined. He was
walking a very fine line and it wouldn't do to put his foot over it
by so much as an inch. Not until he was ready. So, here he was
again, on another Tuesday night, praying nothing untoward
happened.

There was a much livelier crowd here this time, but Stuart's
supercilious smile was just the same. And as William watched
him ingratiate himself with the punters, he realised that being
there might not be so bad after all. If he was patient, and clever,
there might be another way he could protect himself. He could
give himself a little insurance policy, one which would wipe the
smile from Stuart's face once and for all. And to do that all
William needed was information.

With something of a plan in place, he felt a little happier,
and although the hours of drink-fuelled entertainment dragged
interminably slowly, he was eventually rewarded for his vigi-
lance. His attention had been caught by Stuart in conversation
with a bloke at the bar. William couldn't hear what was being
said, but it wasn't the subject being discussed that had
concerned him; more the manner in which the conversation was
being conducted. There was a way in which people ordered
drinks, just as there was a way in which people engaged in
banter with staff, and this interaction fitted neither of those
stereotypes. The conversation was brief, and although Stuart's
head was bent close towards the other man, he never made eye
contact. Instead, he looked past him as they spoke, eyes roving
the rest of the crowd in the room. He checked his watch, gave a
curt nod and the bloke he'd been speaking to returned to where

he'd been standing. Judging by the eager expressions on the faces of the man's two mates, they had been waiting for whatever information he was about to impart, and the glances which subsequently flicked across to where Stuart was now polishing glasses were cautious, but curious.

On his previous shift at the club, William had left as soon as he'd been able, and he did so again tonight. The last of the punters had been ushered out and were on their way home and while it wasn't exactly quiet, it was at least calm, which was exactly how William liked it. Tonight though, his only thought was not how quickly he could get to bed, but where the best place might be for him to wait unnoticed. Pulling his jacket tighter against the chill wind, William lost himself in the shadows.

He didn't have very long to wait. Soon, much sooner than William had anticipated, Stuart came through the club's side door and made his way purposefully down the street where Vipers was situated. The club's neon sign was now switched off so there was nothing to light his way, and Stuart was quickly swallowed into the dark. It was a simple matter for William to slip out behind him and follow from a distance. It was half three in the morning, and there wasn't a soul about. William could hear the squeak of Stuart's trainers as clearly as if he'd been standing beside him.

They had reached the car park now, or what passed for one. For as long as William could remember it had been nothing more than a small, open space between buildings – scruffy, with an air of disuse about it – no barriers, poorly lit and with no security cameras. In short, it was very private.

During the day, a guy sat by the car park's entrance, charging a quid for its use, but he was old when William was a youngster, and was positively ancient now. He knocked off at five though, so those in the know could park there for free after that time. Even so, hardly anyone was there tonight – a handful of cars, and a grey van parked up in the corner. And waiting by the side of it were the blokes from the club.

The car park was dark enough that William could have moved closer if he chose but, as he was pretty certain what was about to happen next, he hung back. No point in getting involved; all he needed were his suspicions confirmed. Following them up could happen another time.

The men were silent as Stuart approached, the greeting between them no more than a nod. And Stuart was quick – he unlocked the van and slid open the side door in seconds. At this distance William couldn't be certain what the men were buying, but he could hazard a good guess. The whole exchange lasted no more than a minute. A quick flash of cash and that was that. It saddened William, angered him too, but he stayed in the shadows, silent and waiting.

The van was the first to leave. It was too dark and too far away for William to get the registration number, but if Stuart had parked there tonight then William was pretty certain he would do so whenever he was on duty. William could easily pop back to check another time.

Now that the men had got what they came for, William could see the mood relax. With Stuart gone, the threat of discovery was over and now they were just mates out for the night, all tanked up and nowhere to go. It was time for William to head home.

Waiting until the men were out of sight, William ambled across the car park and into the road, fishing in his pocket for his keys. The night was catching up with him and he longed for a soothing cup of tea and the relative comfort of his bed. He'd hardly gone fifty yards, however, before the silent night was suddenly filled with raucous laughter and catcalls.

'Oi, giss a bite, love.'

If there was a reply, William couldn't hear one, but whatever was said was followed by another gale of laughter.

'Aw, don't be like that. I asked nicely.'

The familiar scent in the air told William exactly where the men had stopped, and he caught up with them in seconds.

Light spilled into the alley from the open bakery door, and silhouetted against it was a figure, bent double as it tried to retrieve something from the floor. As William watched, one of the men kicked it away amid more raucous laughter.

'Whoops... butterfingers!' It was another man speaking this time, unsteady on his feet.

'Think it's time you lads headed home, isn't it?' William's voice was soft, unthreatening.

Now he was closer he could see the figure was a woman, already small, but looking much smaller in the presence of the three men. One of them moved to block her path back into the safety of the bakery, effectively marooning her in the alleyway. William took several steps closer.

The nearest man turned to William, jabbing a finger at his chest. 'You the sleep police, or what?'

'No, just the voice of reason.'

'Oooh, hark at him.' The second man convulsed with laughter, catching at the arm of the third. 'All right, no need to get your knickers in a twist.'

More laughter followed, which William ignored. He stood silently, his narrowed eyes holding the man's belligerent gaze until a second or two later, his expression cleared.

'Hey, I know you... you were at the club tonight.'

'I was. Which is why I'm asking you to leave before we have to get anyone else involved... like Stuart, for example.' He was aware of the other two men moving closer, but he stood his ground. He could put all three of them on the floor in seconds, but he'd rather not, given a choice. With any luck, somewhere inside their fuddled brains a shaft of reason still existed and given what had just taken place, William didn't suppose any of them were keen to lose favour with Stuart.

'Yeah, and what's it to you? We have every right to...' The man trailed off at a nudge from his mate.

William nodded, acknowledging the wisdom. 'Just call it a night, that's all I'm asking. That way no one's in any trouble.'

For a moment, William thought the mouthy one was going to make something of it, but then, with a broad grin, he slapped William's arm as if he had just told the funniest joke ever. 'Come on then, let's get going. These two have no sense of humour.'

He pushed past William and went swaying off down the street, pitching against the woman as he did so. 'Oopsie.' He giggled.

William watched until all three men were well on their way before turning his attention to the woman still standing stock-still. 'I'm sorry,' he said. 'I don't suppose they meant any real harm.'

'And that makes it all right, does it?' The woman was tiny, particularly in comparison to his bulk, and much older than he'd first thought. In fact, her hair was as grey as his, tied back into a loose plait. William had an overwhelming urge to pick her up and carry her back to safety.

'No, it doesn't make it okay at all,' he replied. 'But it seemed like something I should say.' He held out his hand, palm upper-most in submission. 'I'm William. Tactless, but basically harmless.'

The woman jerked her head in the direction the men had taken. 'Friends of yours, are they?'

'Hardly.'

'But you know them?'

'I've had the dubious pleasure of their company this evening, but that's not the same thing.'

The woman gave him a long look, ignoring his hand with an audible sigh. 'Thanks,' she said. 'It was good of you to inter-vene.' She moved to stand inside the doorway, steadying herself against the door frame. 'Bloody hooligans,' she added, her face pale as she stared down the alley.

'Aye... idiots,' William agreed. 'Too much booze to remember their manners, let alone anything else.'

'So, I'm supposed to ignore them simply because they don't know what they're doing?' She bent to pick up what William saw was the remains of a sandwich, now lying on the floor, its filling spilled onto the cobbles. '*That* was my lunch,' she said pointedly. Then she tutted. 'I suppose I should be grateful it's just my lunch that's ruined.'

William bent to assist her, scooping up some fallen lettuce. 'You didn't deserve anything to be ruined. Don't be grateful to them for—' He stopped suddenly. 'Sorry, I'm not trying to tell you what to do.'

'Good, because I'm not grateful, I'm bloody furious that people think it's okay to throw their weight around... and insinuating that because I don't find their so-called humour funny, there's something wrong with me.' The woman stared at him, holding his look for a second before dropping her gaze.

'Are you okay?'

She swallowed. 'Yes, I'm just... I'm not very good with confrontation.'

With the light behind her, her face was in shadow, but William could see enough of her expression to know that she was far from all right. She looked badly shaken.

'So how come you were at the club tonight?' she asked, holding out her hand for the remains of her sandwich. 'If you don't mind me saying, you look a little older than the average raver.'

William grimaced. 'I work there as a doorman.'

Her mouth flattened into a thin line. 'I see.'

William shrugged. She obviously didn't approve of his career choice, but he couldn't blame her. He didn't think much of it either.

'That must be fun.'

'What can I say? It's not how I'd choose to spend my evening but I don't question how others choose to spend theirs.'

The woman studied him for a moment, her expression inscrutable. 'Sorry,' she said. 'I didn't mean to give you the third degree when you were only trying to help. I don't get any visitors, it's usually just me and the night – quiet, calm and peaceful. I am grateful to you, though.' She looked down at her hands still holding the remains of her sandwich. 'I should get back inside – I've got work to do. And a cup of tea which is probably stone cold by now.'

'Then take a few minutes and make yourself another,' he replied. 'That wouldn't hurt, surely?' She stared at him again and he suddenly realised it might sound as if he wanted one too. 'I'm going to do the same,' he added, moving slightly away. 'It's been a long night.'

She nodded, her expression closed and still tight with anxiety.

William wracked his brain for something else to say. He ought to go, but he also felt the need to stay. 'Listen, I'm sure there'll be no repeat of earlier, but make sure you keep this door locked.'

'I'm never bloody opening it again. I don't usually, and it's always locked. I just wanted some fresh air; it gets hot in here. I guess I won't be doing that again. Thanks, guys.' Her gaze dropped to the floor.

'Sorry, that was thoughtless,' said William, clearing his throat. 'I didn't mean to alarm you. Or make you feel vulnerable.'

'*More* vulnerable...'

He dipped his head slightly, acknowledging her reply. He felt a need to apologise for a whole lot more than just his comment. 'You shouldn't have to change your behaviour because of someone else.'

The woman looked up into his face, one eyelid twitching. She rubbed at it and tucked a wisp of hair firmly behind her ear. It had come loose from her plait. 'Agreed, but some people don't make that easy, do they? They think everything is about them.' Her face was stony.

William nodded. 'True enough,' he replied mildly. '*Some* people... but not everyone.' He held her look for a moment. 'Anyway, let me get on home and leave you to your tea.' He doffed an imaginary cap and turned to go.

'Hang on, wait...'

He turned around to see the woman disappearing back into the bakery. The smell coming from inside was incredible, and it was warm and comforting. He couldn't imagine anywhere he'd rather be on a cold winter's night, and his stomach gave an appreciative lurch. As if reading his mind, she reappeared moments later, carrying a small paper bag.

'Have these,' she said. 'With *your* cup of tea.' The beginnings of a small smile tugged at the edges of her mouth. 'And thank you.'

William took the bag and peered inside, his mouth suddenly watering as the two fat croissants which nestled there released a rich, buttery aroma. He used to dream of food like that.

'Am I allowed?' he asked. 'I don't want to get you into trouble.'

She did smile then. Almost imperceptible, but it was there. 'You won't. It's no problem,' she said.

William was about to reply when he realised that she was leaning against the door frame again, almost as if without it she would slide to the floor. He scrunched the top of the bag closed, patting the contents gently.

'Thank you. You wouldn't believe how long it is since I had these.' He dipped his head. 'Now go and have that cuppa.'

He'd only gone a few steps when he turned back, aware that the door hadn't yet been closed behind him.

'Listen, don't take this the wrong way...' William was torn. He hadn't really thought this through, and he absolutely should not be doing this. Whatever happened to not getting involved? 'I'm not really sure if I should say this or not, but I only live around the corner—' He could see the woman's eyes open wide. 'So, if you ever feel threatened again, or get locked out, or... I don't know, anything, and you need some help, I'm by Turner's estate agents, do you know it? There's a green door to the left-hand side. Just bang on that, it doesn't matter what time, and I'll come down.' He waited, but there was no reply. Had he really expected one? 'Anyway, night then.'

This time he walked resolutely away, so that by the time her voice reached him it was nothing more than a whisper on the breeze.

'Night, William.'

12

Beth

There was something about Frankie which, up until now, Beth hadn't been able to put her finger on. This was the third morning they had had coffee together and in between times Beth retained an image of Frankie in her head which, on meeting again, was nothing like she'd pictured at all. But today, she realised why. It was because Frankie had one of those curious faces which looked so ordinary most of the time – not plain, just nothing in particular to distinguish it – until the moment she smiled. And when she did, her eyes, normally mid-brown, turned to gold and her whole face lifted, lit up as if she had her own personal sunbeam to stand beneath. She kept her smile hidden most of the time, like a secret gift she rarely bestowed, but when she did...

'This is kind of weird, isn't it?' said Beth as she placed two cups of coffee on the table, pushing one towards Frankie.

Frankie looked around her, a blank expression on her face.

'Sorry, I don't mean this place,' explained Beth. The coffee shop they were sitting in opened earlier than most to cater for the on-their-way-to-work crowd, but other than that, was the same as coffee shops everywhere – warm, fragrant and anonymous. 'Just that if we were normal people, working normal hours, having coffee like we are would be the equivalent of meeting up at ten o'clock at night.'

A momentary frown crossed Frankie's face, but then it brightened again. 'Oh yes, I see what you mean – right before bedtime...' She scooped up some froth from her coffee with one finger and popped it in her mouth. 'Normal people, whatever they are... Working the night shift is like living on another planet – but maybe I'm strange, I really like it.' She looked up at Beth, a question hovering in her eyes.

'I don't think I've ever thought about it,' replied Beth. 'It's just something I do. You're on your own at the bakery though, aren't you? Whereas I'm still surrounded by people. The hospital never really sleeps and, even though it is a little different from the day shift, I never get the sense that it's night-time outside, not until I finish my shift and am on my way home. Then it can feel as if I'm the only person alive in the world. Can't say I particularly enjoy that feeling though, not like you.' She took a sip of coffee, looking at Frankie over the rim of her mug. 'I saw you the night Jack fell out of bed,' she supplied. 'You were dancing as if you hadn't a care in the world. And there was this expression on your face, kind of soft. Like you were in the arms of your lover.' She grinned. 'Maybe you were.'

'Huh... in my dreams.'

'You looked lovely. It made me wonder what it would be like to feel so peaceful.'

Frankie wrinkled her nose. 'I love the middle of the night. I find it... calming. It probably sounds stupid, but I can be who I want to be then. In the daytime, there's so much... I don't know what the right word is, really... expectation? Does that make sense?'

'From other people, you mean?'

'Something like that.' She fiddled with the biscuit that came with her coffee. Then she picked it up and bit it in half, chewing slowly. 'It's like I don't know who I am during the day. I feel pressured to be a certain way. Too many years of doing things simply to conform, I think. So now... now that I'm awake during the night, I find it easier to be the person I think I am, rather than the one I always pretended to be.' She shook her head. 'Sorry, I'm talking rubbish.'

But Beth recognised the look on her face. 'No,' she said, reaching forward with her hand. 'No, you're not. I think we often pretend to be something we're not. I do it all the time.' She studied Frankie's expression. It was as if no one had ever said that to her before. 'I pretend I've had enough sleep when that couldn't be further from the truth. I pretend I'm fine when people talk to Jack as if he's a five-year-old, when really, I want to throttle them. But most of all I pretend I'm the most patient person who ever lived, when really my body is boiling with everything I don't say and everything I hold back.' She stared at Frankie, suddenly shy, and not at all sure where that had come from. 'I'd love to be the person I pretend to be, but I'm not, not really. I don't think I do a very good job at all. I don't mean at work,' she corrected. 'But at home, where it really matters.'

'But does Jack expect you to be that perfect person?'

Beth stared out of the window, eyes unfocused. She wasn't looking outward, she was looking inward, at the boxes where she hid her thoughts day after day after day. 'No, I don't think he does,' she replied. 'But I feel like I have to be, because if I wasn't, I don't know how he'd make it through the day. He feels guilty enough about the accident, about changing our lives and the burden he places on me. So, however hard things are, I try to keep it hidden. I try to give him the perfect version of me.' She shook her head. 'Sorry, I didn't mean to offload on you like that.'

'You weren't offloading, and even if you were, it would be

okay.' Frankie tipped her head to one side. 'It's clear you don't think he's a burden.'

'I don't. I love him,' replied Beth simply. 'And I don't care how he is now, he's still the man I married all those years ago. We have no children, so it's just him and me, and I wouldn't change that for the world. Our life is hard, at times very hard, but no, he's not a burden. The difficulty is that if I didn't pretend, getting him to believe that would be nigh on impossible. His guilty feelings would skyrocket and I'm scared of what that could do to us.' She gave a wry smile. 'Trouble is, pretend too often and you forget who you really are.'

Frankie dabbed a finger against a crumb of biscuit. 'I used to think my life was complicated, but compared to yours...' Her eyes were warm on Beth's. 'You must be very good at juggling things.'

Beth pulled a face. 'I think I'm good at throwing things up in the air and praying they don't come down again,' she said. 'Or at least not all at once, and I don't think that's quite the same thing. There's so little room in our lives for anything which throws a spanner in the works – you saw what happened the night Jack fell out of bed. All it takes is one small thing and...' She made a gesture with her hands as if a bomb was exploding.

'So, you work the night shift because it's practical, is that it?'

'Hmm... and that's the only reason. It's a simple equation. Jack obviously needs more help during the day than he does at night when he's asleep, so I needed to figure out how I could look after Jack, work full-time and still find a few hours to sleep myself. The answer I came up with was the night shift. It doesn't really allow me to do any of those things properly, but that's just the way it is at the moment.'

'And you can't get anyone else to look after Jack?' asked Frankie, checking herself almost immediately. 'I'm sorry, that was a ridiculous thing to say.'

'It wasn't,' replied Beth, smiling warmly. 'It was a valid

question, but the truth is that we simply can't afford it. Jack would probably prefer it if I wasn't nagging him all day, but unless we can find a way to bring in more money, we're stuck as we are. And with everything going on at the hospital, my salary is more likely to go down rather than up.'

'How's that work then?' Frankie queried.

'The usual. The hospital needs to save money and because the wages bill is one of the biggest areas of expense, it's the one which gets tinkered with the most. We're going through another round of redundancies at the moment and I'm having to reapply for my job. If I'm lucky enough to hold onto it, I'll end up with a contract which effectively means I'll be doing more work for less money.'

'But that isn't right...'

'Nope.' Beth raised her eyebrows. It was a conversation she'd had countless times before.

Frankie took a deep breath as if to speak and then let it out slowly. She could obviously see there was no point in pursuing the rights and wrongs of the situation. 'I'm sorry,' she said instead. 'That's rubbish.' She looked around her a moment. 'Listen, say if you need to get home but... would you like some breakfast?' She nodded towards a table on their left who had just been served. 'That's making my mouth water and the prices look pretty reasonable.'

Beth checked her watch. 'You know, that's not a bad idea... are you sure you're okay staying?'

'I am if you are.'

'Breakfast it is then.'

Frankie got to her feet. 'What would you like? And I'll get them because it was my idea, so no arguing. You can pay next time.'

Frankie's tone left no room for discussion, but it was obvious this was just as big a deal for her as it was for Beth. 'Then, thank you. Could I have a bacon and egg sandwich? They're a bit of a weakness of mine.'

'Coming right up,' said Frankie, smiling.

Beth smiled back, remembering a conversation she'd had with Jack the week before. As soon as she'd mentioned the possibility of meeting Frankie again, he'd been adamant that she should, adding the rider that she could stay for as long as she wanted, he'd be quite happy lazing in bed until she got home. If she hadn't known better, she might have thought he was trying to get rid of her, but she also knew that *he* knew she would never go unless she had his blessing. So here she was... with Frankie already assuming they would be meeting again. She rather liked the thought of that.

Her sandwich, when it arrived, was pretty much hanging off the edge of her plate it was so big. But God, it looked good... She glanced down at her lap, at her jeans which were stretched tight across thighs far too big for them really, her stomach rolling over the waistband. 'I shouldn't be eating this,' she said. 'Every day I tell myself I'll be good.'

Frankie's eyes narrowed as she looked down at her own plate. 'Do you want to be good?'

'Not particularly, no.' Beth pulled a face. 'That's not strictly true. I'm a nurse, I'm conditioned to worry about my health. But some days I just want *all* the cake.'

Frankie had a rather amused expression on her face. 'I know what you're thinking,' she said. 'But trust me, the grass isn't always greener...'

'Maybe not, but you're so lovely and slim...' Frankie had the kind of body Beth had always envied – pretty much straight up and down, but for someone like Beth, with far too many curves in all the wrong places, Frankie looked perfect. 'If I worked in a bakery, I'd be the size of a house. How do you manage to avoid so much temptation?'

'Would now be a good time to confess that I've put on nearly a stone since I started working there?'

'A stone? Blimey, what were you like before?' Beth slapped a hand over her mouth, blushing furiously. 'Sorry, that came out so wrong. But you look gorgeous on it in any case. I've always struggled with my weight.'

Frankie shrugged. 'My husband liked slim women. Ex-husband, that is. But don't do yourself down – I think you look lovely. And you should absolutely eat your breakfast without feeling guilt of any kind.' She smiled warmly before picking up her sandwich, and Beth had the sudden feeling that Frankie's ex was not a topic she wanted to discuss.

'We're never satisfied with how we look, are we?' she said. 'We're always comparing ourselves to other people. Is that a woman thing, do you think?' She pulled out a piece of stray bacon and popped it in her mouth, chewing thoughtfully.

'I don't know about that,' answered Frankie. 'But what I *do* know is that since I've been on my own I've realised how nice it is to make my own decisions, how free I feel not having to pass every suggestion through someone else's filter.' She gave a slight smirk. 'Although that might be an age thing as well. Since I hit my fifties, I've definitely developed a rebellious streak. I've spent such a large part of my life feeling that kind of crippling self-consciousness which hits when you're a teenager – feeling like you have to *be* a certain way and *look* a certain way – these days I'm trying really hard not to give a damn about what other people think. I don't always succeed – those kinds of chains are not easily thrown off – but I'm beginning to feel better about myself.' Frankie swiped a finger across her plate where egg had oozed from her sandwich. 'Blimey, listen to me. Rant over.'

Beth waved away her remark. 'No, carry on.'

She watched surreptitiously as Frankie munched her way through her breakfast. Her grey hair was tied up in a loose ponytail, the ends curling softly on her shoulders. Her skin glowed with health and her soft brown eyes were warm and calm. She looked peaceful and, despite her words, more *at peace* with herself than most people Beth knew, including herself. She had always believed that people came into her life for a reason, so meeting Frankie now, in the way she had... She took a bite from her own sandwich, sighing with pleasure.

'These *are* good, aren't they?'

Frankie didn't reply, just grinned through a mouthful of food. 'I didn't realise how hungry I was,' she replied after a moment. 'I lost my lunch, so I haven't had a great deal to eat.'

'You lost your lunch? How did you manage that?'

Frankie wiped a smear of sauce from her lips. 'I had the unfortunate pleasure of meeting some drunken louts during the night – they were in the alley outside the bakery – and one of them thought it would be fun to try and steal my sandwich. Funnily enough, I didn't fancy it after I'd picked the remains up off the floor.'

Beth hurriedly chewed. 'Are you okay? I'd have been terrified.'

'I'm okay now. At the time I *was* terrified. And bloody angry that they'd invaded my space. It felt horribly personal. I don't usually go outside when I'm working but hot flush, you know... I needed some air, it was boiling in the bakery.'

'I don't think I'd like being on my own at night.'

Frankie shook her head. 'It's normally really quiet. Occasionally there's a bit of noise when Vipers turns out, but folks are usually headed in the other direction. I've never had any bother before. Just unlucky, I guess.' She took a sip of her coffee. 'A bouncer from the club came to my rescue and saw them off for me.'

'I think I'd be just as scared of him.'

'Yeah, this guy was huge...' Frankie motioned above her

head with her hands. 'About a foot and a half taller than me, and built like the proverbial... well, he was big anyway, but thankfully not that scary at all. He was a bit older than me, I think, and he had grey hair like mine which somehow made him feel less threatening.'

But Beth wasn't convinced. 'Are you sure that's where he was from? He could be just saying that.'

'True. But I think he was legit. He was very polite, in any case.'

'A knight in shining armour then?'

'Maybe, if there is such a thing. I used to believe in them once upon a time, but—' She broke off suddenly, her attention caught by something in the street outside.

Beth followed her line of vision, seeing the colour drain from Frankie's face, but nothing which might have caused it. She reached out a tentative hand to touch her sleeve.

'Is everything okay?' she asked.

Frankie jumped, her knee bumping against the table leg. She stared at Beth, clearly realising she was supposed to be saying something, but having no idea what. Distracted, she looked down, studying her plate before moving it fractionally. She did the same with her mug, *and* the little bowl of ketchup, lining them up against the checked tablecloth.

'We were talking about knights in shining armour,' prompted Beth gently. Frankie's sudden change of mood was concerning. Despite what she'd said, it was obvious that her encounter in the night had rattled her more than she let on.

Finally, Frankie smiled. 'Yeah... no such thing.' She glanced briefly out of the window again before turning her attention back to Beth. 'So, what have you got lined up later today, anything fun?'

'We'll probably go for a walk if it isn't raining, and then I'll pretend I'm having a sleep when really I'll be writing out that job application I was telling you about. Hopefully it will all just be a matter of course and things will carry on as they always have without Jack being any the wiser.'

Frankie looked up sharply. 'Haven't you told him then?'

'God no, can you imagine how he'd feel if he found out?'

13

Tam

There were days when Tam never felt warm. He had mostly learned to live with the cold, but that didn't stop the very bones of his body from aching. And he was convinced the chill wasn't entirely due to the temperature either. There was so little warmth in his life – no soft edges to cushion life's blows, few kind words or welcoming smiles, none of the glow inside which came from the simplicity of a comforting hug (which wasn't from his mother). One which told you that everything would be okay. He missed those human moments more than anything.

He got on well with his colleagues at work, but as kind as Trish could be, he wouldn't call her a friend. Those people didn't know him; they didn't really see him at all. And unless his circumstances changed, even the brightest summer's day wouldn't bring the kind of warmth he longed for.

Sure, there had been plenty of friends in the past, one or two of the closest ones even offered to help when the business went bust, but those friends also had families and lives of their own, and Tam knew that sofa surfing was a surefire way to stretch those friendships to the limit. Maybe he *had* pushed them away, and their offers of help, but none of them had tried too hard to change his mind. It turned out they didn't need much encouragement at all to drift away, and so he lost them too. In fact, Eleanor was the only person he'd call a friend these days, absurd as it sounded.

He'd had many a sleepless night over the last couple of weeks, at times hating himself for the choices he'd made, at times patting himself on the back for having the integrity to make those self-same choices, but mostly just fighting down the rising tide of terror inside him. Because what would he do if he lost his job? Life was bad enough now; he didn't think he had the strength to face what a jobless future might bring. Neither did he have a clue how to change his current situation.

He pulled his sleeping bag higher around his ears and closed his eyes, but the darkness was suddenly overwhelming, and he sat up, fumbling for his blanket which had become as twisted as his thoughts. Strangely, settling down for the night when he was cold wasn't as bad as waking up – knowing that at some point he would have to leave the relative warmth of his covers and face the day. And although he wouldn't have to get up for a while yet, this morning was going to prove more difficult than most.

He looked around the car park, checking the lie of the land. He'd got used to which cars came and went and which stayed overnight. It helped him to tune out the random noises which seemingly posed him no threat – car doors opening and closing, or the occasional movement of vehicles in and out. It meant he could at least get *some* sleep. Last night had been different though, and he stared at the space which had been occupied by the grey van, wondering if it was about to become the latest of his problems.

He'd noticed it before on numerous occasions, but there had

been nothing about it to attract his attention in the past. It usually arrived before he went to sleep, and was always gone by morning, but in his wakefulness last night he'd realised that the opening of the van's side door was accompanied by behaviour he wanted no association with. Drugs spelled trouble, particularly for people like him, and if it had happened once, the likelihood was that the trade was regular. Being sensible, he ought to find somewhere else to stay but, tucked away as it was, this little car park had been perfect. Clearly he wasn't the only person who thought so. He sighed and leaned his head against the back of the front seat. Life could be so rubbish at times.

As he sat there, a woman came into view. He'd seen her before. She was the owner of the clapped-out navy Volvo who always parked as close to the exit as she could. She had on a woollen coat today, buttoned up to the neck, but during warmer weather, he'd glimpsed a nurse's uniform and had always assumed she worked the night shift. It would explain her desire for a fast getaway come morning and he smiled. He didn't blame her – he'd do the same.

She passed by the rear of his car, and he shut his eyes, as if that would magically make him invisible. At least it would spare her the embarrassment of making uncomfortable eye contact; that would be awful. When he first started sleeping in his car, he used to watch people – surreptitiously, of course – but he liked to imagine what kind of life they had. Wondering where they'd been, where they were going... Did they have any pets? What was their favourite colour? Anything and everything, small details, but ones which made up a life. This little window on the everyday used to make him feel connected. It made him feel as if he was still a part of it. But then he realised he would always be on the outside of the window looking in and the opposite happened. He turned his head away and pulled his blanket higher.

The sudden expletive was such a surprise it made him

jump. It was still too early for loud noises of any kind, and certainly not ones as filled with emotion as that had been. And it was soon followed by another, different this time – the woman had quite a vocabulary. He looked over to where she was standing by her car, and he was caught by how utterly defeated she looked. Without thinking, he threw off his blanket and scooched his legs out of his sleeping bag, reaching for his trainers. He had one hand on the car door before he thought to check his appearance. A fleece and jogging bottoms looked harmless enough though, didn't they?

The woman jumped as if she'd been shot. 'Jesus, you scared the life out of me.'

Tam threw up his hands as if she'd pointed that same gun at *him*. 'Sorry, sorry... I wasn't thinking.' He slowly lowered his hands. 'Do you need any help?'

The woman stared at him and then at the car. 'Probably... I don't know.' She kicked the side of the car viciously and Tam immediately saw the problem. The nearside tyre was flatter than a pancake.

'Ah... Have you got a spare?'

She looked about her as if one might happen to be lying around. 'Yeah...' She scratched her head, distracted. 'It's in the boot, I think.'

He gestured at the car. 'May I? I can give you a hand if you like.'

'Yeah, okay...' she muttered, fumbling with her phone. 'No! Wait a minute.' She frowned and placed a hand on top of her head, staring across the space. Tam could see the beginnings of panic stirring.

'I don't have to help,' he added. 'Are you with the AA? Or someone who could come out to change it for you?'

'What?'

'The tyre. Is there someone who could come out to change it for you? A breakdown service, maybe.'

She stared at him again and he winced at his words.

'Sorry, I didn't mean to assume you couldn't change the tyre yourself... Just that it's a dirty job and you're... you might not want to.'

She seemed to be having trouble understanding what he was saying. 'I need to get home,' she said. 'I can't be doing with this...' He cringed as she let fly another volley of expletives.

'Shall we have a look in the boot?' he suggested, hoping to move the situation along.

'There's no point,' she said, her attention suddenly snapping to him. 'The spare is flat too. I never got it repaired. And no, I'm not with the AA or anyone else who could help.'

'Ah...' Tam nodded in commiseration. 'It happens. We always think next week will be soon enough to do these things, don't we? And then suddenly a year has gone by and...' He trailed off. He wasn't helping.

'I know you,' she said, eyes narrowing. 'I've seen you. You sleep here, don't you? In your car.'

Tam took a step backward. 'Right...' He should have known. 'And I suppose you'll be informing the police on me now, will you? Have me moved along? Or arrested for deigning to speak to you?'

'What the hell?' She glared at him. 'Why on earth would I do that?' Her eyes locked on his, the intensity of her gaze rapidly becoming uncomfortable. 'Oh, I see, it's because you kip here overnight, isn't it? So, even though you know nothing about me, you've decided I'm the kind of person who would behave like a—' She broke off. 'Not very nice person.'

'Well, you brought up the subject of me being homeless.'

'Yes, because I've seen you here, that's all. I wasn't being judgemental, far from it. And I certainly wouldn't call the police.'

'So kind of you.'

'Isn't that allowed?' She shook her head. 'I'm a nurse, for

heaven's sake. Every day I see people in hospital who are there when they shouldn't be – because they've drunk themselves stupid for so long their liver is a shrivelled mess, or because they've smoked twenty a day for thirty years and are dying of lung cancer. I've learned not to judge. One, because it's none of my business, and two, because behind every damaged liver or cancerous lung is a person, with a *life* and a *story* to tell. I don't believe in giving someone my opinion on how to live when I haven't walked in their shoes.'

'Well, you're one of the few people who don't,' he muttered.

'So, shoot me,' she said, hands on hips as she glared at him. But then, realising what she'd said, she tutted loudly. 'Fantastic... I'm standing in a car park with a complete stranger in what might as well be the middle of the night, and I've just asked him to shoot me. Let's just tune into *Crimestoppers* now, shall we?'

'Is that a man thing?' he asked. 'Pardon me, but now you're being *really* judgemental.'

Her head dropped immediately. 'Yes, yes, I am... I know, I'm sorry. I just need to get home. Sorry,' she said again. She stared at her car, her face overwhelmingly weary. 'I don't know what to do... Damn it, how could I have been so stupid?'

'Okay, let's look at this logically. You have two options as far as I can see. One, you get a new tyre, in which case you need to contact a garage, or a mobile fitting service might be a better bet. Or two, you get a lift home and deal with the flat later.'

The woman checked her watch. 'Nowhere will be open yet and...' She shook her head in frustration. 'I don't have time for this... and I can't afford a new tyre either. Aren't those mobile places really expensive?'

'I've no idea,' replied Tam truthfully. 'Do you have a phone? You could google it.'

'The garage I use is miles away,' she said, ignoring his suggestion. 'It's not far from where I live, obviously, but I'm not there, am I? And in any case, it doesn't open till nine on a good day.'

'Taxi then? Or... would there be someone at the hospital who could run you home? A friend, maybe?'

She gave him a scathing look. 'You can't just leave a hospital if you're working. And don't get me started on taxis. None of them will come out my way. It's not worth their while, apparently, they'd have to charge too much. Because of the petrol prices.'

Tam nodded. 'Minicabs maybe, but a taxi might be okay. There are probably some by the station.'

'Which is on the other side of town.'

Tam was beginning to regret getting out of his car. Whoever this woman was, he hoped she was much better at problem-solving when she was at work. Right now, she seemed determined to make a drama into a crisis.

As if sensing his thoughts, she sighed heavily before turning her attention back to her phone. 'I'm sorry. You're right, and I know you're trying to help, but I really need to get home *now*. Not in two hours. My husband's disabled and, until I get home, there's no one looking after him. He was coming down with something last night, and...' She vented another sigh of frustration. 'I shouldn't have gone in to work in the first place...'

She began jabbing her finger at the phone screen and, moments later, Tam heard a dial tone ringing out. There was a long pause.

'Hi love, it's only me. Sorry, did I wake you? You don't sound great, are you okay?'

The woman turned away from him, and Tam watched as she placed her hand on top of her head again. It was obviously her go-to thinking pose. She nodded several times.

'Okay, well, I've got a flat tyre, so I'll be home as soon as I can, but... No, it's flat too... It just is, okay? So, I'm going to have to get a taxi or something and I don't know how long I'll be, so... Yes, I'm fine, I'm still in the car park.'

Tam shuffled from one foot to the other. There was a very obvious solution staring him in the face, but he wasn't at all sure how it would be received. He screwed up his face, wrestling with the decision. When did things get so complicated you couldn't even offer a helping hand when one was required? He heaved in a breath and moved to stand in front of the woman. Nothing ventured...

He waved a hand at her, motioning to the phone. 'May I speak to your husband?' he asked.

'What?' She mouthed *no* at him and a deep frown furrowed her forehead.

Tam held his hand out again. 'I have an idea,' he said. 'Please...'

'Hang on a minute, Jack,' she said. 'There's someone here who— No, he's just someone who came over to see if I needed any help. He wants to talk to you... Okay, hang on.' She handed over the phone, still frowning.

'Hi, hello... Jack, is it? My name's Tam, Tam Murray, and I happened to be in the car park when your wife realised she had a flat. I came over to see if she needed any help changing it.'

'Thank you, that's kind but—' The man on the other end sounded groggy, his voice rough. Tam broke in before he could get any further.

'And I thought I ought to talk to you, so you'd know I wasn't some kind of weirdo... Yes, I realise if I was a weirdo that's exactly what I *would* say, but I have a car. And it struck me that in the absence of any other readily available solution, I could give your wife a lift home.' The woman's eyes widened at that, and Tam smiled and nodded. 'She doesn't look very happy about the idea, but look, I work at Chawston House, it's a residential care home in town. If I give you the number you can ring them and speak to my boss, Trish. She'll vouch for me.'

There was a pause. Jack was clearly thinking. 'Again, that's very kind but I'm not sure... We're a bit off the beaten track and...' His voice was ripe with indecision. 'Perhaps I could have a word with my wife again?'

Tam handed back the phone and moved a little distance away to give them some space. In all likelihood he would still be able to hear every word of the conversation, but he could at least look like he wasn't trying to. He forced his attention elsewhere, following the flight of three pigeons who swooped to settle on the roof of the building opposite.

After a minute or so of low murmuring, the woman waved her phone, the conversation clearly ended. She slipped it back inside her pocket. 'Right... Um, are you sure it's okay to drop me home? It's a twenty-minute drive and we live on a farm so it's at the end of a pretty rough road.'

Tam nodded, smiling. 'My car's older than yours, so it's no problem. Not like it's a top-of-the-range sports car or anything. And it's absolutely fine. I'm not due at work until lunchtime.'

'Okay then... thank you.' She held out her hand, suddenly shy. 'My name's Beth.'

Tam could see her run her tongue over the front of her teeth. It was something he did when he was nervous, too, his mouth too dry to speak.

He took her hand and shook it. 'Pleased to meet you, Beth. I'm just over here.' Although, of course, she already knew where his car was.

Opening the car door for her, he prayed that it didn't smell too malodorous inside. He tried to keep it ventilated during the times when he wasn't asleep, but that wasn't at all pleasant when it was this cold, and he obviously hadn't had a chance this morning so... He climbed into the driver's seat, painfully aware of his situation. He really hadn't thought this through. The rear of the car was full of his things, his sleeping bag still open where he'd only recently climbed out of it.

'So, where are we headed?' he asked.

'It's Beacalls Farm, near Lower Bettesfield,' she replied, doing up her seat belt. 'Do you know it?'

Tam knew it well. Not so long ago, it was a journey he made every day. He nodded, swallowing the lump in his throat. Moments later they pulled out of the car park.

14

Tam

A thin, hazy sun broke through the clouds as Tam drew up outside Beacalls Farm. Beth was right, the track to the house would test even the most resilient suspension, but he didn't care – just being back out this way soothed away any tension he had been feeling. He loved it around here, always had. He waited until Beth had climbed from the car before following suit, lifting his head to the sky and taking the morning air deep inside his lungs. He'd forgotten how good that felt. And the birds... He smiled, trying to sort out one joyful call from another.

'There you go,' he said. 'Home sweet home. It's a beautiful spot,' he added, looking around him.

The journey had been quiet, the conversation a little stilted, but now Beth smiled, properly it seemed. 'We love it,' she said. 'And I can't thank you enough. Really, you've been very kind.' She fished in her handbag. 'Will you come in for a moment? My husband wants to meet you.'

Tam was torn. He felt as if he should, but staying here for

too long would almost certainly leave him feeling maudlin. Too much of a good thing always reminded him of what he'd lost.

'Please?' she asked again. 'I can at least make you a cup of tea after dragging you out here.'

'Sure,' said Tam. 'Thank you, that would be lovely.'

He followed her inside to find a warm and welcoming farm-house, with whitewashed walls and worn flags on the floor giving it an air of permanence. It was old, and a little tired-look-ing, but Tam thought it was beautiful.

Beth led him into an airy kitchen, gesturing at a well-scrubbed wooden table which sat in the middle of the room. 'Grab a seat,' she said. 'And I'll put the kettle on. Do you mind waiting a few minutes while I get Jack up? He can't, you see, without me...' She dumped her bag and coat on the table and hurried away, leaving Tam lost for words.

The kitchen had clearly been modified for Jack's needs, or at least in part. The rest of it housed a collection of things which had been 'cobbled together' – furniture which didn't really belong in a kitchen, but which had been repurposed. One of these was a large bookcase which stood against one wall. The top shelves were occupied by a selection of novels, but the bottom few had been put to use housing a whole range of things which Tam guessed might need to be on hand – a bowl of fruit, an opened packet of biscuits, a pair of binoculars, a notepad, pot of pens, iPad, headphones, reading glasses, toaster, and a stack of non-fiction books on their side. Out of habit, he peered at the titles, smiling in recognition at one of them which he pulled from the stack.

He was still leafing through it when a voice came from behind him. 'It's very good.'

Tam spun around, embarrassed to have been caught with one of their personal possessions.

'Yes, I've read it,' he replied. 'Sorry, I was just... reminiscing. It's been a while since I last looked at it.' He replaced the book, standing awkwardly even though the man in front of him was smiling. He didn't look in the least annoyed to find a perfect stranger rifling through his things.

'I'm Jack,' he said. 'And apologies for the rather rough-and-ready appearance.' He ran a hand through thick curly hair. 'It takes a while to get up in the morning, as you can imagine.'

Tam nodded and approached him, holding out his hand. 'Tam,' he said. 'Pleased to meet you.'

The hand which took his was warm, with a firm grip, while the other lay still in the man's lap. He was wearing jogging bottoms and a sweatshirt and Tam relaxed a little, slightly more comfortable in his own clothes.

'I'll get the coffee on... you do drink coffee?'

'Oh, yes, thanks. As long as it's not too much trouble.'

Jack paused a second. 'It's an incredible faff, but then most things are. What's important, however, is that the coffee is made because without it the day doesn't start at all.'

Tam smiled. 'I know what you mean.' It was one of life's small rituals that he missed. He waited while Jack's wheelchair reversed and spun about before following him to stand in front of the kitchen window. 'And it looks as if it's going to be beautiful, after all.' The sun, although still pale in its winter clothes, was gaining in strength, the sky beginning to lose the silvery threads of dawn and finding blue. 'Cold,' he added. 'But give me sunshine over rain any day.'

Jack looked up, his eyes flicking to the window, before turning his attention back to the task in hand. 'It all looks pretty much the same from down here.'

Tam winced, but the words held no bitterness. Jack was simply stating a fact. Tam pulled his phone from his pocket and snapped a quick shot.

'There you go...' He angled the screen so that Jack could see it. 'There's something about the land in winter...' he mused. 'Maybe because it makes us look harder to find its beauty – it's

all so obvious in the summer – but it's there all the same and—'
He stopped, suddenly aware of how inappropriate his words
might be but, to his relief, Jack was smiling, albeit wistfully.

'I was always a sucker for a good hoarfrost,' he said. 'Waking
up to find that the world had been transformed overnight.' He
finished spooning coffee into a machine on a low counter and
set it going. 'Beth won't be long – she's just getting changed out
of her uniform.'

Tam nodded. 'Of course… she works the night shift, doesn't
she? Sorry, I should have realised she'd be desperate for some
shut-eye. Listen, the offer of coffee is great, but I don't have to
stay.'

'It's the least we can do after your kindness. I really am
grateful to you for getting Beth home. Our set-up here doesn't
give us much room for manoeuvre, I'm afraid. We don't have a
back-up plan if anything goes wrong, so…'

'She was very anxious to get home,' Tam replied. 'She
mentioned you weren't well.'

'Hmm… She worries.'

'Occupational hazard, I would imagine.'

Jack smiled. 'I had a raging fever when I went to bed last
night, but I feel fine now, so I don't know what that was about.
Have a seat, the coffee won't be long.'

'So, what do you farm here?' asked Tam, sitting down.

'Farm?' Jack looked down at his legs. 'Not a lot. Not any
more.'

Tam closed his eyes. He was such an idiot at times. 'Sorry, I
didn't think. I just saw all the books and…'

'They're more an exercise in keeping atrophy away these
days.' Jack tapped his head. 'The old noggin feels like mush.
Plus, a little bit of dreaming never does any harm.'

Tam looked up from where he was studying the grain on
the table, one finger tracing a particularly prominent whorl.
'True. Although sometimes it has the opposite effect from what

you intend.' The surface of the wood was beautiful, worn smooth with the patina of use and obviously well loved. 'I find it makes me yearn even more for the things I've lost.' He looked up again to see Jack studying him.

'It is a bit like picking at an old wound, I agree. You know you shouldn't, but...' Nostalgia drew out his words. 'There are worse things to read, though.'

Tam laughed. 'Oh, there are, I've read quite a few of them.'

'Have you seen this one?' Jack lifted a newspaper from the table, revealing a book underneath. 'It's good. I like it because it makes me think that something might still be gleaned from all this chaos.' He waved a hand towards the window. 'It's a bit of a jungle out there.'

Tam studied the book's cover, its edges a riot of ivy leaves and bramble, blackberries and sycamore seeds. At its centre, a beautiful turtle dove was posed among the branches, the softest pink blush to its breast. '*Wilding*,' he read. 'May I?'

With Jack's consent, he picked up the book, turning it this way and that so that the embellishments on the cover caught the light. He flipped it over and began to read the back, eyes widening in delight as he did so.

'You can borrow it if you like,' said Jack.

It was a tempting offer, but totally impractical. 'I'm not sure I'd be able to get it back to you,' Tam replied. 'Not unless your wife has a habit of breaking down in the car park. Thanks, though. I'll see if I can get a copy from the library.'

Jack's reply was stalled by Beth coming back into the room.

'You know, some days I swear it's only the thought of a decent coffee that gets me through the last hours of my shift.' Now dressed in jeans and a hoodie, she looked tired, but more relaxed than she had been up until now. Tam didn't want to pry, but he was beginning to understand the difficulties their life posed. 'Oh sorry,' she added. 'I've interrupted you. Carry on, I'll sort the drinks.'

'I was just talking to Tam about *Wilding*,' replied Jack.

Her face fell slightly. 'Do you take sugar, Tam?'

'Just milk, please.'

Silence fell for a few moments until Beth set a mug down in front of him. 'Just humour him,' she said, rolling her eyes. 'He can go on about it for days.' Her tone was light-hearted yet, for a second, the look on her face was anything but. Tam was a little confused. He would have thought she would be encouraging of something her husband was interested in.

'No, really. It sounds my kind of read,' he replied. 'I couldn't help noticing some of the other books on the shelves there.' He gestured towards them. 'I've read a couple of those too.'

She placed a mug in front of Jack before returning to collect her own coffee. 'So how come *you're* interested in farming?' she asked. 'Is it a family thing?'

Tam shook his head. 'I didn't always work in a care home... But no, I don't come from a long line of farming stock, I'm just interested in our countryside. It's always been a passion of mine.'

She nodded, but her expression was closed. It was clear she didn't want to pursue the conversation. 'I hope Jack has told you how grateful we are,' she said, sitting down opposite. 'I had visions of arriving home to find him in the throes of some hideous bug.'

'He has, but it's fine, honestly. I was glad to help. Will you be able to sort something with your car?'

'Oh yes, I'll give our local mechanic a ring in a bit. Clive's very good, but there's no point contacting him before ten at least.' She smiled. 'He doesn't like early mornings.'

'The man's in his seventies, though,' added Jack. 'You can hardly blame him.'

Tam took a sip of his coffee. Beth was right, it was very fine coffee indeed. It was the kind he would love to drink every morning too. At a table just like this one. In a house surrounded by rolling fields, just like he used to have. He cleared his throat. 'I'll finish this and get out of your way.'

'No rush.'

Beth smiled, but the conversation had faltered, and he was beginning to feel like a spare part. She probably had a million and one things to do, sleep being one of them.

'I ought to get home anyway,' he replied, pointedly checking his watch. 'Got a bit of shopping to pick up before my shift starts.' The coffee was still too hot, but he gulped down several mouthfuls.

Beth dipped her head, acknowledging his statement and ignoring his lie. 'Have you worked there long?' she asked.

'Few months,' Tam replied. 'But I like it.' He swallowed the rest of his drink. 'Thanks again. This is the best coffee I've had in a long while. Anyway, I hope you get your car sorted out. It was nice to meet you, Jack.'

'You too. Are you sure about the book? I'm sure we could come to some arrangement.' He checked himself. 'Actually, take it, please. A small recompense for your help. I can easily order another copy.' He grinned. 'Thank heaven for Amazon.'

Tam opened his mouth to argue, but then closed it again. 'Then thank you. I know I'll enjoy it.' He picked up the copy of *Wilding* and got to his feet.

'I'll walk you to the door,' said Beth.

'It's been lovely to meet you, Tam,' she added softly as they reached the threshold. 'And obviously, I'm very grateful but – don't take this the wrong way – it isn't necessarily a good idea for Jack to go dreaming about this place again. Ultimately he...' She took a deep breath. 'He gets frustrated, and then he gets angry, and then... he gets depressed.' Her look was a little embarrassed. 'I just try to head it off where I can. I'm sure you understand.'

Tam did, but he didn't think she was right. He nodded though. It probably wasn't a good idea for him to stay much longer either. 'No problem. And it's not as if there's any reason for me to stay in touch, is there?'

'No...' She lowered her voice even further. 'You're usually asleep when I pass, but if you ever need anything, maybe I could return the favour some day? Just... I don't know... Maybe leave a note on my windscreen, or something?'

He nodded. 'Thank you. Although I have been wondering whether I ought to rethink where I've been stopping. It doesn't do to stay in one place for too long so...' He let his sentence trail off. He didn't want to explain that in all likelihood drugs were being dealt only a few metres away from where she'd been parking. The grey van had always gone by the time Beth returned to her car, so whatever was going on would never affect her. She had enough on her plate without worrying about that too.

She looked surprised. 'That's not on account of me, I hope?'

'No, no... it's the way it goes, that's all. I'll be there for a bit though, I expect. Got to find somewhere suitable first.'

She wanted to know more; he could see the questions forming in her head, but she held them back. 'Okay... bye then.'

He smiled. 'Bye, Beth.'

15

Beth

'He seemed like a nice chap,' said Beth, returning to the kitchen. Jack was still sitting at the table, mug in hand. He had that look on his face, the one where he was lost in his dreams, far away from the day's reality. 'I was lucky he was around.'

'And not an axe murderer.'

She slid him a look. 'Don't... I all but called him that.'

Jack winced. 'Point taken. Hopefully there won't be a next time, but if there is, call a taxi, just in case. I worry about you.'

'You're lucky if you can find one. Besides, we don't have the money for the rates they charge. They fleece you when they find out you don't live in town.'

'But in an emergency, Beth. It's not as if you jump into one every five minutes, and I'd rather have you safe.'

Beth rubbed the back of her neck. She had the beginnings of a headache and that was where they always started. Too much tension just at the wrong end of her day. She needed to change the subject.

'I was worried about *you*. I'm glad that whatever was ailing you last night seems to have fizzled out. Maybe you were just more tired than usual.'

Jack nodded, picking up the newspaper from the table and glancing at it idly.

'What was the problem with the spare anyway?'

'I dunno. It was flat as well, we did look.' It wasn't an outright lie. She picked up her mug and carried it to the sink, pouring away the remains of her coffee. 'I'll never sleep if I drink this.' Her thoughts were already racing ahead to all the things there were still left to do. Jack might be out of bed, but he was far from ready for the day. Plus, there was washing to put on the line, another load to go in the machine and now the car to sort out as well.

'I can shower later if you want to get your head down,' said Jack, as if reading her mind. She could feel his eyes on her, assessing what he saw. 'You look tired,' he added. 'Bad shift?'

Beth shrugged. 'The usual. I think I'm just hormonal.' She attempted a smile. 'Well, more hormonal than usual.' She was making light of things, but it hadn't been a particularly easy shift – too much chatter about the redundancies which inevitably pulled everyone down. Beth was just as worried as any of her colleagues, but there were always one or two who did nothing but moan and she tried to avoid them as much as she could. No one could change the situation, but you could change the way you coped with it. The bottomless pit of doom, Lisa called it, and Beth agreed with her – it was far too easy to get dragged in.

'Actually,' she said, 'if you don't mind showering later, I might turn in. I'll just give the garage a call and get Clive to sort the tyre for us.'

'I can do that,' replied Jack. 'You get off to bed.' He glanced at his watch. 'Shall I wake you at two? Bit later than usual?'

She grinned. 'With a coffee?'

'Always.'

She was halfway across the room when he spoke again. 'Beth...?'

She turned at the change of tone in his voice.

'Was the spare tyre still the same one from the last time you had a flat? Because that was over a year ago.'

'Yeah, I know.' Beth decided to brazen it out. 'I kept meaning to get it done, and like the stupid idiot I am, it slipped my mind. I won't do that again.'

'I just worry about you...' replied Jack, studying her face. 'You were lucky today that Tam was around to help.'

'I know,' she said lightly. 'But we'll get it sorted.' She smiled and came forward to kiss him. 'Thanks for doing that. And could you ask Clive if he'll invoice us, rather than pay upfront? I'll settle it when I get paid.'

This time she was almost at the door when she heard Jack sigh. A loud, very audible sigh that was designed to get her attention.

'Why do I get the feeling there's something you're not telling me...?'

'I don't know,' replied Beth, turning back around. 'Why *do* you get the feeling there's something I'm not telling you?' She grinned at her teasing of him, just to show it was well meant. But then she sobered. 'I'm not, you know, it's just the same old crap. An unexpected bill we really can't afford, so we'll jiggle a bit, like we always do.'

But Beth's attempts at deflection weren't going to work. Not today.

'Don't do that,' said Jack. 'Pretend it isn't important. It isn't funny and it isn't the truth either. I know what we have in the bank, and there's enough to cover a new tyre, for goodness' sake. There's also enough for the odd taxi. I'm also damn sure your not replacing the spare was deliberate because you're a very organised person, Beth, you don't forget stuff like that.' His eyes narrowed. 'You took a calculated risk hoping it wouldn't backfire, except that today it did, didn't it? I could have waited the extra half hour it would have taken you to walk to the station and get a taxi.'

'I was worried about you.'

'When a simple phone call would have established you didn't need to be. So, what's really going on here, Beth? I know we don't have much to spare, but we're doing okay.'

The pain in Beth's neck had now moved to settle over one eye. And she knew from experience it was a headache she wouldn't be able to outrun.

'I might not have a job next month,' she replied, hunching her shoulders up to her ears. She released them, stretching out the muscles as best she could. The pain was about to get a whole lot worse. 'But chances are I will, and if I worried myself to death every time the hospital went through another round of redundancies, I'd be... well, I'd be dead.' She rolled her eyes at him. 'I refuse to do it, Jack. It's a hard enough job without living your life wound up like a coiled spring. Lisa's told me it's very unlikely I'll be one of the ones to go, and I trust her. She's in with senior management and she *will* get to have her say. So, let's just see what happens, shall we? I'll worry about the sky falling in when it lands on my head.'

'See, you're doing it again. Making light of things. Even the language you use is designed to sound ridiculous so it's easier for you to pretend it doesn't matter, or that it's never going to happen.' He drew in a deep breath. 'And what's worse is that you do it to hide stuff from me, thinking I won't see through your sleight of hand.'

Beth's mouth dropped open. 'I do not.'

'You do. You hide things from me all the time. And don't look at me like that... as if you don't know what I'm talking about. You think I won't cope, so you never reveal anything that might provoke an emotion. God forbid. Just keep Jack on an even keel. Well, let me explain something to you – real life carries on just the same whether you can use your legs or not. There's good... there's stuff which rumbles along the middle... and then there's stuff which has the potential to be monumentally shit and, at the very least, deserves an emotional response. This is one of those times, Beth. So don't fall into the trap of thinking that my brain is as useless as the rest of my body. I can *think* perfectly well.'

'Okay, well how about you then?' Beth retorted, hurt by the unfairness of his remark. 'You do exactly the same. Except you pretend you don't. You make out you're fine with things when you're not. I can see your jaw clench, Jack. I can hear the slight change of pitch in your voice. The bloody air bristles around you when you're seething and yet you go out of your way to pretend everything's okay.'

'So, ask yourself why I do that... I do it so that you don't have to deal with any more of my crap than you already do.'

'Exactly!' She huffed in exasperation. 'Likewise. If I keep things from you, it's because you have to deal with so much crap on an average day, I don't want to add to the pile you already have to wade through. We're both protecting each other, so don't make out this is all my fault. The only thing I'm guilty of here is loving you.'

'*Ditto...*'

Beth closed her eyes, trying to keep calm. She should be grateful to hear that Jack loved her, even if he didn't quite say it, but it almost felt like an accusation.

'I just don't want to spend what little time we have together worrying about stuff which might not happen. We made a pact once, remember? To try to carve out a little time each day to actually live, and not just exist.'

'Except we don't really do that any more, do we? That bloke today, who brought you home, he wanted to ask me what I did, I could see it in his eyes. He did ask me what we farm, a logical question given what I was reading and where we live. But, when I said "not much" he held back on the real question he wanted to ask, which was "why not?"... So why do other people think me capable of doing something and yet I don't?'

'Are you suggesting that's my fault?'

'I'm not suggesting it's anyone's fault.' Jack's tone was mild, and she hated when he did that. You only needed to look at the expression on his face to know he was deliberately keeping it that way. He raised his eyebrows. 'And, yes, straight after my accident, I couldn't have coped. I'll be the first to admit that I was happy to don the "Jack's disabled" label, but however angry and frustrated I got, I still didn't understand that it was a label I could tear off. Maybe now I do.'

'Jack, we're talking about the farm. And I know how much you miss it, and dream that things might be different, but we have to face the facts here. It hurt me to hear Tam chatting away with you earlier, because it was a reminder of what can no longer be. It's too brutal.'

Jack's mouth tightened into a thin line. 'Do you really think it takes a perfect stranger to remind me of that? Do you not realise that I think about it every day? Every *minute* of *every* day? How I feel doesn't go away just because we're not talking about it. But that's your trouble, isn't it? That's the way you like it. You don't like talking about it. And thanks for the vote of confidence, by the way. I'm not hearing any words of encouragement from you, any protestations about all the things I *can* do. You really do know how to make a guy feel useless.'

'*What?*' Beth stared at him in astonishment. 'That's a low blow, Jack. When every single day I deal with the reality of what you can't do.' She held up a hand. 'And don't you dare start accusing me of feeling bitter about it. I don't. I have never blamed you for what happened, nor do I resent doing what I do, but you do not have the use of your legs, Jack. Nor one arm, to all intents and purposes. There are very real limits to what you can do and believing you can do otherwise is only going to end one way. Why on earth would I let you walk willingly down that path?'

'Interesting choice of words.'

Beth let out a strangled scream. 'Don't try to be clever – you know what I mean. Ordinary everyday *life* screws with your head. I'm not about to let you chase some stupid notion you've got into your brain, only to have it blow up in your face. Can you not see what that would do to you?'

'Isn't that *my* choice? You treat me like a child, Beth.'

'Then stop bloody acting like one! You accuse me of hiding stuff from you, but you won't ever talk about the reason why we stay here – in a house that is ill-equipped for your needs, that haemorrhages money on repairs and heating and is never even warm.'

'I don't know what you're talking about.'

'Okay then.' She gritted her teeth and lifted her chin. 'I think we should move.'

Jack stared at her, jaw clenched in exactly the same way she'd accused him of earlier. *Go on*, she willed him, *say it. Actually come out and say the thing which lies behind all of this*. She held his look, one eyebrow raised in challenge.

Jack raised his. Challenge accepted. 'I am not selling the farm,' he said.

'Exactly... You won't ever sell this place even though it's the biggest millstone around our necks, because you're still harbouring delusions that one day you might get out there again. Accept what happened to you, Jack. I mean, *really* accept it. Reading your farming books to "keep your mind active..."' She shook her head dismissively. 'Don't pretend. Those books don't help you, they stop you from having to face up to what's going on here. The dream is over, Jack. And you need to stop hankering after a past which is never going to be your future. And the sooner you do that, the sooner *we* can build a new one.'

'*Wow*...' Jack let out a sharp breath of surprise. 'You really *have* been keeping things from me.' He blinked rapidly, his mouth shut tight to hold back his emotions. She'd never seen him look so desolate.

He pushed his finger against the control stick of his wheelchair, reversing away slowly, gaze still locked on hers, only spinning around at the last moment. 'Thanks for that. And keep me posted about the job thing, won't you? Just so that I can pretend we're in this thing together.' There was a moment's pause and then his chair carried him from the room. 'You're wrong, by the way...'

She'd gone too far. Shit... *shit.* But still she answered, quietly, with tears in her eyes, 'No, I'm not.'

16

Frankie

Frankie wasn't due to meet Beth for another fifteen minutes, but the coffee shop door was the closest one to her and she yanked it open, ducking inside and heading towards the rear. She had been on her way to the greengrocer's, but all thoughts of dinner went out of her mind in an instant. The only thing which mattered was getting off the street.

At that time of the morning the place was quiet, and she had her choice of the tables. She hurried to the furthest and sat down, counting to ten, eyes closed as if that alone could hide her from the world. Not even the world, just the one person who mattered. She was pretty sure he hadn't seen her, but he was looking, he must have been – why else would he be here?

She prayed that the door behind her remained closed and it was several more minutes before she could rouse herself from the table to check the street outside. She thought she'd caught a glimpse of him the last time she was here with Beth, but she'd convinced herself it was just her head playing tricks on her. It was a game her imagination had played far too often in the past.

She thought she was settled, thought those times were over, so why was she seeing him now? There was only one real answer – because this time he was actually here.

She pulled out her phone to check the time and, with one final search of the street, returned to her original seat, her heart still pounding. She'd been so careful, so how did he know where to find her? Only her sister knew where she was and they barely spoke; he would never think to ask her.

Frankie's head was still full of panicked thoughts when Beth tapped her on the shoulder a few minutes later. She nearly jumped out of her skin.

Beth laughed. 'Sorry...! I almost didn't see you right at the back,' she said, sitting down and plonking her bag on the floor.

'I think there must have been some kind of a breakfast meeting here this morning,' Frankie replied. 'So, I just parked myself here. Thankfully they've gone now. There was quite a gaggle of them.'

If Beth noticed the array of scrupulously clean tables, none of which looked as if they'd been recently occupied, it didn't show. 'Sorry, I got a bit held up. Have you been here long?'

'No, few minutes, that's all.' Frankie narrowed her eyes a little, finally taking in Beth's weary face. She got up to lean across the table and give her friend a hug. 'Is everything okay?'

'Fine.' Beth smiled brightly. 'Just a long shift, that's all. God, I need a coffee... Are we having breakfast too? Please say yes.'

Frankie laughed. 'They are rather good here.'

Beth bent down to rifle through her bag. 'What would you like? My shout.'

'Then the usual please, that would be great.' How easily the word 'usual' slipped off her tongue. How easily she had taken for granted that her time here could continue for as long as she wanted. She had made plans, small ones admittedly, but hopeful ones. And she had made a friend. The weight of change bowed Frankie's head and she wasn't sure she could bear to move all over again.

She looked over to where Beth was standing at the counter, at the person next to her, at the couple sat in a window seat, and the young mum cradling a child on her lap, fast asleep, without a care in the world. So much ordinary life going on around her every day, and yet it was impossible to tell what secrets those lives might be hiding, what turmoil was being faced, what heartache... She checked herself. Or what happiness, what joy... The only thing she was sure about was that it could all change in a heartbeat.

'Food won't be long,' said Beth, sitting down again. 'Is it me, or is it boiling in here?' She shrugged off her coat and hung it over the back of her chair. 'I'm forty-nine, for goodness' sake, I'm not ready for hot flushes yet.'

'Don't you believe it,' replied Frankie, rolling her eyes. 'Mine hit when I was younger than you.' The menopause had been yet another reason for Frankie to think she was going mad. If she couldn't trust her own body, what could she trust? Certainly not the thoughts in her head.

'Great, thanks for that,' said Beth, pulling a face.

Frankie smiled. 'If it's any consolation, mine wasn't half as bad as I'd been led to believe it would be. Anyway, enough about the disintegration of our youth. What's happened about your job? Have you heard anything yet?'

Beth shook her head. 'Rumour, that's all, nothing definite. My immediate boss reckons I've got nothing to worry about. She said my record would speak for itself.'

But despite her words, Beth didn't look at all happy.

'So that's good news then... isn't it?'

'Yes, I suppose...' Beth tucked her hair behind her ears, before massaging her neck. 'No, it is good news. It's just that I seem to be constantly on the back foot at the moment. It goes like that sometimes. We can have weeks where everything runs smoothly, and then others where calamity seems to lurk around every corner.'

'Jack-based calamity?'

Beth gave a tight smile. 'He had an off day at the end of last week, nothing specific, feeling tired more than anything. But by the time I was due to leave for work, he had a raging temperature and a thumping head. Course, he did what he always does, which is to tell me he'd be fine and that there was no reason for me not to go to work, but although I put up a token fight, that's all it was. I can't afford any time off at the moment. Or any more occasions like the one when Jack fell out of bed. Lisa covered for me then, and I got away with it, but I might not have. And it only takes one or two black marks on my copybook and that's me gone.'

'But the management team must have families too. Don't they understand that problems crop up from time to time?'

'On a personal level they probably do. But they're not paid to be personal. Some of them hide it better than others, but they're looking out for their own jobs just as much as I am, so...'

'When did we all become so scared?' asked Frankie, scowling. '*How* did we all become so scared?' she asked, shaking her head. 'It's not right, is it? Sometimes I get so... so... *furious* about the state of the country. We're all invisible. Especially if we don't fit inside the neat little boxes we're supposed to. But we all matter, *everyone*... It shouldn't be this way, we shouldn't have to fight just to live a life, a life we're all entitled to.' She rolled her eyes at her outburst. 'Sorry, was Jack okay?'

Beth nodded. 'But, typically, I was panicking like crazy, *again*, because I had a problem with the car and couldn't get straight home. As it turned out there was nothing to worry about – Jack was right as rain – but I didn't know that at the time. The guy from the car park gave me a lift home in the end.'

'He did what?' asked Frankie. 'And which guy? The one who sleeps in his car?'

'Yeah. Tam, his name is. I'd got a flat tyre and, after quite a bit of shouting and swearing on my part, he came over to help. I'm not surprised he woke up, I must have sounded like a drunken sailor.'

Frankie leaned forward. 'So, what happened?'

'Well, after he'd accused me of being judgemental about him sleeping in his car, he offered to change the tyre for me.'

'Sounds like he has a bit of a chip on his shoulder.'

'I guess... but I can't say I blame him. I expect he gets treated like dirt most of the time.'

Frankie raised her eyebrows. 'Sorry,' she said. 'That was rude. I just have a problem with men who throw their weight around.'

'He didn't though. Not at all, now I come to think about it. He even apologised for offering because he didn't want to imply that I was incapable.'

'See?' Frankie shrugged, smiling. 'Don't listen to me.'

'Maybe...' Beth smiled back. 'But I didn't exactly behave well myself. After I'd told him I wasn't in the slightest bit judgemental of his residential status, I then pretty much accused him of wanting to attack me simply on the basis of his being a man. In fact, he probably thought I was completely vile. I don't really remember what I said, I was too busy being stressed.'

'So, if he changed the tyre, how come he ended up giving you a lift home?'

'Because he didn't. The spare was flat too.'

'Ah...'

Beth nodded. 'I know, nice one. So, after I'd panicked some more about not being able to call the garage because it was too early, and not having the time to get a taxi because I'd have to walk to the station, or get any of my friends to give me a lift because they all work at the hospital, he offered to drive me home.'

'So, what was he like then?' asked Frankie.

'Really lovely.' Beth sighed. 'He even insisted on speaking to Jack before we left so he could introduce himself – he works in a local care home – and reassure him there was nothing untoward going on. Jack invited him in for a cup of coffee and they seemed to get on like a house on fire, bonding over their love of the countryside...' She trailed off, gaze dropping to the table. 'I'm such a bitch.'

Frankie stared at her, horrified to see tears welling at the corners of her eyes. 'What on earth makes you say that?'

'Because I made it sound as if I didn't want him there. I shut him down when he was speaking and then, as he was leaving, I warned him off encouraging Jack with his dreams about the farm. Said I didn't want him upset. I could see Tam didn't agree with me, and he told me not to worry, told me in all likelihood I'd never see him again. Then he said he'd probably be moving on from the car park anyway, just to make sure.'

Frankie didn't know what to say.

'And I only said what I did because I was embarrassed about the fact that I'd cut short their conversation earlier. I wanted to explain why but ended up looking like a prize cow.' She shook her head. 'I *am* a prize cow. There was absolutely no reason to behave the way I did.'

'Maybe you were just looking out for Jack,' said Frankie gently. 'Like you always do.'

Beth nodded, but then shook her head several times, no longer able to hold back the tears which began to spill down her cheeks.

'We had a terrible row after he left.'

Now Frankie was beginning to understand.

'It was worse than we've ever had. In fact, we never argue. Maybe that's part of the problem...'

'That doesn't sound like a problem to me.'

'I don't think we're very good at talking to one another. Even after the accident we never really...' She trailed off. 'Emotions were running so high. Jack was in a lot of pain, and he was right, I just took over – organised him, and us, to within an inch of our lives and then simply carried on. It's been that way ever since.'

Frankie hated to see her friend so upset. 'I think... no, I'm pretty certain that would have been the only way for you to deal with things. Of coping with an event that was, literally, life-changing. Don't ever feel bad about doing what you needed to get you through the day. You're a nurse, Beth, you did what you do best. You cared.'

'I smothered.'

Frankie took hold of her hand and gave it a squeeze. 'I doubt that. So don't berate yourself for what you've done. I can't begin to imagine what it must have been like for Jack, but it was equally as bad for you. I'm not the best person to give relationship advice, but you're a strong woman, Beth. You rose to the challenge that life threw at you, and you live that challenge day in, day out. That takes a lot of guts and energy, let alone the sacrifices you have to make. I think we women should stop putting ourselves down. I think we're pretty damn amazing.'

She said it with such force that Beth stopped in her tracks, sniffing. 'So, what do you do to put yourself down?'

'Oh, plenty, believe me.'

'Such as?'

But Frankie just smiled. 'Another time, maybe.'

She sat back as the waitress appeared with two plates, waiting until she had placed them on the table and moved away before resuming the conversation.

'So, how's it been the last few days?' she asked gently.

'Awful...' Beth picked up her bap and stared at it. 'I've eaten so much chocolate since then, and now I've got a humongous spot on the end of my chin...' She swallowed. 'Jack's barely speaking to me.'

Frankie *really* wasn't the best person to give relationship advice, but her heart went out to Beth. 'That must feel awful when the two of you are so close. I'm really sorry, Beth. But you know, not long after we first met, you said you felt as if you were pretending to be perfect the whole time. Perhaps this was a conversation you really needed to have, even if it was an acrimonious one. It's given you both an opportunity to get things off your chest, and it's important to say how you feel. The longer you don't, the more danger you're in of believing the things you tell yourself. We delude ourselves all the time, about little things mostly, but sometimes it's the big things, and it becomes a habit before we even realise.'

'I keep telling myself that.' Beth wiped her chin. 'And I know it's good to be honest with one another, but I said some awful things, Frankie. I didn't mean them, not really, it was just the heat of the moment, but—'

'Not really?' Frankie gave her a sympathetic smile. 'Don't dismiss what you said, even if the words you used were ones which, with hindsight, you wouldn't have chosen. From what you've told me I think the essence of what you said probably *was* true.'

Beth nodded, closing her eyes silently for a moment. 'It was...' she admitted. 'But now I'm not sure Jack will ever forgive me.'

'Have you asked him to?'

Beth looked surprised. 'Not as such, but I did say I was sorry.'

'I asked, because I'm pretty sure Jack will have said plenty too. And like you, they were probably things which didn't sound great when said out loud, but which, *exactly* like you, were things he's had on his mind as well. Things he didn't want to admit to. I don't think it was wrong to say them and now you have a choice, surely? You can say sorry, and gloss over it, and in time get back to how things were, or you can ask each other's forgiveness for the way you've both dealt with things, and set to work putting it right.'

'So, this is a good thing?' asked Beth with a weak smile. 'Even though it feels as if the world is ending?'

'Even though...' Frankie agreed.

Beth shook her head. 'I'm such an idiot,' she said. 'But I'm very glad I met you.' She squeezed Frankie's hand back. 'Thank you...' She sniffed. 'You will let me know if I can help *you* any time, won't you?'

'You already have.' Frankie grinned. 'Apart from anything else, you have introduced me to what are arguably the best bacon and egg baps this town has to offer.'

Beth stared at her breakfast, raising it as if to salute Frankie, and took a huge bite. 'And amen to that,' she mumbled through a mouthful. At least that's what Frankie thought she said.

By the time the two of them parted, Beth seemed happier, or at least had begun to see light at the end of the dark tunnel she was in. Frankie, on the other hand, already anxious, was now a tight bundle of nerves, and desperate to get home. But there was one thing she needed to check first. Forewarned was forearmed.

Scanning the street both ahead and behind, she hurried to the bakery. Fortunately, there was only one other person there aside from Melanie: a woman in a dark red coat. Frankie waited a moment for the customer to be served, her anxiety soon turning to impatience.

She stepped forward. 'Mel, sorry to interrupt, but has anyone been in asking for me this morning?'

Melanie smiled at the customer and handed over her change. 'No, should they have?'

'Not really, just...' She didn't want to explain anything to Melanie, but she had to be sure. 'Would you do me a favour?

And if anyone *does* come in, could you tell them you've never heard of me?'

Melanie's eyes widened. 'Well, I can, but...'

'It's a long story, but it'll be my brother,' Frankie lied. She didn't even have a brother. 'He's got himself in trouble again, and I kept quiet about my job here otherwise he'd only start hassling me for money. Anyway, I heard he's back in town, so if he does appear...'

Melanie nodded. 'Families, who'd have them, eh?' She turned to rearrange the bread on the shelves behind her. 'I wanted to ask you something, actually. Have you heard anything from Vivienne? I wondered if you knew when she was coming back.'

'I had a message at the beginning of the week to say she was still feeling poorly, but that was all. Whatever it is seems to have really knocked her out.'

'Hmm...'

Something about Mel's tone caught Frankie's attention. 'Have *you* spoken to her?'

'No, but I've left umpteen messages on her answerphone, and she hasn't replied to any of them. I can't keep doing these hours forever, I've got other stuff to take care of, and it's been a while now. What if she's really ill?'

'She's probably just got the flu or something, I'm sure she'll be in touch.' Frankie was ashamed to say she hadn't given her boss much thought, but Mel was right – what if Vivienne was really poorly? The longer she was away from work, the longer Frankie would need to open up the bakery of a morning and serve in the shop, in full view of anyone passing by. There was a reason she liked the quiet and privacy of the night shift. 'Tell you what, I'll make her a cake and pop it round,' she said. 'See if everything's okay.' She glanced back towards the street as another customer came in. He might not have been asking for her at the bakery yet, but that didn't mean he didn't know she was there. And, if he'd tracked down where she worked, he would sure as hell have found out where she lived... 'Anyway, I've got to run, but let's keep each other posted, okay?'

She was in such a rush to get to the safety of her flat that she pushed open the bakery door just as someone pulled it from the other side, practically catapulting herself through the doorway. She had the impression of height and dark woollen clothing before she could gather herself sufficiently to apologise.

'Someone's in a rush. I've just come to see you and now here you are.'

Frankie looked up, startled. She hadn't been expecting that at all.

'Vivienne?'

17

Frankie

'What I hope is that whoever buys the bakery will keep you on,' said Vivienne, nursing her mug with both hands. 'And I shall certainly make that suggestion.'

Frankie nodded. 'Thank you,' she said. 'That's very kind. But the main thing is that you're okay.' It seemed like the right thing to say, even though Frankie's brain was still reeling in shock from Vivienne's announcement.

'There are no guarantees, of course,' replied Vivienne. 'But I've been lucky. The tumour was very small, was caught early, and I'm told the treatment has been a complete success. The idea to sell the business took me by surprise, though,' she added. 'It certainly wasn't something I was planning, not for a good few years yet, anyway. But as soon as I began to think about it, I realised it was what I wanted. I'm not getting any younger.' She took a deep breath. 'But that's life, I guess. When a crisis hits it changes you, in ways you may not have imagined, but the one thing it does do is make you look at the decisions you've made in your life. My husband and I realised it was time to take the foot off the gas and do something different with the rest of our lives.'

'Makes total sense,' said Frankie. 'I think if I were in your position, I'd do the same. And who wouldn't want to live by the sea?' She smiled politely. 'Do you know whereabouts yet?'

Vivienne shook her head. 'We've got a shortlist of possibles, so it will be a case of visiting each to see where we like best. Our house is going on the market as well, so it could be some time before we're able to make the move. Of course, it also depends on how quickly the business takes to sell, but I imagine it will be several months yet before anything is finalised. I hope that gives you enough time to make arrangements of your own?'

'I'm sure it will, and I really appreciate you giving me as much notice as possible.'

Vivienne put down her mug of tea on Frankie's coffee table. She'd barely even drunk half of it. 'You must let me know if you need any help and, of course, providing any references you might need goes without saying. As I said, hopefully it won't come to that, but do please let me know.'

Frankie cleared her throat. 'I will, thank you... and... um... will you be selling the flat as well?' She hadn't wanted to ask, but she had to know. There was a tiny possibility things might not be as bad as they seemed.

Vivienne smiled awkwardly, making ready to leave. This wasn't a social call, after all. 'I'm sorry, but we'll need the money from both the flat and the business if we're to make our move.'

And there it was. Every bit as bad as Frankie feared. 'Of course,' she said. 'I understand.' She got to her feet to make it easier for Vivienne, leading her through into the kitchen. 'I was going to make you a cake and pop it round later... I'm glad you're okay.'

Vivienne was starting to look embarrassed. 'That's very sweet, but really it should be the other way around. I should be making a cake for *you*. It's been a tough few weeks, but I'm lucky I can put it behind me now. I appreciate you being so understanding, though. I know this isn't easy news to hear. Hopefully nothing will change but... Anyway, if you need a reference or anything, please let me know.'

'I will,' said Frankie. 'And thank you. I've really enjoyed my time at Duggan's.'

Vivienne dipped her head. 'I will miss it,' she said. 'But I think it's the right thing to do.'

Frankie couldn't sleep after Vivienne left. It had been surprise enough practically barging into her when she'd just been the subject of her discussion with Mel, but even more so when she asked if she might come up and have a chat. And as for her news...

Frankie was also unused to having visitors. It made her feel awkward, self-conscious about the smallness of her home and its obvious make-do-and-mend appearance. She hated feeling that way, especially as Vivienne had been so lovely to let her have the flat in the first place. It was at times like these that Frankie felt her insecurities even more keenly. Part of her almost felt sorry for Vivienne. Actually, given what she'd had to say, Frankie felt terrible, knowing what she'd been through. And the fact that she'd had to impart her news in what were clearly sparse surroundings couldn't have made it easy for her. Vivienne was a nice person, and it was obvious that leaving a ticking time bomb in the wake of her visit was something she really hadn't wanted to do. But Frankie understood Vivienne's position perfectly. Life was short; Frankie was only too aware of that.

She shivered as she crossed the bakery kitchen and peered out the window. She wasn't cold, but the night was, bitterly so. She could only see a sliver of sky from where she was standing – deepest inky blue and shot through with stars. March could be such a harsh month, and although the cloudless days were cheerful enough, they brought with them below-zero temperatures and heavy frosts. The cobbles outside were already glittering dangerously. Frankie gripped her mug tighter, sipping her tea, grateful that she was warm and safe inside. It was just one of the many advantages to working at Duggan's, and she had taken her comfort, along with everything else, for granted. Where would she find another job which suited her so well? Or any job, in fact. Let alone somewhere else to live.

A figure turned into the alley, and she automatically took a step back before recognising the silhouette. It hadn't taken long at all for it to become familiar – the relaxed gait seemingly at odds with the broad bulk of the man. She smiled. William must be on his way home and her tea break seemed to coincide with his appearance more and more often these days.

It had been almost two weeks since she had first met William and, although she'd had no more bother with drunken louts, true to his word he had checked she was okay every day since then. Sometimes he gave a jaunty wave, sometimes it was a cheery salute, and it was oddly comforting, knowing that he was out there keeping an eye on things, even if it was only for a few moments.

A few days ago, while out running errands, she'd even gone to find the estate agents he had spoken of and, sure enough, there *was* a green door to the left of it, just as he'd said. She'd stared at it for quite a few minutes, wondering if he was inside, before tutting and walking back down the street. She felt foolish for having done so, but she had also acknowledged that a part of her felt better. It was most likely that her imagination had been working overtime, but the fear it might not have been never left her.

With a cheery thumbs up, William walked on by, and she watched until he reached the far end of the alley, disappearing from view as he turned the corner for home. She wondered whether he would be having eggs for breakfast, smiling at the thought of him slicing his bread into soldiers. Perhaps he might even put on some music while they were cooking, but somehow she doubted it; William didn't look much like a dancer. With a tut, she swallowed the rest of her tea before turning away from the window. She could feel the cold air coming off the panes of glass – stand there any longer and she'd soon feel chilly herself. Besides, she had work to do.

She left her mug by the sink and was about to collect some maize flour from the store when a thought came to her. And it was such an outlandish thought that it stopped her in her tracks. She rolled it around in her head for a few moments, savouring the unusual feel of it, and wondering what it was that had put it there. It was definitely not the kind of thought Frankie normally had and that in itself was surprising. It was a good thought though. It was a lovely thought, but did Frankie really have the nerve to carry it out? Frances definitely wouldn't, but Frankie... She looked towards the window again, wondering what it must feel like to be adrift on such a freezing night.

Her hand rested on the storeroom door. If she thought about it too much she wouldn't do it, that much was obvious – she'd talk herself out of it. She needed to push open the door quick and get on with it before she changed her mind. Focus on just this one thing, push everything else out of her head and not think about what she would actually be doing...

It had long been a mystery to her why there was a flask and a hot-water bottle in the storeroom, leftovers from some long-ago crisis perhaps but, like everything else in there, Frankie had cared for them – wiped dust from the flask and loosened the stopper on the water bottle in case the rubber perished. The flask was a good size, too, plenty big enough for several cups. The only question now was whether to fill it with tea or coffee.

Carrying both items to the sink, Frankie set the kettle to boil again and, while she waited, busied herself choosing some pastries. She decided on tea for the first time – she could easily ask what he preferred going forward – and she would take some sugar in a little bag instead of adding it to the tea, just in case he had it without. Minutes later, having given the flask a good rinse out first, she made a strongish brew and then filled the hot-water bottle as well, putting both on the side while she fetched her coat. She paused by the door, before shaking her head. *Out you go, Frankie, don't stop to think or you'll never do it.*

After the warmth of the bakery, the cold night air fairly took her breath away, and she nestled her neck deeper into the warm, furry collar of her coat. The action only served to strengthen her resolve. Not everyone had the luxury of a warm place to be, and she hoped he at least had warm clothes and blankets. She reached the car park before she even considered that Tam might not be there. Hadn't Beth said he'd been thinking of moving on? Course, if he was there, he would also probably be asleep.

She almost turned back. Stupid... If he *was* asleep, it had probably taken him an age to get that way and he wouldn't take kindly to her waking him up. Plus, she'd have to rouse him in the first place, and that would be plain awkward. But then she looked at the things she carried, knowing what a difference they could make. Her discomfort was nothing compared to his.

Scanning the car park, she wondered which car belonged to Beth and which might be Tam's. There weren't many cars here at all, and any of them could be his. She spotted one, parked up against the far wall, close to the only light. She moved closer, heart beginning to pound.

As it was, she needn't have worried about having to wake Tam. As she neared, trying to see through the dark glint of the windows, she realised that he was already sitting up. He was also watching her steadily as she approached. She lifted the flask and hot-water bottle so he could see them; what on earth did you say in this kind of situation?

'Hello... Tam?' She peered closer. 'My name's Frankie... I've brought some things for you.'

Tam's car was an estate and with the back seats removed there was quite a large space in which to lie down. Tam, however, was huddled in one corner, leaning against the rear of the driver's seat. She didn't want to open a door or the boot and have all the cold air rush in, neither did she want him to open a window, but practically shouting at him from outside wasn't ideal either. He was still watching her, all but expressionless. She smiled.

'I've got some tea... and a hot-water bottle,' she said. 'I thought you might like them.'

She was beginning to feel very foolish, and very cold herself. She should have worn her gloves. And she didn't know what to do. She didn't blame Tam for being wary of her – he must think her presence odd to say the least, but he could say *something*. Otherwise she might have to leave the things she'd brought on the ground and just back away – which felt horribly like feeding some kind of wild animal. She tried again.

'I'm sorry, this must seem very strange, but I work at the bakery around the corner – on the night shift – and I was thinking how bitter it was outside when I remembered what Beth had said about you—'

At the mention of her name, Tam leaned forward and pulled on the door handle. 'Beth sent you?' he said as the door swung open.

'No, she didn't send me, but I'm a friend of hers and... I just wondered whether you might like these?'

Tam stretched out his arms to take the flask from her. 'I don't know what to say, this is amazing. Thank you...' He paused a moment, as if unsure what to do next. 'Do you want to get in? Sorry, you'll have to go round the other side. I'll shift my stuff.'

'I'll clamber over, don't worry.' She hurried around to the

passenger side and pulled the door open, climbing inside to sit on a relatively clear patch of blanket. She quickly shut the door behind her, but it didn't seem to make much difference. It felt as cold inside the car as it was outside.

It wasn't until she was sitting looking at Tam that she realised how absurd the situation was. He might be known to Beth, but Tam was still a total stranger to her, and it was the middle of the night. Evidently the same thought had just occurred to Tam. He gave a low chuckle. 'Well, this is interesting... I can't say I've ever had this happen to me before.'

'Me neither,' Frankie replied. 'I almost didn't come. But I realised if I didn't do it as soon as I had the thought, I wouldn't do it at all, and it's freezing tonight, that's the point. It had to be now, really, or not at all.' She frowned. 'Not that this wouldn't be a good idea on any other night but... you know what I mean,' she finished, thoughts tied in knots.

'I do,' said Tam. 'And it is bloody freezing. I'm very grateful.' He took the hot-water bottle and shoved it inside his sleeping bag. 'Really, very grateful.'

'I didn't know what you preferred either, so I've brought tea. I hope that's okay.' She fished in her pocket. 'And I have some sugar too if you want it.'

'I don't usually,' replied Tam. 'Although I'll take it this time, if you don't mind. I'm craving sugary stuff at the moment.'

'Perhaps it helps keep you warm,' said Frankie.

'Aye, it could well be that. Worth a try, I reckon.'

Frankie nodded. 'I was worried I'd have to wake you.'

He shook his head. 'I think I've managed about half an hour's sleep so far. I got off okay, but woke up pretty sharpish, and that was it. Once you get cold, you've had it, it's very hard to get warm again.'

'It must be,' replied Frankie, giving him a shy smile. She didn't know what to say that wouldn't sound rude. It wasn't as if Tam could simply put on another jumper. She was certain he would have taken every precaution he could against the chill, and asking if there was somewhere else he could sleep was just plain insensitive – if there was, Tam would already be there. 'I'm sorry,' she said instead.

Tam frowned. 'Not your fault,' he said.

'No,' agreed Frankie. 'But I'm still sorry you're in this situation. I can't imagine what it must be like.'

'The worst thing is there's nowhere to go,' said Tam. 'Nighttime is closed. And it's the loneliest place you can imagine. There's nowhere to sit, or get warm, so I stay here, hunched and cold and uncomfortable, knowing that outside is even worse.'

Frankie suddenly remembered what else she had brought with her and pulled the bag from her pocket. 'Perhaps these will make the night feel a little better.'

Tam took the bag with a look of wonder on his face. 'This is a really kind thing you've done.'

'You did a kindness for a friend of mine,' said Frankie. 'I thought that was worth repaying.'

Tam looked sideways at her. 'Even so, most people wouldn't have.'

'I try not to be most people,' Frankie replied. 'Admittedly I don't know that many, but mostly the things they do or say make me nervous, so I stay out of their way.'

'Then coming here must not have been easy for you?'

'No, I...' Frankie dropped her head. 'I'm trying to feel a little freer about things.'

'And you thought you'd start with me?' Tam grinned. 'I'm honoured and, like I said, extremely grateful. People confuse me, too, some of them anyway. I can never quite figure out what makes them act the way they do.'

Frankie nodded. She guessed that Tam had probably been treated appallingly in the past. 'Sorry, I can't stay long. I'm still at work and I ought to get back, otherwise there won't be enough loaves for sale come the morning.'

'Is that where these came from?' asked Tam, as he opened the bag slightly and peered inside, inhaling the enticing aroma which wafted out. 'Heaven,' he said. 'Did you make them yourself?'

Frankie gave a small nod, grateful that her blushing cheeks would be hidden by the dim light. 'There are always a few spares – ones which go a bit wonky when they're baked. They taste the same,' she added quickly. 'But they're not the prettiest.'

'I don't know what to say.'

'No need to say anything,' said Frankie. 'I should get going and *you* should have some tea while it's still hot. The flask isn't mine, so I'm afraid I've no idea how well it works.'

'I'll have myself a proper midnight feast.'

'At three in the morning?' She laughed. 'Well, enjoy...' She began to shuffle her way towards the car door. 'And hang onto the flask and hot-water bottle. There's no need to return them straight away, so you can pop back whenever you need a refill. The bakery's the one at the end of the lane there.' She pointed to the road leading away from the car park. 'There's a back door a little way along the alley which cuts through to Green Street.'

Tam nodded. 'I know it,' he replied, watching as she pushed open the door. 'Good night, Frankie.'

'Night, Tam,' she replied. 'Sweet dreams.'

She didn't feel the cold at all as she walked back to the bakery.

18

Frankie

Frankie worked flat out when she returned. Not only because she had a little time to make up, but because she felt far more at ease than she had done over recent days. The dark had never held any fear for her, but her last few shifts had been plagued with worries which had spilled over from the day, leaving her cowed and anxious. Feelings she was far too familiar with. The night was hers, and no one was going to take it from her. She had two more people in her life now though, three if you counted Tam. Fledgling friendships they might be, but she felt stronger than she had in a long time. There would be a way out of her situation, she just had to find it.

She picked up her phone and navigated to her playlists. She knew exactly which one she was looking for and, with her favourite songs filling the room, she danced her way through the remaining hours of her shift.

With the last batches of bread cooling on the racks, Frankie began to tidy up, clearing away all the equipment she had used during the night. It was half past six and everything would need to be shipshape before the shop opened for the morning trade. She turned off her music with a smile – time for one last cup of tea and then she'd set to it.

The sun was just beginning to rise, although you'd never know it given the darkness outside. The height of the buildings would ensure the alley was in shadow for a good while yet and, busy in the storeroom, Frankie had no way of seeing the figure approach. She heard it though: the faint clicking of a heel tapping against cobblestones in the lane outside. She froze, listening intently. The noise stopped momentarily, as if whoever was outside had paused beside the window. Even now they might be peering in. Heart suddenly pounding in her chest, Frankie inched closer to the storeroom door. With any luck she might be able to peer through the gap without being seen herself.

She almost cried out as a tap sounded on the window – four sharp retorts in succession. She checked herself – did that sound friendly? The sort of rat-a-tat-tat rhythm you'd make on a friend's door, a casual knock somewhere you were expected. She took a deep breath and, with a broom clutched firmly in her hand, she stuck her head around the door. She let out a laugh of relief as Tam's face appeared and she hurried to let him in.

'Was that for me?' he asked, grinning as she opened the door. She was still holding the broom. 'You looked as if you were about to clout me one.'

'No, I just… Well, yes, possibly. Until I saw who it was.'

'Don't blame you,' he said. 'You can't be too careful.' He smiled again. 'I wondered if I might ask a huge favour.' He was looking past her into the warmth of the bakery. 'You wouldn't have a loo I could use, would you? I got rather carried away and drank the whole flask of tea, with the inevitable consequences…'

Frankie took a step back. 'Of course. Come in.' She pointed to the far corner. 'It's through there, but I'm sorry, the door doesn't shut properly. It has an alarming tendency to swing open at times so...' She pulled a face and handed him the broom. 'Do you want to use this to prop it?'

Tam took it as instructed, cheeks bright red, although that might have been from the cold...

'I'll just... do something out the front,' finished Frankie, murmuring her last few words. The room wasn't overly large, and the cloakroom not very far away. She wondered if she should whistle, or perhaps sing...

'Sorry about that,' called Tam, appearing a short while later. 'There's a gym I go to for my morning ablutions, but it's not open yet.'

'It's no problem, honestly,' said Frankie, coming through the archway which led into the shop. 'It must be rather difficult, I imagine. It's my fault, I should have thought before bringing you an enormous flask of tea.'

Tam was silent a moment, weighing something up. 'Can I ask you a personal question?' he said, and then continued before Frankie had a chance to reply. 'Only I've noticed you always try to take the blame for things, even when you're being incredibly nice.'

Frankie's hands went to her cheeks. 'Oh, do I...? Sorry.'

'And you always apologise for everything, too.' Tam smiled. 'It should be *me* apologising. I didn't mean to embarrass you.'

'No, it's okay,' Frankie replied, clearing her throat. 'You're right, it's a habit I got into... accepting the blame for everything even when it wasn't my fault. Anything for a quiet life...' Her voice faltered. 'Trouble is, once those habits are with you, they're a bugger to break, aren't they?' And Frankie's had been with her a *very* long time.

Beth had told her that Tam worked in a care home, and she could see how that would suit him. He had a kind expression, with gentle, enquiring eyes and, for all that she'd only known him ten minutes, it would be easy to tell him her life story – to explain that although she very much wanted to be Frankie,

Frances still clung doggedly on. *She* was a hard habit to break. Frankie had come close to telling Beth all about her former self as well, but Beth had problems of her own; it wouldn't be fair. And neither would it be fair on Tam.

'Did you sleep in the end?' she asked, changing the subject.

A dreamy smile crossed Tam's face. 'I've not long woken up,' he said. 'I know it was only for three hours or so but compared to what it would have been had you not shown up, it feels like the best night's sleep ever.'

Frankie rolled her eyes. 'You're just being kind,' she said. 'I bet it was nothing of the sort.'

He grinned. 'Trust me, I stopped dreaming about eight hours a night quite some time ago.'

'You've been homeless a while then?'

'A while, yes. Actually, not that long in the grand scheme of things, but long enough. I'm hoping that might change, obviously.'

'Of course,' said Frankie. 'And you have a job, at least.'

'I do... but not one I have a hope of hanging onto for much longer if my situation doesn't change. Employers don't like staff with no fixed abode. It makes them nervous. I'm not saying they'd rather employ Bob the axe murderer, so long as he lives in a nice three-bed semi in Walton Street, but that's the way it comes across. It's as if *I* don't matter. So, despite the fact that being homeless doesn't change me as a person, apparently it does.' Tam held up his hand, smiling. 'You were going to apologise again, I can tell. There's no need, it is what it is. And you've been kind enough, I shouldn't burden you with my problems.'

Frankie stared at him. Wasn't that exactly what she'd just been thinking? 'I *was* going to say sorry, but only to *empathise*, not apologise.' She returned his smile. 'My boss told me earlier that she's selling the business, but I won't burden you with my tales of woe either.'

'Ah... touché. I'm sorry to hear about that though.'

Tam shoved his hands in his pockets, hunching his shoulders. 'I know you said it was okay to keep hold of the flask for now, but I can go and fetch it if you want it back, I didn't want to presume...'

'No, hang onto it. The temperature is set to be well below freezing for the next three days or so,' Frankie replied. 'But you're welcome to bring it by any time for a refill. The hot-water bottle too. I'm here from about eleven—'

A sudden tap on the window made them both jump. Frankie whirled around to see William's concerned face peering at her. He motioned towards the door.

'Everything okay?' he asked as she opened it. 'Only...' His eyes flicked past her to where Tam was standing. 'I was just passing and saw you had company... I thought it best to check.'

'Thank you, but I'm fine. Um, this is Tam, he—'

'Just popped in to use the facilities,' supplied Tam. 'Friendly neighbourhood homeless person,' he replied, a slight edge to his voice. He was about to add something further when he stopped, a puzzled expression on his face. 'I think I know you, don't I? Or I've *seen* you at least...'

William peered closer. 'The car park?' He nodded. 'I've seen you there too.' He stared at Frankie. 'Sorry, I didn't mean to intrude.'

'It was good of you to check on me,' replied Frankie, her cheeks growing a little hot. 'William very kindly came to my rescue one night,' she explained to Tam. 'I got caught up with some lads who'd had rather too much of everything and thought my sandwiches were fair game.'

'They'd been to the club where I work,' added William. 'So, I helped them on their way. I promised Frankie I'd keep an eye on things and I was worried someone else was... you know, being a pain.' He smiled awkwardly. 'Sorry, that was presumptuous of me.'

'You were probably right,' replied Tam. 'And I was just leaving anyway, so...'

Frankie looked from one to the other. 'I need to get on,' she said, amusement in her voice. 'Or I won't be ready to open up shop, but you're both very welcome to a cup of tea, I've not long boiled the kettle.'

'I probably shouldn't,' said Tam.

'I was just passing,' said William.

'But actually, that would be lovely,' said Tam and William.

Frankie grinned. 'Right then, there's the kettle and the mugs, and the tea bags are in the cupboard. Help yourselves. And milk, no sugar for me.' She picked up a couple of mixing bowls and made her way back to the storeroom.

'Where were you headed so early this morning anyway?' she called to William. 'Did you fall out of bed or something?'

William seemed to think her comment enormously funny for some reason. 'Or something,' he replied with a grin, but then his face sobered. 'I don't usually sleep more than a few hours at a time. A habit I've got into over the last few years... too noisy where I was before,' he added in explanation. 'So this morning I thought I'd go for a walk to clear my head.' He glanced at Tam. 'I wanted to check on something, too, but you might be able to save me the bother.'

Tam pointed a finger towards his chest in the classic 'who me?' gesture.

William nodded. 'You wouldn't have happened to notice if there was a grey van parked up by you last night, would you? And if it's still there this morning?'

Tam narrowed his eyes. 'Yeah, I've seen it. Why the interest?'

'It belongs to my boss at the club, that's all. He's up to something and I'd like to know what.'

Frankie was taken aback by the sudden expression on William's face. There was an anger there she hadn't seen before, even when he'd been dealing with the louts the other week.

'Not being funny,' said Tam. 'But I'd steer well clear if I were you.'

'I'd like to,' replied William. 'But the owner of the van is the assistant manager. I just wanted to check a few facts before taking what I know to Danny – he's the club's owner... while also trying to decide whether that's a good idea or not.'

'Why?' asked Tam, taking down some tea from the cupboard. 'Do you think he might be in on whatever's going on as well?'

William looked pained. 'I really hope he isn't,' he replied. 'But if he is, and I blow the whistle... there's every chance I'll be out on my ear and I really need this job.' He stared at the wall over Frankie's shoulder. 'Thing is though, what if he doesn't know and I don't tell him?' He stopped suddenly, looking anxiously at Tam.

'Don't worry,' said Tam evenly. 'I'm pretty sure I know what's been going on too.'

Frankie looked between the two of them. 'Would someone like to fill me in?'

'Drugs,' replied William, his jaw set.

Frankie's eyes widened. 'Well, if it is, then Tam's right. Don't get involved.'

'Don't worry, I don't intend to,' replied William. He took a deep breath. 'But Danny's a young man. I may not like the club much, but he's running a successful business, and although he might not think much of me, he was good enough to give me a job when plenty of others wouldn't. If he isn't aware of what his manager is up to then I think I have a duty to tell him, before the repercussions blow a hole in his life.'

Tam added water to each of the mugs and looked around for something to stir it with. 'So, you're caught between a rock and a hard place,' he commented, eyes alighting on a spoon by the sink. 'I know how that feels. You want to do right, yet if you do, you run every risk of your life going bang. I'm sick of living without a parachute. Or worse, having one which everybody else is trying to sabotage.'

'That's exactly it,' said William, rubbing a hand across his chin. 'Sometimes it feels as if we're all living on the edge. One false move and...' He motioned a plane with his hand, plummeting from the sky.

'So, who's trying to sabotage *your* parachute, Tam?' asked Frankie as she began to fill the sink with hot water.

'No one yet,' replied Tam, raising his eyebrows. He shook his head. 'I'm being dramatic, but my immediate boss saw me sleeping in my car. My probationary period is coming to an end and, although I trust her not to say anything, if the company finds out, I suspect any future I have with them will be over.'

Frankie snorted. 'Oh, for goodness' sake.'

'Sorry,' said Tam, misreading her expression. 'You're trying to work and we're both being miserable.' He handed her a mug of tea. 'This is very kind, but perhaps we should go?'

'You'll do nothing of the sort,' said Frankie, looking between them both. 'Come and sit down. A few weeks ago, pretty much all I did was sleep and come to work. And that was fine. I rather liked it, actually, or at least I thought I did. But then I met Beth, who is one of the kindest people, and now you two as well. You're all three terrified of losing your jobs, and I just found out my boss is selling the bakery, so that makes four of us. I'm not sure what's going to happen about that yet, but for the time being we have this place. At least it's somewhere warm and safe to take refuge from the problems in our lives, if only for a little while. And who knows, maybe there's a way we can figure out how to change things?'

Tam looked at William. And William looked at her.

'I agree,' he said. It's ridiculous that Tam could lose his job because he doesn't have a permanent address. Doesn't your boss understand you're never going to get one unless you keep earning? Well, I live in the town, you can use my address.'

'I can't do that,' replied Tam.

'Who's going to find out?' said Frankie, shoving her hands into a pair of washing-up gloves.

William nodded. 'People do it all the time – they pretend they live somewhere so they can get their kids into the right school, or if they're a politician they do it to claim a pile of expenses they're not entitled to. Stuff that. It's no huge imposition to me. We've got to help each other out, no one else is going to.'

'He has a point,' said Frankie. 'A very good point.'

William's brow wrinkled for a moment. 'I'd put you up if I could, only my flat's tiny, and my landlord—'

Tam held up a hand. 'Honestly, please, you don't need to do that. You both have your own lives to live without me tagging along, and it really isn't necessary. I was able to get my job in the first place because I used a friend's address as my own. Actually, he's not a friend – long story – but he's the reason why I'm in this mess, so I reckon he owes me a favour. I'll make up some reason for my sleeping in my car – say it was only a temporary thing, and that I'm back at that address now. If anyone checks, he can damn well vouch for me.'

'But what if your boss sees you again?' asked Frankie. 'Is there somewhere else you can park?'

'I'll find somewhere,' replied Tam. 'No need to worry.'

Frankie thought for a moment. 'Playing devil's advocate here, but this friend – not friend – is there no way you can stay with him? I know you might not want to, but what if it was just until your review has passed?'

Tam's response was immediate, and unequivocal. 'Absolutely not. It's out of the question.'

Frankie tipped her head on one side. 'Okay then, we'll keep thinking. There'll be a way to sort things, I know there will.

And meanwhile...' She crossed to a counter on the other side of the room and returned with a cake box which she placed on the table, directing both men to take a seat with a wave of her hands. 'I wondered if this might help.' She took the lid off the box.

'God in heaven,' muttered William, leaning closer. 'That smells amazing. What is it?'

'Toffee apple crumble cake,' replied Frankie. 'I thought I might, you know, make something a bit different. What do you think?'

'To the idea or the cake?' said Tam. 'Because my initial thought is that both are wonderful. I would need to confirm that though...' He eyed the cake with a grin. 'And I would probably need a very large slice to be absolutely sure.'

Frankie smiled back. 'I'll get you a knife.'

'What do you reckon, Tam,' said William. 'Half each? That ought to do it.'

'Excuse *me*...' Frankie stood with her hands on her hips.

'Sorry, make that a third each,' said William, catching Frankie's eye.

'That's more like it,' she said, pulling a knife from a drawer and handing it to Tam. 'Now, you know that long story?' she added. 'Would now be a good time to tell it?'

19

William

It was bizarre how those two minutes of William's day had become his favourite, developing into something he really hadn't been expecting. It wasn't even two minutes, just a few seconds, the time it took to walk past the bakery window, but it was there, and it had meaning. Nothing much in William's life did any more. There was something about Frankie which intrigued him – vulnerability mixed with determination. It was an odd combination.

She'd been hugely wary of him when they first met, and he couldn't blame her – *he'd* run a mile if he met himself down a dark alley, too. But then the next time he managed to catch her eye as he passed by, and she had looked up and waved. And smiled. The connection was so slender, it almost didn't exist, and yet he found himself looking forward to his walk home from work far more than any other time of the day. Sometimes she was dancing, and it struck him that he'd met precious few people who could hold that kind of joy inside them. It made something inside of him ache, and that complicated things.

He had come back to this town to keep a promise, but he hadn't reckoned on Frankie, or Tam for that matter. And it put him in an impossible position. Listening to the way Tam had been betrayed by his best friend had made William's deception feel even more poignant. Even if he *was* trying to do the right thing, the truth still mattered and lying hurt. He just hadn't bargained on how much.

So now William was in a quandary. He needed Tam's help this morning, but William had hidden his past for so long that allowing the ties that bound it to loosen wasn't easy, so, much to his shame, he did what he always did and only told Tam as much as he needed to know and no more. Tam had readily agreed to help, but that didn't make William feel any better.

William had no transport, that was the problem. But if he wanted to follow through with his plan then he also needed to follow Stuart, which was why he and Tam were both currently sitting in Curzon Street – far enough away from Stuart's house not to cause alarm, but close enough to keep an eye on his grey van. It hadn't been difficult to find out where Stuart lived. Several of the waitresses at the club had been happy to chat, and Stuart clearly wasn't as popular as he thought he was.

Just as William had suspected, the grey van opened its doors to customers on almost all of the regular club nights, but William had also spotted it on a couple of other occasions too.

'Don't take this the wrong way,' said William to Tam after a few minutes. 'But the less you know about what's going on the better. I'm really grateful for your help, but I don't want to get you involved any more than you are already.'

Tam slid him a sideways glance. 'In other words, don't ask questions,' he said, smiling at William's sheepish expression. 'Don't worry, I don't want to know what's going on. My ex-wife used to laugh at me for being so naive about the ways of the modern world, and I readily admit to being a confirmed wuss. So, I shall drive you where you need to be driven and that's it.'

'Fair enough,' replied William, somewhat relieved. 'I'm hoping that sometime fairly soon, Stuart will be paying somewhere a visit in his van and all I need to know is where that is. I can take it from there.'

Tam nodded. 'Are you going to say, "follow that van"?'

'I can do, if you like.' William slid him a look, smiling at the amusement on Tam's face. 'You really don't get out much, do you?' he teased.

Frankie had plied them with the remains of the toffee apple cake for the journey and William was halfway through his when he spotted Stuart leaving his house. He was wearing his trademark black jeans this morning but had swapped his usual black shirt for a hoodie and baseball cap, jammed on his head the wrong way round. William imagined he thought it made him look super cool and his dislike for the obnoxious man grew.

Tam started his engine as they waited for the van to pull away and, at William's signal, he began to follow at a safe distance. William had been worried he'd never be able to follow Stuart's van on foot, hence the need for Tam's car, but ironically, they only travelled the length of two streets before Stuart turned into a small industrial estate which William knew of old. It had been scruffy when William was a kid; now it looked virtually derelict – the forecourt choked with weeds and littered with abandoned planks of wood and rusted metal signs.

Asking Tam to wait in the car, William picked his way across the scarred ground and began to skirt the edge of the nearest building, hugging the stained and blackened walls. Behind it was another yard which had once served as a car repair shop, and beyond that were three smaller lock-up units and a row of garages, all of which were hidden from the main road. William peered around the corner, holding his breath, but Stuart's van was easy to spot. It was the only vehicle there, the trade in car repairs having long since dwindled to nothing. There wasn't another soul about, but William only waited long enough for Stuart to climb from his van and open the roller shutter of one of the garages, before he retraced his steps. He didn't need to know any more. Not yet anyway.

Tam's eyebrows were raised as William climbed back inside the car. 'That was quick.'

William nodded. 'No point hanging around. I was just interested to see where Stuart went, that's all.'

'So that's it?'

'That's it,' William agreed.

'I might not want to know what's going on,' said Tam. 'But I did think it might be marginally more exciting.'

William didn't return his smile. 'Be thankful it isn't,' he replied.

They were about to return to the car park when William put a hand on the steering wheel. To his surprise, the van was already leaving, and so after the requisite gap had grown between them and it, he instructed Tam to set off in pursuit once more.

This time, they drove right across town, to a large residential estate which had almost trebled in size since William's family had once bought a property there. And new houses were still being built. After a confusing number of left and right turns had been taken, Stuart stopped outside a row of small shops in one of the oldest parts of the estate, just a couple of streets away from where William had once lived. Asking Tam to pull up a little distance away, William swivelled in his seat to get a better look.

The shops were all different from when William had been a boy and sent to buy his dad's cigarettes, but there was still a newsagent there, albeit in a different place. The other spaces were filled by a fish and chip shop, a tanning salon, hairdressers, charity shop and, largest of all, a convenience store-cum-off-licence. There was nothing curious about any of them, but what *was* curious was that, after pulling what turned out to be a bunch of keys from his pocket, Stuart unlocked the door to the tanning salon and went inside. It was already a little after nine o'clock, so presumably the business didn't open until later, but it seemed an odd place for Stuart to be. He had a pale, pock-marked complexion, so if he owned the place, which seemed unlikely enough, he certainly wasn't availing himself of any free sunbed sessions.

William thought for a moment, eyes narrowing in response to where those thoughts were leading him, and then he pulled a piece of paper from his coat pocket, together with a pencil, and made a quick note. Whichever way he turned it in his mind, it was clear there was only one thing he could do now. He needed to follow his thoughts to their end.

'We can go now,' he said to Tam, facing front again. 'All done.'

Tam gave him another sideways glance and slowly drove away.

20

Tam

Tam had hoped that Trish would be pleased to hear his news. Admittedly it was a cock-and-bull story he'd told her, but he thought he'd been pretty convincing. A fictitious argument with an equally fictitious girlfriend had seemed just the thing to explain away his sleeping arrangements, or so he'd thought anyway. He had stressed how temporary an arrangement it had been, even squirming with embarrassment at having to tell his boss such personal information but, from behind her desk, Trish just smiled. Purely perfunctory, she barely even looked at him. And that wasn't like her.

'That's great,' she said. 'I'm glad we've sorted that out.' She gave another smile, tighter than the first and Tam quailed slightly. Trish wasn't stupid – was it really so obvious that he'd just lied?

'So, is that all you need?' he asked, businesslike but breezy.

She looked up at him then, properly, for the first time since he'd stepped into the office, and Tam realised the look in her eyes had nothing to do with what he'd just told her.

'I'm sorry, Tam,' she said, dropping her gaze. 'But we lost Eleanor last night.'

Tam stared at her, confused. *Lost...?* The meaning of her words came to him as if spoken in a foreign language he struggled to understand.

'I know how fond of her you were.'

And he realised then that Trish had been crying.

Despite all their different backgrounds and experiences, death was the one thing which connected all the residents of Chawston House. When he first started working there it had been Trish who told him that death was the only certainty in life, and she had been right. It didn't matter whether you were rich or poor, practitioner of a faith or bereft of any, the journey on to the next adventure was only ever just around the corner – it was just that for some the road took a little longer to travel. And now Eleanor's next adventure had already begun, and Tam hadn't even got to wish her bon voyage. Or remind her to pack enough Jaffa Cakes for the journey.

It was something they had joked about, and he had marvelled at the way Eleanor could laugh about the details of her demise in such a matter-of-fact way. But she had simply smiled and told him that she was determined to enjoy her death just as much as she had her life. Yet he'd still always thought he'd be there for her, waving her off as she – her words – 'skipped down the path, now my blasted hip won't be giving me gip'. But now she had gone, and what hurt Tam the most was that no one had been there to bear witness to such a remarkable woman.

It wasn't the first time that someone had died during Tam's time at Chawston House, but Eleanor had been special and, as Tam walked down the corridor towards her room, he could feel her death like a shroud, cloaking the house and its light, so that the very colours appeared dulled by its presence. In Eleanor's room, however, Tam was happy to feel the old lady's spirit just as if she was still with them. Even her mug with the dregs of last night's black coffee hadn't yet been tidied away and was still on the table beside her chair. She could so easily have popped out for a moment, returning with gossip from the dining room and a pilfered packet of chocolate biscuits. At least it was a comfort knowing that death had been kind to Eleanor – she had simply gone to sleep and hadn't woken up in the morning.

Tam sat gently on her bed, his head bowed. Up until the other night, Eleanor had been the only person who knew about his circumstances. She had winkled it out of him one evening, her astuteness surprising him, but it had forged the connection between them, and it had made Tam feel comforted. Eleanor had seen him, warts and all, and still liked what she saw. They were co-conspirators, and just the thought of her had made Tam feel less alone. And now she was gone.

The rest of Tam's shift passed interminably slowly, and for the first time since he had begun to work at Chawston House, he longed for clocking-off time, even if that did mean another freezing night in his car. He thought about the flask and hot-water bottle nestled on the passenger seat, and about Frankie and the kindness she had done him. About William, too, and his easy acceptance of Tam, and somehow these thoughts were enough to get him through the day.

Frankie practically dragged him through the door as soon as she saw him.

'You look terrible,' she said, appraising Tam with an intensity that almost made him flinch. 'Sit down, I'll get the kettle on.'

She ignored each and every comment he made about it being time to leave and, although she was busy – heaving around sacks of flour and huge metal pans – she also made it clear she had time to listen. And provide more treats: pecan frangipane tarts this time.

'I sat in Eleanor's chair and thought about my mum,' said

Tam, dabbing at the crumbs on his plate. 'Before she had her stroke, she would argue black was white, just like Eleanor did, but they'd have got on like a house on fire. She's still pretty feisty now, mind. She has a little less movement and a little less hearing than she did before, but God forbid you let on, or she'll have your guts for garters.'

Frankie smiled. 'Sounds a bit like my nan,' she said. 'But she's gone now too. Makes you wonder how long you've got them for, doesn't it?'

'I'm lucky,' replied Tam. 'It's been three years since Mum had her stroke and she's a fighter. She made a good recovery, but her living on her own still worries me. Not that she'd have it any other way.'

'Is your dad not with you then?' asked Frankie, flouring loaf tins at speed.

'He died nearly five years ago,' said Tam. 'So now it's just Mum – Rose – and our little tabby cat, Pickle, who I swear is almost as old as she is. Mum still lives in the house I grew up in as a child. It's colder than I'd like, and the garden is too much for her to manage now, but it's woven through with memories, every inch of it. I think, without them, she'd be so much less.' Tam smiled wistfully. 'It's funny, isn't it, how the older you get the more you think about the past? I can remember every crack in the ceiling of my old room, but not what I was doing last week.'

'Nostalgia's a funny thing,' said Frankie. 'So warm, and comfortable, yet it takes something from you too, I think. And leaves a bittersweet taste in its place.' She paused for a moment, eyes warm on his. 'Don't take this the wrong way,' she said. 'But you're obviously close to your mum. Couldn't you go and live with her?'

'No.' Tam's response was emphatic. 'There's nothing I'd like more, especially under the circumstances. But it would break her heart... literally.' He shook his head. 'I couldn't take the risk.'

'Break her heart…? Why would it do that?'

'Because she doesn't know what happened,' said Tam, his gaze dropping to the floor. 'And if she knew, the shock might be too much. She still thinks I live in my little cottage, running my horticultural business. Despite her medication, her blood pressure is too high and every day it edges her closer to a heart attack or another stroke. So, I see her twice a week. I bring the shopping and together we drink tea and eat cake and talk about the pretend life that I've woven to hide the truth. Sometimes my stories about my work, its plants and its customers, are so real, I almost believe them myself.' He shrugged to hide his shame. 'But I'll continue to tell them, because it's as much about ensuring my mum's happiness as it is a reminder that one day I'll have that life again. I only hope we have enough time left for that to happen.'

'But she's your mum,' said Frankie gently. 'She'd understand, surely?'

'She would,' replied Tam. 'But I don't want to ask her to. I want her to still believe in me, be proud of me. How stupid is that? At my age? Plus, she thinks the world of Chris – we grew up together.'

'It's not stupid at all,' replied Frankie. 'No one wants to let down those they love, do they? Except that sometimes we have a choice to make. We either let someone else down, or we let ourselves down. And sometimes the only way to save ourselves is to let others think badly of us.'

Tam looked up, caught by something in the tone in Frankie's voice, as if she was no longer speaking about him. He opened his mouth to ask if she was okay, but she turned away abruptly and disappeared into the storeroom.

'I'm still listening,' she called. 'And you do realise that you don't owe Chris anything? You certainly don't owe him your mum's good opinion of him. I think your mum would surprise you. I think she'd be horrified at what Chris did and any goodwill she had towards him would evaporate in an instant. Mums are like that – they go all mumma bear when anything threatens their kids, even if those kids are *very* grown up. You're still her child. I reckon she'd be firmly on your side and probably quite cross that you hadn't told her. She'd have wanted to help, you see.'

'Perhaps...' Tam sighed. 'But the doctors warned me that she shouldn't get stressed, or unduly upset. I couldn't live with myself if anything happened to her because of me.'

'I get that. But you also have to live with the knowledge that you're not being truthful with her, and that doesn't square with a man who believes in integrity, who literally gave up everything he had so that no one else would suffer as a result of his actions.'

A sad smile crossed Tam's face. 'And *that* is exactly why I don't tell her.'

21

Beth

Beth had given Frankie's advice a great deal of thought, and although she and Jack were speaking to one another again, there was a space between them which hadn't been there before. Or, perhaps there had been and she'd never noticed it, or allowed herself to, for fear of what she might find there.

They had talked a few times since their argument. Only a little – an agreement not to apportion 'blame' and an understanding that both their stances had arisen out of their love for one another, a desire to care and protect – but the conversations were still guarded, and Beth knew it would take a while to convince Jack that she was truly sorry for the wounds she'd inflicted. She also recognised, privately, that saying sorry was not enough; she needed to prove her remorse. And the thought of what that might mean terrified her.

Her head was so full of thoughts as she left the hospital, she scarcely noticed the streets she was walking through, and was surprised how soon she found herself beside her car. Keys in hand, she stopped, because she had been weighing up the pros and cons of a decision all the way there, and now it was time to act on it. Or not. With a tut, she retraced her steps and headed towards Tam's car. If he was still asleep then she would leave him be, but if not...

As it was, he waved before she could get close enough to check.

'Sorry, I wasn't sure if you'd be awake,' she said as she drew level with the rear window.

'Pondering the great mysteries of life,' replied Tam, opening his eyes wide as if to stretch out the muscles.

'Oh those,' said Beth, smiling. 'Slippery little devils, aren't they? Did you come to any conclusions?'

Tam shook his head. 'Not a one.'

Beth was suddenly lost for words. How did she say what she wanted to without admitting how much she'd got wrong? She blinked. Actually, what she really needed to do *was* admit how wrong she'd been. She needed to do it over and over again until she stopped believing she was always right. Hadn't that been the problem all along?

She cleared her throat. 'The other day when you came to my house... and I was a complete cow...'

Tam touched a finger to the corner of his mouth and Beth had the distinct impression it was to flatten the smile which wanted to appear. She continued. 'I didn't like it when you and Jack started chatting, because I didn't want anyone encouraging him to think about the part of his life he'd had to leave behind. But I was wrong. And clearly you thought so too.'

'Did I?' Tam pulled a face. 'Oh dear... I hadn't thought I was quite so obvious. I did my best to hide it.' But then he smiled, making it easier for her. He was a good man.

'Well, you were right, and I wanted you to know that. I also wanted – although I'll understand completely if you say no – to ask for your help.'

Tam studied her face, as if he were peeling back the layers of an onion to see if there was anything different inside. The intensity made Beth feel a little uncomfortable, but she held her ground. Tam had to know that she was genuine. Suddenly, his features changed. His brows relaxed, his eyes crinkled, and his mouth curved upwards into a generous smile.

'I'm very grateful to you,' he said. 'Do you know that because of your kind words about me, Frankie brought me out a flask of tea and a hot-water bottle? To thank me for doing a friend of hers a kindness. So you see, we seem to have come full circle, and the debt of goodwill is now mine to repay. What can I help you with?'

A circle of kindness... Beth liked the sound of that. 'I wondered if you might like to come and chat to Jack again. Only this time to *encourage* him to think about the farm and its future. Either now – with the offer of a shower, breakfast and anything else you might need – or whenever else might suit you. Stupidly, I've only just begun to realise that the farm is a part of Jack; he can no more deny it than he can breathing...' She trailed off, feeling the familiar burning sensation that heralded the arrival of tears.

'You had me at a shower and breakfast, Beth. You really don't need to explain any more.' He smiled. 'But I'd like that. I've shut down a part of my life, too, and perhaps it's time *I* revisited *mine*. We always think the ghosts of our past are out to get us, don't we? But we forget their haunting can also be benign...'

Beth frowned, not entirely sure what he was talking about. 'So, would you like to come now?'

Tam wriggled his legs out of his sleeping bag. 'Give me two minutes and I'll be raring to go.'

Beth was halfway home before she realised that she ought to have spoken to Jack first before springing this surprise on him. He wasn't usually bad-tempered of a morning, but if he hadn't slept well, or was in pain... But it was too late now; Tam was only three cars behind her. One of these days she'd stop making mistakes and get something right for once.

She turned up the track to the farmhouse, pausing a moment to make sure that Tam was still with her. The turning was easy to miss if you weren't familiar with the road, even though Tam assured her that he remembered where it was. Minutes later, he pulled up alongside her.

A steady rain had begun to fall, and Beth hurried them both indoors.

'Come in, come in, at least it'll be warm in here.'

She led Tam through to the kitchen, feeling a little embarrassed to be back in the place where she'd been so rude before. This time, she would make it up to him. And Jack.

'Would you like a drink while I go and get Jack sorted?' she asked, heading for the kettle.

Tam waved her away. 'I can do that if you like,' he said. 'As long as you don't mind me rummaging for stuff?'

'Rummage away,' replied Beth. 'I won't be long.'

At first, her brain couldn't take in what she was seeing. She stood, staring at the bed in confusion for what seemed like an age before the meaning of it kicked in and spurred her into action. Because the bed was empty. And the bed shouldn't be empty. It should be full, of Jack, who couldn't get out of bed unaided...

She rushed to the bathroom, and back again. Stood in the bedroom as if Jack had somehow managed to hide himself on the floor and, even though she knew it was stupid, she lifted the bedclothes to check. And that's when she realised that his wheelchair was also missing.

Her first thought was that he'd left her. That, somehow, he had engineered a way to leave their life and he'd gone. But he would have needed help to do that, and who would he ask?

How would she not know? Sobs rose in her throat. They'd had an argument, a horrible one, but things weren't this bad, surely? They were talking, they were putting things right. She whirled around, checking the room, but nothing was obviously missing, none of the things he would want to take with him. Even his clothes were still on the chair where she had left them the night before. So, where the hell was he?

'Tam!' She yelled his name before she was even back in the hallway and yelled twice more before she arrived in the kitchen, heart beating frantically, fear draining the colour from her face. She skidded to a halt. The kitchen was empty, too. Only the back door swaying in the wind gave her any clue as to where Tam might be.

She wrenched the door wider, looking out into the falling rain and the mud-slicked yard beyond, scanning for any change to the landscape. As she peered through the gloom she spied two figures over by the furthest gate – one in a chair and one standing. It should be impossible, but it wasn't a trick of the early morning light, nor were her eyes deceiving her. Somehow, Jack had managed to get himself out of bed, into his chair and out of the house. What the hell did he think he was doing?

Beth crossed the yard in seconds, immune to the puddles which splashed muddy water over her shoes and up her legs. Even from some distance away she could see that Jack was soaked through. He was also furious... she could tell by the way he held his head.

'Jesus, Jack, what are you *doing*?' She took in his bedraggled appearance, and the state of his chair, the wheels of which were thick with mud.

'Nothing much,' he replied. 'I should have thought that was obvious.'

She flicked a glance at Tam. 'But how did you even get out here? You can't—' She broke off at the look on Jack's face. 'Well, clearly you can, but for goodness' sake, what were you thinking?' Her shock was rapidly turning to anger. 'You'll catch your death out here, you're still in your pyjamas.'

Jack's mouth was a grim, hard line. 'Yep,' he said. 'Maybe no bad thing...'

Beth ignored his comment. 'How long have you been out here? Why didn't you wait until I was home, I would have—'

'I think, perhaps, we should get back inside,' said Tam, shooting her a warning look. 'And maybe save the questions for later?'

She ignored him too. 'You're soaked through. Why didn't you wheel yourself back inside, for heaven's sake?'

Jack's glance was withering. 'Because I'm stuck. And because I can't pull both levers to disengage the drive motor and make this thing manual. I can do this side...' He waved his good hand. 'But I can't reach the other, so after damn near dislocating my shoulder trying to do so, I decided to wait for you to come to my rescue. Again.'

Tam moved to the front of the wheelchair, dropping to his haunches. He tilted his head to one side, then the other, clearly trying to work out the arrangement of levers which Jack had just spoken about.

'May I?' he asked.

He eased the lever forward and, returning to the rear of the chair, grasped the handles and began to push.

The return journey across the yard was made in absolute silence.

The back door was still hanging open, and a pool of water had gathered on the flagstones where the rain had blown in. It was the least of Beth's worries. She scuttled inside.

'We have another wheelchair,' she said. 'I'll go and fetch it.' Whether Jack's electric chair was just jammed with mud and gunk or was actually broken she had no idea, but it was pretty much useless the way it was. As would Jack be. The other chair was manual, and he struggled to use it without her. What on earth were they going to do?

'Right, we need to get you out of your pyjamas first,' she said, returning with the chair. 'You must be frozen. How long were you even out there?'

But Jack ignored her, his mouth still set in a hard line.

She put the brake on the other wheelchair, drawing it up alongside him so that she could try to move him from one to the other. It wasn't going to be pretty. She was about to ask Tam to put the kettle on, as much to get him out of the way as anything else, when he dropped to his haunches again – positioning himself so that he was eye level with Jack. 'I can get you sorted out, if you like?'

The response was scant, but it was there, the merest nod of his head.

'Okay then.' Tam smiled and lifted Jack out of the chair as if he weighed no more than a bag of flour. 'Where are we headed, mate?'

Beth stared after them as they left the room. The bloody cheek of it – who did Tam think he was? She was about to march furiously after him when she stopped, heart still thudding. She took a deep breath and closed her eyes, conscious of the angry rushing sound in her ears. Tam was right to intervene. She was infuriated with Jack and he with her. Some space would be a good idea if they wanted to avoid the situation deteriorating any further. She felt her shoulders beginning to relax and collapsed into a chair, breathing deeply.

The fight had completely gone out of Jack when he and Tam returned. And Beth's heart squeezed as she saw the expression on Jack's face. He was a small child again, lost and hurt and lonely in a world which no one else could truly share with him. Tam stepped away from the chair, turning his back to give them a little privacy, and Beth hurried across the floor to kneel in front of Jack. She wrapped her arms around his torso.

'You scared me,' she whispered. 'I thought you'd gone. I thought...' She couldn't say how scared she'd been that he'd left her, might leave her still.

'Where would I go?' Jack replied, his voice cracking with emotion. 'Why would I want to?' He heaved a sigh. 'I'm sorry, Beth, I just needed to try... I thought I could...' He shook his head. 'It doesn't matter.'

She pulled back, cupping his face in her hands, every line of it so familiar to her. So familiar and so dear. 'It *does* matter,' she replied. 'It matters more than anything. And we're going to sort this, I promise. I don't know how, but we will.' She gently kissed his mouth and then his nose and his forehead, searching his face as she did so. 'Are you okay?' she asked. 'Do you need anything?'

'Maybe some painkillers.' His voice was quiet and small. 'I'm bloody freezing.' Beth knew that whatever pain he was feeling now would be nothing compared with what was to come. His muscles simply couldn't stand such punishment.

By the time she returned with some tablets and a fleece blanket, Tam had placed three mugs on the table. The scent of toast filled the air and Beth's mouth began to water. She was starving, and thirsty too, now that her initial shock had left her. As she settled the blanket around Jack, she suddenly realised that she hadn't even checked to see how Tam was doing.

'Do you have any jam?' he asked, smiling. 'I couldn't find any in the fridge.'

'I'll get some,' she replied. 'It's in the pantry, but you should get changed, you're soaked. I can probably find some clothes of Jack's that would fit you.'

He pulled a face, bending his knees slightly. 'I feel a bit like I've wet myself,' he said. 'But I've got clothes in the car, I'll go and fetch them.'

'No, you won't,' she replied. 'It's pouring out there and you're wet enough as it is.' She laid a hand on his arm. 'Come with me.'

Back in the bedroom, she began to rummage through the drawers of an old tallboy which stood in one corner. Her face was bright red, she could tell. She'd invited Tam over for some breakfast and a more civilised start to his morning, and look what had happened. She felt awful.

'There's no need to be embarrassed,' said Tam from behind her. 'I can tell what you're thinking, but there's no need. It would seem I arrived just at the right moment, so if you're feeling bad about me being here, don't. Someone, somewhere, obviously thought it a good idea, and I agree with them. Let's leave it at that, shall we?'

She turned around. 'I don't know what to say. I'm so grateful to you.'

'Of course you are. You'd be a horrible person if you weren't, and you're really not, so you can stop thinking that as well.'

He held her look for a moment and Beth blushed again, found out. She smiled. 'I don't know what to say to Jack either,' she whispered. 'He hasn't been this down since...'

'Something you warned me would happen on the very first occasion we met, I believe. You were right, and if I've had anything to do with what happened today then I must accept responsibility for it. And apologise.'

'I don't think any of this is down to you at all,' replied Beth. 'It might look that way, but this has been coming for a while, Tam, I just hadn't seen it.'

He nodded. 'Then in that case, I have some thoughts, if you're happy for me to share them?'

She gave him a quizzical look.

'Let me get changed first. How about you go and butter the toast and I'll meet you back in the kitchen?'

Tam had judged things perfectly; the toast and jam were exactly what they needed. And by the time he returned, she and Jack were already several slices down. She got up to add more bread to the toaster and refill the kettle.

'Come and sit down,' she said to Tam. 'And get stuck in.'

Tam took a seat, looking around at the kitchen as if he'd never seen it before. 'So how long have you had this place?' he asked.

'Eleven years, all told,' replied Jack. 'Two of them farmed, the rest...' – he held up his good arm – 'returning it even further to the wild. I say farmed, but what I really mean is that I made a very small start on all the work that needed to be done here.'

Tam nodded. 'I couldn't see that much from the yard, but if I've got my bearings right, then that field of yours to the left would have overlooked a row of greenhouses at one time, poly-tunnels too.'

'It did. Although I haven't been out there in a while, obvi-ously...' He paused. 'Are they not there now?'

Tam turned and stared out the window. 'I've no idea,' he replied.

Beth plonked another pile of toast on the table. 'I wondered what had happened there,' she said. 'I think the land must have been sold fairly recently, but whoever bought it hasn't bothered with them. It's a shame, they've been vandalised, too; some of them are wrecked.'

Tam turned away, a hollow look in his eyes. 'It's such good land, that's the worst of it. All that promise just slowly ebbing away.'

'That's what Jack always used to say about the farm, the thing he couldn't bear to see happen.' She took in his expres-sion, the droop of his shoulders, the doleful tone to his voice. 'You talk as if it's personal to you,' she said gently.

'Hmm...' Tam gave a wry smile. 'That's because the fields are mine, *were* mine. I grew plants, for shops, garden centres, a business I built literally from the ground up, so I know this area pretty well.' His eyes sought out Jack's. 'It *is* good land. It can still be good land...'

Jack's eyes narrowed. 'So, what happened?' he asked. 'You said you work in a care home now – that's quite some leap.'

'What happened is I was stupid,' replied Tam, taking another slice of toast. He bit into it, the seconds ticking by as he chewed thoughtfully. 'It's a long story, but a common one. I wasn't content with what I had, thought I needed to grow and diversify, so I went into partnership with my best mate. And, because I trusted him, I took my eye off the ball and neglected to realise that he was taking decisions which weren't his to take. The business went bust and the only way I could repay all the people we owed money to was to sell up, cash up and walk away.' He pulled a face, looking down at himself as if to say *and here I am*. 'The rest, as they say, is history.'

Beth sighed. 'Which explains your interest in agriculture,' she said. 'That must have all but destroyed you.'

Tam nodded, his lips pursed. 'Down, but not out,' he said. 'Which is, I think, where I come in.'

Jack exchanged a look with Beth. 'Sorry, I'm not sure I understand.'

'Then can I ask you a very personal question?' said Tam. 'How much do you want to do this again?'

'This?' Beth leaned closer.

'Yeah. This – the farm, the smallholding, the land. How much do you want to make it work again? Properly, as a going concern.'

Jack let out a snort of derision, but Tam ignored him, looking him straight in the eye.

'Because if you're going to do it, then at least do it properly. *Don't* go across a yard thick with mud in a wheelchair which won't cope with anything more substantial than a bit of rain. *Don't* go on your own, and *don't* go without a plan of what you're going to do when you get there. Even better, explain what you're planning to the people around you, and then let them help.'

'Sounds so easy,' replied Jack, staring at Tam in surprise. A bitter note had crept into his voice. 'But, as I can't go anywhere without said wheelchair, the one which, as you pointed out, is next to useless, I'm not entirely sure how you think I can do any of that.'

Tam shrugged. 'Then modify it, I don't know. That's a problem to resolve. But I did see a quad bike sitting over there in the barn which might prove very useful.'

'He can't drive that!' Beth's mouth dropped open. She thought Tam might have some sensible ideas, but clearly, she was wrong.

'He can't drive it *now*, I know that,' Tam replied, rolling his eyes. 'But what if it were altered so that he could?'

'I'm sorry, but this is crazy,' said Beth. 'Have you any idea how much these things cost? Jack's wheelchair alone... we can't afford stuff like this.' She gave Tam a warning look. Which he met with a smile.

'I know you think I'm mad, and that I'm talking about something ridiculous which is only going to make the situation worse, but I mentioned it because when I said I'd built my business from the ground up, I did *literally* build it – the hardstanding for the greenhouses, the frames, the fences, the walls – anything which needed doing, I learned how. I made a pig's ear of some of it, but isn't that half the fun?'

Silence filled the room for a few moments, Beth's heart sinking further and further. She tried to imagine how any of what Tam had said could possibly help them, but all she could think was how impossible it all was. She daren't look at Jack to see what he was thinking. She didn't want to see even the slightest gleam of excitement in his eyes, and then have to watch it fade when it all came to nothing. He would fall even further than he had now.

'Tam, I can see you mean well, but this isn't going to happen.' Jack shook his head. 'I'm not sure you appreciate how little I can do. I can't use my legs. I have one good arm, the other only works intermittently and—'

'Then how did you get yourself out of bed this morning? Into your chair, through the back door and across the yard?' Tam raised his eyebrows.

'Because I was bloody fed up of doing nothing,' retorted Jack. 'Of thinking about all the things I could be doing but wasn't. So, I decided I'd have a go and—'

'And you did it.'

'It took an absolute age.'

'But you did it.'

'It damn near killed me.'

Tam smiled and sat back in his chair. 'But you did it.'

Jack closed his eyes, a smirk playing around his lips. He knew when he'd been outmanoeuvred. 'Yes, I did it,' he said softly.

'Yes, and then you got stuck, got soaked to the skin, and had to wait for us to come home and rescue you,' said Beth. 'You said it yourself.'

'But that's exactly my point,' said Tam. 'None of that would have happened if Jack had spoken about his plans. If he was working with someone.'

'So, what exactly are you suggesting?' Beth frowned at him, hoping he had thought some of this through before opening his mouth. She risked a look at Jack, seeing, as she knew she would, the first glimpse of excitement in his eyes. It was a light she hadn't seen in a long while, and she remembered the promise she'd made only moments ago. Perhaps now *was* the time to make good on it. Because if they were going to do this, they really needed to think about it properly.

Tam nodded. 'Correct me if I'm wrong, Jack, but presumably when you bought this place all those years ago, you had plans for what you were going to do with it. It was your dream, it was all you ever wanted, so I'm pretty sure those plans were big ones. And I'm equally sure those plans are still in your head.'

'I mangled my legs, not my brain,' said Jack. 'The plans are still intact.'

'Good. Then I suggest we start talking about them.'

22

Frankie

Frankie didn't read the note at first. She stooped to pluck the envelope from the floor as she opened up the bakery, juggling her keys, lunch box and phone before walking through to the back where she dumped them on the table. She took off her coat and hung it up, along with her bag, and then wandered through to the storeroom to collect a clean apron.

She put her lunch box in the fridge and picked up her phone, immediately opening her Spotify app to search for that night's playlist, and it wasn't until she had set her music playing and boiled the kettle that she returned to see what had been posted through the door.

It had been a week since her conversation with Vivienne and she'd heard nothing more from her since. She assumed it would be a while before anything happened with the sale, but perhaps she'd been fooling herself, trying to allay her panic instead of dealing with the situation. She'd been guilty of that in the past. What she really wanted was to do nothing – to have a new owner take over the business with Frankie in situ, leaving life to carry on as before – but experience should have taught her that ignoring a situation didn't make it go away. So, should she jump ship and look for a job somewhere else? Or should she wait, in the hope of not missing out on the opportunity to stay? They were impossible questions to answer.

It was with these thoughts in her head that she opened the envelope, expecting to see one thing but, instead, seeing another. And what she saw made her stomach lurch in shock.

Hello Frances.

She stared at the note, at the first two words written there, at the handwriting she knew so well, and the name she no longer used. Her hands began to shake in fear. Robert had found her.

There were more words beneath, a whole jumble of them, but she couldn't seem to get the letters to arrange themselves into something she could make sense of, and her eyes remained unfocused on the page. With a cry, she threw the note back onto the table as if it burned.

She whirled about, staring through the window at the dark outside, knowing that she, in the light of the room, stood out with a clarity denied to anyone standing just metres away, hiding in the shadows. There was no one there, and yet... Her gaze returned to the table. There *could* be.

The storeroom was the only real place where she could hide and she rushed inside, standing behind the door with her chest heaving. The air around her felt thick, like treacle, and she could scarcely draw it in. Her head was spinning. She had work to do, but even though the bakery doors were locked, how could she possibly spend the night there knowing that she could be seen? Knowing that he might be out there, watching, waiting until the morning came and it was time for her to leave? He could have her in his sights right now.

Her eyes felt curiously hot and dry, even though they

spilled tears down her cheeks. She dashed them away, anger beginning to burn through her. She had come so far, done things she never thought she'd have to and, against the odds, had achieved so much. What did she have to do to be free of him?

From across the room, her music still played, her phone lying on the table where she'd left it. But who would she call? Not her boss. It was eleven o'clock at night and Vivienne was still recuperating. And Beth? Her first real friend? Frankie remembered how happy she'd been, keying Beth's number into her phone contacts, but Beth would be at work by now and unable to help.

Frankie switched her attention towards the front door of the bakery. She could leave via the back door and run towards the car park, but that would mean the darkness of the alley and the narrow road beyond. Even if she reached Tam, she wasn't sure how he could help her. She needed to be invisible. She needed to be inside, and that meant the *front* door was her only option. Her flat was the only place where she'd be safe. But as soon as the thought entered her head, she realised that wasn't the answer either. Her flat might be safe, but if she went up there she'd be trapped, holed up until... until she came down to find him waiting for her. And besides, there was just a chance he might not know where she lived yet. Thinking hard, she realised there was only one choice open to her. She had an advantage over Robert because she knew this town and he didn't. She could hide somewhere, she could...

Gritting her teeth, Frankie peered around the door of the storeroom, snatching a quick glance through the window before ducking her head back inside. Her keys were hanging up beside her coat and bag, she could be out of the door in seconds – keys then phone – one, two – and then, gone. She took a deep breath and started running.

Her fingers fumbled, the lock was stiff – how had she not remembered that? Then she was through, but in her haste to relock the door she dropped the keys, the noise like a gunshot in the silent night. She swore, crying out in desperation, as she swiped the keys from the floor, hairs standing to attention on the back of her neck. Something was moving, coming closer...

There! She was done, the door was locked. She turned, pushing away with her feet, propelling herself down the street, but the pavement had gone from under her, slick from icy rain.

She crashed to the ground, pain shooting through her wrist, blooming within one knee, and she scrabbled frantically to right herself. None of it mattered. They were small things. Sacrifices in the face of something much bigger. She snatched up her phone, seeing the crack across the screen. It didn't matter. *Get up, Frankie. Run...*

Her gaze fell on the street ahead – it was clear. But then a sound came from behind and her world stood still. How could she have been so stupid? She'd never make it anywhere. If Robert was behind her, he would catch her easily, her short legs no match for his long stride. She focused on something. A possibility. Yes, take it... *move!*

Moments later, her fist pounded against a green door, her fingers stabbing at the doorbell, again and again, as she prayed that William would be home. If he had already left for work, if he wasn't there...

But then a light came on, and the door opened, and he stood before her, tall and solid and *safe...* She didn't care – she pushed herself through the gap, flattened herself against him and slammed the door behind her.

For the first few seconds all she could do was breathe. There were words coming out of her mouth, but she had no idea what they were. There were words coming out of William's mouth too, but all she could hear was white noise, foaming white water, crashing inside her head.

Gradually, the tumult slowed. Her hearing returned, her

breathing softened, and she swallowed, William's shirt glued to her cheek.

He pulled away, his arms gently holding hers. 'It's okay, Frankie, hey, it's okay.' He stared into her eyes. 'Whatever's wrong, we'll sort it. You're *safe...*'

She nodded, feeling her tears begin in earnest as the shock of her situation caught up with her, the realisation of what she'd just done flooding her with embarrassment. She turned her face away, only for William to slide a hand through her hair and gently turn her head back.

'Don't,' he said. 'It doesn't matter.' And then, after another searching look, 'Come on, I think you need to sit down.'

Her legs were still trembling violently and, as she followed William up the stairs, she almost laughed at the absurdity of her movements – hanging onto the banister as if she'd forgotten how to walk.

She emerged through a door at the top of the stairs, knee and wrist throbbing, into a sitting room a similar size to her own. The furniture was basic, just as hers was, but whereas her flat was bright and full of colour, his was more muted, furnished in soft tones of blues and green, colours of the earth, the sky. There were plants everywhere. She hadn't ever considered what William's flat would look like until now, but she must have had a stereotypical image in her mind because the reality didn't match with it at all. Looking around in surprise, she wondered whether she preferred it to her own. She had deliberately chosen bright colours, thinking them to be cheerful and uplifting, but now she wondered whether perhaps she'd been trying too hard. William's room was calming and serene, and with heavy curtains closed against the night outside, a cocoon.

He steered her towards an armchair in one corner, beside a small table holding a lamp and a stack of books – his chair, and obviously favoured over a sofa which sat opposite. She could still see where the cushions held the imprint of his weight. She was about to protest when he interrupted her thoughts.

'No arguments – sit,' he said. 'And I'll get you something to drink. Something warm, or something strong?'

'Warm,' she said, nodding. 'Thank you.'

Taking advantage of his exit, she inspected her wrist and knee for damage. No skin was broken but although the dim light didn't reveal any bruising, she was sure it was there. She tentatively flexed her wrist, gasping at the white-hot flare of pain which shot through it and up her arm. What on earth would she do now? Bread making was not an activity you could undertake single-handed. She shook her head angrily. Stupid, stupid, stupid...

She spent the next few minutes until William reappeared trying not to cry.

From the other room, she could hear sounds of a kettle coming to boil and she sat a little more upright, sniffing and blinking hard. Anything to stifle her emotions and bring back a sense of normality. She took a deep breath.

'I owe you an explanation,' she said, as soon as William returned.

He was carrying two mugs which he put down on a coffee table in front of the sofa.

'Possibly...' He smiled a little. 'I'll admit I'm burning with curiosity, but you don't owe me anything, Frankie.'

'After what just happened? I don't normally go around throwing myself into the arms of virtual strangers.' Just saying the words made her blush.

'I guessed that. And one day we'll probably laugh about this, but right now... I'm not sure which one of us is the more embarrassed. You, for throwing yourself at me, or me, for catching you and hanging on.'

'Did you?'

'Oh yes...' The corners of his mouth twitched. 'Although I'm not sure you noticed so I probably shouldn't have said anything.' He shook his head in amusement and sat down on the sofa. 'In all seriousness though, whatever the reason for it, I'm glad you found your way here.'

'I didn't know where else to go. I was running and then I saw your door, the green door you'd told me about when we first met and, suddenly, it was all I could think of.'

He pushed a mug towards her. 'No need to think about that now. Here, it's hot chocolate, and probably sickeningly sweet, but under the circumstances...'

She accepted it gratefully, wincing a little as she lifted the mug to her nose and inhaled the fragrant warmth. Taking a cautious sip, she smiled. 'Sickeningly sweet, but very, very nice.'

'Good. Catch your breath, there's no rush.'

And suddenly there wasn't. All this moment needed was to sit and be still. No expectations, no judgements, nothing but the slow passage of time. She pushed herself deeper into the chair and, finally, felt her body relax.

She had almost finished her drink before she realised she was in serious danger of falling asleep. Her head was the weight of a bowling ball, her neck far too slender to support it. It was so, so tempting to give in, but Frankie knew if she did so she would probably let out the most horrendous snort and she didn't think she'd survive any more embarrassment. She inhaled sharply, attempting to rouse herself.

'Sorry...' she murmured. 'I'm not exactly being scintillating company.'

But William merely smiled, his eyes catching the light from the lamp as he did so.

'I ought to get back to work,' she said, and then checked herself. 'God, you probably need to get to work, don't you? I'm so sorry.'

'It's my day off, you're in luck.'

Frankie realised just how lucky she had been. 'I don't know what I would have done if you weren't here.'

A startled look came over his face. 'Those lads didn't pay you a repeat visit, did they? It wasn't anyone from the club giving you grief?'

Frankie shook her head. 'No, nothing like that.'

'But someone was following you? You said you were running.'

'I don't even know if they were,' admitted Frankie. 'I think so. I heard noises and...' She stopped. The only way to explain was to explain properly, but after all this time, holding everything in, never admitting to anyone who knew her what had happened, Frankie wasn't sure she could.

Yet if she were to tell anyone, she'd like it to be William. He was sitting on the sofa opposite, with one leg tucked beneath the other, in a pose which he obviously favoured. He radiated such an air of still calm, it was like a soothing balm. She could feel her blood pressure lowering just by being in his presence.

'You really don't need to tell me,' he said, sensing her hesitation. 'I'm guessing that whatever got you this upset is not something you would normally share with a virtual stranger. And that's okay.'

She stared down at her mug, still clasped in her hands. It wasn't okay, and it would never be okay unless she let people into her life. People who might understand.

'There was a note waiting for me when I got to work this evening,' she said. 'Someone had pushed it through the bakery's letterbox.' She shook her head. 'Not someone... I know who it was.' Was she really going to do this? William had been so kind to her, and she had ruined his evening, *was* ruining his evening...

'I was married. Am married... The note was from my husband, and he—' The breath caught in her throat. 'He shouldn't know where I am, but he does, and now... I don't know what I'm going to do.' She swallowed. 'It took me such a long time to get away.'

There was silence. She didn't want to look at William and see the irritation in his eyes, the realisation that she'd just shoved him straight into the middle of a marital dispute. She didn't want him questioning her motives. But, as the seconds ticked by, she found she couldn't bear it and, looking up, was surprised to see an altogether different expression on his face.

'He hurt you?' he said softly.

'No...' She frowned. 'He didn't hit me. That's what you mean, isn't it? He wasn't violent, but he did hurt me. And sometimes I wish he *had* used his fists, at least then I'd have something to prove what a monster he was. A monster I lived with for nearly thirty years, stupidly believing for most of them that I was happy – that I was married to a man who loved me, and cared for me, and would do anything for me. But it was only when I had reached rock bottom, when I depended on him almost for my very existence, that a teeny spark inside of me began to wonder if it was him who was the problem, not me. And, as soon as I realised, that's when the monster appeared.' She winced. 'They call it gaslighting now, coercive control, and I'm glad, finally, to have some way of labelling his behaviour. To know that people recognise it, talk about it even. Before, it was just me, losing my mind, making a fuss about a man who was so kind and considerate. No wonder people thought I was mad.'

William nodded. 'I'm from the same generation as you so I'm learning about the terms for these things too. I'm sure they existed in the past, but I don't think people understood, not really.'

'He made me depend on him for everything. Even the things I believed in came from him – his mind, his opinions. He changed the way I thought, how I felt even, and if I found myself disagreeing, I told myself it was because I didn't understand, or I was stupid. You lose all faith in yourself, in your abilities, but it happens so gradually you never even notice.'

'Like the boiling frog analogy?'

She stared at him. '*Exactly* like that, yes. It all starts off so innocuously. In fact, when we first got married, I congratulated myself over and over at how lucky I was to be with a man like him. Someone who wanted nothing more than to take care of me. It wasn't until I woke up one day and realised he controlled every aspect of my life that I understood he was the very opposite of kind and caring. The trouble is that, even now, when people recognise this kind of behaviour, they still don't understand how you could let yourself be fooled by it, and to such an extent. They don't believe they could be so easily manipulated, so they don't understand how *you* could be, *therefore*... maybe there was some truth in the things he said about you.' She bit her lip. 'I thought at the very least my family would understand, but I hardly speak to them now.'

'Your family?' William's expression was unbelievably sad.

Frankie nodded. 'They'd joke about me when we were all together, saying, "What are you like?" rolling their eyes and smiling as if they were indulging *my* behaviour. And I wondered why they were saying such things. Now, of course, I know why. But even though they knew me, could see the reality of the situation I was in, suggestion is a hideously powerful tool. All it takes is for an idea to be planted, and he was so good at that – idea bombs – scattering them like seeds and watching them grow.'

William cleared his throat a little, swallowing. 'But you got out? What did you do?'

'I tried staying with a friend for a while, no more than a couple of weeks, but it was enough to show me that it would never work. How even my friends had bought into the lies he'd spread. She was sympathetic, and consoling, but deep down I could see she believed him over me. She wasn't sure about me, and it showed. He was just so nice, you see, so reasonable – so full of concern for me and my mental health, which had been deteriorating bit by bit over the years. At times, it truly felt like I was going mad, and I almost believed I was, *almost*. But not quite. Some part of me still wanted to fight.

'And it was the same with *all* my friends. Their sympathy was ever so slightly condescending. They'd say things like, "Robert's devastated, I've never seen him so upset." They'd acknowledge *I* was upset, but they all expected me to "feel better" after a while and realise that Robert only wanted what was best for me. He'd convinced them, you see, just like he'd tried to convince me. And, because it was drip-fed to them, slowly, slowly, over time, no one had any reason to question what was actually going on.'

'They don't sound much like friends to me.'

'I don't think they were either,' replied Frankie, fumbling in her pocket for a tissue. 'And for the longest time that was one of the biggest hurts. Until I realised that I could never make any true friends when all I had to offer was some watered-down, projected version of me. Until I could reclaim who I really was... am... nothing would change.'

William nodded, getting up from the sofa and fetching a box of tissues from the kitchen. He laid it on the table between them and Frankie took one, nodding in gratitude. She took a deep breath.

'So, I cut my losses,' she continued. 'Did what research I could, and I ran away. I had no money of my own, but I managed to save a tiny amount, literally enough to buy a train fare, and I threw myself on the mercy of a women's refuge. And wow, that really opened my eyes. But it also gave me strength, and although Robert found me, I got better at planning, at hiding, and so here I am, nearly eighteen months after I first left.' She gave a nervous smile, even now anxious that she be believed.

William was silent, deep in thought and, although his brow was furrowed, his expression gave nothing away. She swallowed, dropping her head to hide her face. She didn't think she could bear his dismissal.

'So, what did the note say?' William asked eventually, pursing his lips.

'I don't know,' she admitted. 'When I saw who it was from, I panicked. I threw it down and then... came running in your direction.'

'So, it's still back at the bakery?'

She nodded.

'Well then, we need to take a look. Find out what he wants and then work out what to do. Together. *I* believe you, Frankie, and you're not alone now, not any more.'

Relief flooded through her; relief, and something else too which brought heat flooding back into her cheeks. Before she could reply, however, he grinned.

'Would you like something to eat? I'm starving and I've a slab of fruit cake if you'd like some? Shop-bought, I'm afraid, so not a patch on yours.'

'No thanks,' she said. It was an automatic reply, born out of years of being careful about what she ate. 'You see! I can't even decide whether I want cake or not. What I meant to say was, yes please, I'd love some cake.' She tutted, cross with herself.

William grinned. 'With cheese?'

'Cheese?'

'Wensleydale... it's a surprisingly good combination.'

She stared at him, amused. 'Okay, that's completely weird, but cheese it is.'

23

Frankie

Hello Frances,

You'll think I've been stalking you, hunting you down because for some reason you've got it in your head that I'm out to hurt you. But please believe me when I say that nothing is further from the truth.

I have obviously found out where you're staying but only because there are things we need to resolve. You've made it very clear how you feel about our relationship and I'll admit that made me more upset than I've ever been. I really thought we were good together. But I'm also not stupid and I can see that you have made your mind up – using your maiden name again is proof enough of that. However much I want you back, I know I also have to be realistic and see that it's time for me to move on with my life.

That's all I'm asking for, Frances, just a chance to put things right going forward, to be practical and make arrangements so that we can both begin again, properly. I love you so very much, and I hope you know I've only ever wanted what was best for you. It breaks my heart to say it, but I can see now that we're probably better off apart.

You know my number. Get in touch, and we can have a chat, that's all, just a chat about where we go from here.

Much love,

Robert

William's brows drew together, his lips working as he reread the letter for a second time.

'It could be worse,' he said. 'Sorry, I know that's not helpful, but at least he's not threatening you.'

Frankie shook her head. 'He'd never do that, not when there's a chance that someone else could hear him or see what he'd written. That's not the way he works. He's always so *reasonable*... But what he's written here is a pack of lies, William. His very first sentence gives away what he's really done. He *has* stalked me, hunted me down. He draws attention to the very thing he's guilty of and then refutes it, makes it sound crazy, like it's something which could only have come from the mind of someone unhinged. Don't you see that?'

She stared at him in exasperation, but to her surprise, he nodded.

'I don't know Robert,' he said. 'But you do. You've lived with his behaviour for years, so if you say that's what he's doing then I accept what you say.'

'He's looking for a way in – just a chat – it sounds so casual, but that's how he works. If I meet him, he'll be charm itself – friendly, complimentary – he'll make me believe that I'm in control, and then he'll slowly take it away.'

'Except that now you know what he's like, you won't fall into that trap again.'

'But what if I do, William? I'm scared. It happened before. I fell victim to his behaviour for well over twenty years. Whichever part of me allowed that to happen is still within me.'

'And so is the part which worked out what was happening and fought back.' He studied her face. 'Plus, correct me if I'm wrong, but weren't the weapons he used on you dependent on one thing – your desire to please him? Not because you were weak,' he added quickly, 'but because you loved him. That's no longer the case, surely?'

Frankie shook her head several times. 'I hate him,' she said. 'I hate him for what he's done to me. For taking half my life and making it his.'

'Then you'll be fine,' replied William. And suddenly, for the first time in a long time, Frankie felt she might be.

'*Plus*, you also have me now, don't forget,' he added. 'I'll make sure you don't get led astray.'

She smiled at his easy assumption that he would be there for her. She felt safe, she realised, and she hadn't felt that in a long while.

They'd been in the bakery half an hour or so by then, and leaving the sanctuary of William's flat had taken nearly all of Frankie's resolve. But William had walked with her, step by step, until they reached the door. Even then, it had taken a reassuring touch on her arm before she could step over the threshold. William relocked the door, checking both the street outside and the alley before taking up a stance in the middle of the room while she read the letter. If Robert had wanted to see her reaction when she read it, he would be in for a big surprise.

'So, what do I do?' asked Frankie. 'Do you think I should meet him?'

William nodded. 'Yes, because you *do* need to sever ties, legally and irrevocably. But you do so on your terms. Meet him when you want, where you want, and trust me when I say you'll be okay.' She fidgeted under the intensity of his gaze. '*Do* you trust me?' he asked.

Did she? The question had never even entered her head, but her actions seemed to suggest that she did. She had acted on instinct, and if the last two years had taught her anything, it was that the one person she *could* trust was herself. She nodded, uncertain of this new feeling within herself – allowing herself to be vulnerable in the presence of another – but, she reminded herself, she had to do this if she was to have any kind of meaning in her life.

'Look at me,' William added, 'and tell me what you see.'

She blushed, knowing that what she had first seen when she met William was certainly not what she saw now.

As if reading her thoughts, he laughed. 'And don't be polite. First impressions, go on...'

She pursed her lips. 'What I actually thought, which is extremely ironic under the circumstances, was that I wouldn't like to meet you down a dark alley.'

William was still amused. 'Thought so. And I'm hoping that Robert will be no different. I'm fifty-two. I've had a life, Frankie, and I've done things I'm not especially proud of. So, although I wouldn't hurt a fly *now*, it wasn't always the case. And *that* is what people see when they look at me. They see my height and my build, and they see capability.' He smirked. 'Robert won't try anything while I'm around.'

She nodded. But even though it seemed one problem might now have a solution, she had another quite pressing one to deal with. She looked at her watch and groaned.

'I'm in so much trouble,' she said. 'It's nearly one o'clock and I'm way behind where I should be. I should have called my boss to let her know what was going on, but...' She lowered her eyes. 'I needed this job, William, so I wasn't exactly truthful about my past. Vivienne has no idea about Robert, about any of it.'

'She knows you're a damn good baker, and that's all she needs to know.'

'But what am I going to tell her when I can't open the shop tomorrow because there's hardly any bread to sell? I need her to recommend me to any prospective buyers, not tell them I'm a useless liability.'

'You're hardly that. When have you ever let her down before? And you're not going to let her down now either. There are two of us here tonight, and believe me, I'm very used to taking instruction. Tell me what to do and I'll help.'

'But I can't ask you to do that. You'll be up all night.'

'I would have been up a considerable part of it anyway. I told you, I don't sleep all that well. Besides, I'm not leaving you here on your own, so you might as well put me to good use.'

Frankie thought quickly. Was it possible? *Could* William help her? If she concentrated on the items which were ready to be baked, then it might work. Whether they would have enough time to prepare the various doughs ready for the next day was a different matter, but she would worry about that later. 'Okay, let's make a start,' she said. 'And see what's what.'

It was something she did every night, several times a night and so, as she had on every other occasion, Frankie gave no thought to opening one of the fridges, sliding forward the huge tub of dough and hefting it from the shelf with a practised pull.

The cry left her lips before she could stop it, pain searing its way up her arm, leaving a vapour trail in its wake which burned its way back down to her wrist. The tub lurched sideways, and she fought to control it, but with only one hand, it was an impossibility, and she twisted her hip and knees to catch it on the way down. It was almost on the floor before two strong hands appeared beneath it and lowered it gently the rest of the way. They lowered her gently to the floor as well, cradling her arm as she cradled her wrist, tears running freely down her cheeks. She let them fall.

The shock of the sudden pain had brought them, together with the burning embarrassment of her vulnerability but, as she let herself lean into William's solid bulk, it was also the realisation that it was okay to cry. That, this time, there was someone to catch her when she fell.

If she had cried before at the relief of reaching a place of safety, at the tumult of thoughts which had assailed her as she fled from Robert's presence, this time she cried for all the times she'd been unable to, the times when she'd put on a brave face, the times when she had denied herself her true feelings, and the years she had lost. But mostly, she cried for the young woman who had set out on her life with such hope, such faith for the future, and had lost *herself*.

Eventually, for the second time in as many hours, she pulled away from William's arms, only slower this time, as new thoughts rushed around her head. The realisation that this man, whom she barely knew, had rekindled the faith and hope she once held. But, more than that, in doing so he had shown her the woman she could be, the one who still believed in friendship, in kindness, and who didn't push people away, but who instead could draw them to her. It was a heady sensation.

It took a lot of courage to meet William's eyes, but when she did, she was surprised to see her own shyness and a certain awkwardness reflected back. And, as the corners of his mouth began to curve upwards, there was humour there, too.

'I'm too old to be sitting on the floor,' she said, smiling, aware that her knees were now joining in the protest so brilliantly led by her wrist.

William groaned. 'I'm not sure I can feel my feet,' he said, wincing as he extricated them from under him and stretched out both legs.

Laughing, they helped one another to stand, grimacing at their stiff limbs and, in William's case, a bad bout of pins and needles. It was several minutes before they were able to face one another again.

'And before you say it, there's really no need to apologise,' said William, turning his attention to her wrist. 'Why didn't you tell me you were hurt?'

'I slipped over... I didn't think...' She screwed up her face as she very slowly tried to rotate her wrist. She stopped almost immediately.

'Here, sit down,' said William, pulling out a stool from under the worktable. 'I'll get something cold. Do you have any ice?'

She shook her head. 'But there's a cold pack in the bottom of the freezer.'

He assessed her for a moment, eyes missing nothing. 'Okay, so we'll sit for a while and see if that helps, and then I think a trip to A&E might be in order.'

'No.' Her reply was louder than she intended. 'Sorry... I didn't mean to shout. But I can't go to the hospital.' She looked around the room with anxious eyes. 'There's so much to do, and besides, I'm sure nothing's broken, I just wrenched it, that's all.'

William's only reply was to raise his eyebrows.

'Honestly,' she said. 'I'm happy to sit for a bit, but after that...' Her eyes widened. 'What on earth am I going to do?'

William opened the freezer. '*You* are going to stay there and put this on.' He handed her the cold pack. '*I* am going to get to work, and *we* are going to sort this.' He picked up the fallen tub of dough, which, thankfully, seemed none the worse for its sudden descent, and placed it on the worktable. 'What do I need to do first?'

Frankie sighed with relief as the fire in her wrist began to abate slightly. She nodded towards the far side of the room where the storeroom lay. On the wall beside it was a whiteboard, sectioned into grids and covered in green writing. 'That's the plan,' she said. 'Every type of bread we make, and each

pastry, quantities and weights. It hasn't been updated much
since I got here, but what isn't written down is up here.' She
tapped her head with her good hand. 'And that' – she pointed to
the tub of dough – 'is for the first batch of sandwich loaves. We
need to divide it up into equal weights, shape it, put it into the
tins, which need to be prepared first, and then leave it to rise
again. Basically... There's a little more to it than that.' She gave a
wry smile.

William just grinned, holding up both hands. 'Better wash
these then, hadn't I?' He moved towards the sink but then
stopped, turning. 'I assume I get a pinny as well?'

'A pinny?'

'Yeah... an apron.'

Frankie rolled her eyes. 'I know what a *pinny* is.' She smothered a smile. 'Just that it seems such an...' She didn't want to
offend William. 'Old-fashioned word...' she finished, wrinkling
her nose in amusement.

'*And...?*' William's eyes twinkled in challenge.

'And... it's hanging on the back of the storeroom door,' she
said, trying her hardest to keep a straight face.

It seemed impossible. And improbable. Given all that had
happened, how could she simply watch while William worked?
Yet that's exactly what she did, effectively ignoring everything
until something which had, at first, seemed insurmountable,
gently assumed new proportions, less scary ones, until what
she'd thought of as the hugest of obstacles became one which
could be simply stepped around with ease.

At first, she explained every detail, every action William
should take, every process he should follow, but as the minutes
turned into hours, she gave less and less instruction, becoming
aware that she had swapped from watching his every move to
simply watching him.

'You've done this before,' she said.

William barely looked up. 'Once or twice,' he replied. 'Like

I said, I've had a life, Frankie. I've made the odd loaf of bread in my time.' He flicked her a glance. 'Not like this, but this is good. I'm enjoying it.'

It was true. Frankie could see it in the way he moved, his body relaxed and at ease. His face was the same. He had been concentrating so hard in the beginning, but gradually his initial anxiety at getting things right had been replaced by a simple peace. And *she* felt peaceful, too. It was a spell she really didn't want to break.

Eventually though, light crept into the room as the rising dawn gained mastery over the night.

'What do we do now?' asked Frankie, looking around at the result of William's labours. They hadn't finished, but they had done enough. William had done enough. But she wasn't referring to the to-do list.

'About what?' replied William, although it was clear he understood her meaning.

The word *us* seemed to hover in the air but Frankie turned her head slightly so as not to see it. 'This... me... the situation. And me crying all over you.'

William cocked his head to one side. 'Do we have to do anything about it?'

Frankie thought for a moment. 'I suppose I thought you'd want to talk more about stuff – me, and what happened. And I don't mind, if you want to ask me anything.'

William's look was warm. 'I could do, but your situation didn't happen overnight. It's taken time to rise, but now you've been punched down, it'll take a while before you—'

'That's really corny,' interrupted Frankie, laughing.

'I know.' He grinned. 'But it's a pretty good analogy, all the same.'

'So, what now?' she said, amused. 'Into the oven with me?'

He scratched his head. 'That's where it kind of falls apart. But what's important here is that I understand this is not something which has only just happened to you. It runs deep and will take time to come right again. Poking it every five minutes to check if it's okay will probably have the opposite effect.' The corners of his eyes crinkled. 'So I'm trying really hard not to.'

He was giving her space. She understood. And his honesty endeared him to her even more. 'That actually makes a great deal of sense,' she said. 'And it isn't that I don't want to talk about my life, but...' She was grateful for the opportunity not to.

He nodded. 'Frankie, we can't know everything there is to know about each other in just one night. And that's okay.'

She smiled at the slight warning note in his voice. And she nodded, it really was okay. Perhaps, for the first time in a long time, Frankie could simply get used to breathing in the company of another.

'But on a purely practical note,' continued William. 'What *do* we need to do now?'

'Put the kettle on?' she suggested.

24

William

'You know, you probably should have had this X-rayed,' said Beth. 'It's not massively swollen, which is good, but you might still have a fracture.'

William met her raised eyebrows with a nod. He'd only been introduced to Frankie's friend five minutes ago, but he had liked her on sight.

Still in her nurse's uniform, Beth had dumped her bag on the table and knelt on the dusty floor beside Frankie with a look of such kind concern, he had immediately warmed to her. Plus, she had batted away Frankie's apology for having dragged her over on her way home from work.

'I'd have been furious if you hadn't,' she said, her gentle fingers probing the tender spots on Frankie's wrist. She sat back on her heels. 'How long ago did this happen?' she asked.

Frankie flicked William a glance, unsure. 'Maybe about eleven?' she replied. William nodded.

'Last night?' Beth looked around her for the first time since arriving. 'Tell me you haven't been working since then,' she said. 'How on earth did you manage?'

Frankie shook her head. 'William stepped in. There's no way I could have done it otherwise. I couldn't even lift a tub of dough out of the fridge.'

Beth smiled at him. 'The knight in shining armour,' she said, giving him an appraising look. 'Frankie told me how you came to her rescue once before.'

If she had said *and now here you are again*, William wouldn't have been the least bit surprised. Instead, she nodded, a generous smile aimed in his direction.

'Good,' she said. 'I'm glad you had someone with you. Have you put any ice on it?' The question was directed at William. 'And what about painkillers?'

'No painkillers. Sorry, I didn't think, but a cold pack, yes, to start with.' William ran a hand through his hair. It should have been one of the first things he thought of as soon as he knew how badly Frankie had been hurt.

'Then let's get your arm raised, pump you full of drugs and we'll take it from there,' said Beth. 'You also need to get home and have some rest,' she added, pointedly. 'Now I know you have a first-aid kit here because I've used it myself.'

Frankie nodded. 'It's on the far shelf, bottom left.'

William didn't need to be asked. Frankie looked exhausted. There were dark smudges around her eyes, and she looked pale and wan. He'd carry her up to her flat if necessary.

Beth made short work of putting Frankie's arm in a sling, motioning to her bag as she did so. 'There are some paracetamol in there somewhere. Can you have a rummage for me?'

William stared at the soft bundle of leather on the table. 'In there?' he asked. He couldn't go rummaging through that; it was her bag, and private. Women's handbags were sacrosanct; his mother had drummed that into him the day he tried to find the bag of sweets she'd taken from him for swearing.

Beth nodded. 'Hmm... they'll be at the bottom, they always are.' She adjusted the length of the sling before deftly tying a knot on the front of Frankie's shoulder. 'Honestly, it's fine.'

William slid his hand inside Beth's bag as if it might contain a mousetrap and began to fish about. Keys... a phone... something hard and oblong, a purse, perhaps? Numerous bits of paper... Eventually he made contact with a small square box and pulled it free. 'I'll get some water,' he said, keen to hand over the tablets.

He watched while Beth finished the last of her ministrations. Frankie was fading fast. She looked as if she could fall asleep in her chair, and yet they still had to get the shop ready for opening. Then serve goodness knows how many customers until Frankie's colleague, Melanie, could come to relieve them. And William couldn't see how Frankie would manage any of those things.

As if reading his mind, Beth stood up, sliding her bag across the table and pulling out her phone. 'I'm going to give Tam a call,' she said, 'and see if he can come and help.' She smiled at Frankie. 'I'd stay myself, only—'

'No, you need to get home,' said Frankie, her face creased with pain. 'I've delayed you long enough as it is.'

'Jack will be fine,' replied Beth, the expression on her face making it clear she would hear no argument. 'I do need to get home, but only because Tam is due to visit later this morning and I need to get Jack up and ready for him.'

'Tam is?' Frankie was clearly puzzled. 'And since when did he have a phone?'

Beth shrugged. 'It's just an old pay-as-you-go we've had sitting in a drawer at home, but it works. I thought it might be useful for him to keep in touch with folk. And for us to keep in touch with him.' She slid a glance towards William, and he wondered if what she wanted to say next was private. 'He's been over to see Jack a few times now. They've been discussing the farm, making a few plans. Did you know he used to grow plants for a living? Who'd have thought...'

Frankie nodded, smiling.

'Anyway, it's early days, but...' Beth left her sentence hanging, and although the warmth of the bakery might be responsible for her rosy cheeks, William was pretty sure she was blushing.

'Oh, Beth...' Frankie reached over to squeeze Beth's hand. It was an awkward movement given that one of her arms was strapped up, but there was no mistaking the pleasure she was feeling. 'I'm so pleased for you. And for Jack – that's lovely news.'

Clearly there was an importance to Tam's visits which William knew nothing about.

'Let me call Tam now,' said Beth, 'and see if he can come over.'

She moved away and William took the opportunity to slide into the chair next to Frankie.

'I didn't know she and Tam knew one another,' he whispered, his head dipping in Beth's direction.

'I'll tell you about it later,' murmured Frankie, sighing. 'Sorry, this is causing no end of problems for you all.'

Without thinking, William covered Frankie's hand with his own. It seemed the most natural thing in the world, especially seeing that Frankie had just done the same to Beth, but as soon as he slid his fingers over hers, he realised it wasn't the same thing at all. He pulled his hand back, grimacing at his clumsiness.

'Sorry, I...'

But Frankie just smiled. 'It's okay,' she said, pulling his hand back and pushing it flat to the table. She laid hers over the top. 'Thank you. I don't know what I would have done if you hadn't been here.'

William's heart thudded in his chest. He should probably

reply, but words suddenly seemed far beyond his reach. He smiled instead, feeling the seconds tick by as Beth continued her phone call, each one seemingly longer than the last. He scrutinised the grain on the table, tracing the whorls back and forth with his eyes until he heard Beth saying goodbye. He gently straightened, withdrawing his hand.

'Right, all sorted,' said Beth. 'Tam's on his way. I'll hang on until he gets here, and then head home, if that's all right. Are you sure you're going to be okay?'

Frankie nodded. 'I'll be fine. Honestly. It's feeling better already.'

The look on her face would suggest otherwise and William could see she wasn't fooling Beth either, but he let it go. He'd get her home as soon as he could.

Tam arrived in what seemed like a surprisingly short space of time, until William remembered that all he had to do was climb out of bed, literally, and a makeshift bed at that. His hair was tousled, sticking up on one side, and his shoulders were hunched, his face pinched and drawn. The morning was still bitterly cold, and it was clear Tam hadn't had much sleep.

'Come in,' said William as he pulled the door wider. 'And I'll make you a drink.'

'Thanks.' Tam shivered at the sudden blast of warmth, as if it reminded him how chilly he was. 'A black coffee would be good.'

There was a sharp intake of breath. 'Tam, you didn't come to get your hot-water bottle filled. Or your flask. I'm so sorry, I should have realised.' Frankie's hand shot to her cheek, her mouth open in dismay.

Tam's smile was easy. 'I didn't think it was that cold,' he replied. 'Won't make that mistake again.'

'Are you sure you still want to come over to the farm?' asked Beth. 'We can easily do this another time. When's your next day off?'

'No, no, today is fine,' Tam assured her. 'I'm better if I keep busy. I'll seize up otherwise.'

William hung his head as he crossed the room to sort out some coffee. It had never even occurred to him what Tam would do when he wasn't at work. Sitting in his car couldn't be much fun, but where would he go otherwise? And what would he do? Keep moving because there was nothing else *to* do? He deserved so much better.

Tam slid into the chair that William had not long vacated. 'What happened?' he asked Frankie. 'Are you okay?'

She pulled a face. 'Long story,' she said. 'But the short version is that, like an idiot, I fell over. Sprained my wrist a bit, that's all.'

William had no idea whether anyone knew about Frankie's situation besides him, but it was a reminder that Robert was still out there, somewhere. And that Frankie would still be terrified. He carried the kettle to the sink and began filling it with water, his head racing with thoughts. So much so, he almost missed what Frankie was saying. All he heard was the word 'amazing'. He turned around to find both Tam and Beth smiling at him. Was that what Frankie had said? That he was amazing? He swallowed, murmuring something non-committal.

'But I'm afraid the job's not over yet,' continued Frankie.

'So I gather,' said Tam. 'Beth mentioned you need help opening up.'

Frankie nodded. 'The shop opens at half eight, but nothing's laid ready yet. I'm not sure if I'll be able to serve either, and the first hour is one of the busiest.'

Tam eyed the doorway which led into the shop. 'I might be able to help with that.'

He returned in less than a minute. 'Yup, all sorted. I had a till just like that in my shop... glorified shed. I might be a bit rusty – in fact I'm sure of it – but there's nothing like being thrown in at the deep end, is there? It'll be fine. And if it isn't, then William and I will just have to use our innate charm to keep the punters happy.'

William snorted. 'Speak for yourself,' he said, but he was pleased to see Frankie smile.

'In that case, I'll get going,' said Beth, with a quick glance at the clock. 'But only if you promise me you'll go home and get some rest.' She crossed the room to drop a kiss on Frankie's cheek, giving her shoulder a squeeze. 'And you'll call me if it gets any worse.'

Frankie nodded. 'Promise.'

'Come over whenever you're ready, Tam. I'll probably be asleep by the time you arrive, but don't be afraid to wake me up if you have any problems.' She paused, giving a sheepish smile. 'Don't go too mad either...'

Tam merely grinned. 'I won't. See you later.'

Once Beth had gone, Frankie roused herself into action, but William could see that it was only the thought of falling into bed soon which was keeping her going. Despite protestations that he and Tam would manage, she insisted on coming through to the shop to help, where she sat, perched on a stool, looking for all the world like she would topple off at any minute. But they were both incredibly grateful for her presence.

Tam fared far better than he did, serving customers politely and, even though he got confused about which bread was which, at least he was able to help. William felt utterly lost. He was too big, for one thing, all but filling the space behind the counter, and constantly getting in the way. In the end, he retreated into the back room and began to wash up, stowing the last few bits and pieces in the storeroom. He would be back there tonight, and without the luxury of a fridge full of risen dough, would probably have to work twice as hard. Even so, he was smiling as he ran a finger lightly along one of the shelves. He was looking forward to it.

25

William

William hovered by the doorway to Frankie's flat. He didn't want to leave her but she insisted she'd be all right and he could hardly argue. Being a shoulder to cry on was one thing, as was helping her out in the bakery, but inviting himself into her flat was crossing a line which, although it was one neither of them had drawn, was there just the same. Plus, he needed to get some sleep himself, even though he'd just arranged to meet Tam shortly. There suddenly didn't seem to be enough hours in the day.

'You're sure you'll be safe here?' he asked, looking up at the window above the bakery.

Frankie nodded. 'If Robert does turn up, he'll have a long wait on his hands. I won't be going anywhere until this evening. And you'll be back then, won't you?'

William wouldn't miss it for the world. 'Okay then.' William stared at his feet. And then at Frankie's cheek, where he'd seen Beth drop a friendly kiss. Could he do the same? Dare he? He told himself it wouldn't mean anything, but who was he trying to kid? He couldn't think of anything he'd rather do. As it was, he'd spent nearly all of the last twelve hours with her, and the thought of the next twelve without her felt inexplicably odd.

He passed Frankie her bag, opening the door for her and dropping his gaze once more. He shuffled his feet. He had only seconds left before Frankie would be gone...

'Bye, William...' Frankie raised her good hand and touched his jacket, just light enough for him to feel. She leaned forward and... 'I'll see you tonight,' she added. A moment later, she slipped through the door.

Not once during the last thirty years or so had William met anyone like Frankie. And that changed everything. Because his past had been lived with no real thought for the future, and most of the time he hadn't much cared what happened to him. Now, though... So, although he knew what he ought to do about Stuart, *should* and *would* had suddenly become two entirely different things. And that was a problem.

'What are we up to today then?' asked Tam as William greeted him. 'Another spying mission?'

William grimaced. 'Not quite, but I do need your help again. You had a business, didn't you? So does that mean you know about accounts and stuff?'

'In theory, although I'm not sure how useful I'll be. My business went bust, remember? Why are you asking?'

'Because I need some information, but I'm not sure how easy it will be to find. I thought you might know. Can I possibly borrow you for ten minutes before you go to Beth's?'

At Tam's nod, William glanced around him at the street, busy with morning shoppers. 'Is there a way to check a company's accounts? I don't need the detail, just how much money they're making.'

'Companies House has an online database – would that

help? You can search for a list of directors, when the business started up, turnover, that kind of thing.'

'That's exactly what I need. But I don't have a computer or a mobile phone, or not one where you can do that kind of thing, anyway.' He pulled a face. 'I'm a bit of a dinosaur, I'm afraid. Frankie might have one, I suppose. Or Beth... I've never asked.'

Tam smiled, fishing in his pocket and pulling out a battered wallet. 'No need,' he said. 'Not when you have one of these.' He winkled out a dog-eared card. 'Library membership,' he added. 'Books, maps, newspapers, audiobooks, and... a computer suite, all free to use.'

'Perfect,' replied William, grinning.

It was quiet in the library at that time of the morning, and the computer suite quieter still.

'Go and grab a seat,' said Tam. 'I'll book us in.'

William did as Tam suggested, heading for the computer which was furthest from the door. There weren't many folks around, but he didn't want to take the chance that someone might overhear what they were about to discuss.

He picked up a leaflet, idly reading it while he waited for Tam to appear. It was more to give his hands something to do than any interest he had in learning how to research his family tree, however. If he did this thing, and found the information he needed, did that mean he absolutely had to follow it up? His head had one answer, and his heart another, and right now, William had no clue which would win.

William was no angel; his life thus far had been littered with lies. Some of them were no more than the schoolboy fibs of his youth. Some might come under the umbrella of a certain kindness, an accommodation of how you felt in order to spare someone a harsh reality. But some of them had been much worse. And then there were the lies of omission, where he hadn't revealed what he should. Kept things to himself in order to cover the truth of his past... but wasn't that just as bad?

He had told Frankie and Tam that he didn't need much sleep because he'd been living somewhere noisy, implying as much anyway, but he'd *lied*. He'd told Frankie he'd made the odd loaf of bread, implying that it was a leisurely pastime, something he might do of a weekend, but he'd *lied*. He had also left an apologetic message for Danny on the club answerphone saying that he wouldn't be at work for the next few days because he had flu, but he had *lied*.

The *truth* was that he would be working with Frankie until her wrist was better because there was nowhere else he'd rather be. But his relationship with the truth was complicated. He glanced at the computer screen in front of him. If he and Tam found what he suspected they might, then the biggest truth of them all was about to stare William in the face. The question was whether he could bring himself to tell it.

'Sorry,' said Tam, appearing by his side. 'Would you believe the computer which allows us to use the computers was on a go-slow. I'm loving the irony.'

William smiled and shuffled his seat over so that Tam could sit down in front of the screen. 'I'm not much good with technology,' he admitted. 'It's kind of passed me by.'

'Well, I'm no expert,' replied Tam. 'But I reckon I can find us what we need. Let me just log on and then I can take a look. Have you got the exact name of the company you're trying to find?'

William pulled a piece of paper from his pocket and spread it open on the desk. He'd been carrying it around ever since they'd followed Stuart's van to the row of shops just around the corner from where he used to live.

'Sun City Tanning Studio...' read Tam, squinting slightly at William's untidy scrawl. 'Isn't that the place we stopped outside the other day?' He frowned. 'I know you said it was better if I didn't know what was going on, but I think the time for that has passed. You obviously think it's something dodgy.'

'I didn't mention it before, but I used to live a couple of streets away from those shops when I was young. I know them very well. The tanning salon was a greengrocer's back then, and I've been inside it many a time. It isn't very big, none of the shops are. They're only small businesses, useful and viable, but not the sort to make you a millionaire. So how much do you reckon the tanning salon takes in a year?'

Tam pursed his lips. 'We can do a quick search of similar businesses for sale, if you like,' he said. 'That would give us a rough idea of turnover, but I don't suppose it's more than forty or fifty thousand a year. A shop that size, in that location...' He shook his head. 'Definitely not going to make you a millionaire.' He began to tap at the keyboard. 'Let's have a look, shall we?'

William watched while Tam brought up a series of pages, most of which meant nothing to him, but after a couple of minutes, Tam indicated the screen. 'If we want more detail, we have to pay, but this should give us the basics.' He began to type the company name into a search box.

The screen was suddenly filled with a list of names – all either identical or very similar to the one they were looking for, businesses all over the country. Tam drew his finger down the list. 'There,' he said, tapping the screen. 'It's the only one with the right address.'

A couple more clicks of the mouse and the screen changed again. Filled with numbers this time, against terms William had no understanding of. 'You'll have to tell me what we're looking at,' he said.

But Tam was silent, brows drawn together as he digested what he saw in front of him.

'What does it mean?' urged William.

'That I was in the wrong line of business,' Tam replied. 'I can't believe they're making that much money... Is tanning really that lucrative?'

William stared at the screen. 'No,' he said. 'That's just it, I don't believe it is. This is about ten times what I think it should be, but, sadly, pretty much what I expected to find. I'm no expert, but if what I suspect about Stuart is right, then he's going to need some way of making his ill-gotten gains seem legit. He needs to make his money clean.' He raised his eyebrows at Tam, not wanting to say the actual words out loud.

Tam looked furtively around the room, leaning closer. 'You mean they're laundering it?' he whispered.

William nodded. 'I can't think of any other explanation. And businesses like tanning salons are prime examples of how they do it – ones which operate primarily on a cash basis. They simply mix in the dirty money with the legitimate takings, and it all comes out clean in the end. But what you end up with is a business that has far more money coming through the door than you would expect.' He thought for a moment. 'Is there a way to check who owns this company?'

'Sure,' replied Tam. 'Hang on, I'll get the page back up. So yes, here's Stuart, and apart from him, there's just one other guy listed – a Paul Morris. Does that mean anything to you?'

William stared at the second name on the list, unsure whether to be relieved or not. A big part of him had been worried he'd find Danny's name, but Paul Morris meant nothing to him. He picked up the piece of paper which held the details of the tanning salon and, spying a biro that was lying on an adjacent desk, he scribbled down what he'd seen on the screen. 'Thanks, Tam, this is exactly what I needed.'

Tam slid him a sideways look. 'I'm not sure you should be thanking me,' he said. 'This is serious, William. What are you going to do?'

William closed his eyes, inhaling deeply as he opened them. 'At this moment in time, I'm not sure. But something. I have to do something...' He swallowed, staring at the wall behind the computer as if the answer could be found there. 'I have a promise to keep.'

26

Tam

It was a beautiful day and Tam could feel his spirits lifting with every mile he drove. After weeks of rain, grey skies by day and freezing temperatures at night, this morning had heralded the return of the sun. Tam could feel spring beginning to stir. He'd become attuned to the slightest change in temperature and this morning there was a softness to the air that he hadn't felt before – a faint promise of what was to come. Faint, yet there all the same. It was the perfect day for what Tam had in mind.

Jack looked like a kid on Christmas Eve when he opened the door, grinning from ear to ear and, Tam was pleased to see, looking far more relaxed than when Tam had first met him. Just the thought of what they were about to do had been enough to smooth the lines from his face and chase away the grey pallor to his skin.

'Good morning for it,' said Tam as he followed Jack down the hallway of the farmhouse.

'Pathetic fallacy,' replied Jack, as he wheeled ahead of him. ''Twas clearly meant to be.'

'It's still pretty cold though,' cautioned Tam. 'I hope you've got plenty of layers on.'

'I feel like the Michelin man. I reckon I'll be okay.' He paused. 'Actually, I don't care if I'm not, we're doing this anyway.'

'Then we'd better crack on,' said Tam. 'The sooner we make a start, the sooner we can find out whether this will work, or if it's just a really, *really* silly idea.'

Jack stopped as he reached the kitchen and spun around. 'It has to. If it doesn't, Beth is going to kill me. And you, for that matter.' He raised his eyebrows at Tam, who laughed.

'And don't I know it. Come on then.'

One of the first things Tam had done during his last visit was to sweep up and clean the yard. The area immediately outside the back door was fine but, as Jack had already discovered to his detriment, the further you went towards the barn and the boundary fence, the muddier it got. Run-off from the field, that's all it was and, understandably, Beth had never seen the need to clear it. Neither she, nor Jack, had ever expected him to venture that far. Now, at least, Jack's wheelchair could cross the yard and enter the barn without becoming stuck.

According to Jack, the barn had been a neat and orderly place a few years ago, but you'd never know to look at it now. Since Jack's accident it had become a dumping ground for anything which no longer worked, which they had no need of, or which they had no room for in the house. As such, it was now home to a wonderful assortment of things which Tam was hoping to cannibalise – old bikes, a metal bed frame and a chair which used to be in the kitchen, but which had been moved to give Jack more space to manoeuvre. It was also home to the quad bike which Tam had spied on the day he'd helped bring Jack inside after his little 'adventure'.

Tam was already poking around inside when he realised that Jack was no longer with him. He turned, and then smiled when he saw there wasn't a problem at all. Jack was simply sitting with his face turned up to the sun, a gentle smile on his lips.

'I've denied myself this for so long,' he said. 'I must have been mad. Why did I do that, Tam? Why haven't I ever just come outside simply to soak up the day?'

'I think you know why,' replied Tam softly. 'Because we try to protect ourselves from the pain of what's been lost.'

Jack nodded. 'And in doing so, become so fearful of what might hurt that we stop living. Then after a while we forget how to.'

'It's human nature,' replied Tam. 'One of our fundamental flaws – we close ourselves off to the slightest reminder of what we can no longer have.' Hadn't he done exactly the same in his own life? Sold everything he owned to appease his guilt when his business failed and, in doing so, denied himself all hope of ever owning one again? Denied himself hope, actually. It was a hard lesson to learn, and even harder, perhaps, was finding the courage to ask for help.

'We might be flawed,' added Tam. 'But we're also capable of doing extraordinary things.' He grinned, looking back at the barn. 'And on that note, point me at your toolbox.'

The design had been in Tam's head for a while now, his thoughts of it a good way of eating up the hours when he was too cold to sleep. But the vision he had of it, and his ability to create that vision, didn't necessarily match up. There had been tweaks to the design, complete alterations to it and a good deal of swearing but, as he wiped a filthy hand down his jeans, he was pleased with what he saw.

Having removed the quad bike's original seat, what Tam had made most resembled something he remembered from his mum's bike when he was a child. Effectively a metal 'cage', it bolted onto the quad bike allowing Jack to sit inside where he would be supported by means of several cushioned pads which also protected him from the hard metal sides of the cage. Another cushion secured in front meant that Tam could sit and drive. Pretty, it was not, but effective? Only time would tell.

'What do you reckon?' he asked.

Jack looked frozen, having essentially sat still for several hours while Tam worked, but he still grinned. 'I'm going to feel like a child at a play park. You know, in one of those swing seats for toddlers with bars round it.'

Tam wrinkled his nose. 'Yeah, there is that – sorry. Or... you could see it like a howdah, a stately noble sitting atop his elephant...?'

'Let's go with that, shall we?' replied Jack, a broad smile on his face. 'Either way, can we just try it, please?'

'I think we should.' Tam grimaced. 'Are you sure you're ready for this? And, just as importantly, will Beth still be asleep?' At his answering nod, Tam continued. 'This might be a teensy bit undignified.'

'I lost all dignity years ago,' said Jack. 'Just manhandle me into it. I'll shout if it hurts.'

Manhandle was definitely the operative word to describe what happened next, but, with much puffing and panting, plus assurances from Tam that they would find a way to do it more smoothly, Jack was installed on the quad bike. He looked around, then down at his 'seat', before snorting with laughter.

'Definitely more toddler than stately noble,' he said, '*and*, I'm happy to confirm, complete loss of dignity... Apart from that, I can't quite believe it.' He grew more serious. 'This is incredible, Tam. What you've done is...' He looked away for a moment, blinking hard. 'Way beyond what I could ever have imagined or dreamed of. I don't really know what to say, except thank you, and that doesn't begin to cover it.'

Tam nodded, feeling a surge of something approaching happiness. This was what he used to be good at – solving problems, making things work. Running his business hadn't been easy – there had always been something to fix, or a solution to come up with. Mother Nature herself threw up all kinds of hurdles, but he had truly enjoyed every minute. He turned his thoughts back to the matter in hand before his own emotions got the better of him. He needed clear vision for what came next.

'Don't thank me yet,' he added. 'Not until we've had a test drive. I need to make sure this thing doesn't unbolt itself after ten minutes.' He stared at the gate which led out of the yard and into the wild unknown. Then fussed over the cushions supporting Jack, pushing them firmly down each side. 'Are you sure you're ready for this?'

'As I'll ever be.' He signalled ahead with his hand. 'Let's go!'

'Oh, wait, hang on a minute.' Tam dashed back inside the barn and returned carrying a cycling helmet. 'Safety precautions,' he said. 'And no arguments.'

By the time Tam had helped Jack on with the headgear and clambered aboard the bike, his heart was beating wildly. This could well be the most stupid thing he'd ever done, or the most genius. Either way, they were about to find out. With the entirety of Jack's wellbeing resting on his shoulders, Tam started up the bike.

He turned a couple of slow circles in the yard. So slow, in fact, that anyone walking alongside them would have had trouble keeping their speed in check, but Tam wasn't taking any chances. Once he was satisfied that both the bike and Jack were stable, he scrambled off again and opened the gate. It would be the first time Jack had been through it in nine years.

Progress was slow, and not just because of the uneven ground. There was so much to see, and so much to say, that Tam had to keep stopping in order for Jack to relay what they were looking at. From what he'd said before, Tam knew that the farm needed a lot of work, but nature had been running riot for the last decade or so and she hadn't held back.

The trees in the orchard were overgrown and diseased, the

area choked with weeds, and the wall which bordered it had tumbled to the ground in more than one place. Beehives had rotted, their inhabitants having long since made off for superior accommodation, and the pig sties and chicken coops were overgrown and derelict. The hedges and fences which had once formed borders between fields had either disappeared entirely or taken liberties with whatever space had been available to them. There were five acres in all, and every bit of it needed an enormous amount of work. But none of that mattered today.

As if to welcome Jack home, the wind, which had still been a little too chill for comfort, had turned balmy, rustling the leaves in the trees and swaying the tops of the tall grasses. Every inch of greenery glowed bright under the sun's rays, and the birdsong swelled around them, jubilant and joyful. For quite a considerable amount of time, Jack said nothing. He simply sat, drinking in everything around him in a silence so profound with emotion, Tam swore he could see the air rippling with it.

Eventually, when they had seen their fill, Tam turned the bike to take them home – back to the farmhouse where Beth would still be sleeping. Jack had left her a note in case she woke early, but she had gone to bed with strict instructions not to set her alarm. Safe in the knowledge that Jack would be with Tam all day, she had readily agreed. Now though, both of them were thirsty and starving hungry – lunchtime had been some while ago. It was time to head back inside.

Ten minutes earlier, possibly even five, and they might have made it home without Beth catching them. As it was, she met them just as they were coming back through the gate into the yard.

'What the bloody hell...' She stared at the quad bike, brows so furrowed her eyebrows were almost touching, her lips pursed in a thin line.

'Have you been out there on that thing?' she asked. 'I mean, properly out there, on the farm?'

Tam nodded, dropping his head and waiting for the explosion that was surely coming.

'The orchard, the fields, the pig pens, the hen houses, all of it,' said Jack, leaning so far forward Tam could feel his breath on the back of his neck. 'I've seen it all, Beth, every last inch of it.'

Beth was clearly still trying to come to terms with what her eyes were seeing, but her expression began to change as she took in the enormity of what Jack had just said. 'And how do you feel?' she asked. Her voice was thin and wavering.

Jack lifted his hands to the sky as best he could. 'Absolutely bloody fantastic,' he yelled.

Beth stared at them for a moment. Looked first at Jack, then at Tam and back again. And then she burst into tears.

27

Tam

Transferring Jack from the bike and into his chair again was just as ungainly a process as it had been in reverse. Eventually, though, with Beth still hiccupping through her tears, they made it back to the kitchen, where Beth immediately began to make some tea. Tam understood – it was an emotional time for her, and she and Jack needed a little space. After bustling about for a few minutes, she returned to the table with a collection of mugs on a tray and a packet of chocolate biscuits.

'I'm black and blue all over,' said Jack wearily, pulling his tea towards him. 'But I don't care. My heart feels whole today, Beth, and I can't tell you how good that is.'

She sniffed. 'I'm not crying because I'm upset, I'm crying because... The look on your face, Jack. I never thought I'd see it again.'

He took her hand. 'You have to come out with us next time, Beth. It's all still there, just waiting for us. It's tired and broken and overgrown, and in one hell of a mess, but it doesn't matter. All it needs is time.'

Beth smiled, and almost caught Tam's eye, but she looked away at the last moment. He took a biscuit, cramming half into his mouth as he reflected on what he needed to say. It was important to get this right.

'Of course, it also needs a lot of hard work,' he said, deliberately staring at Beth so that she would know he was looking at her. For so many years now, Beth had had to be the voice of reason, the one who trod the thinnest of lines between being encouraging and being realistic. Tam didn't want her to take that role any more. They both knew what lay ahead of them but it was important that *he* be the one to voice *her* concerns. If they were to make any progress at all, they had to take it slowly and thoughtfully.

'And I'll be the first to admit that the amount of work seems overwhelming,' Tam added. 'There's also the issue of how much putting things right might cost. But the bones of the farm are there. Initially, a lot of the work will simply be clearing and housekeeping, getting Mother Nature back in check.'

Jack nodded. 'And there's also a huge difference between me sitting on the back of the quad bike and very slowly touring the land, and physically doing the work. Because I can't, obviously. I know that. But what I *can* do is plan, and research, and perhaps, with help, do some of the very simple stuff myself.'

Beth opened her mouth and then closed it again, repeating the action before finally taking a sip of her tea. She must have questions threatening to burst out of her ears, and Tam would be the first to admit they didn't have all the answers – nor even the majority of them – but what they did have was an agreement, in principle, and from there they would begin.

'The most obvious question, of course, is who exactly is going to do all this work?' Tam snaffled another chocolate biscuit and grinned at Beth, who blushed furiously.

'Yes, I know, I know, I'm a boring spoilsport,' she said. 'So, thank you for jumping in so I didn't have to, but these are important things. Someone has to say them.'

'They do,' said Jack, his voice suddenly forceful. 'But you are not a boring spoilsport, Beth. You're the one who's kept us going. Kept us going and kept us from going under. You're the only reason I'm here today. Without you, none of this...' He broke off, swallowing. 'I don't even want to think about what my life would be like without you. Sound of mind might be open to debate, but you've kept my body and my heart sound, Beth. All these years...'

Beth's lip trembled as she gave Jack a look which tugged on Tam's heartstrings, never mind anyone else's.

Tam blinked rapidly, clearing his throat slightly. The room was so still, though, it sounded unnaturally loud and he grimaced in apology.

Beth simply smiled and, taking a deep breath, she looked from one to the other.

'So, who *is* going to do all the work then?' she asked. 'As much as I'd like to help, and I will where I can, there just aren't enough hours in the day to—'

Tam leaned forward slightly. 'I don't want to be presumptuous,' he said. 'Today wasn't about that. It was about giving Jack a way to get back out on the land, but I'd love to help you with the farm – if you want me to, that is.'

Beth stared at him. 'Of course we want you to.' Jack was nodding in agreement. 'But what about your job?'

'I've been thinking about that,' Tam replied. He'd been thinking about little else. 'And I reckon I could work around my shifts. I might even be able to tweak my hours. Summer's coming and the days will be drawing out, I could potentially put in a good few hours each day.'

'But that would mean you'd be working almost every hour of the day,' said Beth. 'And hard, physical work at that. I'm not sure that's fair. I mean, we couldn't even pay you, Tam. I wish we could, but we barely keep our heads above water now as it is.'

Jack sighed in frustration. 'She's right, Tam. I can't ask you to take all this on. I feel so much better from just being outside all day, and being able to see our land, its potential, is the icing on the cake. It's given me renewed determination to make something happen here, but it's too much to ask of you – you'd end up being exhausted. The work would begin to feel like a chore, and you'd come to hate it. It's the very worst thing that could happen.'

Tam's heart sank like a stone. After everything they'd accomplished today... but even as he opened his mouth to argue, he knew that what Jack had said made sense. He was letting his own desire run away with him.

Up until today, their conversations about the farm had been just that – discussions about ideas and plans. None of them were based on the reality of what lay beyond the yard gate, and without this, they might as well be meaningless. He'd seen for himself how much work there was to do, and he knew how hard that work would be. His job at Chawston House wasn't physically tiring, but sleep was hard to come by at times and spending hours at the farm as well would tax his body to its limits. He'd be in real danger of falling at the first hurdle, and if he did that then all Jack and Beth's plans would fail. Again. It would break Jack's heart, and it would be Beth who would be left to pick up the pieces. There was no way Tam could do that to either of them. As much as it hurt him to push aside his own dreams, he knew he must, for everyone's sake. He shook his head.

'Sorry, I was letting myself get carried away by this place. And you're right. No pun intended, but it's never a good idea to run before you can walk.'

'We *will* find a way to make this work though,' said Jack, his warm smile showing how much he understood Tam's disappointment. 'I'm convinced of it, but it's important to take our time and not rush in. For now, maybe we should just focus on something small. Getting even a tiny aspect of the farm up and running would be a huge achievement.'

'But you're still welcome here any time,' put in Beth. 'Come and make plans with Jack for a few hours and help him work out what's feasible. He'd love that. We both would.'

'I really would,' agreed Jack. 'Help me keep the dream alive.'

Tam glanced at his watch. It was probably the best solution all round, and he brightened his smile. 'In any case, I reckon the quad bike will need a fair few adjustments if it's going to be viable for the longer term. I could come and have another tinker, perhaps.'

Jack shifted in his chair, moving his weight from one side to the other and wincing as he did so. He rolled his eyes. 'A little more padding, maybe?'

'I'll put it on the list,' said Tam, grinning. 'I really ought to get going now, and leave you two to the rest of your afternoon.'

'But you haven't even had any lunch,' exclaimed Beth. 'Chocolate biscuits don't count.'

'They do with the number I've eaten,' replied Tam. 'And it's no problem. I'll get dinner when I'm on shift tonight.'

'Rubbish,' replied Beth. 'How about a fat bacon sandwich before you go? Bacon and egg, even?'

There had been no way Tam could pass up crispy bacon and oozing, drippy egg, but he was paying for it now. He practically had to run down the road to get to Chawston House on time. Tam had never been late yet, and he wasn't about to start now. Today would not be a good day for that to happen.

As it was, Trish caught him by the door as soon as he entered, looking unusually flustered.

'She's done it again,' she said, clearly exasperated. 'I told her we didn't have time, but she never listens, and you know what Enid is like if we rush her. She won't be happy, and it's completely unnecessary. We could move her tomorrow when we've got more time and then everyone will be happy. You know, I think she winds the residents up on purpose, just to keep us on our toes.'

Tam blinked, surprised by the force of Trish's words. She was usually so calm. In fact, he couldn't remember ever seeing her so riled before. He also had no idea what she was talking about.

Trish's face softened, no doubt in response to his blank look. 'Sorry,' she said, shaking her head in irritation. 'It's Donna. She's convinced herself that Enid and Roberta aren't getting on and wants to swap their rooms around. And she wants it done before Roberta's daughter arrives so that she can prove she's resolved the situation before she complains.'

'But I spoke to Fiona the day before yesterday,' said Tam. 'And I doubt very much she's going to complain. She laughed once I explained about her mum and Enid pinching each other's biscuits as soon as backs were turned. In fact, she said it's just the kind of thing her mum *would* do. Apparently, she's always enjoyed "being cheeky", as she put it.'

'They're both as bad as one another,' said Trish. 'Just two old ladies who delight in causing trouble. They might grumble about it, but secretly they probably both live for the excitement.' She shook her head. 'But what do I know? I've only worked here eleven years.'

Tam gave her a sympathetic smile. 'So where are we moving Enid to?'

'Eleanor's old room. Which Enid will hate because it's too cut off from what's going on in the lounge. Sorry, Tam, but would you mind giving me a hand?'

'Sure, let me take my coat off, and I'll be on it.'

Trish touched his arm. 'Thank you,' she mouthed and rushed off.

Eleanor's room had been empty for just over a week now and Tam hated to see it so forlorn, stripped of everything that had made it hers. Her daughter had been in for her belongings the day after she died and since then it had lain, cold and impersonal, until needed by a new occupant. They could put as many people in it as they liked; to Tam it would always be Eleanor's room. He stood in the doorway for a moment, thinking of better times. Eleanor would have understood how he was feeling.

Trish wasn't the only one up against the clock, however. Tam had only fifteen minutes to go before his review meeting with Donna, and although it had already been explained to Enid, several times, that she was moving, if she decided she didn't want to go at that precise moment, that time could disappear in the blink of an eye. He hurried back down the corridor, praying that Enid would prove willing.

Half an hour later, his meeting over, Tam stood outside the door to Donna's office, swallowing hard. He had no idea what he was going to do. He, and all his paltry belongings, had hitherto been balanced precariously on a very small rug, and now even that had been pulled from under him. There'd been a complaint, Donna had told him. Well, not a complaint as such, but it had been brought to her attention that he'd been sleeping in his car and didn't actually have anywhere to live. She had a duty of care, blah-blah-blah... She hoped he understood. So, no permanent contract for Tam. No job at all, in fact.

Dazed with shock, he walked down the corridor and through the lounge as if none of it were really there. None of it mattered anyway. There was only one thing he wanted to do.

'Tam!' Trish's voice carried loudly over the hubbub of background noise as she hailed him from across the room. 'Wait a minute.'

He slowed his pace, but only slightly. Trish would have

known what was due to happen today. She had known for a while now. How long? Hours? Days? A week? And she had said nothing. In fact, it might have even been her who had told Donna he was homeless. Instead, Trish had begged for his help this morning and then let him walk into Donna's office completely ignorant of the fate which was about to befall him. He had no wish to talk to her.

'Tam, stop, please...'

She caught up with him quicker than he expected, a sharp tug on his sleeve pulling him to a halt.

'I know you're angry, Tam, and you have every right to be, but please just listen to what I have to say.'

Tam stood silently waiting, eyes closed against her empty words.

Trish touched his arm. 'I've agonised over whether to say anything to you or not, but I didn't because I was still hopeful that we might not be in this situation at all.'

'We? Forgive me, Trish, but how are *we* in this situation?'

'I've made a formal complaint about the way you've been treated,' she replied, colouring at the harsh tone in his voice. 'And they have to respond to it. There's still a chance they might overturn their decision.' Her lips thinned into a hard line. 'It might take a few weeks to resolve, but if they found in your favour, you could come back.'

Tam shook his head. 'I appreciate it, but it doesn't change anything. Even if they do change their minds, I don't want to work for an organisation that has to be bulldozed into expanding their tiny minds. I'm so tired of having to explain who I am to people who don't care. I'm done here.'

'But what are you going to do?'

'Go home. Well, when I say home...' He let his sentence dangle, knowing it sounded bitter, but he was past caring. 'I'm sure I'm owed some holiday, or sick leave. Maybe even compassionate leave... If not, tough.' He made a derogatory noise. 'I don't really care either way, so I'm leaving now. I'm sorry if that makes you short-staffed for the rest of the evening, Trish, but that's Donna's problem, not yours. Perhaps this is one you should let her handle.'

'Oh, I will, don't worry. Donna is very aware how furious I am. I hope you know this had nothing to do with me,' she added. 'You explained the reason why you'd been sleeping in your car so I know it was only a temporary thing. I gave you my word I wouldn't say anything, so I don't know how Donna found out.'

'Except it wasn't temporary, Trish. I think we both know that.' Tam sighed. 'It doesn't much matter now anyway.' He turned to go.

'It does matter, though,' said Trish. 'Of course it matters, and the way I feel now, I've a mind to come with you.'

Tam softened. 'Trish, you can't do that. The residents here love you. What would they do without you?'

'They love you too, Tam. Please stay, we can work something out.'

He shook his head. 'Thanks for everything you've done, Trish, I appreciate it. It's been nice working with you.'

Trish opened her mouth to reply, but instead she leaned forward and kissed his cheek. 'You too,' she said. 'And I mean that. Keep in touch, and take care of yourself, won't you?'

Tam dipped his head and walked away. He was pretty sure that Trish stood watching him, but he didn't look back. He turned the corner into the corridor where Eleanor's room lay and stood on the threshold for a moment, looking around for one last time. Everything was different now. The chair was in the wrong place, the bedlinen was new – too modern for Eleanor who, if it didn't have roses on it, didn't want to know – and the picture hooks were bare of all the joyful family photos she had so loved. He got on well with Trish, but it was Eleanor who had made his time at Chawston House so enjoyable. There really *was* no reason for him to stay. He collected his coat from the staffroom, and without a backward glance, silently pulled the front door closed behind him.

The car park looked different at this hour. It had a purpose to it, a life that was missing at the tail end of the day or in the early morning, and he was unused to there being so many cars. He stood next to his own, pondering what to do with the hours which unexpectedly lay ahead of him. But, as usual, there was very little choice. He could either sit in his car and read, or maybe listen to some music, or he could do what he did on his days off, which was to visit any one of the few places where you could linger, unchallenged, for a reasonable period of time without the need to spend any money. The library had been his salvation on more than one occasion, but it wasn't open today. Unlocking the car, he dumped his bag on the back seat and, straightening, zipped his jacket up to the neck. He would head for the river before it got dark.

It was always beautiful there, and Tam did his best to let the gentle ripples of water calm his soul, but even the blackbirds calling from the tops of the bushes didn't move him like they usually did. His head was full of crashing thoughts, too many to single one out and make any sense of it, so he walked until dusk had fallen. Then he turned slowly back into town where he nursed a solitary black coffee in a run-down cafe for another hour.

After that, there was nothing else for it but to head back to his car. With the sun gone the air was rapidly becoming colder and he climbed into the front seat, laying his head back against it. He wouldn't get any dinner now he'd left his shift early, and although his stomach was beginning to growl with hunger, he didn't regret what he'd done. He sighed heavily as the same parade of thoughts began their march around his head. He just couldn't understand how Chawston House could have found out about him. Granted, someone from there might have seen him in his car, in the same way Trish had, but he didn't think another member of staff would be so cruel as to dob him in. What did it matter to them? A member of the public then...? A concerned citizen? But again, it made no sense to Tam why anyone— His thoughts crashed to a halt. It suddenly made a great deal of sense...

He scrambled from his car, slamming the door hard enough to make the vehicle rock, and then took off at speed, anger fuelling his every step.

Fifteen short minutes later, he reached his destination and knocked on the door in front of him.

'Tam...' He was gratified to see the look of surprise on Chris's face. 'Did you want to come in?'

'No, I'm fine here.'

'Okay... but at least come into the hall if you're not staying, it's freezing with the door open.'

'Nice and warm in there, are you?' asked Tam. 'Got a nice little fire going?'

Something in Tam's tone must have registered with Chris because his expression instantly changed from wary to down-right uncomfortable. 'I do, as it happens. But like I said, you're welcome to come in.'

Tam wasn't about to give him the courtesy of an answer. They stared at one another for a moment, silent in the dark, empty street.

'Oh, hang on a minute.' Chris's face grew suddenly animated as a thought occurred to him. Something he no doubt hoped would ease the conversational difficulties. 'Another letter came for you today, I'll just go and fetch it.'

He left the door open, disappearing back down the hallway and, without his bulk standing in the way, Tam could feel the warmth from the house seeping towards him. He wasn't the sort to wish ill on anyone, but vague thoughts flitted through his head – like how much he would love to drag Chris from his complacent, smug life and lock him out of his house – see how he liked a night in the cold. Except that people like Chris would never have to suffer like that – there'd always be someone, somewhere he could take advantage of.

'Here you go.' Chris attempted a jovial grin which Tam would have dearly loved to wipe from his face. 'Not working today?' he asked.

Tam silently shook his head.

'Day off then. Been up to anything nice?'

'Nope, no day off.' Tam stared at him, hoping Chris could feel his seething contempt. 'In fact, I was there earlier. I had my review meeting today, the one where they should have appointed me to permanent staff now that my probationary period is over. But you know what, Chris, they didn't do that. Instead they... I believe the kind term for it is "let me go". Sacked. Terminated. Call it what you like. I don't have a job any more.'

Chris's face registered shock. 'Mate, that's awful. I don't know what to say...'

Tam regarded him coldly. 'No? How about I'm sorry?'

'I don't understand... I...'

'Don't you? Are you sure about that, Chris? Because the funny thing is that when my boss explained that she'd had to fire me on account of me being homeless, I wouldn't have given the question as to how she came by that information much thought. Not until she mentioned that it would have been far better for me if I hadn't lied to them in the first place. If I hadn't given them a false address when I started. And as soon as she said that, I began to wonder... Because how would they know that, Chris? How could they possibly find out when no one else knew, apart from you? I thought you were a bastard before, but now...' He turned away in disgust. 'I don't even have the words for what you are.'

Chris's face grew hard. 'It was an easy mistake to make.'

'A mistake? Is that what it was?'

'Yes!' Chris glared at him. 'I was trying to do you a favour. A letter came and it looked important, so I dropped it off at the care home. I didn't know she was your boss when I spoke to her...'

'What did you say, Chris?' Tam's tone carried a warning.

'I can't really remember,' he replied, looking flustered now. 'But maybe I did mention you didn't actually live here, I don't know.'

It was all beginning to make perfect sense to Tam.

'Oh, I think you do know, Chris. I think you remember exactly what you said.'

'So what if I did? I've done you a favour, mate, but you're so pig-headed you can't even see it.'

'You've done me *what?*'

'A favour. I asked you before to come and work for me, well, now you can. It's a proper job, Tam. You wouldn't have to degrade yourself any more, you could do something you enjoyed. Get back to how you were before.'

Tam closed his eyes, more angry than he could remember being in a long while. 'I don't believe this. How could you even think I'd be remotely interested after what you've done? Once was bad enough...' He shook his head furiously, clenching his fists by his side.

'You and your stupid pride,' muttered Chris. 'For heaven's sake, man, can you not see where it's got you? Nowhere, that's where, and with *nothing.*'

'I have my honesty and my integrity. They might be nothing to you, but they're the only things that have been keeping me warm at night.'

'See? That's exactly what I mean. You say those words like they're the holy grail, Tam, but it's bollocks. They're *meaningless* when you have nothing. I'm offering you a real job. A job with good pay, solid prospects. A job which I know you'd give your eye teeth for. Back in the game, doing what you love.'

'Don't you dare kid yourself you're helping me, Chris. Not when the truth of it is that you're talentless. You don't have it in you to run a business. Look what happened when you were left to your own devices the last time. I trusted you, Chris, and I'm not about to make the same mistake again. You only want me on board because you know you'll fail without me. There's nothing altruistic about this. Just selfish need, same as always. I'm just gutted I never saw it before until it was too late.'

'You'd be mad to pass this up.'

Tam's mouth gaped open. 'Or surprisingly sane,' he hissed, and walked away.

28

Beth

Beth winced in sympathy as Frankie struggled to fill the kettle with water.

'Here, let me,' she said, taking it from her and pausing to study her face. She looked pale, and there were dark smudges under her eyes. Beth acknowledged that this might be due to the soft lighting in her flat, but Frankie's smile also seemed tired, and perhaps a little forced? She turned off the tap and set the kettle to boil.

'Sorry to call by unannounced, but I'm on my way to work and I couldn't virtually pass your doorstep without checking you're okay.' She eyed the sling which Frankie was still wearing. 'How's it feeling?' she asked.

'Okay, I think. I haven't tried to do anything, just in case. And I've been asleep, so... I'm pretty sure it's just a sprain though, like you said.'

'Even so, I'll feel happier if I take a look.'

'Are you sure you've got time?'

Beth gave her an admonishing look. 'I'm positive. Now... mugs?' There were several by the sink, still dirty, but she didn't want to presume. 'I'll wash these, shall I?'

Frankie immediately got to her feet. 'I'll do them.'

Beth gently gripped her shoulders and steered her towards the table. 'You'll do no such thing,' she said. 'Sit down and enjoy being waited on. Washing a couple of mugs isn't going to kill me.'

Frankie gave a rueful smile. 'Thank you. I'd have done them but a very good friend of mine told me I should rest my wrist.'

Beth grinned and turned to the task in hand.

'I hope you're not going to work tonight,' she added as she began to run water into the sink.

'I have to, there's no one else.'

'But how on earth will you manage? The fact that there's no one to take your place isn't your problem, is it? Surely the owner should sort that out.'

Frankie's gaze dropped a moment and she shrugged. 'She's not well herself, and I don't really want to bother her just now. And I'll be fine. William is going to help me again.'

Beth was about to respond with a teasing reply when she realised that Frankie didn't look as pleased about the prospect as she thought she would. 'Is everything okay?' she asked. 'You look a little... preoccupied. Not your usual cheerful self.'

Frankie gave a wan smile. 'I had a phone call just after I got home this morning, and it's rather thrown me for six. Not to worry though, it'll sort itself.' She visibly brightened her face. 'You, however, look like all your birthdays and Christmases have come together.'

'Do I?' Despite its wetness, Beth put a hand to her cheek. She hadn't come to talk about herself but she was bursting with happiness and dying to tell Frankie her news. 'I've had a brilliant day. Well, Jack has... we both have.' Her excitement was hard to contain.

And for the first time since she opened the door, Frankie's face lit up, her beautiful smile back in place.

'Good job we're having tea then,' she said. 'You can tell me all about it.'

'What I hadn't given Tam credit for is how easily he looks after Jack,' said Beth a few minutes later, once they were settled. 'He's not awkward in his company. He doesn't step politely around his disability, nor dodge potentially embarrassing questions. It's as if he has this inbuilt knowledge of how to act...' She broke off. 'Sorry, that sounds a bit rude. I'm not implying that everyone... or maybe I am...' She smiled. 'It's just that most people we come across see the chair first before they even consider Jack as a person.'

'Does he take sugar?' said Frankie, nodding in sympathy.

'Yes, exactly that. But Tam is different. He makes no assumptions either. He's actually built a – I'm not sure what you'd call it – a cage thing that fits over the seat of the quad bike so Jack can go on the back of it. It's extraordinary. He took Jack out today, toured the whole farm just so that he could see it again.' She paused, feeling her throat tighten at the memory of Jack's face earlier. 'It's been nearly ten years,' she added. 'Can you imagine? I never thought I'd see Jack look so happy again, and I can't thank Tam enough for what he's done.' She dropped her head.

Most of her thoughts had been happy ones, but they also rode tandem with a whole bunch of others she was struggling with. 'I also can't believe I got it so wrong,' she said. 'All those years I denied Jack, discouraged him from doing anything which reminded him of his old life. I've let him quietly decline just like the farm has, mouldering away until there was almost nothing left.'

'Oh, Beth...' Frankie squeezed her hand. 'You mustn't be so hard on yourself. You're the reason why Jack is here in the first place, why he's *still* here. And everything you've done has been because you love him. Even if events are now showing you a different way forward, you mustn't ever think what you've done is worthless. Without you, none of this would be happening. Without Tam, too. What goes around comes around, Beth. You've made a friend of Tam, and I don't think he has too many of those. We don't always know why things happen the way they do, but recognising magic when it comes into our lives is a special talent only a few people have.' She gave her a pointed look. 'And yes, I do mean you.'

Beth's cheeks flushed in response, and she was reminded of how pleased she'd felt when Frankie said yes to her invitation to have coffee. It seemed such a long time ago, but Beth knew that Frankie had been just as pleased as her. Tam wasn't the only one who needed a friend. They all did.

'*You've* made a friend of Tam as well,' Beth replied. 'And me, and William too... Seems like I'm not the only one with a special talent.' She grinned. 'And I'm very glad you have William looking after you,' she said. 'You have to admit, there is a little of the knight in shining armour about him.'

Frankie laughed. 'There is, I—' She stopped, swallowing. 'Beth, can I tell you something? I should have shared it before, but it's not something I find easy to talk about.'

'Of course you can... Are you sure everything is okay? I thought there was something wrong when I arrived.'

Frankie nodded. 'But this kind of has to do with William as well, so...' She frowned. 'I'm not going to make you late, am I?'

Beth shook her head but held up her hand to stall her slightly. 'Let me look at your wrist while you talk.' She began to undo the knot on Frankie's sling with deft fingers.

'When I slipped over last night, it was because my feet wouldn't move me fast enough. I was running away from the bakery because I was terrified that someone from my past had caught up with me.' She cleared her throat. 'That someone was my husband. I think I mentioned him before, only in the past tense, as an ex-husband. I don't use his name any more – Nightingale is my maiden name – but technically we're still married…' She winced slightly as Beth lowered her arm. 'He'd shoved a letter through the door of the shop and, when I found it, the only thing I could think of was getting away. I've been running for a long time, Beth, and yet, when I was really scared, I ran to William… and I'm kind of having a hard time dealing with that.' She grimaced. 'My head's all over the place.'

Beth drew her brows together. 'Hold on a minute, that's a lot of information.' She stilled her probing fingers on Frankie's wrist. 'You're saying you're *still* married? And to a not very nice man, by the sounds of it. Why were you so scared? What has he done?' She thought quickly. 'Maybe this is something you should be telling the police.'

But Frankie shook her head. 'No. I've been down that road before… And Robert hasn't done anything, not recently anyhow.'

'But he's been abusive in the past?' And suddenly, threads of their previous conversations came back to her. How Frankie had once said her life was complicated, how she was revelling in being able to make her own decisions now that she was on her own, but most of all how she loved the calming darkness, away from people and their judgements of her. A time when she could reclaim the person she was, instead of the one she had pretended to be.

'It's why you work the night shift, isn't it?' she said. 'You've been hiding from him. Hiding from everyone. Oh, Frankie…' She moved her fingers away from Frankie's wrist so that she could gently squeeze her hand. 'You tried to tell me before, didn't you? And I just waffled on about my own problems, how I was feeling about Jack, my job… I'm so sorry.'

'Don't be,' replied Frankie. 'My problems are no more important than anyone else's. And you needed to express how you'd been feeling, too. The simple fact of saying the words aloud has probably helped you get to the point you're at now.'

Beth returned her attention to Frankie's wrist, partly out of necessity, but partly because she needed time to process what Frankie had said. To acknowledge the truth of it and recall how easy it had been to confide in her. To tell her things which she had kept hidden, even from herself. She'd been right to trust her instincts – Frankie *had* come into her life for a reason. Which meant that the reverse was also true.

'You said that Robert put a note through the door of the bakery, but do you think he knows about your flat too?'

Frankie shook her head. 'The letter implied that he did, but I don't know for sure. I haven't seen him here. Although, to be fair, I didn't *see* him at the bakery either, his letter just spooked me. I think I was seeing shadows at that point.'

'Understandable.' Beth gritted her teeth, furious that a man she hadn't even met was causing Frankie such anguish. 'So, what does he want? Because whatever it is, he isn't going to get it.'

'He claims he wants to meet up – just so that we can attend to the practical arrangements for moving forward with our lives. And by that, I assume he means a divorce. But that won't be what he wants, Beth, it's just the civilised face he's putting on things. That was always the problem. He's incredibly good at appearing to be the model husband – kind, loving, extremely caring, and ever so reasonable. It took *me* years to figure out what was really going on. Most of my friends never took the time to work it out though, or listen when I told them. My family were the same. They still see the break-up of our marriage as my fault. We hardly speak now.'

Beth looked up, stunned. 'What? How long ago did this happen?'

'Eighteen months. But we were married for nigh on thirty years, so they had a long time to listen to Robert's lies about me, his insinuations about my mental health, his control disguised as love. If I were in their shoes, I'd probably think the same.'

Beth doubted that very much. Frankie was far too astute, and far too kind and understanding. 'Is that what he did? Made out you were going cuckoo?'

'Kind of,' replied Frankie, smiling sadly at the memory. 'It was more that I had my little "difficulties" – things they should be considerate of – and it doesn't take long for suggestions like those to be taken at face value. Trouble was, by the end, he had eroded all my self-confidence, all my ability to make decisions for myself. I'd practically become the person he'd convinced everyone I was. And yet, there he was doing his utmost to look after his wife. It's easy to see why everyone sided with him, how they felt sorry for him.'

'But surely that was his plan all along? Wasn't that the point?'

'It was, of course it was. But it meant that I had very little to fight with. Even now, I'm not sure how I managed to get away.'

The almost unbearable pain in Frankie's eyes was hard to look at, but it also struck something deep within Beth. Something deep and determined. 'Have you decided to meet him? Because if you have, there's no way you're doing it alone. I'll come with you... Or I'll sit somewhere close by ready to charge in and batter him if he puts a foot out of line.'

Frankie smiled. 'You know William offered to do much the same, but... would you really do that for me? Are you sure you don't mind? It *is* time I stopped running and faced up to him, and if you were there, I don't think I'd be so fearful. It's the fear that gets in the way of everything.'

Beth was resolute. 'Nothing would give me greater pleasure,' she said. 'In fact, if William has offered to do the same, perhaps he should be there as well? I don't know what Robert looks like, but William's a big bloke – he could scare the pants off him.'

'I know. I was very tempted to take him up on his offer, but I don't think it would give quite the right message. It would make it look like William and I were... you know, a thing.'

'A thing?' Beth returned a teasing smile. 'And what exactly would that be?'

A rosy bloom welled up Frankie's neck. 'Don't. I'm giving myself a hard time over him as it is.'

Beth pointed a finger at her chest in amusement, as if to say *who, me?* 'Just tell me what's so horrific about being in a thing with William?'

'I don't know, that's what's so stupid. But I don't want to give him the wrong idea. I've already turned up at his flat, thrown myself into his arms and cried all over him. Twice, actually.'

'But you were scared, hurt and upset. What's wrong with that? Would you be worried if you'd done that to me? Because I doubt it. Why does him being a bloke make it different? He's still your friend.'

'It's not him being a bloke that I'm worried about per se. I mean, it is, but only because...' She paused, looking sheepish. 'Because I wanted him to kiss me. There, I've said it.' She dropped her head. 'I mean, I really, *really* wanted him to kiss me. And believe me, that's not something I've thought about in a very long time.' She shook her head. 'I think there must be something wrong with me.'

'On the contrary,' said Beth. 'I think, given all that we've said here tonight, there's something very right with you. I think it's proof of how ready you are to consign Robert and everything he did to the past. The future is what's important now. Perhaps it's time for the nightingale to fly again.'

To Beth's surprise, an anxious expression came over Frankie's face. 'Except that it's not that simple, is it? You know that phone call I mentioned earlier?' She sighed. 'It was from my boss, the owner of the bakery. She thinks she's found someone to buy the business. I knew it was going to happen, but I really thought I'd have more time, and what's worse is that the prospective buyer is a property developer, so he wants to buy the flat too.'

Beth's mouth dropped open. 'I don't know what to say... that's awful news. Can she do that? Yes, silly, of course she can. But there must be something we can do. Has she said how soon it's going to happen?'

Frankie shook her head. 'She and her husband still need to sell their house before they can move and buy something else, so I guess it will be as long as it takes for that to happen. She hasn't said yet whether this person will want to keep me on, but if they don't, there's not a lot I can do.'

Thoughts were whirling in Beth's mind. There wasn't any sense to them yet, but... 'We'll sort this, Frankie. I don't know how, but one thing at a time, we'll sort this.' She glanced at her watch and pulled a face. 'I'm really sorry, but I'm going to be late if I don't get a move on. Are you sure you're okay being here on your own?'

Frankie nodded. 'I won't be on my own, William will be here soon. He said he'd walk me to work.' She rolled her eyes. 'All of the four steps from my flat to the bakery's front door.'

'Good. And make sure you don't do anything. Your wrist won't take it kindly if you do, and it'll be a few more days before you can even begin to test it. Keep it in the sling and, if you can bear to, just rotate it gently every hour or so to keep it mobile.'

'Don't worry, I'm quite happy to let William take over. He's got the makings of a surprisingly good baker.' She checked herself as if a thought had suddenly crossed her mind. 'Shouldn't you hear about *your* job soon?' she asked.

Beth swallowed. 'It might even be tonight. And I'm hopeful things will be all right. I passed Matron in the corridor as I left this morning and, although she didn't say anything, she gave me a huge thumbs up. You wouldn't do that if you were about to make someone redundant, would you? Besides, I can't believe the universe would be so unkind now, not when for the first time in a long time there's a little glimmer of hope.'

Frankie got up to walk Beth to the door, pulling her into a one-armed hug at the last minute. 'Sometimes all you need is hope,' she said.

29

Frankie

Frankie knew she shouldn't, but she couldn't help but watch William while he worked. And while it was true that she did need to keep an eye on what he was doing, there were plenty of occasions when her gaze lingered even though she knew he was quite capable of performing the task in hand. For a big man, he was surprisingly agile, and had an economy of movement that fascinated her. It was no surprise that he lifted the huge tubs of dough with ease, likewise the sacks of flour, but he could also handle pastry with an unexpectedly light touch. He caught her looking once or twice, fixated by the way the tendons rippled in his arms as he kneaded dough, but he didn't say a thing, simply smiled.

Just as he promised, William had called by the flat a few minutes before she was due to leave. It had felt odd after being on her own. Odd, but oddly nice, too, even if she did feel a little awkward. Her confession to Beth about wanting William to kiss her was still far too fresh in her mind and she was sure it would show in her face as she greeted him. But, if it had, William gave no sign that he noticed.

Her awkwardness aside, however, she was still incredibly grateful for William's help. For all she knew, Robert might be watching her, but he would never show himself if William were around. Despite Beth's offer to be at their meeting, the thought of seeing Robert again still terrified her, but she had an even more pressing problem now. She had no idea what she would do when the bakery sold, and the possibility of losing her job and her home was a reality she couldn't ignore.

'Penny for them?' said William, as she stared vacantly out of the window.

'You're good at this,' she said. 'I was just wondering if you'd like a job, which is a bit of a bugger really given that Vivienne thinks she might have found a buyer for the business.'

William paused mid-knead, up to his knuckles in as yet sticky dough. 'What?' he said. 'How soon?'

Frankie pulled a face. 'I don't know, she didn't say.' She quickly relayed the contents of the conversation.

Dismay tugged the corners of William's mouth downward. 'So, you still don't know what that means for you?'

'Nope. But I get it. Who wouldn't want to go and live by the sea given half the chance? I know she's been poorly, but I like it here, William. And just when it looked as if things might be getting better, too. Great timing.' She paused. 'Sorry, that makes me sound horrible...' William's impression of her was suddenly very important. 'And I'm not, honestly. I understand perfectly how she must be feeling, but—'

A knock on the door interrupted her. It was Tam, peering at them through the window. Frankie hurried to let him in.

'I'm glad you're here,' she said. 'William's such a hard taskmaster, he won't let me stop for a second, and I'm dying for a cup of tea.'

William snorted. 'As if.'

Tam eyed her wrist. 'Is it feeling any better?'

'Much better... as long as I don't move it.'

Tam winced. 'Well, if you need any more help... I'm not sure how much use I'll be, but the spirit's willing.'

'Thanks, Tam. I'll see how the new apprentice goes and let you know.'

'Oi,' muttered William, pretending to be offended. 'The new apprentice is doing just fine, thank you.'

Frankie held her hand up to her mouth as if to shield her words from William, and stage-whispered, 'I'll be in touch.'

'Anyway, he already has a job,' said William. 'He's not having this one.'

'*You* already have a job,' replied Frankie, grinning.

'Oh yeah... good point.'

'Actually, I don't have a job,' said Tam quietly. 'They've let me go.'

The room became suddenly hushed.

'What?' Frankie looked between the two men. 'How have you lost your job? That can't be right.'

Tam took a deep breath. 'It came as a surprise to me as well. But I had my review meeting earlier – my probationary period has come to an end – and, as far as I was aware, everything had been going well. I was expecting to be offered a permanent position, not have it taken away from me.'

'Well, I hope they had the decency to say why.' She frowned. 'It's not more cutbacks, is it?'

Tam shook his head. 'No. It's because some kind soul let them know I don't have a permanent address and am sleeping in my car. Apparently, that doesn't fit with their expectations of a model employee.'

'But can't you complain about it? Take it further?' Frankie ushered him to the table to sit down. 'That's disgusting.'

'It is, but there's nothing I can do,' he said, laying down the flask and hot-water bottle he'd been carrying. 'That's exactly what a probationary period is for – so they can get rid of you if they need to. My manager's a bit officious, but even she had the decency to look embarrassed. Said she has a duty of care and had to act upon the information she'd been given. Not that she took the decision lightly – she wanted me to know that. She'd gone to head office and consulted with HR, but their advice was clear. She was sorry, but they wouldn't be offering me a permanent contract.'

'That's bullshit,' retorted Frankie. 'Sorry, but it is.' She looked at William for agreement.

He nodded, joining them at the table. 'Of the worst kind,' he replied. 'But legally, I expect they are in the clear. Morally, I hope they find it hard sleeping at night. That doesn't change the situation though.'

'No, besides, it's too late for that. The deputy manager's a decent sort, and she's made a complaint, saying the company should reconsider their decision. She reckons I stand a good chance of being reinstated. But I wouldn't go back, not now. I walked out, actually – I couldn't bear to be there knowing what they thought of me.'

Frankie studied him for a moment, such a kind and gentle man, and began to feel angrier than ever. Tam was exactly the sort of person they *should* be employing, and yet they had tried to disguise their spineless action as being in the best interests of their residents. They should be standing up for people like Tam, not grinding them further into the mire. 'This is just the kind of shallow-minded behaviour that infuriates me,' she said. 'That good, honest people get treated so appallingly because they don't fit perfectly into the little boxes we're all supposed to occupy. It's short-sighted. And cowardly, too. Plus, you should have a choice, not have to be so snivellingly grateful for a job that you put up with working for people like that,' she added. 'And if you have the audacity to have any principles, well, you need to forget those pretty sharpish. It's very easy to have morals and principles when you're wealthy, and virtually impossible if you're not. It's just plain wrong, on every level.' She shook her head in disgust, catching William's eye as she did so. He looked astonished by her outburst. 'Sorry,' she said. 'I'm ranting. Things like this make me so angry.'

'Oh, I agree with you,' replied William, giving Frankie a curious look which, unaccountably, made her blush.

'I agree with you too,' added Tam. 'It's an impossible situation.'

Frankie smiled. 'And me ranting doesn't help you either. I wish I could think of something which would. What will you do?'

Tam shrugged. 'Look for another job. And keep myself busy in the meantime. I've been over to Beth's today, giving Jack some help with the farm. There probably aren't enough hours in the day for everything he wants to do there, but at least now I might be able to give him a few more.'

'Beth mentioned you'd been over,' said Frankie. 'In fact, mentioned isn't quite the right word. Talked about you in very glowing terms would be more appropriate. You've made a big difference to Jack's life, you know. I'm not sure if you're aware quite how much it means to him, and Beth.'

'It's made a big difference to me too,' replied Tam. 'Losing my business was like losing the most important part of myself, the part which sustained everything else. And the fact that it was ripped out from under me...' He broke off, and Frankie could see the rigid tension in his jaw. 'So, getting back out on the land has been a joy. Despite what's happened today, I'm really looking forward to going back there. I've missed that sense of optimism, of excitement.' His face suddenly fell. 'Don't mention the job thing to Beth though, will you?'

'I won't if you don't want me to,' replied Frankie. 'But why ever not?'

'Because I know she feels she ought to pay me for the work I do, and I don't want her to feel awkward about it. They can't afford it and they're going to need every spare penny if they want to make the farm a going concern again. But I know Beth – if she finds out I've lost my job, she'll feel even worse, and I don't want to put her in a difficult situation. I don't spend much, and I still have some of this month's salary left. I'll be okay.'

'But what will you do for food? I know you used to have at least one meal while you were at work.' She watched as Tam tried to formulate an answer, knowing that he would want to spare their feelings by insisting he'd get by. She frowned. 'Wait a minute... you said you walked out. What time was this? Tam, have you actually had *anything* to eat today?'

He looked up, mouth open, but then glanced away, too embarrassed to reply.

'*Tam...*' Frankie felt terrible. 'Why didn't you say something? You're among friends here, and in case you hadn't noticed, countless loaves of bread and an abundance of pastries too. What would you like?'

'You honestly don't have to do this, Frankie. It's very kind of you, but—'

Tam didn't get any further as his stomach suddenly let out a loud growl. Frankie's hand went to her mouth and for a moment she wasn't sure what to say. She glanced at William, only to see that he was trying desperately hard not to laugh.

'Well, that's your argument right out the window,' he said, grinning. 'Betrayed by your own stomach...'

Tam groaned. 'I don't believe that just happened,' he said. He shook his head in amusement. 'Talk about timing...'

'Your stomach obviously knows what's good for it,' said Frankie.

'Aye, I reckon it does...' He pursed his lips. 'I'm not very good at asking for help,' he said. 'But I think I need to start practising.'

Frankie nodded. 'You do... so, being serious for a minute,

will you have something to eat with us? Not only now, but whenever you're hungry. Obviously, I'm only here at night, but you're very welcome to come up to the flat and have something with me. I have to eat too.'

The tips of Tam's ears were pink but he smiled, a little shy but also, she could see, touched beyond measure. 'Thank you,' he said. 'Really, that means a great deal.'

William, who had been sitting with two fingers placed across his lips, clearly thinking about something, leaned forward. 'Listen, I made out before that staying at my place would be a problem. It might be, but I should stand up for what I believe in. I'm quite happy to take on my landlord if it comes to it, and although it's not a huge place, you're welcome to stay there. I appreciate you might like your own space, even if it is only your car, but I want you to know it's not your only option here.' He held up a hand. 'And don't dismiss it outright because you don't want to impose on me. Think about it, please.'

Tam nodded. 'I will. I promise I will. And thank you, that's—'

'No thanks required. I should have offered it ages ago. And even if the answer's no, then going forward, you can use my address as your own. At least that might help you with your job hunting. You mentioned before your mate didn't like you using his.'

'Yeah, well, he's definitely no mate, and after what I said to him earlier, I very much doubt I could use his address even if I wanted to.'

Frankie frowned. 'How so?'

'Because he was the person who ratted on me to my employers.'

'But why on earth would he do that?' she said, horrified on Tam's behalf.

'Because he's a nasty piece of work, by the sounds of it,' said William.

Tam nodded. 'Yes, that, and because he wants me to work for him. He said he hadn't meant to tell them and then, in the next breath, told me he'd done me a favour and I should jump at the chance of his job.'

'Of all the slimy... Are some people really that stupid?' asked Frankie. 'How on earth did he think you'd work for him after he's betrayed you not once, but twice now?'

'I reckon he was banking on you being desperate,' said William. 'Which is the worst kind of blackmail if you think about it.'

Frankie shook her head. 'No one should ever be that desperate. Don't do it, Tam. Something else will turn up, I'm sure of it.' William gave her a pointed look. 'Yes, I know I'm a fine one to talk but...'

'Don't worry, I'm not about to,' replied Tam. 'Nothing would—' His forehead suddenly furrowed. 'Why are you a fine one to talk?' he asked.

Frankie shook her head as if to bat away his question. 'I've just found out the owner of this place might have found a buyer. But that doesn't matter now. What matters is that—'

'Of course it matters,' interrupted Tam. 'I'm banging on about my job when a potential bombshell of your own is about to explode. How long will you have?'

'I have no idea yet,' replied Frankie. 'Vivienne will ask them to keep me on, but I'll have to wait and see.'

'And what about your flat? Will they let you stay there too?'

'Possibly, but the chap who's interested is a developer. I expect he'll want to do the place up and then rent it out for a price I haven't a hope of affording. No doubt the bakery will get a makeover too, become "artisanal".' She put quotes around her last word with her fingers. 'Although I suppose it could do with a bit of something... I mean, it's fine, but it's never going to win any awards, is it?'

'I guess not...' Tam's gaze travelled around the room. 'I

hadn't really thought about it, but maybe it could do with a little sprucing up.'

'I'm not sure Vivienne's heart is in it any more. Even before she got sick she didn't bother much with the place, and she's had it for years. There's actually some beautiful display stuff she no longer uses in the storeroom – she just sits the bread straight on the shelves. I hadn't thought much about it either until now, but it's not exactly inviting. A bit utilitarian, maybe. And the use of the space here doesn't work all that well, I've thought that for a while. There's all this room out the back and yet the front is so cramped you can hardly get anyone in there. Three people and the shop's crowded out.'

William gave Tam a knowing smile. 'I think someone else might like to own it,' he said.

'Who?' Frankie frowned at his expression. 'What, me? God no, I wouldn't know the first thing about running a business. Baking the bread I love, but I wouldn't want the responsibility.'

'Not even if it meant you'd be sitting in the driving seat instead of being a passenger?' said William. 'Responsible for the things which happen in your life instead of feeling as if someone else was in control?'

Frankie's mouth gaped open. William wasn't criticising her, she only had to look at the warmth in his eyes to know that. He was telling her her life was worth it, that *she* was worth it. She swallowed. Was she? She was about to reply when Tam cut in.

'From the man who lost his business this might sound like a load of rubbish, but as long as it's something you truly care about, then running a business is no different from anything else in your life. We take care of the things we love, the things which bring us joy and which make us happy. Learning how to do that is never a chore. I wouldn't want the responsibility of baking bread which is going to be sold to members of the public, yet *you* love it.' He raised his eyebrows as if to challenge her. 'So, you might find it isn't all that difficult after all.'

William sat back in his chair and folded his arms, an amused expression on his face. 'Playing devil's advocate for a minute then... If you *were* running this place, what would you do?'

'Oh, nice try,' replied Frankie. 'But it's never going to happen, is it?'

'Humour me,' said William. 'I'm just interested, that's all.'

Frankie held his look for a moment before pushing back her chair and getting to her feet. 'I'll put the kettle on,' she said. 'And then I'll get you something to eat, Tam.'

'Go on,' said William. 'I really want to know.'

Tam grinned. 'And me.'

Frankie was on her way to the sink, but she stopped, half turning. Thinking better of it, she turned back, but then spun around, this time looking directly at Tam.

'You know the very first time we met you told me that the worst thing about being homeless is that there's nowhere to go at night? How alone it feels? Well, that's what I'd do,' she said. 'I'd open up this place. I'd make the night a little less closed.'

30

William

Ever since leaving Frankie that morning, William had been in an agony of indecision for most of the day. First of all, there'd been that moment on her doorstep when he'd come so close to kissing her. An action which, had he gone through with it, would most likely have destroyed any chance of their fledgling friendship continuing as it had. And yet, there had been something, he'd been certain of it. Something which danced in the air between them and... Or perhaps it was simply that he wished there was. Which, after all this time, was a problem.

Because William was a bad bet. He hadn't meant to, and maybe it was just that he hadn't responded all that well to the blows life had dealt him, but, all the same, he'd let down everyone who ever meant anything to him. And he didn't want that for Frankie. Couldn't bear the thought of it. When he was younger, it was easy to tell himself that grief was to blame for his actions. That he hadn't been himself, hadn't been thinking straight, and maybe that was true, it *had* been hard to come to terms with, but he wasn't a kid now and no longer had any excuse. Fifty-two years on the planet and he thought he'd be settled by now. Or at least feel the wisdom of his years. So what did he do now that he found himself thinking things might be different?

Finding out what he had at the library meant he was finally in a position where he might be able to make a difference, if not to keep his promise exactly, then at least to uphold the spirit of it. But taking that chance could spell disaster, and if things blew up in his face then he didn't want Frankie anywhere near when it happened.

He stole another look at her, head bent, as she sat at the table and nursed another cup of tea. It was three in the morning and Tam had long since gone, but the conversation which had started while he was there had continued for a while afterwards. Listening to Frankie talk about all the things she would do if the bakery were hers had tugged at his heartstrings even harder, and he marvelled that this woman, who had been so afraid of life that she hid herself away from it, could be so caring and generous. She had also been very open and honest with William, something he had failed at miserably. Her past had literally caught up with her, and even though she was scared, she had allowed herself to be vulnerable before him.

She deserved so much better than William, that was the truth of it. And yet, what she'd said about having morals and principles had struck a chord with him. It was easy when you were wealthy, she'd said, and virtually impossible if you were not. She so clearly understood Tam's dilemma, and the desire to do the right thing even when circumstances meant you couldn't. So might it be possible she could understand his? Was now the time to be honest with *her*, just as she had with him? He sprinkled a little more flour on the worktable and turned out another batch of dough onto it.

William could see why Frankie liked it here, in the warmth of the bakery, alone with her thoughts every night. There was something comforting about the rhythmic kneading and shaping of the doughs, almost relaxing, despite the physicality of it. When he had made bread before, even though the steps he followed were essentially the same, he had never felt as if he were creating anything, never felt the magic of one of the oldest processes in the world. Here, it was different. Here, it was a magic he could touch, one which leapt from his own fingers. He found himself smiling despite the mess of confusion inside his head.

'It gets you like that, doesn't it?' said Frankie, looking up at him. He could see she was tired, and possibly still in pain, but her look was warm, her eyes soft on his.

'Sorry?'

Frankie indicated the dough he had been kneading. 'I said it gets you like that. You look like you're away with the fairies.'

William nudged his forearm against his nose to chase away an itch. 'I think I was. You lose yourself in it, don't you – the rhythm. It's almost hypnotic.'

She smiled. 'I've put right many a wrong since I've been here, standing just as you are now. I swear sometimes I'd get to morning and not even realise I'd made all the bread. It just sort of happened while my brain was off somewhere, doing its thing.' She tipped her head to one side. 'So, what's your brain wrestling with?'

William shrugged. 'Nothing much. Load of nonsense, probably.'

'With that look on your face?' she replied. 'I don't believe that for a minute. I've been watching you the last half hour, deep in some conundrum or other. Your eyebrows have been doing quite the dance.'

'Have they? What were they doing, a waltz or a foxtrot?'

He expected her to laugh, to smile at least, but Frankie's face remained curious. And watchful.

'Come on,' she said. 'Out with it. I've spilled all my beans, time for you to offload yours. I know we said before about not knowing everything there was to know about each other, but I know virtually nothing about you. That doesn't seem right somehow.'

'How long have you got?'

But Frankie wasn't buying into his attempt at levity. 'Quite a few hours yet, as well you know. Plenty of time for some life history, *and* to tell me what's got you so perturbed.' Her eyes narrowed. 'Are you worried about your job, about the thing with Stuart, is that it? Only I've seen that expression on your face a few times now – a kind of angry, yet sad, determination.'

Damn, she was perceptive, too. Inwardly, William groaned. It would be wonderful to tell her, to unburden himself and even ask her opinion about what he should do, but to do so would mean risking the one thing which had given him any hope for the future. He swallowed. She was still waiting for a reply, and given what she'd suffered in the past, she deserved some honesty. Besides, she was bound to find out in the end, and how much worse would it be to hear about that past from someone else? He took a deep breath, his hands stilling themselves on the dough.

'I said before that I've had a life, done things I'm not espe-cially proud of... Most of it started when I was in my early twen-ties. That was thirty-odd years ago, and sometimes I wonder how I could have been so stupid – but I was young, I guess. We all do stupid things when we're young.'

'That we do. And paying off that debt can take a very long time.' She smiled. She understood. So far, at least...

'I met my Louise when I was twenty-two, and straight off we both knew we had something special. Most of my friends were still being lads, most of her friends were unattached too, but suddenly, within about the space of six months, we were making plans.' William pulled at the ball of dough, turning it over and slapping it back down again.

'Within a year we were married, against everyone's better judgement, it seemed, but somehow that made us even more determined to make a go of things. And that's the part where being too young took its toll,' he continued. 'If we'd listened to each other, focused on what we had rather than what we didn't, we'd have been okay. But we didn't, and I'll never forgive myself for not being strong enough back then. We were both working, but folks didn't go to university when I was young, not like they do now, so neither of us had what my dad would have called prospects. She was working in a shop, and I was labouring for a guy I knew. Money was tight, very tight. We'd both sunk everything we could into getting a place of our own, and to start with it was great fun – weren't we the bee's knees? – but then, while all our friends were out partying and having a rare old time, we were stuck home night after night. It didn't take much for us to be seduced by the lure of something different, something we thought, wrongly, was better than what we had.

'We both started going out, drinking, spending money we didn't have, and it didn't take long for the debts to start piling up. Before we knew it, the life we had, the good life, was teetering on the edge. Trouble was, the guy I was labouring for was nice enough, but his view of what was right and what was wrong was a little blurred around the edges. He wasn't that bothered where he made his money, or who from, and so, after a while, neither was I. I was stupid, I know that now, but I was also desperate, and one thing led to another and... it was petty stuff really, but I ended up in prison for burglary. Not that I'm condoning what I did, far from it...'

He risked a glance at Frankie, but she still wore the same kind expression she'd had when he'd started. If she was shocked, or disgusted, she hid it well.

'I was only in for a few months, but when I got out I discovered Louise was pregnant.'

Frankie's hand had strayed to the middle of her chest, right over her heart. 'The baby was yours, though?' she asked.

'Oh yes, Louise would never... and the dates fitted, but... it wouldn't have mattered. Louise was my wife, the baby was my responsibility.'

William dropped his head, staring at the lump of dough in front of him before driving his fist into it. He looked up immediately, ashamed of his anger, but Frankie simply held his gaze, her eyes full of empathy, of understanding. She thought she understood, but she didn't, not yet. William's head dropped even lower as he was engulfed in a tide of emotion he'd kept at bay for years. He swallowed.

'When I went to prison, I left Louise on her own with no money to speak of and... I don't think she'd been looking after herself very well, hadn't been to half the check-ups she should have and... I'm not saying it was her fault at all, but her blood pressure was sky-high. She developed pre-eclampsia and died shortly after giving birth.'

He wasn't even aware that Frankie was no longer sitting at the table until he felt her behind him, one arm gently turning him round so that she could reach up to lace her fingers around the back of his neck, softly cradling his head and bringing it to her shoulder.

'I'm so sorry,' she whispered, inches from his ear. 'So, so sorry.'

He stayed like that for some time, at first unable to move from under his grief. Grief that was almost as fresh as the day he'd first worn it. But shame came all too soon. There was so much more she didn't know.

'That isn't all,' he managed. 'I have something else to tell you.'

She nodded. 'Okay then, but come and sit down before you fall down. Much as I'd like to, I don't think I can catch you and hang on.'

He looked up, catching her eye, seeing her smile as she repeated the same words he'd said to her.

She waited until he was sitting opposite, before sliding a hand across the table to take his. 'Go on,' she said.

William licked his lips, his mouth dry. 'The baby was only tiny – he'd been born too early, you see, when they rushed Louise into hospital. I was worried about him, but it never even occurred to me that *she* might die. In my naivety I thought everything would be okay. I promised I'd look after her, her and the baby, make everything right again, but then I lost her and... the baby needed so much care, I couldn't...' William broke off, his voice wavering. He swallowed. 'I couldn't cope, I was so scared. I knew I didn't have it in me to look after him so I took off. I left him.'

'I don't suppose it was that simple,' said Frankie gently. 'These things never are.'

But William shook his head. 'No, it was. I was a coward. She had a sister, Louise did, and I knew that she, or someone, would look after the baby, so I ran, went overseas... I worked on the rigs for years, the kind of life that cuts you off from everything. I kidded myself it was the best for everyone concerned, but I didn't even stop to find out, so how would I know?'

He hardly dared to look at Frankie, even though he was very aware that she was studying him intently. Studying him but saying nothing.

'I wanted children,' she said after a moment. 'Desperately. But Robert didn't so that was that. He pretended he did, for a while, but there was always a good reason why we should wait – until we had a bigger house, until he got the promotion he wanted, until he knew our finances were secure... but now I know it was just pretence. He didn't want them because they would have messed up his perfect life, but also, of course, because it would have meant sharing me, and he wasn't prepared to do that under any circumstances. Now I'm glad we didn't have children. What kind of life would they have had living with a monster like him?'

'They would have had you.'

Frankie shook her head. 'I wouldn't have protected them the way I should have. I believed Robert's lies, even about myself – especially about myself. He'd have been able to control them just as he did me. So although I grieved the loss of ever being a mother, perhaps it's better that those children never existed than to have caused them irrevocable damage. Sometimes what we're convinced is wrong can turn out to be right.' She squeezed his hand. 'What I'm trying to say is that perhaps you *did* make the right decision. And what you see as your desertion, this terrible, shameful thing, has actually given your son a life he could never have had with you... Although I'm very aware that that in itself is a terrible burden to bear.'

She gave a weak smile, quiet for a moment as she watched him, her head cocked to one side. He saw clearly the moment when she realised that wasn't the end of his story. Her eyes widened, a quick intake of breath whistling between her teeth. 'You know, don't you?' she said. 'You know what kind of life he's had?'

'I made a promise,' he said. 'And, eventually, when I got my head out of my arse I came back home to see what I could do about keeping it. And what I found was that my son was turning out to be just like me, wasting away his life, mixing with the wrong sort, making stupid decisions... I don't know why I was surprised; they say the apple never falls far from the tree.'

'Oh, William...' Frankie's eyes were warm on his. 'What did you do?'

'Kept my distance, for one thing. I'd been no part of his life for the first eighteen years so I reckoned I had no right to be a part of it then. But I kept my eye on him, saw which way his life was heading... and then tried to do something about it. Stupid, is what it was.' He shook his head. 'I'm a bad bet, Frankie. I don't make good decisions.'

Her brow furrowed. 'What happened?'

'I tried to be clever. Thought if I put myself in the way of something my son had got involved in, I could make it all right. But I should have known better. He'd got friendly with a couple of local lowlifes – you know, the kind who flogged dodgy TVs and laptops from the back of a van on a Saturday night. He was doing a bit of driving for them and I figured that if *I* did a bit of driving for them, he wouldn't have to. As it turned out, they were doing a bit more than flogging gear, they were nicking it too. I got caught and done for possession of stolen goods.'

Frankie nodded. 'I think I can see where this is going.'

William nodded too, realising he probably didn't need to say any more, but having come this far he didn't want there to be any grey areas that could be left open to interpretation. It was all or nothing. He wanted Frankie to hear the words, to know exactly what had happened so there would never be any misunderstandings. And at least she was still holding his hand...

'I had a previous conviction for burglary so the judge came down hard. I was sentenced to and served nine years. I've been out just shy of one – eleven months and four days, to be precise.' He ventured a smile, although there was nothing light-hearted about what he'd just said.

'On days when I'm trying to be kind to myself, about my actions, and my understanding of them, I tell myself that it was grief which fuelled them. To an extent it was, but I think what I was actually driven by was a subconscious desire for my own self-destruction. I'm sorry,' he said. 'I ought to have been upfront about this from the start.'

'Should you?' Frankie looked puzzled. 'I was a virtual stranger then, I don't think "ought" comes into it. Besides which, I like to form my own first impressions of people. I'd rather they didn't tell me what to think straight away. That makes it more about how they *want* to appear, rather than the actual truth of who they are.'

'So, what *would* you have thought if I *had* told you straight away? Before you knew me a little more...?'

Frankie thought for a moment. 'I'm not sure,' she said. 'But, probably not good.' She held his look, unflinchingly honest. 'What I don't understand is what any of this has to do with Stuart, with—' She broke off, eyes widening. 'Stuart's your *son...?*'

William shook his head sadly. 'No, but Danny is...' He let his words sit between them for a moment. 'He doesn't have a clue who I am. Doesn't treat me any better than I deserve, and that's okay, but what's not okay is that I haven't a clue what to do now. Stuart is clearly mixed up in some serious stuff, and I have no idea whether Danny is involved or not. If he is and I go to the police... well, you know what comes next. But if he isn't, then he needs to know before he *does* become implicated. There's also the small matter of my own criminal record. If I do the right thing then the chances are it won't end well for me, but if I do nothing, then Danny's future is on the line, not to mention the fact that Stuart will be free to carry on peddling his wares.' He swallowed, feeling the familiar tightness in his throat. 'See? I told you I was stupid. I should never have come back here... Thing is, though, there's quite a large part of me that's very glad I did.' He smiled, unsure of himself. Foolish really, that he could still harbour hope that she—

'William...' A soft, slow smile curved the corners of Frankie's mouth. 'You asked me just now what I would have thought of you if I'd known all this from the start. And it wouldn't have been good. But you didn't ask me what I think now, now that I *do* know... Because now, I see someone like me. I may not have endured a life behind bars, but it was a prison just the same. So I see your guilt writ large across your face, just as I see mine when I look in a mirror. Although it's not actual guilt, of course, but something you believe yourself to be guilty of, and that's not the same thing. We don't have responsibility for other people's lives, William. Not our husbands or wives, our sisters or brothers, and not our children either. We think we do, because we love them and want to care for them, but we don't. Everyone is responsible for their own actions. I spent years blaming myself for the way Robert behaved, and by the time I realised how wrong that was, it was almost too late. It isn't your job to save your son, however much you want to. Just as it isn't for you to decide how he lives his life in the first place – only he can do that. So there's nothing to feel guilty about, William. And just in case you're still not sure, you gave up your freedom for him. You may not have been able to look after him when he was a child but the sacrifices you've made for him show me exactly the kind of man you are. The past is the past. It's what you do about the present which counts.'

He nodded. Deep down, he knew that, yet somehow he'd never allowed himself to believe it.

'Never doubt that you've been faithful to the promise you made, William.' She leaned forward, holding his look with a warmth that made his heart leap about his chest. 'So, if you ask me what do I see *now*...? I see someone who's had a life, who's done things they're not proud of, who's been stupid because that's what we do when we're young, but who has learned from their mistakes and is putting them right. I also see someone who, if I'd met them in a dark alley not long ago, I would have probably run in the other direction, but who I know now I'd run *towards*. I see *you*, William. I *see* you.'

31

Tam

Tam arrived at the bakery earlier than planned, but he'd found it hard to sleep, again. It had been good to talk last night about what had happened, but as soon as he was back in his car and left alone with his thoughts, the reality of his situation crowded in. He had no job, no home, and no money coming in now either, and yes, he might find another position but there was still the small matter of the last of his debts to finish paying off. Miss those and problems multiplied; he knew that from bitter experience. Even if he found something straight away, with all the checks that needed to be done it could be weeks, even a month or two before he'd be earning again. A lot could happen in that time. His only saving grace was that, with work on the farm and the odd bit of help in the bakery, he had the means to keep himself busy.

He was about to knock on the door when he paused, arrested by the scene through the window. William and Frankie were seated on opposite sides of the table, their bent heads almost touching, with Frankie's slender hand lying over

William's considerably bigger one. The morning was still dark but the bright overhead lights in the bakery lit every line of their features, and Tam was moved by what he saw. They both looked unbelievably tired and he was reminded of how fragile Frankie's situation was too, but there was something else written on their faces. Something warm and... solid, steadfast. And he smiled, pleased. Good for them.

He moved into the shadow of the doorway and coughed, scuffing his feet a little on the cobbles before sounding a cheerful rat-a-tat-tat. Obviously, he had seen nothing.

'Reporting for duty, ma'am,' he said as Frankie opened the door.

She grinned. 'And just in time for breakfast, too.' She pulled the door wider to invite him in. 'I'm sorry, it looks as if a bomb has gone off in here. We were racing against time to get everything finished, and with me next to useless,' – she lifted her sling to make the point – 'there's still quite a lot left to do.'

'No problem,' said Tam. 'I am here to do your bidding.'

Frankie winced. 'The washing-up? We've got an hour before the shop opens but we've still got the cinnamon swirls to ice and the sticky toffee blondies to cut up.'

'Oh, is that what they're called?' William rolled his eyes. 'I've just made twenty-four of the little darlings and had no idea what they were. It's all a bit of a blur.'

'Is that okay, Tam?' added Frankie. 'Sorry, it's the worst job of them all.'

'Just point me at the Marigolds,' said Tam, holding up his hands and waggling his fingers.

'*Thank* you... I don't know what I would have done without you two. The sooner I'm back in action, the better.' She glanced at William, colouring slightly. 'I've been working this poor man's fingers to the bone. We were just having a little pause for breath.'

Tam gave a bright smile that he hoped would communicate

that he hadn't seen their pause for breath at all. 'Excellent,' he
said. 'To the pausing for breath thing, not the other, obviously...'
He cleared his throat. 'Right, washing-up it is.'

The chatter fell silent for a while as everyone got on with
their tasks, and twenty minutes later, the room looked much
improved.

'That's so much better,' said Frankie, coming out of the
storeroom where she'd been one-handedly putting things away.
'I can't think straight when everything is in such a muddle. If we
get the shelves set up ready in the shop, I think we've just got
time for a cup of tea and a bite to eat. And, rather fortuitously,
there are some millionaire's tarts which fell apart when I took
them out of the trays, all gooey with caramel.' She grinned. 'I'm
so cack-handed at the moment, it's terrible.'

Tam was about to reply when there was a tap at the
window. It was Beth, her nose squished up against the glass, and
mouth in a wide grin. She rubbed at the mark it left with her
sleeve, mouthing an apology. She virtually bounced through the
door as Frankie opened it.

'Sorry,' she said, beaming. 'I wasn't thinking.'

Frankie laughed. 'I keep the inside clean, the outside... not
so much. But someone looks happy...'

Beth's response was to throw her arms around Frankie
before pulling away and practically dancing on the spot. 'I've
just come from work,' she said. 'But I had to call in here first
before going home.' Her smile grew even wider. 'I've kept my
job!' she exclaimed. 'Oh God, I'm so happy.'

Tam stepped forward, opening his arms as Beth reached for
a hug. 'That's bloody brilliant news,' he said. 'I'm so pleased for
you. And Jack, too...' He felt unaccountably emotional at her
good fortune, suddenly realising how much he cared about
them both. 'This is it, Beth. It's all going to happen now.'

She grinned at him, eyes shining. 'Oh, I hope so. I'm just so
relieved. I don't have all the details yet because they're still

finalising them with senior staff, but they wanted to let me know as soon as possible, and I've been told that Matron will be in touch soon. I can't thank you enough for everything you've done, and Frankie, for keeping me sane and...' She flashed Frankie a huge smile before moving to embrace William, who was hanging back a little. 'Thank you too,' she said. 'For everything you've done.'

'Me?' he replied.

'Yes, for helping Frankie, and Tam, making sure they're okay, being a friend. It's important.' She pulled a face. 'Sorry, I'm gabbling, but I'm so happy. Did I say that before?' Her eyes sparkled with joy.

'We were just about to have some millionaire's tarts,' said Frankie. 'Would you like one, to celebrate?'

Beth looked torn. 'Oooh, I would, but... I really want to get home, to Jack.'

Frankie flapped her hands as if to shoo her away. 'Yes, of course you do. Go on, go... I'll wrap a couple to take with you, but we need to have a proper celebration at some point.' She wagged her finger in amusement. 'And that's an order.'

Beth whirled around. 'I promise,' she said, grinning at them all. 'And now that we know my job's safe, Jack will be itching to get stuff done on the farm. Shall I ask him to give you a call, Tam? If you've got any free time, we'd love to see you.'

'Actually, I had thought I might pop over this morning, but perhaps I'll give you a head start, so you and Jack have some time to celebrate on your own.' He gave her a teasing look.

'Good idea,' she said, flashing Frankie a coy smile. 'But do come over. I don't feel much like sleeping at the moment, but I will have to at some point. Are you sure that's okay? What about work?'

'Oh... day off,' said Tam, swallowing his lie.

'Great, well, that's settled then. See you later!'

And with that, Beth was gone, rushing out at just the same speed as she'd rushed in. Tam felt quite breathless.

'Well, now I'm really tired,' said Frankie, laughing. 'But what lovely news, I'm so happy for her.' Her eyes drifted to the side where the rest of the millionaire's tarts lay waiting.

'I'll put the kettle on,' said Tam.

By the time he reached the farmhouse a couple of hours later, the kitchen table was covered with a multitude of stuff: several notebooks, an iPad, two mugs, pens, pencils, a packet of biscuits, a glass of water and sheets of paper of varying sizes. As he drew closer, Tam could see they held a series of scribbled drawings.

'Someone's been busy,' he remarked.

Jack grinned. 'I'm knackered and my arse is black and blue but, bizarrely, I've got far more energy than ever.'

Tam, who hadn't, wondered if he would be able to keep up with the pace of Jack's excitement, but he nodded.

'What have you been working on?' he asked, studying a couple of the sheets of paper and trying to work out what he was looking at. 'Is this the hen house?'

Jack nodded, wheeling himself closer. 'I'd never be able to get into the current coop, even if it wasn't falling down. So, I thought about what I might be able to achieve and started to redesign it. Except that led me down another rabbit hole and got me thinking about transport as well.'

Tam took a seat. 'Okay... where do you want to start?'

'The transport? I think that might be trickier to put into place. More expensive certainly, and while the quad bike is brilliant—'

'For a first attempt...'

'Yes, brilliant for a first attempt but, ultimately, I need something I can use independently, and preferably something a trailer can be hitched to...'

'A trailer?' Tam searched his brain for a solution, mentally adding another set of equations to those already in his head.

'Yes, because I have no means of carrying anything at the moment. But I *might* be able to get what I need into a trailer and then pull it to wherever I need to go.'

'So, an all-terrain wheelchair then?'

Jack winced. 'Ideally, but they're hideously expensive. We virtually had to take out a mortgage to afford this one.' He looked down at the wheels beneath his seat. 'Is there any way we could adapt this? Or the manual one we keep for emergencies?'

Tam thought for a moment. 'Don't know... but leave it with me. There must be a way. Or maybe some further modifications could be made to the quad bike...'

'I thought that, but I find it difficult to balance now, hence why I'm black and blue. Even if we could somehow alter it so I could drive, I'd get thrown about all over the place.'

Tam's eyes narrowed. 'We need to lower your centre of gravity then. Make something you sit *in* rather than sit *on*.' Jack was nodding. 'I want to say a go-cart type of thing but that's probably ridiculous. In any case, we're rather putting said cart before the horse. What we need to do first is make areas accessible to you, as many as we can. The ones closest to the house are easiest, so...' He caught the amused look in Jack's eye. 'Ah... which is exactly why you were thinking about the hen house.' He tapped his forehead as if to say, *idiot*... 'Okay, no pun intended, but let's park the transport issue for a minute. Tell me about your designs.'

Jack slid one of the pieces of paper towards him. 'First and foremost, I need to be realistic. What I'll be capable of achieving here is very limited. It's not going to be as I planned or dreamed of all those years ago. In all likelihood the vast majority of work here will have to be undertaken by someone else and—'

Tam leaned forward. '*However...*'

'*However...* there are some things I *can* do. Extremely slowly and with modification, but I reckoned the hen house could be the place to start.' He tapped the paper. 'The problem with the old coop is that the door into the run isn't wheelchair accessible, and then the house itself follows a traditional layout – meaning that the nesting boxes are raised off the ground. The chickens prefer it that way, but it makes the boxes too high for me to collect the eggs. I'd probably also struggle with the lids. So, with a bit of lateral thinking, and some internet trawling, I've come up with a way to potentially install the nesting boxes on the *outside* of the main house, using runners. The chickens would still access them from inside, and if I rigged up a pulley system, I could raise or lower them. What do you think?'

What Tam actually thought was how brave Jack was. How very restricted his life was to the extent that even the simplest tasks required detailed thought if he was to accomplish them. He nodded. 'A bit like those lifts in big old houses – dumb waiters, I think they're called. And that way you could collect any eggs, and presumably clean the boxes too. But what about food? And water? And whatever else chickens need?'

'Ah, that's where the trailer comes in,' replied Jack. 'They'll be free-range during the day, so in summer, apart from a bit of grain, that's pretty much it. I can take care of that, provided I can get the grain there. Same for their winter feed. There's already a standpipe for water, and I should be able to find something to transfer that into their hoppers. What I really need is a way to reliably get from the house to the coop so I can shut them in at night and let them out after laying.'

'And by reliable, you mean independent?'

'I guess I do, yes.'

Jack was silent, ostensibly looking at the plans in front of him, but Tam could tell they weren't the focus of his thoughts.

'Can I just say something, Tam, before we go any further?'

His expression had grown suddenly serious. 'I'm very aware how simple I'm making these things sound, when the reality would be anything but. I have to try, though. I have to do something, however small, however pointless-seeming or...' He broke off. 'I just have to.'

Tam held his look. 'I know.'

'And the other point is that none of this will ever work without my having someone with me. I've fucked up my life once already by doing something I shouldn't have – doing something on my own when it was a two-person job. If I did it again, Beth would kill me. I mean, she might not have to, but you get the gist...'

Tam nodded.

'And whoever that person is would be doing ninety-nine per cent of all the work, while I'd still consider this my farm. And I'll still be the one having the final say on decisions and that probably doesn't seem fair, but...'

'It's exactly how it should be. Maybe not the division of labour...' He grinned. 'But circumstances are what they are. So, it's not a problem.'

'No?'

Tam shook his head. 'Nope.' He paused a moment, looking back down at the drawings. 'Shall we go and look at the hen house?' He eyed the chair next to him on which a plump cushion lay. He picked it up. 'You might want to take this,' he added. 'For a bit of extra padding.'

Beth's expression was so fierce, Tam felt like a naughty schoolboy in front of the headmistress. He stared at the floor and the rapidly growing pool of water.

'Are you two going to make a habit of getting wet?' she asked. 'Only there are such things as coats, hats, brollies...'

'Um...' Jack looked as if he was crying, rivulets of water

dripping from his hair to track down his cheeks. 'In our defence, it didn't look like it was going to rain when we went out. And then it just sort of came down.'

Tam nodded in agreement. 'One minute fine, and then the next...' He mimed a cloudburst with his hands which, he conceded, might have looked more like a bomb exploding. 'And the trouble is that we'd wandered a bit further than we thought, so getting back here quickly wasn't really an option...' He shifted his feet slightly, his boots squelching with mud. 'Sorry. I'll clear up the mess.'

Beth pursed her lips, silence lengthening as she glared at them, but then, like the wind, her expression changed and she laughed. 'You should see the look on your faces, but honestly, what are you two like?' And then she gave a coy smile. 'Just as well I'm in such a good mood,' she added, looking directly at Jack. 'You should go and get changed, you're absolutely soaking. Get out of those wet things before you catch your death.' She looked at Tam. 'I'm not sure what we do about yours, but I can dry them and, in the meantime, you'll have to borrow some old clothes of Jack's again.' She stopped. 'What?'

Tam smiled. 'I have some other clothes in the car. I can easily get changed into those.'

Beth's hand flew to her mouth. 'Oh God, you have, haven't you? Tam, I'm so sorry, I wasn't thinking, I...'

'It's fine,' he replied, shaking his head at her horrified look. 'And you have to admit, carrying all your possessions with you comes in pretty handy sometimes.'

She gave him a look. One which acknowledged the light-heartedness of his comment, but one which also let him know how much she cared.

'Then the very least I can do is wash and dry them for you. Unless you have a tumble dryer stashed in your car I know nothing about.'

Tam grinned. 'Nope, so thank you. Damp clothes in a car

aren't great. They kind of stay damp, and then everything else... It's a bit like camping holidays when you were a kid.'

'Good. Whip those off while I help Jack get changed and I'll get a wash on. It shouldn't take too long.' She glanced at the clock on the wall and then at the falling darkness outside the window. 'What am I saying? Tam, this is crazy. Why don't you stay here tonight? It's filthy out there now and getting colder by the minute. Plus, it'll be at least an hour and a half to get your things sorted. Possibly longer, you know what jeans are like for drying. And in any case, it will be gone dinnertime by then, and you'll have had nothing to eat either. So, it makes far more sense to eat with us, and then just stay... You can have a shower too, if you like and—'

'Beth,' said Tam softly. 'I don't need persuading. Thank you, I'd really like that.'

Which is how, several hours later, Tam came to be preparing for sleep. Only for the first time in a long while, in a bed, within an actual bedroom, with a proper duvet (even if it did have pink flowers all over it) and crisp white sheets. His car lay outside on Beth and Jack's driveway, now just a vehicle.

He folded up his freshly laundered clothes and was about to put them back in his rucksack when he stopped and, instead, laid them over a chair which stood in one corner of the room. And now that the idea was in his head, he set about removing all his other clothes from his bag and, feeling somewhat sheepish at the liberty he was taking, placed them in the chest of drawers opposite the bed. It wouldn't hurt for just one night.

He took out his small travel clock, placing it on the bedside table before fishing out his library book from the bottom of the bag. His head was whirling with thoughts – nice ones for a change – but he knew that he'd never sleep unless he could persuade some of them to calm down. He and Jack had spent the evening considering how they might go about rebuilding the hen house and had already drawn up a to-do list of the steps

they needed to take. It was a lengthy list, much of which
wouldn't, or rather couldn't, be tackled for a while yet, but it
didn't matter. Tam would wake up in the morning warm,
without stiff and aching limbs, and actually be looking forward
to his day.

He climbed under the duvet, sliding his legs back and forth
across the sheets, revelling in their smooth expanse. A soft
fleecy throw lay across the bottom of the bed in case he grew
cold in the night, and he pushed his toes beneath it, sighing with
pleasure at the warm weight of it. He reached behind to plump
his pillows and, library book in hand, he lay back, marvelling at
the soft give of the mattress beneath him.

It was as he opened the book that the letter fell out. He
stared at it, curiously at first, wondering where it had come
from, and then he remembered it had been given to him by
Chris. He was about to cast it aside, not wishing to sour his
mood by thinking of their last encounter, when he realised the
letter had a stamp on it. An actual stamp, and an embossed logo
he didn't recognise. It certainly wasn't the junk mail he had first
assumed it to be. He laid down his book and picked up the
letter, peering at it more closely before sliding a finger under the
seal to open it.

After that, despite the luxury of his surroundings, and the
deep, enfolding comfort of his bed, Tam hardly slept at all.

32

Frankie

The coffee shop was busy, which was one of the reasons why Frankie had chosen to meet Robert there. The hubbub of background noise would make talking easier, less self-conscious, but it would also mean Robert would have to be a little more guarded about the things he said. They weren't the only reasons, though. The coffee shop was where she had first come with Beth, where a friendship had blossomed and her new life had properly begun. It seemed the perfect place to end the old one.

Careful timing of her arrival meant that Robert would get there first and have to sit and wait for her, instead of her always being the one to dance to his tune. It was a small distinction, but important. She was still terrified, however, her stomach a squirming mass of butterflies as she walked among the tables to join him. She passed Beth, seated at a table in front of theirs, ostensibly reading, but instead metaphorically holding her hand, and Frankie lifted her head a little higher.

Robert got to his feet the moment he saw her, his eyes flying to her hair, clocking her jeans and boots. Hair she no longer dyed blonde, clothes so very different from the skirts and blouses she used to wear.

'Frances...'

She was about to correct him, when she stopped. Frankie was not a name she wanted Robert to use. *Frankie* didn't belong to him.

He leaned forward, about to kiss her, when she sat down, leaving him pecking at air. He frowned but quickly recovered himself.

'You look... goodness, so different. But beautiful as ever. I wouldn't have thought grey hair suited you, but you know...' He studied her. 'I think it does.'

Frankie didn't care. Frankie didn't dye her hair because Frankie didn't want to. Frankie liked her hair grey, with its soft silvery waves which framed her face, and that was all that mattered.

'Hello, Robert,' she said.

She *had* wondered how *he* would look. Whether he would still favour the preppy, boyish style which he thought portrayed a suave elegance, and which, in the early days, she had too. So she was almost amused to find that everything about Robert remained unchanged, right down to the carefully cultivated stubble, and his wedding ring which looked as if it had been polished for the occasion. Or perhaps it was simply that she noticed it in contrast to her own, which was no longer on her finger but, instead, lying in a drawer in her flat, collecting dust.

'Are you well?' he asked, attempting to take her hand which was lying on the table. She removed it and slid it onto her lap. 'I've been so worried about you.' He stared into her eyes, his own soft, almost beseeching. 'I can't help it, but all I want to do is take you home and look after you.' At one time he could look at her that way and she would do almost anything he asked.

She ignored his comment. 'I'm really well, thank you.' Clearing her throat, she continued. 'Have you ordered a drink?' The table between them was bare.

'No, I... I thought we could go somewhere a little more... Somewhere nicer. Perhaps for lunch. A nice country pub, or—'

She pushed her chair back from the table. 'Well, I'm having a coffee. Would you like one?' Frances would never have bought Robert a drink; it was always the other way around. Frankie, on the other hand, rather enjoyed the novelty, although she inwardly cautioned herself not to get too carried away.

'A cappuccino then,' he replied, also getting to his feet. Frankie waved him away. 'No, I'll get these.'

She received another frown but, by the time she returned to the table, Robert had regained his composure.

'So, you're working in a bakery then,' he said. 'I should imagine that's quite a change. Are you enjoying it?'

Frankie nodded, sipping at the foam on her coffee. 'I love it. If you remember, that's what I was doing when we first met. I'm not sure why I ever gave it up.'

'But darling, it was such a twee little shop, wasn't it? Someone with your skills was deserving of so much better.'

'Perhaps.' Frankie wrinkled her nose. 'But I never did go on to anything better, did I? Or, in fact, to anything.'

'But you liked being a housewife,' replied Robert. 'You always said you did. And you were so good at it.'

It was true, Frankie had enjoyed it. She'd enjoyed the novelty of it when all her other friends had been working, particularly when those friends had been juggling full-time jobs with bringing up children. She had enjoyed furnishing their home and looking after it. Just as she had enjoyed having the freedom to do other things. Until, of course, she realised that she had never had any say in the way the house was decorated, or the way she looked after it, because Robert liked things just so. Until she'd realised that her freedom was limited to the house, and one or two other places which Robert deemed 'safe'. Until she'd realised she would never be going back to work, or volunteering, or doing any of the other things she'd thought she would enjoy. She was about to reply when Robert continued.

'Of course, if you want to carry on working, I'm sure we can sort you out something. I'll help. You can do anything you want to do, of course you can. You could even start driving again.'

'*Start* driving? Robert, I'd never have stopped if it wasn't for you.'

His chin dropped so that he looked at her from under his eyelashes. It wasn't endearing; it gave him a rather unfortunate double chin. 'Frances... let's think about that for a minute, shall we? If you recall, it wasn't me who stopped you from driving. In fact, I did all I could to encourage you, but you were always so nervous and timid about it. I understood, just as I can understand you not wanting to admit to it either, but we could take it slowly, try to build up your confidence again, and—'

Frankie held up her hand. 'Robert, we're not here to talk about any of those things. We're here to talk about the fact that our marriage is over and that there are things we need to put in place so that we can both move on with our lives. I thought you understood that.'

'I do understand, really I do. I know that's what you think. But you haven't ever given me a chance to put my side of the story. Instead, you've convinced yourself I'm some sort of monster. You were obviously confused and upset when you ran away, but perhaps now that all these months have passed, you've calmed down a little. I had hoped you would see how much I tried to help you. The driving is just one instance of that, but there are many more, if you'd just listen to what I have to say.'

'First...' Frankie leaned forward. 'I was not *confused* when I ran away. On the contrary, it was when I began to see things very clearly. And as you've mentioned my driving, again, let's *do* think about that for a minute. Let's think about how a friend once told me she knew I didn't like driving. And how, when I looked surprised, she said she'd always got the impression I didn't. How, when I challenged her, she couldn't recall who had given her that impression, but then admitted it might have been you. I liked driving, Robert. I learned just after my seventeenth birthday, couldn't wait to get my licence, in fact, and my independence, but then, when I met you, you automatically drove whenever we went anywhere.'

Robert shook his head. 'And being a gentleman is wrong, is it?'

'There was nothing gentlemanly about it. It was a deliberate action designed to undermine my confidence. *But*, you were good at it, I'll give you that. So kind and considerate, so caring. *I'll drive, darling, you've had a busy day.* And then it was, *why don't I drive so you can relax*, or, *are you sure you want to drive? You don't much look like you want to.* And even when I argued that I was perfectly fine, you'd tell me that *you absolutely didn't mind*.' She held up her hand again to stop him from interrupting. 'And do you know what? At first, I thought it was lovely. But then the weeks went by, then the months until, suddenly, it was eight months since I had last driven myself anywhere. Consequently, the first time I *did* go out, I *did* feel a little anxious, and of course you picked up on that, told me not to put myself through it when there was no need. Told me I was bound to be nervous. But you know, Robert, I never was a nervous driver, I loved it. Yet somehow, all too easily, I became one. And even then, you didn't stop. You'd offer to come with me, telling me I'd feel better if you did, and even though you didn't say anything, I could see from the way you were holding your body that I was making you feel uncomfortable. Could tell by the ever so slightly unconvincing encouragements you used to give, that I wasn't such a good driver after all. And so I *doubted* myself, and that's all it took.'

'Well, I really think... I can see that's what you believe, Frances, but if we're being honest with each other, you always were a little bit fanciful... Not that I mind, it's one of your most endearing qualities actually, but—'

'You've got a bloody nerve. You systematically made me doubt *all* my abilities. In every area of my life, you made me believe I was useless. At work, with my friends, even my family... so don't you dare—' She stopped. She'd promised herself she wouldn't get angry, wouldn't end up justifying herself and her beliefs all over again. It was exactly what Robert wanted. She inhaled, slowly and steadily, and then sat back in her chair and drank her coffee, praying he wouldn't notice that her hands were shaking.

Robert gaped at her, frowning, before shaking his head sadly. 'Frances, I'm really not sure what's got into you today. I came here wanting to be civil, to look constructively at our current situation and to offer solutions.'

Frankie shook her head. 'No, Robert, you didn't. You came to persuade me that *you* are the solution to my problems. But I don't have any problems. I never did have, actually, and, in fact, the only problem I have now is you. I ran away because I couldn't bear watching myself disintegrate before my own eyes. And I *kept* running because I knew that all I needed was some time – to find myself again, to pick up the broken pieces of the person I once was and put them back together again. And that, is exactly what I've done.'

'But we love each other.'

'No, we don't. You don't love me, and you certainly don't want me to love you in return. What you want is someone who is prepared to worship you, to constantly massage your ego. But most of all you want someone willow-like, someone you can shape and bend to your will, someone to be so taken in by all the care and attention you lavish on them that they can't see what's really happening – that it isn't care and attention at all, it's controlling and coercive. You're the one who's broken, Robert, not me. You need help, but I'm not going to be the one to give it to you.'

His face flushed with anger, his mouth hardening into a thin line before he could stop it, before he could paste his charming smile back on and adopt his oh-so-concerned expression. And to think that less than two months ago she could well have been sitting here, just as she was now, but with all the same doubts and insecurities that she had suffered from for most of her life. She might even have been tempted by the lies Robert offered her, ones which, now, she saw so plainly. She had a life now, she had friends, she— A slight movement of Robert's head allowed her to see behind him, to another table where a gentle giant of a man sat calmly sipping his coffee. She had *William...* And she smiled, feeling warmth wrap around her heart. She hadn't thought she wanted him here today. Hadn't known he was coming. Was too wary of being thought of as in a relationship with him. Now, she realised, that was *all* she wanted. And she didn't care who knew it.

'I'm not sure what you hoped to achieve here today,' she added. 'But I really don't think it was any of the things you declared in your letter. It wasn't to agree that our relationship is over, neither was it to be practical and formalise arrangements so we could both move forward. And, because I suspected that might be the case, I've already taken the liberty of doing so on our behalf. I've been in touch with a solicitor, Robert, and you'll be hearing about divorce proceedings shortly.'

He looked at her, with that still boyish smile on his face, a mixture of sadness and patient understanding. 'Frances... I can understand how you might think that's what you want, but I hate to see you like this.'

Frankie was about to tell him exactly what she wanted, when she stopped and checked herself, instead focusing on his last words.

'Hate to see me like what?' she asked.

Robert squirmed. 'You know, if you didn't have the money for clothes which suited you better, you only had to ask. That flowered dress I loved you in, remember that? Goodness, you looked so beautiful. I'd love to see you in something like that again.'

Frankie nodded. 'Yes, money has been tight...'

He smiled. 'There now, you see? And hairdressers, too, cost a fortune these days.'

'They do. That's certainly true.'

'I could help you, Frances, if only you'd let me.'

She lowered her gaze, as if she was thinking about his words, as if she was taking a long time to consider the implications of them, and then she raised her eyes and smiled. 'You see, the thing is, Robert, that even if I had a million pounds, I wouldn't dye my hair or buy those hideous dresses again. Because I don't want to. Because I like my hair this colour. Because I like what I'm wearing. When you say you hate to see me like this, what you actually mean is that you hate to see me happy. You hate to see me, finally, a strong, independent woman who isn't yours to command any longer. That's what you really hate. But you'd better get used to it, Robert, because that's not about to change, and neither am I.'

Fire flashed in Robert's eyes. 'You've never been able to make good decisions, have you? That's been the problem all along. I put up with it, I tried to help as best I could and what do I get for it? I've had to *hunt* for you, Frances. My *wife*. I've had to employ people to look for you. Have you any idea how that makes me look? But I've found you now, so you can stop all your silly games and just come home again where you belong.'

'No, thank you.'

'Don't make me force you, Frances.'

From the corner of her eye, she could see William getting to his feet. He sidled into the seat next to Robert and leaned up against him. 'And just how, exactly, are you going to do that?'

33

Frankie

The three of them sat in the coffee shop for some while after Robert left, William beside her and Beth sitting opposite. They must have made quite a spectacle, hugging and laughing the way they had, but Frankie didn't care. Robert had told her she had made out he was a monster and she realised that's exactly what he was. Not the scaly monster with saliva-dripping teeth of horror films, but, instead, the type which lay under the beds of children the world over – a monster who, at night, seemed so scary, casting such fear deep into their hearts, but who, in the light of a new day, turned out to be an old, discarded teddy bear that was no longer played with. Robert held no power over her now.

And if Beth had been loud and exuberant, pulling Frankie into a fierce hug and then releasing her only to do it all over again, then William had been her opposite, quiet and calm. But the way he enfolded Frankie in his arms and pulled her head into his shoulder before kissing the top of it left her in no doubt as to the way he was feeling. He didn't need any words at all to tell her that.

'I am so proud of you,' said Beth. 'What a slimy, snivelling creep Robert turned out to be. But you were amazing. You held your ground, and said all the things we'd rehearsed, even when he tried turning to his old tricks again.' Her expression suddenly sobered. 'But what he did to you was awful, Frankie. I can't imagine the life you must have had. And I'm so sorry I didn't know you then – I like to think I'd have helped.'

Frankie squeezed her hand. 'I'm sure you would have, but perhaps it's better that you came into my life when you did. Without you, and William, and Tam too, I'd never have found the courage to face up to Robert.'

'It's funny how we all came together, in different ways and at different times,' said Beth. 'I was thinking that the other day. Do you ever get the feeling it was meant to be? Or does that sound silly?'

'Not at all,' said Frankie. 'I'm convinced of it. I have been since the first day we met, when you slipped outside the bakery and scraped your knee.'

Beth nodded, smiling at the memory. 'It wasn't even that long ago, but so much seems to have happened since then. I'm certainly in a very different place to the one I was in before.'

'I think we all are,' said William. 'And if Tam were here, I know he'd say the same.'

'Speaking of whom, where has he gone?' asked Beth. 'He was all set to come today and then had to dash off at the last minute. He was most mysterious when I asked him about it.'

More than likely gone for a job interview, thought Frankie, shaking her head in response, but Tam had asked that she keep news of his unemployed status from Beth, and so that's what she would do. It seemed a shame, though. Was she the only one who could see what a huge benefit there was to having Tam at the farm? As if reading her thoughts, Beth sighed.

'He's been with us four days now,' she said, smiling at the thought. 'I don't know why I didn't think of inviting him to stay before. I feel rather ashamed I didn't, but' – Frankie looked up at the concern in Beth's voice – 'although it's fantastic having him there, it worries me. He says he's taken a few days' holiday which was owed to him and, grateful though I am, he's been putting in some very long hours. I don't want him spending all his hard-earned break with us.'

'Perhaps he wants to,' countered Frankie.

'It certainly seems as if he does, but I'm worried Jack will come to rely on him too much. I know my job is safe now, but we don't have anything left at the end of the month, so there's still no way we can pay Tam. Especially not now we might need any extra money we do have for getting the farm back up and running. I feel we're taking advantage of him, and Tam doesn't deserve that. He's been let down enough in the past as it is.'

Beth's phone rang before Frankie could reply and she pulled a face. 'Sorry, it's the hospital, I need to take this.' She excused herself and hurried outside to take the call in the relative quiet of the street.

William took the opportunity to slip his hand into hers.

'How are you feeling?' he asked.

A rush of thoughts flooded Frankie's head. How *was* she feeling? The word 'elated' took up space front and centre and she considered it for a moment. It wasn't a word which she would ever have used to describe herself in the past, but yes, today, that would do very nicely. Elated and grateful, proud – of herself – happy and... giddy as a schoolgirl. She leaned her head into William's shoulder. 'Very good,' she replied. 'And most definitely *not* a Frances.'

He drew back slightly so he could look at her, an amused smile on his face. 'Not a Frances?' he said. 'I noticed that's what Robert called you, but what's that all about?'

'Frances is the woman I used to be,' replied Frankie. 'I didn't really like the name even when I was a child. There was something too fussy about it, too prim, and the way my mother used to say it when I'd done something naughty... As I got older, I grew to hate it even more, mainly because of the way Robert said it, which made my teeth clench and my stomach churn. It's a name for someone subservient, compliant, far too meek and with no thoughts of their own. In short, a person Robert owned... So, when I got away and came here, I decided that *Frankie* could be someone I liked. A free spirit. The kind of someone I think I *could* have been. And so I determined that *she* would be *me*, but I rather had to grow into her first. I wasn't sure if I could.'

William held her look, the corners of his mouth curving slightly as he studied her face. 'Well, in the nicest possible way, I think Frances is well and truly dead,' he said. 'I don't think you need to worry about her any more.'

They were still smiling at one another when Beth returned to their table and Frankie was horrified to see tears on her friend's face.

'Beth, whatever's wrong? It's not Jack, is it?'

Beth might have been crying, but she was angry now. She shook her head furiously. 'No, thank goodness. But I can't believe it, Frankie. They've changed my shifts for this new job. After all this, and they go and do something like that. They *know* I can't work days, it's impossible.'

'Come and sit down,' said Frankie, hating to see Beth so distraught. 'I'll get us another drink.'

But Beth shook her head. 'I have to get home...' A look of horror crossed her face. 'What am I going to say to Jack? He'll be devastated.' Her hand flew to her face and Frankie could see her eyes welling with tears again. 'It's so bloody unfair! Just when everything was going so well. And I'm supposed to be ecstatic because I've even got a slight promotion, which is a joke in itself – it's only enough to pay for an extra packet of choco-late biscuits a week. It's nowhere near enough to pay—'

'Can't you ask them to look at the shifts again?'

Beth shook her head. 'I have, but it doesn't work like that. This is a new position. It's what the hospital does to get around various employment laws. Basically they sack us all and then rehire some of us, but on new contracts, with new hours and new rates of pay. From the beginning of next month my current job will no longer exist. I couldn't carry on doing it however much I might want to.'

'Oh, Beth...' It was a particularly bitter blow after this morn-ing's celebration. 'Saying I'm sure everything will work out sounds a bit pathetic,' added Frankie, silently admonishing the universe for being so bloody awkward. 'But I do hope you can get it sorted. If anyone deserves a break it's you and Jack.'

Beth nodded, weary now. Life was an uphill battle at times, and it showed. 'I'd better get home,' she said. 'Not that I'll sleep now, but I probably ought to get some rest... and try to work out what the hell we're going to do.' She blinked hard before giving Frankie a wan smile. 'I've ruined your day of victory now, too.'

'No, you haven't,' admonished Frankie. 'I couldn't have faced Robert today without you, and I wouldn't have even considered doing so a couple of months ago. I'd have turned tail and run, just like I have in the past. You've made a big differ-ence to my life, Beth, and don't you forget it. There'll be a way through this, I know there will.'

'I hope so...' Beth dashed a hand against her face, but even as she did so more tears began to fall. Frankie got one last look at her anguished face before she rushed away.

William was still holding Frankie's hand, albeit under the table, and he gave it a silent squeeze. Neither of them knew what to say. Eventually, Frankie loosened her hand, pulling it reluctantly away.

'I guess I'd better get home too,' she said. 'Although I don't much feel like sleeping either.' She made to stand but then sat back in her seat, feeling the pull of William's presence. There was so much she needed to say to him. To thank him for being there for her today. For all the days he had been there for her. Her wrist was already feeling a lot better, and it wouldn't be long before she could fully resume her duties at the bakery. What would happen if she told him how much she would miss having him there? What would happen when the bakery sold and the only job she could find meant she had to work during the day? Would she even see him at all? But mostly what she wanted to say was how easily William had become a part of her life, and the thought of that changing was... She drew her thoughts to a close and leaned against his shoulder.

'Is your head as full as mine?' she asked. 'I feel as if it's about to explode.'

'Probably,' he replied. 'Nothing's simple, is it?'

She closed her eyes. 'And yet it should be,' she said. 'I feel like it wants to be, but somehow we're all still... I don't know, stuck? Is that the word I'm looking for?'

'It's one word, certainly. And I'm not sure I have a better one.' He smiled and took her hand. 'Come on, I'll walk you home.'

The sun had appeared since they'd been in the coffee shop, bathing the street ahead in a gentle glow, warming the mellow stone of the buildings and bringing the faded winter colours to life. It was how she felt – as if some part of her had been reawakened. It was the first time she had walked through this town without any thoughts of Robert in her head, and she realised that to some degree or other he had always been there. Like a shadow – sometimes in front of her, sometimes behind, but always present no matter where she stood. Now he was gone it was as if she could see the world differently.

The bakery and her flat wasn't far now; it would take perhaps a minute more to reach it.

'William, don't go...' She met his eyes. 'Sorry. This is going to sound really stupid, but I don't want to be on my own, I don't know why. Normally when my head feels this way, I crave solitude, but today... And I'm not very good at this...' She held up the hand which was still attached to William's. 'It's been a long time since I thought myself a part of anything.'

'Me too,' said William. 'I've been in prison for the last nine years, remember?' The edges of his eyes were crinkling. 'Don't underestimate what you did this morning,' he said, his head tipped to one side. 'You've said goodbye to a big part of your life, and while that might feel good, it's also left behind an empty space, which is what you're feeling now. It won't take long for it to fill back up again though, and this time it will be with good stuff.'

He stopped to study her face, but whereas she had always hidden herself from Robert's gaze, hating the cloying, claustrophobic weight of it, William's look was warm summer sun and the touch of a light, refreshing breeze. There was room to grow beneath it.

'Then will you come in with me?' she asked. 'Say if you'd rather go home.'

But William shook his head. 'I don't want to be on my own either,' he said. 'I don't think I can possibly drink any more coffee, but a cup of tea would be nice. As would several of your pastries... What would be really nice, though, is several more hours of your company. No expectations, just...'

'Breathing in and out... getting used to being with someone.'

He nodded, a slow smile working its way up his face. 'Breathing in and out... I can do that.'

· · ·

Frankie watched as a shaft of sunlight travelled the wall in her living room. She and William were shoulder to shoulder on the sofa, feet up on the coffee table, comfortable and safe, yet still her brain would not cease its endless chatter. They had talked for almost two hours. She had told him some more about her life with Robert, and he had told her about Louise and the dreams he once had as a much younger man. But mostly they talked about their present, about Beth, and Tam, and the situation they were all in. The past was behind them, feeling more and more distant with every passing day, and yet the future was still such an uncertain place, it was hard to see a way into it.

'I can hear your thoughts whirring from here,' muttered William. He nudged her elbow and Frankie smiled.

'Sorry, I shall ask them to keep the noise down.' The sun was almost halfway across the wall now. 'I was just wondering what you're going to do,' she added.

William squinted across at her. 'I wasn't planning on doing anything much. Your sofa's way more comfortable than mine.'

'I meant about your job. About Stuart, and your son.' He had some difficult decisions to make, and she wasn't sure she wanted to hear the outcome.

'Ah...' William let out a long, slow breath. 'About my job – try to find a new one, I think. Apart from how much I'm enjoying being a baker, I'm going to find it almost impossible to stay on at the club. And about Stuart... nothing.'

Frankie craned her neck to look at him. 'Nothing?' She looked back at the golden light on the wall. Might they be able to face the future together?

William looked up at her. 'I've thought about this every which way I can, and I can't risk it, Frankie. Not now. You don't mind throwing things away when you've got very little to lose but... I don't want to lose the things I have now.' He paused. 'I don't want to lose you.' He had the warmest brown eyes.

'I don't want to be *lost*.' She laid her head on his shoulder.

'But surely if you went to the police and explained, they would listen. Just because you have a criminal record doesn't mean they won't take you seriously. Or am I just being incredibly naive?'

'I was done for possessing stolen goods, Frankie. And I served nine years. I've been out less than one. I should be as far away from anything illegal as I can be.' He paused a moment, looking down at his hands. 'I haven't told you this but a few weeks back Stuart offered me cash in hand to help him out at a mate's party. To help the guests have a good time, was how he put it. And I'm pretty certain the mate wasn't actually a friend in the traditional sense, more like someone Stuart was keen to oblige... for financial gain. My guess is that he's been holding illegal poker games, or something very similar. I should have mentioned it before, but it's linked in with all the rest of it and...' He held up a hand in a helpless gesture. 'I refused, but as you can imagine that didn't go down all that well. Stuart doesn't like people who say no to him and he can cause a lot of trouble for me. One word in Danny's ear and I'll be out of a job. So, doing what I have been – checking out the score with Stuart – has been a kind of insurance policy, so that *I* have something on Stuart, if he decides to invent something about *me*... What I don't know, however, is if Danny has any knowledge of the things Stuart has been up to. My first impression is that he doesn't, but what if he does? I don't like the idea of Stuart getting away with what he's been doing, but I have to face an unassailable fact – either my son is mixed up in something illegal, or he's innocent. Either way, my taking action could cause me irreparable harm.'

'Caught between a rock and a hard place,' she said, lifting her head to look at him. 'I know you want the best outcome for your son, but isn't there some way you can speak to Danny? Let him know what you've found out, at least give him the chance to prove himself innocent, if that's what he is? Then at least you'd know. Maybe now's the time to let him know who you are.'

William's response was instant. 'No,' he said, shaking his head. 'When I came back here I never imagined for one minute I'd get a job working at Danny's club, but when the opportunity came up I thought it was like a sign, or something, that I was in the right place to finally come good on my promise. But you were right, Frankie, I was acting out of guilt because I thought putting something right in his life would make up for all the wrong I'd done to him. I've been using that promise as a crutch for all these years. I've been allowing it to feed my guilt, keeping it nice and fresh and kidding myself that I needed it to give my life a purpose, a reason to carry on. But if I let go of my guilt, and give my life new purpose, then I no longer have need of the crutch that used to prop it up.' He swallowed, his fingers sliding into hers. 'I don't deserve to be a part of Danny's life, and I simply have to accept that. After all, he's never made any attempt to find me, has he?'

Frankie thought about his words for a moment, feeling the sorrow behind them but knowing that they also held the truth. 'But then he'll never know the sacrifice you made for him.'

'I shouldn't need him to. I'd only be telling him to make myself feel better, and that's never the right reason for doing anything.'

'I think that's incredibly brave, and selfless.'

William gave a wry smile. 'Not that brave. I'm also terrified of telling him who I am because at best he'll find out he has me for a father, someone with a very dodgy past who deserted him as a baby, and at worst, I'll find out that he's up to his eyeballs in illegal activities and I'll lose my job and probably a lot more besides.'

Frankie squeezed his hand. 'There must be a way around all this. We'll think of something,' she said, shuffling her feet across so that she could nestle them against his.

'Are you playing footsie with me?' asked William, his voice warm with amusement.

'Blimey, is that still a thing?' she asked.

'I've no idea,' replied William. 'But your feet are cold.'

She was still smiling ten minutes later, time during which neither of them had spoken. The shaft of sunlight was now playing across the edge of the coffee table and pretty soon it would reach them. She felt blessed by its presence.

She felt blessed by so many things and yet, in many ways, her existence was as precarious now as it had been when she first fled from Robert over eighteen months ago – more so, in fact. She had no idea what she would do if there was no job for her when the bakery sold – find another one, obviously – but the bakery was far more than just a place where she worked and lived. It had brought more kindness, and in such a short space of time, than her life had known before, and it had given her hope and peace, too. It had become her sanctuary, transforming the long, dark hours of the night, and within it she had found everything she thought was lost forever. She had found herself. And now William. And the thought of leaving was unbearable.

She thought about their circle of friendship, too, with Beth and Tam. It was a circle which bound them together, the type of bond which made you feel courageous, as if you could do anything because they would always have your back. And yet, none of them were settled. Beth might have kept her job, she and Jack might have found new ways to live the life they'd always wanted, but their problems were far from over. Tam might have found a way back to doing the things he loved, but he'd still lost his job, was still homeless and had now been betrayed not once but twice. All four of them had made tentative steps towards a new future, but each of them still bore the weight of chains which were holding them back, chains which were seemingly impossible to throw off, and yet...

A thought drifted into Frankie's head, and then another and

another. She was convinced that things could work out, for all of them, so if fate hadn't yet had time to bestow all her gifts upon them, then perhaps it was time for Frankie to give her a helping hand.

She nestled deeper into William's warmth beside her, his breathing now deep and rhythmic, and she felt her eyes begin to close. There was work to do first, but tomorrow was another day. First thing in the morning, she would...

34

Frankie

Frankie leaned up against her sink and contemplated what to have for breakfast. It was a little after nine and the lack of sleep over the last few days was catching up with her. She felt overwhelmingly weary, yet her head was still buzzing with all that she needed to do. She and William had woken with a start yesterday evening, surprised to find they had both slept for several hours, but both of them feeling the effects of falling asleep on the sofa – he with a dead arm, where Frankie had been lying on it, and she with a painful crick in her neck. She smiled at the memory, at the slight shyness that still existed between them, fuelled by worries that they might have snored, or worse, dribbled, in their sleep. But any potential embarrassment had soon turned to laughter and last night's shift at the bakery had flown by.

It was one of the things which had made her more determined than ever to act on her decisions of the day before. Even in the short time William had been helping her, the thought that he would no longer be doing so wasn't something she wanted to contemplate. Having him there felt so right. And there was nowhere else she'd rather be. She had to make this work, one way or another. William had gone back to his flat, needing to run a few errands and catch up on some sleep of his own, so it was perfect timing. It wasn't that she was keeping things from him, more that she needed certain confirmations first before she spoke to him.

She glanced at the clock on the kitchen wall. There were a couple of things she had to take care of before she called Vivienne, and with any luck she just had time to catch Beth before she went to bed.

Not surprisingly, Beth's voice sounded flat and lifeless. After rushing home in tears yesterday morning, Frankie suspected that whatever sleep she had managed hadn't come easily.

'How are things?' she asked, fervently hoping for some good news.

'As you might expect,' replied Beth. 'It's all a bit rubbish, actually. Jack is alternating between feeling everything is hopeless, burning with anger that the hospital could have done what they have, and a brittle optimism that somehow I'll get another job with far more money and the roses will start coming up again.' She sighed. 'And I guess that's where I am too. I spoke to Lisa at the hospital last night – she's my line manager – and she's furious too. She's done everything she can to get them to change my shifts, but they won't budge. The whole workforce has been completely restructured, and if I don't like it then I know what to do. One of the nurses who *has* been made redundant would no doubt jump at the chance of my job... It's not that I'm not grateful, but I kind of stopped listening after that. Nothing changes.'

'Oh, Beth...' It was about as bad as Frankie feared. 'What will you do?'

'I still have no idea. I can't even think straight right now.

Get some sleep, I guess, and then attempt to work out some way for us to manage. At the moment I can't see how on earth I can work during the day *and* look after Jack. We simply can't afford any help.'

Frankie nodded, feeling her stomach tightening a little. Now that the time had come to say what she needed to say, the doubts were beginning to creep in. Was she doing the right thing? Or was she just plain meddling? 'About that,' she said. 'I've had a bit of an idea...'

Tam was busy when she rang him, slightly out of puff from sawing up planks of wood, but sounding remarkably chipper. Frankie had already written her questions down beforehand so she wouldn't forget anything, and although Tam was surprised by them, he was more than happy to give his advice. He still made light of any experience he had on the subject, just as she knew he would, but she also knew she could trust what he said. It would stand her in good stead.

'There's just one more thing, Tam,' she said. 'Before I let you go, I wondered if I could talk to you about William.'

'William?' Tam sounded bemused. 'Is everything okay?'

'More than,' replied Frankie, knowing he would hear the smile in her voice. 'It's just that I've had a bit of an idea...'

Frankie's stomach growled. She still hadn't made any breakfast and she should probably eat before calling Vivienne. It might help settle her stomach. Then again, it might make her feel even more queasy... And besides, she needed to get this over and done with. She had to know whether it was even a possibility.

Vivienne answered on the third ring.

'Frankie, hello. I was just on my way out. Is everything okay?'

Frankie bit her lip. 'Yes, it's fine. But I wondered if I might have a chat about something. I can call later though, if you're busy?'

'No, no, now's good. I was only popping next door to take some magazines to my neighbour. I read them first and then pass them on, but I can do that any time. What can I do for you? I'm afraid I don't have any more news about the sale, I'm still waiting to hear back from the people I spoke to you about.'

'Yes, that's why I'm ringing, really,' Frankie replied, winding a curl of hair around her finger. 'It's just that I've had a bit of an idea...'

35

Frankie

Frankie turned the key in the lock and pushed open the bakery door. It was her and William's last shift together, and the way she was feeling it might as well be *her* last one, too. But William was right behind her, so she kept the smile on her face and held the door wide for him before closing and locking it. She was determined they would have a good night.

'Well, here we are,' she said, as they walked through to the back and she turned on the lights. 'I bet you'll be glad to see the back of this place. The boss is an absolute tyrant.'

William grinned. 'Worst I've ever had.' He paused, looking at her. 'Are you *sure* your wrist is going to be okay?'

'William...'

'I know, I know. I have to go back to the club sometime, but you can't blame me for trying. It's been good though, hasn't it?'

'You know it has. And no being maudlin,' she teased, wagging her finger in mock severity. 'I've no idea how long I'm going to be here for yet, so I'm going to make the best of the time I have.'

'And I'll still be able to call by on my way home each night,' he said. 'And get to spy on you when you're dancing around the room, with a bowl in your arms, singing like you're Doris Day.'

Frankie rolled her eyes. 'I'll get you dancing yet, just you wait.' She hung up her things and went to the storeroom. 'Right, pinny for each of us and then we'd better get rolling. Or Vivienne will sack me, never mind the rest.' She winced slightly, glad she had her back to William; she really hadn't wanted to mention Vivienne.

She handed him an apron and was about to switch on the ovens when there was a series of knocks at the door – jaunty ones – rat-a-tat-tat. Two heads appeared in the window.

'Is this your doing?' she asked William, an amused smile on her face as she went to open the door. 'What are you two doing here?'

'Day off,' said Beth, grinning. She was holding a large round tin.

'And I just came for the cake,' said Tam, taking the tin from Beth's arms. 'Get the kettle on and I'll sort some plates,' he said.

Frankie looked at William, but he shrugged. 'Nothing to do with me,' he said.

'You do know we're supposed to be working,' she said. 'Although if you've brought cake, I suppose a quick cup of tea won't do any harm.'

'They're brownies,' said Beth. 'And blondies. I wasn't sure which you liked. Probably not a patch on your pastries, but...'

'She's lying,' said Tam. 'I sneaked one earlier.'

Frankie laughed. 'Lovely as it is to see you, why *are* you here?'

Tam cranked the lid off the tin and set it down on the table. 'It's your last night working together, so we thought we'd come and surprise you. Plus, we're celebrating my new job, of course.'

'You've got a new job?' said William. 'But that's brilliant! Fast work, too. Where is it?'

Tam grinned at Frankie. 'You haven't told him, have you?'

'Well, in my defence, I didn't know for certain that you'd accept it, so...' Frankie took a seat at the table and pulled the cakes towards her, breathing in the heavenly aroma of chocolate. She looked up, giving Beth a warm smile.

'Okay... would someone like to tell me what's going on?' William's hands were on his hips.

Tam bustled past with a stack of plates. 'That pinny suits you, you know.' He sat down beside Frankie. 'It's very simple, really. Actually, Frankie, why don't you explain?'

Frankie helped herself to a blondie, looking at William with a smile. 'It was after I met with Robert yesterday,' she said. 'And you and I got talking. Well, I got thinking... about us – all of us – and all the things which have happened recently and all the things which haven't.'

'Carry on,' said William, sitting down.

'And I realised that without you guys, none of those things would have been possible. I'd never have dreamed of meeting Robert if I didn't have you. I'd run away so that I wouldn't have to stand up to him. Because I couldn't. Didn't ever think that I would. And the only thing that made that meeting possible was knowing you had my back, knowing that I had people to talk to who would understand, being buoyed up instead of weighed down. It gave me the strength I needed.'

She took a bite of her blondie, chewing thoughtfully. 'Then, of course, I realised it's the same for each one of us – shared friendships, shared kindnesses which have brought so much good into our lives in so many ways, and yet... we're still stuck in the same position we were in before – Beth having kept her job, but unable to find a way to have the life she and Jack so deserve, Tam without a home or the means to get one, and you, William...' She sent a warm look in his direction. 'Perhaps beginning to move on with a part of your life and yet unable to resolve an issue from your past. And once I'd realised all that, then the rest was easy. Because if the reason we've all come so far is each other, then we're also the reason to go even further. Because, as someone very wise once said, if it's not all right in the end, then it's not the end...'

Beth leaned across the table to give Frankie's hand a squeeze. 'Which is when, I suspect, she rang me. Isn't that right, Frankie?' At Frankie's shy nod, she continued. 'And what she had to say made a lot of sense, at least it did when I stopped arguing, telling her all the reasons why it wouldn't work, and instead started thinking about all the ways in which it might. Because what I didn't know at the time was that Tam had lost his job. And what *he* didn't know was that despite having kept my job at the hospital, Jack and I were in a worse position than ever before.

'I should have realised that Tam was at the farm not because he was on holiday, as he claimed, but instead that his holiday had started on the day he had his review at work. I should have realised it was no coincidence. Frankie felt awful about breaking her promise to Tam – not telling me he'd lost his job – but she was right to do so.'

Tam, who had been about to snaffle a brownie of his own, sat back with a broad smile on his face. 'And I forgive you, Frankie, obviously... You see, I was worried that if Beth knew I'd lost my job, she'd feel even more awkward about the fact she couldn't pay me for the work I was doing. She might also feel that *I* was taking advantage of *them* – working at the farm when it suited me, only to take off the minute I got another job, leaving Jack to flounder again. I couldn't do that to them.'

'A fact I very helpfully all but pointed out to Tam in case he didn't come to the conclusion himself. Because *I* was worried that we were taking advantage of *him*. Using him for free labour, because there was no way we could pay him. And given how badly he'd been taken advantage of in the past, I wasn't going to have him think we were doing the same. So there we both were, both fearing we were taking advantage, and it was all a bit of a pickle really.' She gave William a wry smile. 'It took Frankie to point out that taking advantage needn't necessarily be a *bad* thing. In fact, the clue was in the name. What we needed to do *was* to take the advantage that was being given to us. So, I offered Tam a job.'

'The pay is rubbish,' said Tam. 'Actually, there's no pay. But we hope in time there will be. But what I do get is full board and lodging... that's all the cake I can eat, and the chance to do something I love, working on the farm. The downside is that while Beth is out working her new day shift, I get to look after Jack, but... fortunately, I really like him, so it's not a problem. I've been working as a carer, after all, so that side of things isn't much different from what I've been doing. It's a win-win. We just needed to put our pride in the bin and see the solution that was staring us in the face. And it's all thanks to Frankie.' He picked up a brownie, saluted her with it and then took an enormous bite.

William beamed at her. 'I knew there was something about you the minute I saw you...'

'You did not. The remains of my sandwich were all over the floor and I suspect I was very rude to you.'

William waggled his head from side to side. 'Okay, maybe not the first time... But soon. It was very soon after that.'

Frankie caught Beth's eye and grinned. 'I'm just so pleased for you. I'm glad it all worked out.'

'It has,' Beth replied. 'But we didn't come here just to tell you about *our* situation.'

Tam leaned forward. 'No, because after Frankie rang Beth, she made another phone call, to me. Another little idea she'd had, and one I was happy to help with. Have a cake, William, you haven't got one yet.'

William looked up, clearly perplexed by the tone in Tam's voice.

'Frankie didn't tell me all the details, William, because they're not hers to tell, but I'd be daft if I hadn't realised there was more to your interest in Stuart and his grey van than simply being a concerned citizen, or a diligent employee. And all that cloak-and-dagger stuff...' William held up a hand to interrupt, but Tam shook his head. 'Let me tell you something first.' He took another bite of his brownie. 'I couldn't remember all the details of where we went and what we looked at, so I did a bit of backtracking and I wrote it all down. I won't do anything about it yet, because the one thing we need to be sure of is that, when I do, there can be no repercussions for you, William. So, I thought that perhaps in a few months' time, when you might have been able to distance yourself from the nest of Vipers, I could put in a call to the local police and tell them everything I know. As a concerned member of the public who happens to use the car park, I think it's my duty, don't you? I also think the police will be very interested to hear what I have to say.'

William shook his head incredulously. 'I can't believe you'd do that for me. Why even would you?'

'So you won't have to,' answered Tam simply. 'I don't need to know why it's difficult for you to go to the police yourself. But I was just as much a witness as you were, except that I have absolutely nothing to lose in telling them. Your name won't even be mentioned, to anyone.'

William swallowed, his hand, Frankie noticed, shaking as he ran it through his hair. 'I don't know what to say,' he said. 'Thank you doesn't even begin to cover it.' He looked at Frankie, his eyes a mixture of emotions, but very clear, top of the list, was how he felt about her. Blinking suddenly, he tore his gaze away. 'Actually, I do know what to say. Because keeping secret the details of my interest in Stuart is wrong – it's not the way friends behave. You've done something so selfless, so generous, you deserve to know why.'

And so, with a halting voice, William told his story. About

Louise, about his son, and about prison too. And when he had finished, just as Frankie knew there would be, her friends' faces were filled with nothing but compassion and understanding. Here, in this little bakery, among the battered tins and dented work surfaces, Frankie had found what she thought she'd never have, and she hugged the thought to her, knowing that whatever else they might have to face in the future, they had each other. And really, that was all that mattered.

'And what about you, Frankie?' asked Beth softly. 'Keeper of friendships and weaver of dreams, what about your future? You can't leave this place, we won't allow it.'

'Ah...' said Frankie. 'Well, I don't know for certain I'll have to, so, until I find out, I'll just have to make the most of the time I've got. I had thought I might have found a way to turn things around, but it wasn't to be.' She smiled sadly, looking down at her plate. She didn't think she could say much more.

Tam cleared his throat. 'Actually, there's something else I need to say,' he said. 'Something that I need to tell Frankie. Something that only I know, but we're not all here yet, so...' He looked towards the door and then down at his watch. 'Perhaps we should just talk among ourselves for a few minutes.' He gave a sheepish grin.

'Tam, you're making it sound like there's been a murder or something,' said Beth, tutting with amusement. 'And we're all waiting for the detective to come in and reveal the big dark secret.' She looked at the blank faces around her. 'Okay, just me then. Never mind.' She waved a hand in Tam's direction. 'As you were.'

He shrugged. 'I promise I don't have a big dark secret, so—' He stopped, looking startled. 'It's not dark, anyway...'

Beth waved her brownie in the air. 'Oh, for goodness' sake, Tam, out with it.'

'No, honestly, I—'

'Wait a minute,' said Frankie. 'What was that?' She

frowned. 'It sounded like...' She jumped up from the table. 'Bugger...'

'Was that the front door?' asked William, also getting to his feet.

Evidently it was, because Frankie hadn't even gone three steps before Vivienne appeared through the doorway. Frankie's hand flew to her mouth.

'Vivienne! Oh God... I'm so sorry. I can explain, we were just...' She gestured to the table behind her where her three friends were still sitting. She was about to make an excuse when she stopped herself. Admittedly, she ought not to have them here during work time, but she wasn't going to lie about them. 'We've just had some good news, and my friends brought in some cakes so we could celebrate. But I'll go without my break later to make up the time.'

'Hello, Beth,' said Vivienne, dipping her head. 'And Tam, William... Please, sit down again. I'll join you, if I may.'

Frankie stared at her. 'How do you know...?' She looked at William, and then at Beth, but they looked as astonished as she did. Only Tam was still smiling.

'I won't stay long,' said Vivienne. 'Because it's *way* past my bedtime, and I'm sorry I'm late. I couldn't find my damn car keys.' She shook her head. 'Never mind.'

Frankie waited until Vivienne had taken a seat before joining her at the table, throwing William a horrified glance. She had no idea what was going on.

'These look lovely,' said Vivienne, peering into the cake tin. 'May I?'

'Yes, please do,' said Beth, blinking hard. She looked stunned.

'I'll probably get horrific indigestion eating this late, but you know what they say? Life's too short...' She smiled. 'Anyway, I won't keep you, Frankie. I expect you're wondering how I know the names of your friends, but before I let Tam explain, I should tell you that I'm here tonight because he asked me to come, and I readily agreed. The circumstances are very special indeed.' She took a brownie from the tin and laid it on a plate which Beth quickly pushed towards her. 'What Beth and William don't know is that before they both came to see me today, I'd had a call from you, Frankie. Do you know, I never did get to deliver those magazines. No matter.' She shook her head. 'Frankie, do you want to tell them what you asked me?'

Frankie could feel her cheeks beginning to blush furiously. 'Um... I asked if you might consider me running the bakery for you, instead of you selling it. Because I'd like to buy it one day.' She swallowed, aware that both William and Beth were staring at her.

'Yes,' replied Vivienne. 'But sadly, I need the money from the sale of the business in order to move, so I had to turn Frankie down. You were very eloquent, though – I wish I hadn't had to.'

Under the table, Frankie felt William's hand slip into her own. 'You were very kind,' she replied. 'And I knew it was a long shot. Worth asking though.' She gave a tight smile to hide her disappointment.

'It was,' replied Vivienne. 'And I was still thinking about it when my doorbell rang, and I opened it to find Beth on my doorstep. She asked me pretty much the same thing – whether there was any way to ensure that Frankie could carry on working here. She was very eloquent, too.' She smiled at Beth, who went bright pink. 'And then there was William, who arrived about forty minutes later. He was the most eloquent of all.' She smiled at Tam. 'Not that you weren't, dear, you were, but William... Let's just say I could see he had a special reason for asking. So that's partly why I came here tonight, Frankie – because I thought it was important for you to know what wonderful friends you have. None of them knew you had already been in touch with me, nor did they know that the others had either, or that they planned to. Yet they had each tracked me down, and came, separately, to plead your case. I was incredibly touched by that.'

Frankie's nose was beginning to smart. She had a horrible feeling she would burst into tears, and she gripped onto William's hand as if her life depended on it. She nodded, and that was all she could manage. Words were quite beyond her.

'Perhaps Tam might like to explain the rest,' added Vivienne. 'While I eat this delicious-looking cake.'

Tam cleared his throat again, his eyes shining. 'So, I already mentioned that Frankie phoned me earlier today to ask for my help, but she also asked me for some advice, and although she didn't say why, it was easy to guess what her motives were. She asked me whether at some point in the future I could help her write a business plan and apply for a bank loan. She also wanted to check that if I was given a set of accounts for a business, that I'd be able to tell her how well that business was doing. My answer to all those questions was yes, of course. It was something William had said to her, she explained, about her wanting to be the driver in her life instead of just the passenger. I think that's something we've all felt keenly over recent weeks. And so of course, as soon as I ended the call, I knew exactly what *I* needed to do.'

He reached inside his jacket pocket, took out an envelope and laid it on the table. It was a little battered and looked as if it had been opened several times. 'Chris gave this to me, and I'd almost forgotten I had it. It wasn't until I stayed over at Beth's that first night that it fell out of a library book. But...' He smiled at Frankie. 'I think you should be the one to read it first.'

Frankie eyed the envelope as if it were a ticking bomb, brow furrowed into puzzled creases.

'Go on,' urged Tam. 'It's okay.'

Conscious that all eyes were on her, Frankie opened it, drawing out the sheet of thick cream paper. 'It's from a firm of solicitors,' she said, peering at the letterhead. 'In Cambridge.' Her eyes tracked further down the page, widening in shock as she read on.

'What does it say?' asked Beth, all but grabbing her arm.

'Oh my God, that's incredible news, Tam. I'm so happy for you! It's Eleanor, his friend from the nursing home, the lady who died. She's left him some money in her will.' She did burst into tears then, clapping her hand over her mouth to stifle the noise she was making. 'Sorry...'

'I didn't do anything special,' said Tam. 'And I didn't believe it at first, but I went to see Eleanor's family, or what's left of it – just a daughter – but it's real. That's where I was yesterday. Beth thought I'd gone to work, but instead I drove down to Cambridge to meet her. I'm sorry I couldn't be here for you when you met Robert, Frankie, but I made the judgement that this might be something I needed to do.'

Frankie waved aside his apology. 'You were a friend to Eleanor, Tam, at a time in her life when she needed it the most. There's no one more deserving.' She could see his eyes beginning to fill with tears and she gave him an embarrassed smile.

He stretched his face, blinking and sniffing. 'It was important to me that I had Margaret's blessing – that's Eleanor's daughter – and she gave it to me. Said her mum had always been a good judge of character.' His voice was beginning to break a little and he took a deep breath. 'Nothing like this has ever happened to me before. Some people might say it's not a huge amount of money, but to me, it's everything. It's exactly enough. Because there's enough to pay for a few things on the farm, Beth – an all-terrain wheelchair for one, and a trailer, 'cause Jack's going to need one of those. And it's also enough to pay for this...' He opened his arms a little. 'I've bought the bakery for you, Frankie. It's yours. You get to stay. You get to do whatever you want with it.'

Frankie's chair made a hideous scraping noise against the

floor, but she didn't care. She scrambled to her feet, pulling Tam from his chair and into the fiercest of hugs.

It took a few moments for her to realise that someone else had got to their feet. 'Frankie, I couldn't be happier,' said Vivienne. 'I know without a shadow of a doubt that you'll make a go of things here. So perhaps in a few moments, when I'm gone and you've all caught your breath, you can open this.' She took out a bottle from her bag and placed it on the table. 'I wouldn't normally encourage drinking at work, but on this occasion... Perhaps you'd better put a sign on the door for the morning, saying you might be a little late opening. I'm sure folks won't mind... just this once.' She smiled and turned to go. 'I should tell you, too, that you've made me a very happy woman. My husband and I viewed the most perfect house at the weekend, and now, if we're quick, we might just be in time to buy it.' She waved a hand in farewell. 'Now get that champagne open. I'll see myself out...'

It was quite some time before any of them could speak properly. But there were lots of tears, and hugs, and so much excitement, that anyone walking past would have wondered what was going on.

As yet, there'd been no baking at all, but that would come, in time...

Frankie was the first to sink back down at the table. She still couldn't believe any of what had happened, but she only had to look at the faces around her to know that it had. True friends. The best of friends.

'You know, this all started because of you, Frankie,' said Beth. 'A little nightingale, the symbol of love and renewal. You started a chain of kindness that just kept on growing. It's right that we should be here tonight. All of us.' She looked at each of them in turn, smiling.

'What will you do, now that Duggan's is yours?' asked Tam as he busied himself finding glasses and opening the bottle of champagne. 'Apart from think of a better name, that is.'

Frankie grinned. 'I have a list... But one of the first things will be to get some tables in here so people can sit in. And open up at night, when everything else is closed.' She directed a warm look at Tam. 'I've realised how important that is.' She paused for a moment. 'There is one other thing, too...' She lifted herself out of her seat and leaned across the table, taking William's head in her hands, and kissing him gently. 'I'd like to offer you a job, William. You're turning out to be a damn fine baker, and I'm going to need an extra pair of hands. There's no one I'd rather have by my side.'

He pulled back gently. 'Will there be croissants for breakfast? Those raspberry and white chocolate ones?'

Frankie smiled. 'Always...'

'In that case... I'm happy to accept.'

'So, what shall we drink to then?' asked Tam, filling everyone's glass. 'There's quite a lot to choose from.'

'Let's drink to all of it,' said Beth. 'To the bakery.'

'To the farm,' said Tam.

'To friendship,' said Frankie.

'To love,' said William. He was about to sip his champagne when Frankie laid her hand on his.

'There's one missing,' she said. 'To hope. Let's drink to hope...'

And that, is exactly what they did.

36

SIX MONTHS LATER, SEPTEMBER

Tam

It's autumn on the farm now. The landscape is changing, becoming softer, the colours mellowing into shades of yellow through to gold and deepest bronze – honey to ochre, copper to russet, blush to ruby. It's Tam's favourite season. It always has been, but this year will be different, as will the winter to follow and the spring after that. He will wake every day knowing that just outside the kitchen door is a place filled with riches, and all of it just waiting, for him and for Jack.

June was glorious in the orchard. Frothy, delicate blooms of palest pink everywhere you looked, drifting on the breeze to settle on the freshly mown grass. And the scent... Tam couldn't get enough of it – pulling down bough after bough to inhale the sweet perfume as he'd walked among the trees. He'd felt as if he was in heaven.

Ideally, they should have pruned the trees much earlier in the year but, almost as if she knew what they'd been through, Mother Nature decided to forgive them, and so as Tam stares upwards now, into a bright blue September sky, the results of their labours are burgeoning, or rather *his* labours. But for every day he had spent at the top of a ladder bringing life back to the neglected trees, Jack had spent it sowing row after row of seeds. The raised beds that Tam had made were just the right height for him to work at, and slow and awkward work it might have been but this year they will have a harvest, the first in a very long time.

Tam reaches upwards to pluck another apple from a tree. These ones he's promised to his mum, along with the first of the runner beans. She still can't get enough of his stories, but this time his tales about life on the farm are all true. She was horrified to hear what Chris had done – just as Frankie had said she would be – but she was also immensely proud of her son and delighted to hear about his new life. There's no need to talk about anything in the past now, and Tam rarely thinks about it. Why would he?

He polishes the apple against his jumper, fills his lungs with clean, cool air and stares out across the farmyard towards the house. Towards his home. Magic, that's what it is – pure magic.

* * *

Beth

The wee small hours are the ones Beth likes best. When she wakes, warm and drowsy, her body relaxed and at rest. Her alarm will sound in a couple more hours and her day will begin. But it will be a different day to the ones she used to have. Before. Gone are the days filled with rushing and juggling and that scattered feeling that nothing was right. Gone, too, are the nights, which were filled with anxiety, pulled between two places and fully existing in neither.

Now, Beth's days are measured by routine, by hard work, but work which, for the first time in a long while, has focus and clarity. No longer does Beth feel torn in two, lost between a need to care for herself and provide for another. She leaves the house every morning, her shoulders unbowed, and returns every evening tired but happy in the knowledge that every moment she has been away, Jack has had Tam by his side. The truest of friends.

The evenings are spent in so many different ways. But the biggest difference is that Beth is Beth and Jack is Jack: no longer do they have to pretend to be anything they're not. They have both gained so much, but becoming true to themselves is one of the biggest gifts Tam has bestowed on them. So, there is laughter, and much talking, nights simply spent snuggled reading, or balmy evenings spent outside, eating, drinking and dreaming. Because always there are things to talk about. Always there are plans to be made and hope to be made room for. Always, there is each other.

Beth turns and pushes her head closer, feeling the softness of Jack's skin on her cheek. He is lying on his back, she on her side, but after so many years of nights apart, they found they still fit together, are still able to sleep as they once did. She nestles into him, their fingers entwined. Safe. And sound.

Frankie

Despite owning the bakery, Frankie still works the night shift. The daytime no longer holds any fears for her, but she prefers it that way, working each night with William by her side. It's called Frankie's now, of course – no longer Duggan's, no longer tired, and no longer a place to hide from the world. Now it is

Frankie's world. Yet it also belongs to others, because everyone is welcome, at any time of the day. Or night.

There are spaces for customers to sit, to eat, to talk or simply to be, whiling away a cold night when the air outside is too harsh or the wind too fierce. And there's a board on the wall now too, something that Frankie's is becoming known for. On it are pinned gifts of food or drink: receipts for raspberry and white chocolate croissants – still William's favourite – coffees, teas and soups, loaves of bread or cinnamon swirls, paid for by anyone who wants to, and gifted to anyone who might have need of them. Frankie's happy to see the board is nearly always full. There is a whole world of people out there, invisible people, just like she once was, just like Tam and William and Beth, who, for all sorts of reasons, move through their days – and nights – in ways which are different to everyone else's. They all have a story to tell and slowly and surely, bit by bit, Frankie and William are getting to know them all.

William

William hasn't worked at Vipers for over five months now and, true to his word, once he had left, Tam paid a visit to the police. The surprise came shortly after that when Danny paid a visit to William. He wanted to tell him all about Stuart, just in case he hadn't heard. He wanted him to know how shocked he was, how horrified that one of his employees could have been up to something so awful almost under his very nose. He also wanted to assure William that if he was in any way worried about there being any repercussions for him, then he shouldn't be. The police were happy that neither Danny nor any of his other staff had been involved, and that was where the matter would end. Danny was only too aware how anxious

William might be, given his past history, so Danny had been careful to stress to them what a model employee William had been.

Danny still doesn't know who William is, but that's okay. Danny's an honest man, earning an honest living and living a happy life, and that's all William really needs to know. One day, when William has more things in his life that he's truly proud of, he might get back in touch with Danny, and the way things are going, that could be sometime soon. Until then, he's happy to live his own life. It's a life that's turning out to be better than he could ever have imagined.

And lastly…

As for William and Frankie, they're taking things slow. But Frankie's a baker, after all; she knows the benefit of that. The end result is always better for not being rushed. William smiles and says he's proving himself to her. She groans at his pun, but hugs the thought tight. He's proving to be the perfect partner in more ways than one.

Frankie never dreamed that she would ever rid herself of her past life, that the butterfly would ever emerge from the hard shell she'd been hiding inside, transformed and finally free, but now she is truly learning to fly… She has a warm, safe and fearless place to live, is surrounded by the best of friends, and has a business of her own, doing what she loves day in, day out. Sometimes it's hard to believe it's really happened to her, but she only needs to look at William to know that it's true. Because William is the truest treasure of them all.

She never dreamed she would have someone like him in her life, someone who doesn't seek to change her, but who loves her for who she really is, who fills her days with laughter and shares the same hopes for their future, one which will be brighter than they ever dared imagine.

It's only right then that they stand side by side in Frankie's, sharing not only in everything the day brings, but the night, too. Opening the bakery to anyone who has need of them – the lost or the lonely, the needy or the invisible.

In fact, to anyone who needs a little light in the dark.

A LETTER FROM EMMA

Hello, and thank you so much for choosing to read *The Midnight Bakery*. I hope you enjoyed reading it just as much as I enjoyed writing it. If you'd like to stay updated on what's coming next, please do sign up to my newsletter here and you'll be the first to know!

www.bookouture.com/emma-davies

For those of you who follow my writing (a huge thank you!), you'll know that the writing of this book accompanied a big change in my own life, one I'm still adjusting to. But, like Frankie, there is much to be hopeful for. I have some amazing friends who have walked close beside me this last year or so, gently supporting me and encouraging me onward, and an amazing family without whom I could never have written Frankie's story. They truly are the best.

I'm also incredibly grateful to my wonderful publishers, Bookouture, for their unfailing support. They have very generously moved deadlines when my life didn't want to fit around them and made the process of writing this book far easier than it otherwise would have been. So a big thank you to the whole team, who have been so caring and considerate, and, in particular, my editor, Cerys Hadwin-Owen, for her sage advice in making Frankie's story the very best it could be.

And finally to you, lovely readers, the biggest thanks of them all for continuing to read my books, and without whom none of this would be possible. I'm just like Frankie, doing what I love every day, so you really do make everything worthwhile. My next book will be out just in time for Christmas, with another story of love and hope and friendship. I hope to see you then.

Having folks take the time to get in touch really does make my day, and if you'd like to contact me then I'd love to hear from you. The easiest way to do this is by popping by my website, where you can read about my love of Pringles, among other things. You can also follow me on Facebook or over on Substack, where I share my writing together with other thoughts on my publication *At the Still Point*, subscribing to which is free.

I hope to see you again very soon and, in the meantime, if you've enjoyed reading *The Midnight Bakery*, I would really appreciate a few minutes of your time to leave a review or post on social media. Every single review makes a massive difference and is very much appreciated!

Until next time,

Love, Emma xx

www.emmadaviesauthor.com

atthestillpoint.substack.com

 facebook.com/emmadaviesauthor

PUBLISHING TEAM

Turning a manuscript into a book requires the
efforts of many people. The publishing team at
Bookouture would like to acknowledge everyone
who contributed to this publication.

Commercial
Lauren Morrissette
Hannah Richmond
Imogen Allport

Cover design
Debbie Clement

Data and analysis
Mark Alder
Mohamed Bussuri

Editorial
Cerys Hadwin-Owen
Charlotte Hegley

Copyeditor
Jenny Page

Proofreader
Emily Boyce

Marketing
Alex Crow
Melanie Price
Occy Carr
Cíara Rosney
Martyna Młynarska

Operations and distribution
Marina Valles
Stephanie Straub
Joe Morris

Production
Hannah Snetsinger
Mandy Kullar
Ria Clare
Nadia Michael

Publicity
Kim Nash
Noelle Holten
Jess Readett
Sarah Hardy

Rights and contracts
Peta Nightingale
Richard King
Saidah Graham

Made in the USA
Las Vegas, NV
23 May 2025

22604539R00194